THE
BURDEN
OF THE
DESERT

D1634392

JUSTIN HUGGLER

First published in 2014 by Short Books
3A Exmouth House
Pine Street
EC1R 0JH

10 9 8 7 6 5 4 3 2 1

Copyright © Justin Huggler 2014

A CIP catalogue record for this book is available from the British Library.

ISBN 978-1-78072-200-9

Printed and bound in Great Britain by
CPI Group (UK) Ltd, Croydon, CR0 4YY

Cover design by Leo Nickolls

To Anuradha

"Babylon is fallen, is fallen; and all the graven images of her gods he hath broken unto the ground."

Isaiah 21:9

PART ONE

Summer 2003

Chapter One

Hell City

3 August 2003

Lieutenant Rick Benes never forgave himself for the night
he killed the children. It was one of those Baghdad nights when
you could feel the heat crawling down your spine, invading
your nose as you breathed, and drying out your throat until it
was hard to swallow. The heat was a thick presence; it stood
up off the road and blocked your way. You could smell it, the
scent of Baghdad—dust, heat and oil; dark and sulphurous, it
always reminded Benes of the stories he was told as a child of
the fumes of hell. The wind brought no relief; it blew hot in
your face day and night; at midnight the air burned. And the
sound of the guns was always there: sharp, single cracks that
broke the night sky, followed by volleys of fire that echoed across
the rooftops. Somewhere across the city, an American patrol had
just been ambushed and a soldier as young as the ones Benes had
with him now was lying with his head in a halo of his own wet
blood, or somewhere else amid the anonymous brown apartment
blocks, looters had just shot their way into a shop, and the owner,
bleeding to death, watched as they emptied the cash box.

Benes could feel the eyes on him as they drove through the
city. Behind the empty windows flashing by, in the cars that
hurried past when they saw the Americans, he felt the eyes
around corners and behind walls, watching and waiting. The
Humvee was a target drifting through the city, every street an
ambush, every window the one from which the bullet would
come, sliding effortlessly through the thin, unarmoured sides.
Jackson, on the gun above them, was even more exposed, his
head sticking out into the night.

Benes saw an Iraqi on the street ahead, sitting outside his

house on a plastic chair, prayer beads playing through his fingers. He looked up at the sound of the Humvee and went inside, taking his chair with him. No one wanted to be close to the Americans; you never knew when someone might start shooting at them. A second Humvee followed; you never went out alone. Everything was green and unreal through Benes's night vision goggles, as if he were in an alien world. He glanced across at the massive form of Gibbs, so tall he had to stoop at the wheel. A bead of sweat was forming on his lip, and out of the corner of his eye, Benes watched as it budded and swelled into a tiny globe, hung precariously for a moment, and then fell, shimmering briefly before it was lost in the darkness.

"Damn, it's hot," he said to break the monotonous sound of the engine.

"Roger that, sir," Gibbs said. "Hell City. You notice something? No flies."

"What?"

"No flies, sir. Since it got hot, even the flies are gone. It's too hot for flies, and we're supposed to live in it."

Gutierrez laughed from the back seat.

The checkpoint loomed ahead, a light dancing in the road, one of the soldiers waving a torch to warn them to slow. Moon leaned in at the window.

"What's up?" Benes said.

"Not much, sir," Moon grinned. "Only thing I'm fighting out here is this heat." Zivkovich stood a little way off, providing cover.

"Any problems?"

"No, sir, just a few civilians heading home."

"Only a couple more hours to go. Then Hajji should be safely tucked up in bed, and you should have a quiet night of it."

They drove onto the second checkpoint, where Hernandez reported the same, nothing, and they went on. The street was deserted. When they reached the house, Benes could hear angry shouting coming from inside.

"Friendlies coming in," he called out. Murray opened the door, and the unfamiliar odour of the house enveloped Benes: foreign cooking, unfamiliar soap and women's perfume.

"What's up?" he asked.

"Not being cooperative, sir," said Murray.

"They never are. Which way?"

Murray pointed him to a door, and Benes pushed into a room where he felt the cool of an air conditioner on his sweat-soaked clothes. Hawkes, the platoon sergeant, was being shouted at by an Iraqi who was trembling with anger, his face dark with blood, while Faiz, the translator, looked on.

"You have to understand, we are going to establish a position here whether you cooperate or not," Hawkes was saying. He broke off, and the Iraqi, as if understanding Benes was in command, turned and started speaking to him in Arabic. Benes felt Hawkes's eyes on him; he was always watching, gauging Benes's performance in his first command. Benes was supposed to be his superior, but he often felt as if the sergeant saw it the other way around.

"What's going on?" he asked.

"Not cooperating, sir."

"He the owner of the house?"

"Yes, sir."

"Mr Anwar," Faiz said nervously.

Benes was tired, he had been on duty for twelve hours, and he was being shouted at in a language he didn't understand, but he forced himself to remain calm.

"What's he saying, Faiz?" he asked.

"He is asking if you are the one in charge."

"Yes," Benes said. "Tell him I'm in charge." As Faiz translated, Benes looked around the room: ugly brown armchairs pushed up against the walls, a gold-painted chandelier with light fittings in the shapes of flower petals, a bowl of plastic fruit on a table with a lacy white tablecloth.

"He says, I'm sorry, but he says please tell your men to get out," Faiz translated. "He says you cannot stay here." On one wall was a large picture Benes recognised as Mecca, on another a framed photograph of a studious-looking boy. "He says your men might see the women of the house. I'm sorry, sir," Faiz played with his glasses nervously, "but you know this is not allowed in our culture." The room was meticulously clean, everywhere little signs of individuality: lace covers on the seat backs that looked home-made, a jumbled collection of jars and boxes on a shelf in the corner. "He says your men will break his things. He says if the neighbours see your men here, they will think he is helping you and when you are gone someone will come and take revenge on him." Benes had heard it all before in other houses, other streets.

"Tell him we have to be here," he said. "We've got a check-point in the street to ensure the security of this area, and we need a position here to provide cover for it. We will be here for one night only, the position will be on the roof, not in the house, and we will try to disturb your family as little as possible."

"He says his children have seen your men with guns and they are scared. He says they are crying and please go somewhere else."

Benes felt exhaustion drumming against his skull.

"I'm sorry, we have to be here and that's it." Benes looked at the floor and saw his heavy army boots and the dirty prints they had made in the carpet. "I'd better take a look at the roof," he said.

"This way, sir," said Hawkes, starting towards the door.

"OK, sergeant, I'll find it. Stay here and keep an eye on Mr Anwar." Hawkes gave him a rueful look. As Benes made his way up the stairs, he heard the shouting start up again. The stairs were unlit, and he felt his way up. Somewhere in the darkness, he could hear the muffled sound of children's voices: they were trying to whisper but their voices kept rising. Then they stopped; they had heard Benes on the stairs. He moved up, calling out to let the soldiers know he was coming.

He could smell rust from the door that led onto the flat roof. Washing was hanging in a corner. There was a skeletal television aerial and a few flower pots. Usually, the Iraqis slept on their roofs in summer to catch what little breeze there was, but the neigh-bours had retreated inside when the Americans came. Ramirez and Hunt knelt hunched against the parapet wall, training their rifles towards the checkpoint. The city was spread around, a map of deserted streets and concrete houses. The night was moon-less, but Benes could make out palm trees against the city lights bleeding into the sky. Gunfire sounded in the distance.

"How's it going?" Benes asked.

"Both checkpoints covered, sir," Hunt replied. Below, Benes could see the two checkpoints set up as he had ordered, perfectly aligned, one at each end of the street, so each provided cover for the other, and both of them were covered from the rooftop. Ramirez and Hunt had an uninterrupted view of the streets—no one could approach either checkpoint without crossing the sights of their rifles.

"Keep your eyes open," Benes said. "First sign of any attack, you provide covering fire."

Back inside the house, in the dark of the stairs, he could hear a young woman scolding the children. One of them was crying. He told Hawkes he was heading out, and then left quickly, before Mr Anwar could start on him again.

In the street, he felt the invisible eyes on him once more. He could hear the sound of the gun moving above him as Jackson jerked it nervously from side to side. His head throbbed. As they drove, all the lights around them went out: the streetlights, the few lights still on in the houses; only the headlights remained. The power cuts happened every day. Then he heard gunfire close by, from the direction of the checkpoints. Gibbs was already swinging the big Humvee round in a single arc, jumping over the edge of the pavement.

"Get on the radio," Benes ordered Gutierrez. All that came back was static. Then: "Three-two under attack…Three-three under attack." *Both* the checkpoints were under attack. "Three-one under attack." The rooftop as well? It made no sense: the checkpoints and his covering position at the house were all being attacked. They swung into the street behind the first checkpoint: through his night vision goggles, Benes could see flashes from the soldiers' rifles, and a car stopped just in front of the checkpoint, its windscreen shattered from gunfire. Benes could hear incoming fire slapping the air around them. Then it was out of the Humvee and into it.

"Gutierrez! With me!"

Trying to make out what was happening. Outlines of houses and flashes from the guns. Diving to the ground. No breath. Trying to push himself through the concrete of the pavement.

Where to aim? Gunfire behind him. Bullets hitting the wall. Car next to the checkpoint not moving. No explosion. Gutierrez's face. Where was the enemy? "Stop shooting!" Hunt. From the radio. "Stop shooting! You're shooting at us!"

"No, you're shooting at us!"

Then Benes understood. The incoming fire was all coming from one position: the roof where Ramirez and Hunt were. There was no enemy fire: they were all shooting at each other. He grabbed the radio from Gutierrez.

"Cease fire!" he shouted. "Cease fire!" One by one, they stopped. There were a few final shots, a silence that hurt the ears. The smell of cordite hung in the air. Gutierrez was kneeling opposite him, rifle in hands, staring at Benes with big frightened eyes. Jackson was hunched over the gun of the Humvee, and beside him, Gibbs was crouched over his rifle looking dazed. Up ahead, Moon and Zivkovich still had their rifles trained on the car. Moon looked back, an urgent question in his eyes. Hawkes's voice came over the radio, asking what was happening. Gingerly, expecting it all to start again at any moment, Benes stood up and made himself walk up the street to Moon and Zivkovich. Somehow, none of them was hurt. Benes spoke into the radio and Hawkes's voice came back, saying there were no injuries at the house.

"Came up on us real fast out of the dark," Moon was saying beside him, "had no lights on and when we ordered him to stop he just kept coming..." Through the shattered windscreen of the car, Benes could see the driver, the sole occupant, with half his face missing where the bullets had hit him. It looked like a suicide attack, an unlit car coming up fast on the checkpoint.

"Everyone back from the car," Benes shouted. He told Gutierrez to get on the radio and call the quick reaction force for backup. Even if it weren't a car bomb, the petrol tank could still go up. Off to the right, a man burst out of one of the houses and started running towards them. Moon and Zivkovich turned on him, rifles raised.

"Get back!" Benes shouted. The man stopped, terrified, and nervously retreated to the door of his house. People began appearing at the doors and windows of other houses; with a dead

Iraqi in the middle of the street there could be a riot. He could see half the young driver's brain pooled on the car seat beside him, a thick red soup. Another voice from the radio, Hernandez, from the other checkpoint: somehow in the confusion, Benes had forgotten the second checkpoint.

"We have civilian casualties," Hernandez was saying.

Benes got back in the Humvee and signalled to Gibbs to drive. They set off down the street fast, people at the door of every house now. As they came up on the second checkpoint, Benes could see another car full of bullet-holes. Iraqis had advanced beyond their houses and were close to the car, while Hernandez and Steele stood nervously watching.

"Everybody back," Benes shouted, getting out of the Humvee. Jackson trained the machine gun on the most vocal section of the crowd and they quieted, moving back a few paces. Then, as Benes came level with the car, he saw them. Inside a child lay dead in the front passenger seat, a boy who couldn't have been older than twelve, with a neat red bullet-hole between his eyes. The expression on his face was so clear he seemed alive, until you noticed the entire back of his head was gone. Beside him in the driver's seat a man sat still alive, his shirt front soaked in blood that kept pumping out, his fingers, sticky with his own blood, clawing feebly against his chest, staring at them with a look of astonished incomprehension. In the back seat there was a small girl with a wet red space where her eyes should have been, as if that part of her face had simply been ripped off, leaving only blank flesh. And next to her was what must have been her mother, her body thrown over another daughter as if to try to shield her from the bullets, fragments of broken glass strewn across her hair and body.

"They came up in the middle of the shooting," Hernandez said. "We thought they were part of the attack." His rifle shook in his hands. "We thought they were part of it."

And then Benes heard the moaning, a desperate whimpering sound from the back of the car, like an animal in distress. The mother was moving, she was still alive, and so was the daughter under her.

He heard himself screaming for medics.

Chapter Two

Ali Babas on the Road to Baghdad

5–6 August 2003

THE BORDER POST was a huddle of buildings in the desert night. Zoe Temple had expected something more dramatic, something to herald the fact they were crossing into occupied Iraq. A flag stirred; the metal cord it hung from sang eerily in the wind. Dust crept unnoticed across the road, a ghost in the night: from time to time, the wind would pick it up and dance it across the road like a puppet, then abruptly let it fall. The ground, where it showed at the edge of the road, was barren rock and sand; the night sky was vast and so crowded with stars that it shone. A lone American soldier sat leaning against the wall. Half asleep from boredom, his rifle by his side, he barely looked up as they drove in. A long line of parked trucks had been waiting on the other side of the border to cross in the morning, but theirs was the only car to venture here now, in the dead of night. They had been driving for three hours, and they had another five to go: they had come by night to avoid the armed bandits who plagued the road to Baghdad.

Zoe was in Iraq at last, the place the eyes of the entire world were fixed on, and fear and excitement pounded in her mind. A door opened in the border post, and an official appeared, buttoning a greasy uniform jacket. His boots were open, as if he had just slipped them on, and the laces trailed after him. As he leaned in at the front passenger window and murmured in Arabic to Sa'ad, the driver, his eyes wandered to the back and lingered on Zoe. He was speaking to Sa'ad but looking at Zoe, looking her up and down yet avoiding eye contact—she felt as if he were sizing up her body under her clothes. Sa'ad passed the official their two passports, and Zoe watched as he surreptitiously removed the $10 bribe from under the cover of the top passport and slipped it into his pocket, glancing to make sure the American didn't see. He turned Zoe's passport over and looked back up at her.

"Britani?" he asked.

"Yes."

"Journalist?"

She nodded again. He turned and took the passports into the office. For a while, they sat in silence. Zoe watched as the American lazily traced patterns in the dust with his boot, and the wind wiped them away. After a while, a second official came over and spoke to Sa'ad, shooting a hungry glance at Zoe.

"Customs," Sa'ad told her, reaching behind his seat back to open her door. "Please." Zoe got out and felt the cold night air. When he saw her step out of the car, the American soldier seemed to come to life, slowly getting to his feet.

"How's it going?" he asked Zoe. He towered over her, but for all his size he was shy and awkward, a nervous boy. He stood with his feet wide apart and stooped, as if to bring himself nearer to her height.

"All right," she smiled.

"Headed for Baghdad?"

"Yes. Long drive."

"Yeah," he nodded. "You got a cigarette?"

"Sure." She fumbled in her bag for her pack. Sa'ad had opened the back of the car, and the customs official was looking through her bags. She watched him warily out of the corner of her eye.

"You're English, right?" the American asked.

"How can you tell?" She smiled as she held out the pack of cigarettes, but he didn't get the joke.

"Oh, from your accent and all," he said. "First time in Iraq?" He pronounced it Eye-raq.

"Yes."

"Well it's not so bad, s'long as you like sand," he grinned. "You with the CPA?"

"No, I'm a journalist."

"Oh, OK. You on TV?"

"No, I'm a writer. For the *Informer*. It's a newspaper in London," she added when he looked back blankly.

"Baghdad," he mused. "Pretty rough over there. No place for a...for a lady. You want to take care over there."

She made herself keep smiling.

"Don't worry, I'll be fine." While they were talking, the customs official finished checking the car and returned their passports to Sa'ad.

"Well, I'd better be going," she told the soldier.

"Yeah. Take care." As they drove off, she heard him calling out, "Hey, what's your name, case I read any of your articles?" but by the time she could reply he was gone. She peered through the window, trying to make out something of the country as the border post slipped into the distance, but all she could see was the darkness of the land beneath the shining sky. It was out there, all around her, the place she had spent the last three months watching on television. Her irritation at the American who thought Iraq was "no place" for her because she was a woman quickly faded. He had probably never even been to Baghdad. The road had broadened out to a six-lane highway, and they were going at speed now, racing through the night. Sa'ad was hunched over the wheel, his eyes bleary with exhaustion. He was a gloomy man with a wispy moustache—Zoe had thought his name was unusually apposite until he told her it was Arabic for "happy". He had already been exhausted when he turned up to collect her from the hotel in Amman, and once, on the winding road in Jordan, he fell asleep at the wheel and she had to shake him awake to avoid veering into a deep ditch. After that she had given up hope of sleeping on the journey.

She thought how her colleagues in London would envy her now. She had watched with frustration from her desk as other, more experienced journalists covered first the war in Afghanistan and then the invasion of Iraq, but now, three months after the fall of Saddam, she was on the road to Baghdad. She knew they still had hours of monotonous driving ahead of them and then a dangerous final hour into Baghdad on a road frequented by armed bandits. It had sounded adventurous when they talked about it in the comfort of the hotel lobby in Amman, modern-day highwaymen the Iraqis called "Ali Babas", but now she was nervous. Within a few hours, she could have one of their guns to her head. She had her money hidden in various places around the car in case they were stopped: some under the roof lining where Sa'ad had pulled it up and shown her, some behind the central armrest, some in her sock and money belt, and a healthy amount in her pocket to hand over. In the open luggage space behind her was a bulletproof flak jacket, and in the laptop bag at her feet was a satellite phone that supposedly worked anywhere, but if anything did go wrong, there was no one she could call who could help her here. For the first time in her life, Zoe realised, she was completely on her own, and it gave her a strange sense of exhilaration.

It had been a grey July day, rain intimate against the window, when Nigel Langham, the foreign editor of the *Informer*, had walked across the newsroom, sat casually on the edge of her desk and asked if she was interested in going to Iraq. The newsroom had been alive with approaching deadlines at the time, phones ringing and being slammed down, fingers hammering at keyboards, men and women swearing, but Zoe remembered how the drama had seemed to fade away into insignificance when Nigel asked her about Iraq.

"Yes, I'll go," she had said, but Nigel seemed not to hear her.

"It'd just be a matter of filling in for a few weeks, really," he went on, in his Estuary whine. "Martin's been there eight weeks and he's exhausted, so he needs to come out. David can't go in right at the moment because of his back. We need someone to do a holding job, basically, and the Editor seems to feel you're the right person." As he spoke, he had pushed a notepad covered in her scribbled notes of an interview distractedly around her desk. Dishevelled, with what was left of his dark hair turning grey, Nigel looked and sounded as if he felt no one alive could match him for problems. "It's only a case of keeping the seat warm until David can get there, of course," he went on, "but it would be a learning curve and a chance to dip your toe in a really big story."

"I'm up for it," Zoe said, but again Nigel went on as if she had not spoken.

"Obviously there are risks involved, and there'll be bullets flying around. So you need to think pretty seriously if that's something you're really up for." It was almost as if he were trying to discourage her. In front of her lay the half-written story she had been working on all day, about a new fashion line designed in hemp being launched to promote environmental awareness: she had been struggling against her own boredom to finish it. Across the room, the news editor was looking in their direction, and she sensed another celebrity story heading her way. Later, she would think of that moment, in the busy newsroom, in the midst of the city with ten million people crowded into its streets and buildings, facing a hundred million decisions—to marry or divorce, have a child or an abortion, whether they were in love, how to pay their debts, whether to find the end in a handful of sleeping pills—and think how easily she decided to risk all she had or ever could have on that single choice.

"Yes, I'll do it," she said. "When do you want me to leave?"

He paused and looked at her, as if sizing her up, then said, "Well, Martin wants to be out by Sunday, and the Editor wants us to keep Baghdad staffed on a daily basis, so you'd need to start travelling by Friday."

That had left her two days to prepare, but she hadn't complained. After working her way up through provincial newspapers, reporting mundane local issues, she thought she had arrived when she won a job on a national newspaper, only to find she was reporting the same mundane issues: gossip and petty crimes. News executives held long, earnest-faced meetings about how to report a celebrity wedding in two thousand words across a double-page spread, while a war in Africa in which three million people had died was reduced to three hundred words in the bottom corner of a page or a few amusing paragraphs on barefoot soldiers stealing the passports of foreigners. Journalism was becoming an art that trivialised the serious and took the trivial seriously. And now she was being sent to cover the biggest story in the world. It wasn't until after she had agreed to go that she realised she would have to tell her mother. When she called home that evening, she didn't admit she had already agreed to do it.

"I need some advice," she said. "The paper's asked me to go to Iraq. What do you think?"

She heard the familiar sounds of home down the telephone, the quiz programme on the television, the hum of the washing machine, the chime of the clock on the mantelpiece. And she lied to her mother, told her that she would barely leave the heavily guarded hotel complex in Baghdad, told her details she didn't know herself. And of course her mother replied, "You must do it. Your father would have been proud of you."

They were slowing: ahead, in the car lights, Zoe could make out a gaping hole in the road. There was a small dip in the landscape, and a bridge had been built so cars could continue across without slowing, but most of the bridge was a mess of concrete rubble and twisted metal, a casualty, she supposed, of air raids. A narrow path to one side appeared to be undamaged, and they drove gingerly across.

She winced at the memory of her arrival in the Middle East. Nigel Langham had given her the number of the newspaper's local contact, a Jordanian woman called Alia, who would arrange her papers and a car and driver to cross the border. She called and arranged to meet, but when she reached the hotel lobby it was full of Arab women covered from head to toe in loose black, and she wondered how to recognise her contact. She was summoning the courage to begin asking if any of them were Alia when she heard an American accent behind her.

"Zoe?" She turned in surprise. She didn't recognise the woman who had spoken, a blonde, her long hair uncovered, dressed in white jeans and cowboy boots. "Are you Zoe?" she repeated. Zoe nodded in confusion.

"And who are you waiting for?"

"I'm looking for a Jordanian lady called Alia."

"And she didn't arrive yet?" The woman was grinning, and Zoe realised her mistake.

"I...I...I'm sorry," she stammered.

"Don't worry, dear," Alia said, laughing and taking her hands. "We don't all live in the Middle Ages."

Alia had arranged for Sa'ad to drive her to Baghdad and given her the permits that would enable her to cross the border. And it was Alia who, over tea and cakes in the hotel lobby, with the black-robed matrons looking on, had told her about the Ali Babas.

"Whatever you do, dear, don't think of arguing," she said. "If they stop you, just give them the money."

The first hint of dawn was showing, and Zoe began to make out the landscape. It was even emptier than she had imagined. Red began to show at the horizon, and within minutes, the rising sun set the sky aflame in the east over Baghdad. Sa'ad's eyes were weeping as he tried to keep them on the road, one hand up in vain to block the sun's rays. It was an alien world Zoe found herself in, an inhospitable place of heat and light. The sky was not blue, but a burning white. The land was a vast emptiness of rock and dust that stretched on forever. It was not the movie desert of wind-sung sand dunes and camels shimmering out of the mirage; it was relentless, barren, dead. The only thing that broke the monotony was the black smear of the road disappearing into the distance. When they stopped the car to stretch their legs, the silence screamed. Their ears strained for the slightest sound, but they heard only the emptiness howling back at them. There was no scent, just the terrible clean air of the desert. This was what the world would be like without life, Zoe thought, stripped of the thin teeming skin of forests and animals, cities and villages, birth and decay: the world she knew was a fragile layer between the vastness of sky and the immensity of rock that could be swept away in an instant. Only the wind would remain.

And still the desert went on. Baghdad was cut off from the world by this wilderness; it was as if you had to travel off the edge of the map to get there. All the while, almost imperceptibly, they were going down, descending from the plateau of the Jordanian desert, and as they got lower, the heat grew. For a while, Sa'ad turned on the air conditioning; then he said they were low on fuel and they had to conserve it to be sure they would make Baghdad, so they had to endure the heat. The monotony numbed Zoe's mind, and she must have drifted into sleep because she awoke with a start, blinking the world back into focus to see hints of green on the horizon and other cars on the road. They were coming to the end of the desert, Sa'ad was looking nervously from side to side, and she realised the cars on the road were all bunching together, like a herd huddling for safety when it senses a lion.

24

"What's going on?" she asked.

"Ali Baba."

"Where?" Sa'ad shrugged and kept scanning the horizon. He was dangerously close to the last car in what had become a makeshift convoy; he seemed to be almost racing with it, and more than once Zoe flinched when he came within inches of hitting it. Still, she looked in vain for a sign of the Ali Babas. And then ahead, slewed across the road with the black trails of its own tyre marks snaking out, as if it had stopped and skidded, there was a bus. Beside it were two cars, and standing at the door of the bus, Zoe saw with a shock of fear, were three men holding guns. A frightened passenger was climbing down from the bus; one of the men had a gun pointed at his head. Sa'ad breathed in sharply.

"Ali Baba," he said. They were going very fast now, and Sa'ad lurched the car sickeningly to follow the rest of the convoy cars through the narrow channel of open road past the bus. Zoe could feel the blood pounding in her ears. The passenger was handing something over to the gunmen, who seemed too busy with the bus to take any interest in the cars. Just as they passed, one of the gunmen turned, and for an instant, his eyes met Zoe's. His face was hidden, his head wrapped in a red-checked headscarf, but his eyes were uncovered, and the hard, unrelenting gaze stayed with Zoe long after he had disappeared from sight.

"We saw them, this close!" Sa'ad was laughing with relief, holding up his finger and thumb an inch or so apart: it was the liveliest he had been for the entire journey, as if the tension had lifted from him. The sides of the road were becoming more built up, and the convoy of cars had separated and slowed down. Zoe began to relax: everyone was behaving as if the danger was past. They had reached the suburbs of Baghdad. Sa'ad put the air conditioning back on, to Zoe's relief. She heard a sound like someone hammering on hollow steel. There was a tank in the road ahead, firing into the buildings opposite. It was on the other side of the highway, across the central divide, and the cars on that side were swerving and trying to head back the way they had come. Zoe ducked down and gazed out of the window. As they got closer, she could see the tank was not firing from its main cannon, but from the machine gun beside it. They passed so close she could see the bullet casings arcing out of the gun, glinting in the sun, and the back of the head of the soldier who was firing it.

"What was that about?" she asked Sa'ad when the tank was safely dropping into the distance. In the rear-view mirror she saw him shake his head, his eyes wide with fear, and realised he had no idea.

As they drove on, the streets became more crowded, and pedestrians peered into the car in curiosity. Zoe stared back at them in fascination. But she had not seen much when Sa'ad patted the seat.

"You tired, lie down," he said.

"No, I'm fine."

"Please. People look you. See American. Not good." So, feeling self-conscious, Zoe lay down across the back seat. An ignominious way to arrive in Baghdad, she thought. She found herself looking up at an elderly man who was peering in through the window at her in puzzlement. They continued through the streets; then Sa'ad just as urgently asked her to sit up. Confused, Zoe got up to see a checkpoint. A man in an ill-fitting security guard uniform was standing by a metal barrier, a rifle hanging from his shoulder. She felt a blast of heat as Sa'ad opened the window, and a second guard looked in at her for a moment, then stood back and signalled to his colleague, who swung up the metal barrier to let them through. They drove in to what appeared to be a small area of city streets that had been cordoned off from the others. In the midst of them was a tall building that had been surrounded with thick concrete blast walls.

"This your hotel," Sa'ad said.

When she stepped out of the car, the heat hit her like a hammer: it was so hot she stood dazed for a moment, looking up at the dirty brown concrete tower of the al-Hamra Hotel. Almost all the windows had masking tape stuck across them diagonally in large Xs, presumably to stop them shattering if there was an explosion nearby. Sa'ad helped her unload her bags from the car and carry them in. She stepped into gloom—curtains had been drawn across the windows to keep out the heat. By the main entrance there was a small table at which a man was selling what appeared to be bizarre novelty gifts, watches and cigarette lighters emblazoned with smiling pictures of Saddam Hussein in full military uniform. Beyond, the reception area was dark and drab, with silver paper that must once have been the height of fashion slowly peeling from the walls. The smell of unappetising cooking drifted across the lobby. The receptionist handed her a key and directed her and Sa'ad to the "second building", through a door that led out to a fresh blast of the furnace heat and an open courtyard that contained a surprisingly clean-looking swimming pool. A man with enigmatic eyes was leaning against the wall, smoking a cigarette, long hair pulled back in a ponytail. He watched lazily as they crossed the courtyard.

Inside the second building, another receptionist, friendlier than the first, rushed to take the bags. Zoe counted out the money she owed Sa'ad in $100 bills. She felt a tug of emotion as he stuffed the money in his pocket and shuffled out of the building: he was the nearest she had to a friend here, and now she was alone. She followed the receptionist up a flight of stairs. He showed her into the dingy sitting room of a suite, with a rudimentary kitchen in one corner, a tired old sofa and a set of stained armchairs set in front of a large television, and a dining table and chairs that had been rearranged to serve as a desk. French windows, with the same Xs of tape plastered across them, led onto a balcony. It was blissfully cool: a heavy, old-fashioned air conditioner rumbled against the wall.

After the receptionist left, Zoe explored further, finding two bedrooms that contained nothing but beds and a basic but clean tiled bathroom. In the sitting room, she found a pile of tattered old paperbacks, presumably left by Martin Dalton and David Wilson, the two other correspondents for the *Informer* who had stayed here. Martin had departed for Amman the night before, leaving behind a shirt, a half-finished bottle of gin and a hastily scrawled note that wished her luck.

She had been alone for five minutes when there was a knocking at the door. She answered it to see two tall, heavily built Iraqi men. The taller and nearer of the two looked down at her coldly, his arms bulging under the short sleeves of his shirt. Zoe stepped back; there was no other exit except to the balcony, from where it was a sheer drop to the ground. She cursed herself for opening the door without checking who was outside and wondered if she should call out for help—and whether anyone would come. The shorter and fatter of the two men grinned.

"Miss Zoe?" asked the tall one solemnly, holding his hand over his heart and respectfully lowering his eyes. "My name is Ali. I am your translator, and this is your driver, Mr Mahmoud. Mr Martin asked us to meet you."

Chapter Three

A Night at the al-Hamra

6 August 2003

THE CITY IS fallen, and everywhere lie signs of her defeat. The liberators move through the streets in armoured cars, while the people look on with the eyes of the oppressed. The traffic is jammed because entire roads have been cordoned off behind razor wire by the new rulers. Tanks stand at busy junctions. A delivery driver stands seething with humiliation beside his truck as he is patted down before foreign soldiers at a foreign checkpoint in his city, on the route he has driven for the past fifteen years. A father feels fear and rage as they come into his house, speaking a language he does not understand as they search through his children's toys with the muzzles of their guns. The veteran soldier returned home sits in shame before his children, his army defeated and disbanded, his meagre pension unpaid, wondering how he will provide for his family. The doctor who laboured through war after war to keep his patients alive finds his pay has been suspended because there is no one at the ministry to approve it. The policeman, dismissed because he rose too high under the old regime, watches helpless as his neighbour is robbed and murdered. The bookseller who was tortured and crippled in prison because he once opposed the old regime watches from the shadows as the exiles who railed against the tyrant from the safety of far-off countries are welcomed like heroes in the palaces of the new rulers. Babylon is fallen.

It is a city of the desert. The low buildings are the colour of the desert, as if they were made of dust blown here and piled up by the desert wind. But the houses have new tenants: seizing their chance of a new home before anyone else could, entire families of poor Iraqis have moved into the villas left empty after the grandees of the old regime fled, leaving behind family photographs to be torn up by the vengeful mob. The barracks have been taken over by the army of the new rulers, but there is not enough room and they have taken over the airport as well and spilled out into cities of tents under the relentless desert sun. The city is ruled from the same palaces as before only the occupants have changed, but they have brought so many staff and so much confusion with them that some are sleeping on the palace lawns. Along the banks of the River Tigris, there is a new concrete wall to protect the new rulers from the people they have liberated. Babylon is fallen, is fallen.

And everywhere they are wiping away traces of the old ruler. All over the city, the names have changed. On the new road signs someone has had time to put up, even though there is still rampant looting and no electricity for much of the day, Saddam International Airport has become Baghdad International. In Firdos Square stands the empty plinth where, in the heady days after the fall of the city, the statue of Saddam Hussein was dragged down before the cheering crowds. All that is left is the plinth, barely noticed by the passing traffic, a monument to the vanity of the man who built it and to the vanity of the men who pulled it down. The statue turned out to have feet of clay; it had appeared to be solid bronze, but it was hollow. At the time, much was made of this by the victors, little thinking that their own success was built on as weak a foundation. Put up a new statue of the conqueror, twice as high, that it should have twice as far to fall. In every public square, in every public building, they have defaced the portraits of the tyrant: on the murals and the posters they have scratched out the face of Saddam, as Muslim invaders once scratched out the faces of idols. In some there are bullet-holes where the locals have practised their target shooting. In others, the concrete behind the mural has been torn out of the wall by the army of the new rulers. Babylon is fallen, is fallen, and all the graven images of her gods he hath broken unto the ground.

This was the city Zoe saw around her. Despite the exhaustion that was now screaming in her head, she had come back out of the hotel in search of a story for the *Informer*. Baghdad was nothing like she had expected. There were no crowded bazaars heavy with the scent of spices, no narrow winding lanes with ancient buildings tottering overhead and people flattening themselves against the walls to let a donkey pass. It was a low-rise concrete sprawl, shops with plate-glass windows, and wide streets choked with six lanes of traffic. But for all that, there was no mistaking you were somewhere different: there were office blocks and flyovers, but they looked nothing like the West. The whole place was run-down and dilapidated, as if it had been built to impress twenty years previously and left to slip towards ruin, a dust-coloured city in the sun.

Of the Baghdad of her imagination, there was little sign. In one square, they passed a bronze statue of Aladdin on his flying carpet, and in another an elaborate sculpture of Ali Baba and the Forty Thieves, which looked nothing like the modern Ali Babas she had seen on the road. But that was all there was of the fabled Baghdad of the Thousand and One Nights. The mighty Tigris called out to her from half-forgotten school history books, but when they came to it, it was just a muddy river flowing between concrete embankments.

She sat in the back of an ancient Mercedes, its red paint peeling and rust showing beneath, to which Mahmoud had shown her after a hurried late breakfast of greasy omelette and stale bread. Despite its poor condition, the car was clearly a source of great pride to Mahmoud: he had led her to it with barely disguised pleasure, while she wondered whether it would start. At least Ali and Mahmoud didn't make her lie down on the back seat: when she started to duck out of sight, Ali politely asked her not to, saying it would just arouse suspicion. He had also stopped her bringing the flak jacket with her from the hotel for the same reason.

"This will attract too much attention," he said.

"What if there's shooting?" she asked.

"If there is shooting this will only stop one bullet, or maybe two," he said. "In Baghdad, they will keep shooting, and this will not stop rocket-propelled grenades. It's better to keep a low profile."

She felt nervous as they made their way through the traffic. People stared into the car with hard, resentful eyes, and they didn't look away when she met their gaze. Often she found herself looking down at her feet to avoid them, only to look up again and find their eyes still on her. She wasn't at all sure she should be plunging straight into the city so soon after arriving, without taking time to find out what was safe and what wasn't. The reason she was out, rather than sleeping at the hotel, was Nigel Langham.

She had called London on the satellite phone to let them know she had arrived safely, only for him to ask, "What have you got for us today?" There was something almost threatening in the urgent tone of his voice. She had recognised it immediately; everyone in the newsroom knew it. Nigel was suffering a Crisis of Conference, the panic that gripped the section editors ten minutes before morning conference, the meeting at which they would discuss what to put in the day's paper, as they realised they had no substantial stories to offer. "The Editor's demanding daily big hits from Iraq," Nigel said. Henry Haight, editor-in-chief of the *Informer*, was always, and only, referred to in the newsroom simply as the Editor, as if he were some form of minor deity. Zoe suggested a piece about her journey to Baghdad, Ali Babas, tanks and all, but Langham had dismissed it. "We've already run pieces like that by Martin and David," he said. "I know you've just arrived but just head out there and get us something."

There were no other journalists around she could ask for advice. And so, against her better judgment, she had headed straight out into the streets of an unfamiliar and dangerous city. She realised her experience as a journalist in London bore very little relevance to reporting in a place like Iraq: there were no PR releases or press offices to turn to for stories about life under the occupation. She could call the US military, but they would give her the standard line that was running on the wires, and she needed a story of her own. So she had fallen back on that perennial stand-by of the journalist under pressure, the vox pop, a piece gauging opinion on the streets.

She had asked Ali and Mahmoud to take her to another place in Baghdad whose name had been changed, the great sprawling Shia slum that used to be called Saddam City and was now Sadr City. It was a slightly desperate idea, she knew, but it was becoming obvious that Iraq's Shia majority, long oppressed under Saddam, was going to be crucial in the months ahead, and she wanted to get the view from the slums in which the poorest of the capital's Shia lived. That the area used to be called Saddam City was a bonus, an added irony that could make for a good intro. The ambitious rush in where even fools fear to tread.

Ali, the translator, who was her only source of advice, didn't seem to think it would be too dangerous to visit Sadr City. After the initial menace of their arrival, he and Mahmoud had proved friendly, though they seemed somewhat uncomfortable around a Western woman. She was conservatively dressed in loose jeans and a long-sleeved shirt, but she noticed both men avoided looking at her. Ali, the quieter of the two, spoke excellent English and was clearly intelligent, but she felt she had to make a stand when he tried to talk her into covering her hair with a headscarf, a hideous shiny black polyester thing. Ali insisted it was so she would not stand out as a foreigner, but she thought that with her pale features it would just make her look like a Westerner in disguise, someone with something to hide, and she half suspected it had more to do with his own ideas on how women should dress. Mahmoud was more ebullient; he spoke little English, but that didn't discourage him from trying. "This place I am drive in war," he told her. "Huge bomb blast. Very frighten." He seemed confused about English greetings; he always said "Hello" twice—"Hello hello"—as if he had it confused with "Bye bye". She noticed he had begun to incorporate fragments of English into his Arabic conversation. When another car cut in front of them, he swore loudly, "Son of bitch!" and pounded his fist against the gear stick. Both men were wearing brightly coloured shirts that appeared to be the local fashion.

"God, it's hot here," Zoe said.

"Yes, I think it is very hot for you," Ali said, turning to face her over the back of the seat. "You have come at the hottest time of the year. We say in the last two weeks of July, and the first week of August, even the nails in the doors get hot." He laughed nervously. "There is a joke about this. An American, a British man and an Iraqi all die and they are sent to hell. When they arrive in the burning fires of hell, the Devil comes to them and says each one can have a last request. First the American says, 'Is there any way to reduce the heat?' but the Devil says no, that is part of hell, so the American says he would like to telephone his home in New York and tell his family where he is. The Devil agrees and gives him a telephone. When the American is finished, he tells him, 'That will be $10,000 for the call.' Then he offers the British man, who is suffering from the terrible heat. He asks for the same thing, a call home to London. When he is finished, again the Devil says, 'That will be $10,000.' Lastly he comes to the Iraqi, and he wants to call home to Baghdad too. When he is finished, the Devil says, 'That will be 50 cents.' The other two are furious. 'How come he only has to pay 50 cents and we have to pay $10,000 each?' they ask. 'Oh,' says the Devil, 'but he is only calling Baghdad. That's a local call.'" Zoe laughed and Ali smiled back.

The traffic had thinned and the streets had changed; there were large desolate spaces of empty desert between the houses. In one, a few boys played a desultory game of football, kicking up the dust. The buildings were shabby things with bits of steel rod poking out of the concrete, as if they had never been properly finished.

"Now we are in Thawra," announced Ali.

"Thawra?"

"Sadr City. The real name is Thawra. Then it was Saddam City. Now it is Sadr." He waved his hand dismissively. Zoe looked at the half-empty streets in surprise—Sadr City was supposed to be a crowded slum.

"Are you sure?" she asked.

"This is the beginning. The centre is…not so safe."

"But we need to speak to the locals."

"You want to speak with the people here?"

"Yes, that's why I came."

"That could be…It is OK to look but the people here, they are not…educated. Maybe they will make a problem for you."

Zoe sat undecided. She had told Nigel Langham she was going to Sadr City.

"Why do you want to speak with them?" Ali asked.

"To get the opinion of the Shia."

"So ask me," Ali smiled. "I am of the Shia." Zoe was surprised: with his expensive-looking clothes and his good English, she had assumed Ali was a Sunni. The Shia, oppressed under the old regime, were supposed to be the poor of Iraq. She couldn't turn back: if she gave up now, Nigel would know she had lost her nerve.

"But I want to get the view from Sadr City."

Ali considered for a moment.

"All right," he said reluctantly. "But we must be careful here," he said. "And it is better if you wear this." He held out the head-scarf again. Zoe was about to refuse when she thought better of it and took the black thing.

Mahmoud drove on and the streets became narrower, although the buildings still had a shabby, unfinished look. They turned into some sort of market street, where there were crowds of people, and the Mercedes began to attract attention. They pulled up opposite a shop with a group of older men standing together outside, the only women in view hurrying past, covered from head to toe. Even in the headscarf, Zoe felt she was attracting hostile looks.

"We can talk to these," Ali said, gesturing to the men. As soon as Zoe stepped from the air-conditioned car she felt the heat again, and there was the added discomfort of the black polyester headscarf. She felt a prisoner, forced to hide inside her black mask, as Ali began explaining who she was, and hard eyes looked her up and down.

"Amriki?" one of the men asked in a hostile voice.

"Britani," Ali replied, and the eyes did not soften. There was more discussion she could not understand, then someone pushed a white plastic chair out of a shop and gestured her to it. As she sat, the men crowded round, staring. She pulled out her note-book and pen and looked enquiringly at Ali.

"They will speak with us," he said. An older man had sat down next to her, and she looked over at him and smiled. He looked gravely back at her. His eyes were watery and had red rims, and she could see the veins snaking under his loose skin. "What is the first question?"

"OK, can you thank them for speaking—"

"I already did that. What do you want to ask?"

"Well, uh, how do they feel about the Americans being here?"

Ali asked the men in Arabic and several began to answer at once, then they let the older man who was sitting next to her speak first. When he had finished, before Ali could translate, another man began to give his answer.

"Uh, Ali, can you translate one at a time?" He gave her a warning look and said nothing. When the second man had finished, he quickly started to translate before a third could begin.

"They say they are happy Saddam is gone but they do not want the Americans to stay. If the Americans want only to put away Saddam and leave, then they are happy. But they say the Americans cannot stay in Iraq."

"What did the second man say?"

"The same. He said almost the same. What is the next question?" Zoe needed more than one quote for her story, even if the men said essentially the same thing as each other.

"Please could you translate the second man too?"

Ali looked strained. "He said, 'We are grateful to the Americans for putting Saddam out of power, but now they must leave.' The next question?"

"How do they feel about life in the city at the moment, the power cuts, the looting?" Ali started speaking in Arabic. Zoe heard two of the men start talking casually to each other behind her. She felt calmer, the hostile looks she got at first had subsided, and the men seemed eager to speak.

"They are not happy about the situation at the moment. This gentleman," he gestured with a glance, "says the power cuts are worse now than they were even under Saddam. Before there was no power for two, maybe three hours, now it is for seven or eight. This gentleman," he continued, looking at another, "says there is no safety in the city now. The criminals are free to do what they want, and the Americans do nothing to stop them. It is not safe for their wives and children even inside their houses. We must leave now."

The tone of his voice did not change: he spoke quietly and

calmly, as if he were still translating. She looked up in surprise: he was looking intently at her as if trying to communicate something without any of the others noticing. "We must leave right away. The situation became very dangerous."

"Well, I just need to get their names." But Ali was already thanking the men and shaking hands with some of the older ones. She turned and smiled at the man seated beside her; he avoided her gaze and looked down. Ali gestured to her, and in confusion she stood up and walked towards the car. As they left, she heard hostile murmuring behind her. As soon as they were in the car, Mahmoud drove off at speed and began questioning Ali in Arabic. As Ali explained what had happened, he let out a low whistle and looked back at Zoe in the rear-view mirror.

"What was that about?" she asked, irritated at their abrupt departure. "Why did we have to leave?"

"The two men behind you, they were discussing whether to kill you," replied Ali.

"To kill me?" She was stunned.

"Yes."

"Seriously?"

"Very seriously." He turned and looked back at her.

"Why?"

"They don't like foreigners. I told you, these people are not educated."

Zoe sat in silence. That dusty street corner seemed too shabby a place to die, too far away from everything she knew. Her friends, her mother wouldn't be able to imagine such a place existed.

→━◉⊙◉━←

When she got back to the hotel, badly shaken, all that was left of the day were the last embers of the sun dying red on the windows, though the heat still hit her like a wall. She found the al-Hamra transformed. It had a reputation as the journalists' hotel in Baghdad, and now she could see why. The courtyard was alive with journalists returning from the day's work around the city; they sat in knots at the white plastic tables, talking loudly around a growing litter of empty beer cans. In front of every journalist was a satellite phone, all their plastic aerials pointing in the same direction to pick up a signal. In one corner, a man was speaking excitedly into his, leaning over awkwardly to try to keep the antenna angled right. Now and then he would become so involved in the conversation he moved out of position, and he would curse as he tried to find the signal again. On a balcony three floors above, a television reporter, picked out by the camera lights glaring white against the evening sky, was speaking live by satellite to somewhere across the world. From below, Zoe could see that the crew had carefully chosen a backdrop that included the only palm trees visible from the hotel. The television correspondent looked incongruous up there in her flak jacket. Doubtless it looked dramatic on screen, but from beneath you could see that no one else was wearing one, not even the cameraman—although the television correspondent may have been the wiser, Zoe thought, given the sound of gunfire that echoed in the distance. Every so often, American helicopters passed overhead: at first, there was a distant clatter of sound, then, as it grew in volume, a few of those in the courtyard would peer up to see which side it was coming from; by the time it was a shattering roar, everyone would have their heads craned up, scanning the little rectangle of sky overhead. The helicopters would burst abruptly into view—they always came in pairs for some reason—keeping so low you thought for a moment they would slam into the building opposite. Then they were gone, and the sound slowly died after them.

At one table, a reporter was hunched over a laptop, stabbing at the keys, pausing only to gulp from a can of beer, not noticing as drops of condensation fell silently from it onto his keyboard. Someone was doing gentle laps in the pool. Shouts of laughter rose; the journalists were telling brave stories:

"…was on an embed last week where the Humvee in front of us got hit by an RPG…"

"…translator completely lost his nerve. Refused to go into Ramadi…"

"…another thirty seconds it would have been us…"

"…told him if you want this job, you're coming in…"

"...Americans called up air support. Hit them hard..."

"...ambush. Spent the next half-hour face down in the dirt, bullets flying..."

"...that's nothing. You should have seen us in Samarra..."

"...it's nowhere near as bad as Beirut. Now *that* was dangerous..."

The women leaned forward and toyed with their drinks, sizing up the men from beneath their eyelashes; the men leaned in with careless smiles, their eyes straying down the women. After all, Baghdad was a dangerous, exciting place, and everyone was a long way from home. Across the street, on the upper floors, Zoe could make out local people standing on the balconies of their apartments, staring down at the strange scene around the hotel swimming pool. Still frightened from her experience in Sadr City, Zoe wondered what the watching Iraqis must think of these people who seemed to be having such a good time in the midst of the occupation of their country. She sat down at a table and looked in vain for someone she recognised from London.

When she had called the *Informer* in London, Nigel Langham was all charm and bonhomie; he had safely negotiated the morning conference.

"The Powers That Be want to go big on America today, so it looks like you're off the hook," he told her blithely. Just as Henry Haight was always the Editor, his deputy, a small, balding man by the name of Rob Driscoll, was, for reasons that had always been a mystery to Zoe, only ever spoken of in the newsroom as The Powers That Be, as if he were the head of some cabal that was secretly in control of the newspaper—in fact, he and the Editor detested each other, and he only got to make decisions when Haight was away. When Zoe suggested the piece from Sadr City for the next day's paper, Nigel was unenthusiastic. "I mentioned it at conference, but the feeling here is we've already had lots of vox pops," he said. "We really need you to get your teeth into something solid for tomorrow." She had risked her life for a piece that would never have made the paper, she thought ruefully—unless she had actually been killed. And all because she was too ashamed to turn back. She wondered how many journalists had been killed by shame. She cast her eyes over the courtyard. A lot of the men and women, she noticed, were wearing loose photographers' waistcoats covered in pockets. They looked almost like caricatures of foreign correspondents. It was the sort of thing Zoe wouldn't be seen dead in at home, but here she was beginning to regret her jeans and loose white shirt, and not only because of the heat. There seemed almost a deliberate attempt not to be stylish among the reporters. In one corner she saw the strange, Native American-like man she had seen that morning, ash glowing in the darkening air as it cascaded from the end of his cigarette, talking with a knot of young reporters she didn't recognise. Across from them was a table of men who looked different—big, muscled white men with hostile eyes who kept casting sour looks whenever another table broke out in laughter. On the other side of the courtyard, Zoe noticed a man looking straight at her. She glanced back, wondering if he was someone she knew from London, but she had never seen him before in her life. He gazed back at her unperturbed, without smiling or acknowledging her in any way, and she quickly looked away again. He wasn't good-looking, but there was something about him she wouldn't forget all the same, and it wasn't just the unkempt, overlong dark hair or the several-day stubble; it was something in his eyes and in the way he sat slightly apart, leaning back when all the others at the table were eagerly leaning into the conversation.

"Haven't seen you around before." Zoe looked up: the voice was Australian and standing over her was a slim woman in a loose T-shirt with her long blonde hair tied back in a ponytail. "I'm Kate," she said, holding out her right hand.

"Zoe. I just arrived."

"Why don't you come over and join us?" Kate said, adding with a mischievous smile, "The guys have been asking who you are." She led Zoe to a large table with men and women sitting around it. A can of beer was pushed across to Zoe. The can had so much condensation running down the outside it was clammy in her hand. Kate made the introductions, and Zoe was delighted to discover that sitting across the table from her was one of the most famous foreign correspondents in the world, Bernard J. Randell of the *Washington Report*. Randell—everyone seemed to address him by his surname—had covered the fall of Saigon and the Yom Kippur War. Zoe had studied his reports at university, and now she was sitting with him in Baghdad, covering the same story. But he was nothing like she had imagined from the thunderous, authoritative voice of his writing. He was a small, unimposing man with a nervous manner who constantly jumped into the conversation, self-consciously mentioning the famous people he had met. He often seemed to be trying out snippets of his next article, dropping them into the conversation.

More appealing was Peter Shore, seated immediately to Randell's left: even better-looking in the flesh than he was on television, he was how Zoe had imagined the young Randell, the image of the fearless war correspondent, tall, high cheekbones, tousled golden-blond hair, blue eyes. He had an ethnic-looking blue silk scarf that must have been some sort of turban knotted around his neck and was smoking a cigar. Peter was British, a reporter for MTN, Meteor Television News, one of the twenty-four-hour news networks based out of London, and Zoe had heard plenty of stories about him, how he had ridden into Sarajevo on top of a tank and taken lines of cocaine off the dashboard of his car while driving through an Israeli air raid in Lebanon. There were even rumours of an affair with a minor royal. Zoe was not unhappy to find him glancing in her direction, and she found herself worrying how she looked and wishing she had taken more time over her appearance.

Across from him was Janet Sweeney, a small dark-haired American reporter for the *Los Angeles Record* whom Zoe immediately disliked. She was competitive and interrupted everyone's stories, announcing each time, "That's nothing," before going on to tell a story of her own daring. She was always ready to defer to Randell and was respectful to him to the point of obsequiousness, but she behaved as if she was competing with everybody else.

Beside her was Mervyn Pile, a young English freelancer who was in Baghdad selling stories to papers that couldn't afford to send their own correspondent. Freelancers were paid by the word, usually badly, and it was a risky way to operate: they often didn't even have insurance, but it was a quick way to make a name for yourself. Like Zoe, Mervyn seemed new to war zones.

Constantly rolling cigarettes between his fingers and cracking jokes, he was charming and self-effacing, and there were signs of mutual attraction between him and Kate.

Zoe warmed to Kate: she had an easy manner and seemed to be the keystone holding the table together. She was relaxed and friendly with everyone, even the prickly Janet. Kate worked for Australian television and had been in Baghdad since the invasion. Lastly, there was a French man who looked remarkable: he was wearing the same sort of baggy waistcoat as many of the others, but he had so many different devices clipped to his— walkie-talkie, satellite phone, camera, GPS—that he looked like a sort of commando journalist. He was sipping orange juice instead of beer and said very little. When he slipped out to the bathroom, Zoe asked Kate about him.

"Oh, you mean the Journonator," she said, laughing.

"Journonator?"

"That's what we call him. His real name's Alain...Alain Martin. He lives for journalism—it's all he ever does. Always carries two of everything in case one fails: two satphones, two laptops. Doesn't drink or smoke. He's a complete fitness freak."

Apart from Mervyn, they all seemed to have known each other a long time. As the evening wore on, Zoe began to understand that Baghdad was something of a reunion for them—they were old friends who never met at home, only at various wars and disasters around the world. As the memory of the afternoon receded, and the beer began to take hold, Zoe started to feel secretly pleased that she had been easily accepted by this group of experienced war correspondents as one of their own. When Peter described a recent visit to the insurgency-hit town of Fallujah and told her, "You have to keep your head down, but I'm sure it's no worse than places you've been before," she felt no need to correct him. They called Baghdad "Baggers" and agreed Iraq was the only place to be at the moment, or, in the language of the tribe: "It's the only show in town." At home in London, her friends would be in the pub as usual, and here she was in Baghdad, with Bernard Randell and Peter Shore...and Peter kept glancing at her across the table.

When the food arrived, Zoe was surprised to find it was

vaguely Chinese. Kate was telling the story of the last time she met Peter, in Bethlehem, during an Israeli military operation.

"So we were in the narrow lanes of the old city, and things were looking really dicey. It was deserted, I mean, I've never seen Bethlehem like that. There was no one about, a lot of the buildings were blackened and there were these crushed cars the tanks had just driven over. It was eerie. You could hear the tanks moving about in the background, and no one was really sure how safe it was to be there. If we thought the tanks were coming our way we'd duck into a doorway or an alley. You could so easily get mistaken for a militant and shot. Every now and then you'd see the Hamas and Islamic Jihad guys run past with AKs at the end of the street, dressed all in black like something out of the movies. And everyone else was inside their houses. I mean, you could tell they were there, looking out at you, but you couldn't see them. They were all just keeping their heads down. I ran into Jim Heston from the *New York Times*, and we're both hiding in this dead-end alley thinking this is looking bad, we should get out of here, when I see the most extraordinary sight: there's this guy walking down the middle of the street, and he's carrying a huge flag. I mean a *flag*, and it's got TV written on it. And coming up behind him is a cameraman walking backwards, and after him Peter, doing a fucking piece to camera, walking through the middle of this. It was fucking surreal." Across the table Peter tried unsuccessfully to look sheepish. Zoe wondered if she imagined it or if his false modesty seemed to be particularly aimed in her direction. "And then, when he's finished, he walks up to the front door of the nearest house, starts knocking on it and saying 'Can we come in? We're from British TV.'" Kate was laughing now. "You had to see it to believe it."

"And they let you in?" Alain asked, smiling from the end of the table.

"Oh, yes. Well, you know about hospitality in this part of the world," said Peter. "They never turn you away. Got a great piece. But we got stuck in there for hours when the Israelis came down the street. The Palestinians were terrified of them finding out we'd been in there and wouldn't let us go!"

Zoe heard a voice from behind her.

"Nothing lowers the tone of a hotel like the international press in pursuit of a story," it declared to no one in particular. "And this place didn't have much of a tone to lower in the first place." There was a distinct Irish accent. She looked around in surprise and saw the dark man who had stared at her across the courtyard standing over the table with a smile.

"Jack. We *are* honoured," Kate said with more than a touch of irony. "Take a seat. This is Zoe Temple, by the way; she just arrived for the *Informer*. Everyone else you know."

"Jack Wolfe," he said, holding out his hand to her. She knew the name: she had been reading his bylines. No one had heard much of him before, but he had covered the invasion for the London *Daily Post* and been here ever since. She sensed there was not much love for him around the table. Janet was telling a story about her own first meeting with Peter Shore, in the Balkans.

"So we're in this town, Tetovo, and it's going off. The rebels have taken the hill that overlooks the city, and they're firing down, and the government's basically letting them have everything, trying to get the hill back. They're firing mortars, artillery, everything they've got. The streets are deserted, and we've been wandering around when the army turns up. Suddenly, things don't look so good: we're stuck in a dead-end alley with the military stationed at the only exit. There are four or five of us, and we're around the corner where they can't see us, but there's no other way out, so we decide the best thing is to walk up with our hands in the air. We've all got press IDs so we think we should be all right. Then Peter speaks up. It was the first time I'd met him. He's crouched at the end of the street with the rest of us, and he says, 'You guys go ahead, but you'll have to leave me. I'll find a different way out.'

"'Why don't you just come with us?' we asked, and he said well, he couldn't give himself up to the soldiers. What the hell's this? I thought. It's not like he's a rebel or something. And then he showed us: he had a combat knife with him in his bag. I mean a for-real, twelve-inch *combat* knife! I mean, what the fuck were you doing with that in the middle of Tetovo?"

"God knows," Peter smiled and shook his head self-deprecatingly.

"So we had to leave him there. The rest of us go up to the soldiers and they're pissed and tell us to stay at the hotel. But when we get back there, Peter's already there: he climbed over the roof and through somebody's back garden!"

The table dissolved into laughter, but Zoe couldn't help being distracted by the new arrival sitting beside her. She realised what it was in his eyes that was so unusual: it was the way they seemed to look where they wanted without asking anyone's permission or caring what anyone thought, just as he had interrupted their conversation and joined their table without hesitating. He was younger than most of the others, closer in age to her and Mervyn. He was thin and wiry, without an ounce of spare flesh on him: beside Peter Shore, he was a distinctly unimpressive figure, yet there was something about him that held her attention. When Janet's story was finished, he turned abruptly to Zoe and asked, "So you're the latest addition to the international press *corpse* out here, are you?"

Zoe coloured, unsure whether he had made a gauche mistake in his pronunciation or it was some sort of macabre joke. Janet said loudly from across the table, "Don't you mean corps?"

"No, corpse," Jack replied evenly. "They're a lifeless bunch."

"They seem pretty interesting to me," Zoe said. He smiled.

"Well, you've met the best of them here," he said. "Took over from Martin, did you?"

"Yes."

"You've got the best fixer in town then, Ali," he said.

Zoe smiled awkwardly, thinking of how just a few hours ago Ali had probably saved her life. Then Jack abruptly leaned across the table and interrupted Randell, who was talking to Peter.

"Still convinced it was such a great idea to invade Iraq then, Bernard?" he asked. Randell had been one of the leading supporters of the war in the US press. Despite the light-hearted, joking tone of voice in which he asked the question, Zoe got the impression Jack wanted to needle Randell—no one around the table, not even the experienced Peter Shore, had so much as challenged the legendary Randell on any of the pronouncements he had made about Iraq all evening.

"Well," Randell leaned forward and adjusted his glasses, "I'll grant that not everything has gone quite as we hoped. But what we're talking about here is the opportunity to transform the Middle East. You don't cut and run from a job like that just because of a few setbacks. Right now we're facing some pretty determined opposition from the Sunni Iraqis, but the Shia have decided to give us a chance. The Sunnis have always been on top, and now the Shia want their turn. So far they've welcomed our presence."

Zoe thought of her experience with the Shia in Sadr City that afternoon—she hadn't felt very welcome. But she was reluctant to get involved in the argument so soon after arriving in Baghdad, and she said nothing.

"So it's not liberators any more?" Jack said to Randell. "It's the old colonial world of divide and rule? What happened to the weapons of mass destruction then—found any yet? Seems to me the only person you've succeeded in disarming is that poor kid Ali who got his arms blown off by one of your bombs."

"Jesus, Jack," Peter Shore breathed out. It seemed Wolfe's humour was too dark even for him. The Americans at the table looked horrified.

"Who do you do it for, Jack?" Kate asked across the table. He looked surprised at the question. "It's just that you obviously don't give a shit about the Iraqis. And you seem happy that things aren't going to plan for the Americans. So who do you write your stuff for?"

"Myself, the same as the rest of you."

"Oh no, Jack. That may be true for you, but some of us aren't in it just for ourselves," Kate said, and several of the others murmured in agreement.

"Aren't you?" Jack replied, lounging back in his chair. "I'm here to build a career and visit some interesting places along the way. I'm in it for myself, not to make the world a better place, and if you were honest so are the rest of you. There are saints in Baghdad, but none of them are journalists." Janet was shaking her head, and Randell looked scandalised.

"Well, I think it's time to get some sleep," Peter said, dismissing Jack's comments and getting up from the table. "See you all tomorrow."

The crowd by the pool had already thinned considerably, and one by one, the others got up from the table. When Zoe got back to her room, she could hear the telephone ringing before she opened the door—not the satellite phone, which was in her pocket, but the hotel phone. Wondering who could be ringing at such a late hour—it couldn't be the paper because international calls to Iraq were impossible—she hurried in and answered it. Through the static down the line she managed to make out Ali's voice, very faint and indistinct.

"Miss Zoe, can you hear me? I have found out about a story. A few days ago the Americans killed a family near here. My neighbour says it was a mistake and that the Americans were shooting at each other. The father and two of the children died. We can go to see the mother tomorrow, if you want."

Chapter Four

Hollywood Part One

7 August 2003

THE CAFE IN Adhamiya lay on an unremarkable dusty square. Two small boys were fighting outside, but no one paid them much attention. Electric cables snaked across the square at roof level like jungle creepers; the square lay on the dividing line between two local electricity grids, and the locals had run home-made wiring across so that when there was a power cut on one side, they could take electricity from the other and get a contin-uous supply—or as near to continuous as you could aspire to in Baghdad, which in practice meant less than half the time, since the power was usually out on both sides. It was out now, and inside the cafe the fans were silent and the hot air lay still. The room was choked with cigarette smoke. "Cafe" was too grand a word; it was just a large open room full of battered wooden tables and chairs that did not match, at which men—there wasn't a woman in sight—sat sipping from glasses of black tea so strong you couldn't see the light through them. There was a big window on one side looking out onto the square.

It was early morning, but already the heat was building, and Adel Anwar al-Duleimi could feel his shirt sticking to his back with sweat as he toyed with a glass of tea. From time to time he would take a half-hearted sip. He sat with his closest friend since childhood, Selim, in silence. Adel's eyes were red, with great dark patches under them from lack of sleep, and he was nervous: whenever the door opened, he would look around expectantly at the newcomer, then turn to Selim, who would give a barely perceptible upward tilt of his head to answer no, not this one, and Adel would return to his melancholy study of the tea glass. He had barely slept in three days—but in those three days he had buried his father, his brother and his youngest sister. Now he had come to Adhamiya to join the resistance.

Outside was the patchwork of narrow alleys and lanes he had known since childhood, Adhamiya, the Sunni citadel of Baghdad. Any outsider, Iraqi or foreign, unwise enough to venture into these streets uninvited after dark might never be seen outside them again. At night, Adhamiya belonged to the resistance, and arms and ammunition were openly distributed to the people to attack the Americans. To Adel, this was home, where he grew up, even if his family—the family that was now all but gone, dead, murdered by the Americans—had moved out to a more expensive house in a better neighbourhood many years before. The alleys were haunted for him now; as he passed down them he could see his younger self walking hand in hand with his father, nine years old and bursting with pride, sitting at the table opposite the one where he sat now on the first day his father brought him to this cafe. He could see his father with his stern military face breaking into a smile as he looked down at him, taking a drag on his cigarette; and he could see him as he found him three days before, stretched out on the mortuary slab to cool, stripped of all his futile dignity, a grey piece of flesh that bore only a poor resemblance to his father, the face a mask worn by someone else, without his father behind it to animate the muscles, inhabit the features and wear his face as it should have been worn—stretched out on the slab with a look of surprise frozen on his face and a great hole torn in his chest with the blood turned black all around it. And beside him, Adel's brother Yassin and his sister Rana, their bodies so tiny and feeble, smaller than he remembered them alive, Yassin with a small blackened hole in his forehead, yet an expression so calm it was hard not to believe he was sleeping and would wake in a moment and stretch; and Rana, his little sister, with half her face missing and the flesh torn away where her eyes should have been. Just hours before, he had seen her playing with her dolls and giving them glasses of imaginary tea, smiling and murmuring to herself. That was the moment when Adel's heart gave in, when he saw Rana lying there without her eyes.

And so he had come to meet the foreigner and join the

resistance. His father would not have approved of what he was about to do, his father the colonel who had deliberately kept his eldest son out of the army. He heard his father's ghost whisper in his ear: *If you must join the resistance, go and speak with my friends in the army, fight alongside Iraqi soldiers, don't hide in the shadows with these foreign friends of Selim's.* But those ideas have done nothing to save his father; he hadn't been able to defend his own wife and children from the bullets. Adel recoiled with a stab of guilt from the thought. Again and again over the last three days, Adel had blamed himself that he was not there to protect his family when it happened, even though he knew, in the end, that it would have made no difference, he would have died with the others or lived with the guilt, as his mother and his other sister, Maki, had lived. What chance would anyone have had, unarmed, against American soldiers who opened fire without reason or warning? He would not be unarmed any more.

Adel had not been with them that night, on the visit to his uncle's house, because he had to work late in the office job his father had secured for him. He had returned to find the house empty. At first he hadn't been concerned; he'd wondered idly what had held them up—but as time went on and the curfew loomed, he began to worry. He couldn't phone his uncle's house because the lines in that part of the city had been down since the invasion and were still unrepaired. It was too late to risk going out himself; the chances were he would miss them on the way and get stranded on the streets after curfew. So he sat and waited, growing more anxious. Twenty minutes after the curfew began, he decided to take the risk.

Just as he was gathering his courage to leave, Selim arrived breathless at the door: his family…the Americans…check-point…opened fire on them…mother and sister in hospital…father and brother taken away…no one knew where…in a bad way. Adel rushed straight into the night despite the curfew, rode to the hospital on the back of Selim's motorbike and found his mother, who had held him in her arms and made him feel safe all his life—even when he was a boy and his father was away for months in the war in Kuwait—he had found his mother helpless for the first time in his life, sitting by his sister's bedside pale and shaking, unable to cry, unable to speak, other than to murmur the names of her other children, Yassin and Rana, who had been taken away by the Americans. And Maki lying in bed unconscious, with bloodstained bandages around her head and chest, and tubes and wires connected to her body. The doctors told him they were out of danger and needed rest, so he had gone out again to find his father; they rode from hospital to hospital but could not find him. After a near miss with an American patrol, when they had to duck the motorbike into a dead-end turning and switch off the light, Selim had insisted they go home till the curfew ended at dawn. Adel had sat, unable to sleep, waiting for news and trying to hold back the rising dread.

When light began to show in the sky, mad with fear for his father and brother and sister, he rushed out again. They asked the police, the ambulance drivers…no one had heard anything. Adel asked Selim to show him the place where it happened, but Selim held back. Eventually Adel persuaded him, and as soon as they reached the spot he knew why Selim didn't want to bring him there. The blood—his father's blood—was still smeared casually across the road, as if to mock him. This is all your loved ones are, it said, flesh and blood to be smeared in the dirt. There were bullet-holes everywhere, in the walls, in the cars parked at the side of the street, but no sign of his family or their car.

When the local people realised who he was, they came out to tell him what they had seen. At first they were evasive, but one old man looked him frankly in the eyes and told him: he had seen the Americans take his father, brother and sister from the car, and they had been dead. Unable to comprehend it, a terrible sickness in his stomach, begging fate for the old man to be wrong, he had ridden with Selim to the mortuary and found the bodies. He barely remembered arranging the funeral, bringing his mother and sister home, watching while they lowered his father and brother and sister into the ground, and when it was finished, he had finally lost himself in the emptiness, fallen out of existence and ceased to feel until Selim came to try to talk him out of the madness. Adel had told him he wanted to join the resistance.

The door opened again and Adel looked round: a young man he recognised but didn't know well came in, a friend of

Selim's called Daoud. After they had both shaken hands with him, Selim took Daoud to one side and they spoke together, then Selim leaned across the table to Adel and said, "Our host is waiting. Shall we go?" He left some money on the table for the tea as Adel stood and followed the others out into the street.

They turned left onto a narrow street and into the doorway of a house. Adel followed the other two inside, blinking in the darkness after the sharp sunlight outside. They were shown into a small living room full of chairs with the curtains drawn shut, ostensibly to keep out the heat but in truth, Adel knew, to hide what was about to take place inside. In the gloom sat a man who looked like a Gulf Arab, probably Saudi, though he was dressed in the typical clothes of a young Iraqi man, jeans and a shirt. A taller Iraqi, the owner of the house, introduced him as Abu Khalid, but Adel knew that would not be his real name. Selim greeted him respectfully, addressing him as sheikh, and Adel followed his lead, mumbling his own greetings, and then sat in one of the chairs facing the foreigner. Selim, who was making the usual polite enquiries about Abu Khalid's journey to Baghdad, had told Adel he should not think of him as a foreigner, that there were no borders between believers. He had arrived that morning from Fallujah, west of Baghdad. It was not safe for him to stay in the capital, and he would return before nightfall.

As Adel's eyes adjusted to the darkness in the room, after the brightness of the street and the cafe with its large windows, he found himself surprised by the appearance of the man he had come to meet. Selim had said he had fought against the Americans in Afghanistan, but he showed little trace of it. He looked barely older than Adel himself, and he spoke softly and politely. Adel was almost disappointed, and yet he heard his father's ghost at his ear again, warning him: *Don't be fooled, these are not your people. If you avenge me, do it my way.* But the resistance of his father's old army comrades, who had disappeared into the provinces to fight a war of attrition against the Americans, was too cautious for the grief that was in him now. Abu Khalid and the foreigners had vowed to turn Iraq into a burning hell for the Americans and to pursue them wherever they went across the world.

"Our friends told us about the martyrdom of your father," Abu Khalid said to him from across the room, murmuring the usual condolences. Adel felt a surge of pride at hearing his father called a martyr. As the foreigner spoke respectfully, Adel felt at ease with him. Selim was right: there were no borders between them.

"And what about you?" Abu Khalid asked. "Are you ready to become a martyr?" Adel started. He had heard this language before; he suspected Abu Khalid was asking whether he was prepared to be a suicide bomber. Adel was ready to risk his life in battle and avenge his father, but not for suicide bombing. He couldn't be sure that was what Abu Khalid was asking or how he would react to a refusal. He glanced at Selim for help, but his eyes were on the carpet.

"I...if my fate is to die in battle," he began haltingly.

Abu Khalid smiled back at him.

"Sure, I know what you mean," he said. He seemed relaxed; perhaps Adel's imagination was getting the better of him. "There's something I'd like you to see," Abu Khalid said, and he turned to the owner of the house, who stood up, went across to the television in one corner and began fiddling with the DVD player beneath it. After a while, the picture flared into life. Adel stared in puzzlement: they were showing him what appeared to be a recording of American television footage of the invasion, three months before, the American journalists' voices droning in the background.

"Sorry for this, we had to hide it in the middle of this, so the Americans wouldn't find it," Abu Khalid explained. The picture on the television changed. There was a flicker as it steadied, then the face of an American soldier came into view, but this one was not riding in triumph through Baghdad: he was kneeling on the floor, surrounded by men masked in black, a tall, pale man with his fair hair shaved close. The picture quality was not good; it was a home-made video, and it jerked around. One of the men in black drew out a long knife. Someone was speaking; it sounded like some sort of live commentary—the sound quality was too poor for Adel to make it out. There was fear in the American's eyes, desperate terror. The masked man put the knife to the

American's throat, Adel's heart was pounding, but he couldn't take his eyes from the screen. The knife slid into the American's throat at the side, below the ear, and, still alive, he tensed as if trying to cope with the pain. Adel heard him gasp. A small trickle of dark blood emerged from the wound. The masked man kept pushing the knife in, deeper into the American's throat, then he pulled it forward, slicing open his neck. Much more blood came out and the life seemed to drop from the American. Adel watched him die. The masked man set about carving off the remains of the neck connecting the head to the body. There were muffled cheers on the tape. The masked man held up the severed head to the camera, and the picture flicked back to old news footage. Adel found he was shaking; he had never thought he would be happy to watch a man killed, but here was one of his father's killers, dead and humiliated.

"Hollywood," said Abu Khalid from across the room, chuckling. "They gave us their Hollywood, now we'll give them ours. This was made by our brothers in Chechnya, but, God willing, soon we'll be making our Hollywood movies in Iraq." Not an American then. Adel tried to hide his disappointment. "He was Russian," Abu Khalid said dismissively, as if in answer to Adel's unspoken thought, "but God willing, the next one will be an American. Or British. We need the help of our Iraqi brothers to capture one."

"Capture an American soldier?" Adel asked.

"A soldier would be best. But any of them will do. The businessmen who come here to steal the wealth. The journalists who come to film, so they can pretend to show Iraq humiliated and defeated. Any American will do: they're all the same." Adel heard his father's voice nagging at his ear: *They are not the same,* it said. *A soldier would never*...but he silenced it. An hour ago he had felt powerless against his father's killers. Abu Khalid's Hollywood had made him feel capable again.

⇥●⇤

Zoe stood in a quiet suburban street, outside a low concrete house, trying to ward off the effects of a violent hangover from the previous night's drinking. She hadn't drunk that much, but the relentless heat and aridity of Baghdad had magnified the effects out of all reason: there was a hammering in her head and a greasy unease in her stomach. The dry desert air was like sandpaper against her parched throat. Now, when she longed to sink back between the sheets in the air-conditioned cool of the hotel, she was standing in the sun on a hot, dusty road while Ali tried to work out if they were in the right place. On top of that, she was distinctly nervous of being in the open after her experience the previous day.

"This is the house, I'm sure of it," Ali said. But there was no answer when he knocked at the door. "My friend told me they would wait for us." Across the street, Mahmoud was sitting back lazily inside the Mercedes. Zoe had managed to drag herself from bed when she was awakened by the persistent ringing of the phone. It was Ali calling from downstairs to say he and Mahmoud had arrived. She had overslept by an hour, and she had to make the two Iraqis wait while she ate a quick breakfast. Now she was facing the possibility that, because she had made them late, the family she was planning to interview had gone out, and she would be left without a story. Ali knocked one more time and was answered by silence. He turned to her.

"I think they have gone."

She was about to turn reluctantly from the door when she heard a bolt being pulled. The door opened a crack, and a woman's face peered out nervously. Ali spoke to her in Arabic, gesturing towards Zoe. The woman looked mistrustful. After some more conversation, Ali turned to Zoe.

"Please come." The woman opened the door, and let her inside, but Ali did not follow. She looked around questioningly.

"Her son has gone out," he explained. "That is why she did not answer. She cannot let me inside if there is no man. She will let you because you are a woman."

"But how will I—"

"She is sending the neighbour's son to bring her brother-in-law. I will come in a minute." Zoe followed the woman uncertainly into the house. Now she saw her close up, Zoe could tell this was the woman she had come to meet. Grief sat like a mask upon her face; her eyes stared out from behind it as if haunted by images of the dead. She showed Zoe silently to a living room with seats arranged around the four walls and turned on the air conditioner, then went out with a whisper from the long, loose dress she wore.

Zoe looked around the room. There were no family pictures, just a large embroidery of Mecca. She sat and wondered if it had been wise to come inside without Ali—but he had seemed to think it was all right. After a couple of minutes, the door opened and the woman reappeared, carrying a tray with a glass of water on it, which she offered to Zoe. Unsure whether it was safe to drink—she knew the tap water in Baghdad was not—but reluctant to offend, Zoe took it and sipped gently, though she would have preferred to drain the glass and slake her thirst. The woman smiled sadly at her and nodded encouragingly. Fearing she would suffer for it later, Zoe tipped back the glass and swallowed most of the water; it tasted harmless enough. Then the woman went out again, and Zoe sat in silence. There was no sign of Ali, and she began to worry. She was close to getting up and trying to walk out of the house when the door opened and Ali came in with an older Iraqi man who nodded respectfully to her, then sat down at the far side of the room. Ali introduced him as the brother-in-law, then sat between them and leaned across to murmur to Zoe: "Sorry to keep you waiting. I think this lady will be here in a minute. She had asked her son to wait for us, but he had to go out this morning. She says he will be back soon. This gentleman is her brother-in-law, and he has agreed to be with us."

The door opened and the widow came back in, half-supporting a young girl, no older than fourteen, who stumbled into the room in a daze. Her head and side were heavily bandaged, and she seemed traumatised: she looked out at the world as an unfamiliar, hostile place. They sat in silence, and Ali murmured what appeared to be condolences. The mother nodded slightly to acknowledge him, but the daughter did not even look up. Both were in another place of their own. Zoe looked hesitantly at Ali. He gestured for her to begin.

"Please, could you tell them I am sorry for their loss, and

thank them for speaking to me," she asked him. He translated, and the mother nodded back in the same absent way. "Could I take her name, please, and the name of her daughter?" The mother's name was Zaynab. Zoe started at the initial Z…there were not many other women's names that began with a Z, not many she knew of anyway. Her dead husband's name had been Anwar al-Duleimi. The daughter who sat beside her was Maki. Her dead children, Zaynab went on, unbidden, were Yassin and Rana. Zoe wondered how to begin to ask her about their deaths. The silence lengthened. "Could you ask her to tell us what happened?" Zoe asked.

And Zaynab told her about that night, how the family had been returning from a visit to her brother's house, how they had come to an American checkpoint and her husband had done everything they were told to do, had dimmed the lights and approached slowly, and how the Americans had started shooting at them for no reason. How she had shielded Maki, who was closest to her, with her own body. "The bullets were coming into the car," she said, "they were all around us. They kept hitting my children again and again." There was no emotion in her voice; she spoke in an even tone: it was as if she had no emotions left to feel. She seemed to speak out of an untouchable numbness. As she spoke, Zoe felt that she had uncovered a real story, a tragedy that needed to be told to the world. She, Zoe Temple, would demand justice for this poor woman and her daughter.

"What did the Americans say?" Zoe asked. It was the brother-in-law, from the other side of the room, who answered.

"Nothing," Ali translated. "They have said nothing. No one has come to us; no one has spoken to us." Zaynab murmured something. "She says, 'They have destroyed my whole family, but for them I do not exist,'" Ali said.

"What about Maki? How are you now?" Zoe asked. But when Ali translated, the girl kept her eyes on the floor, her reverie unbroken, and it was Zaynab who answered.

"The doctors say her wounds are not serious and she will be fine," Ali translated. "But Mrs Zaynab is worried about her. She does not speak any more. She does not want to eat and they have to feed her." Zaynab got up and drew something from the folds of her dress. She held it out to Zoe, a photograph of her children sitting together. Zoe recognised Maki; beside her was another girl, shyly looking down, and a boy smiling up into the camera. Behind them stood a young man, the oldest son, the one who wasn't with them that night. Zaynab did not let go of the picture, but held it in her hand for Zoe to see—it might have been all she had left of her dead children. Zoe looked up into her eyes, but all she met was the same bewildered grief.

"How old is she?" she asked.

"She is thirty-four," Ali translated.

"And her children?"

"Adel, the eldest—the one who is not here—is eighteen—"

"So she was only sixteen when she had him."

"Yes," Ali nodded. "It is not unusual here." He gave the ages of the other children. Rana, the little girl in the picture, was only five.

There was an abrupt electronic ringing from Zoe's bag—the satellite phone. She looked to Ali in consternation. Sensing the problem, he spoke to the family. The brother-in-law replied.

"Please answer your phone," Ali translated. "They do not mind."

"Please apologise for me," Zoe said, fishing for the phone in her bag. "I have to go outside to get a signal."

"No problem," Ali said, explaining to the others in Arabic. The brother-in-law quickly stood and opened the door. Zoe stepped back out into the heat and panned the phone's aerial around the horizon, looking for a signal. When she found one, the ringing tone changed and she answered. It was Nigel Langham's voice, breathless down the line from London.

"Zoe, we're getting reports of a massive bomb at the Jordanian Embassy. Can you get there as quick as you can and let us know what's happening?"

"OK, but I've got a fantastic story. I've found a woman whose—"

"This looks huge on the wires. It's all the Editor is going to want today, so just drop whatever you're doing and get there."

"I'm in a slightly tricky position, Nigel. I'm in the middle of an interview with a woman whose children have been killed—"

"Not now, Zoe, I've got to head straight into conference. Just get over there."

"OK," Zoe said reluctantly, wondering how she was going to extricate herself from the house. She went back in and spoke to Ali, trying to keep her voice even. "There's been a bombing at the Jordanian Embassy."

"OK, it is close to here," he said. "We will go after—"

"They want us to go straight there."

"We cannot leave now," he said. "And if we go, it may not be easy to return."

"Well…I have the story."

"So ask a few more questions. Then I will explain we are finished."

She asked Zaynab about her husband. It had been an arranged marriage; he was a colonel in the Iraqi army; he fought in the war with Iran and in the invasion of Kuwait. He was a good man. Zoe wrote it all down, her mind racing on, wondering whether they would get to the bomb scene in time, feeling guilty she was not taking Zaynab's tragedy seriously enough. She asked what Zaynab thought of the Americans, but Zaynab said nothing, just shook her head slightly. Ali brought the interview to a close, thanking Zaynab and her brother-in-law while Zoe gathered up her notes. As they were leaving, she had a thought.

"Can we arrange for a photographer to come and take pictures of them?" It would give her a chance to accompany him and ask more questions. Ali spoke to Zaynab, and she agreed. As they drove away, Zoe realised she had not met the oldest son, Adel.

Though the Jordanian Embassy was nearby, they moved slowly though the traffic. Eventually, Zoe saw smoke rising ahead, and as they turned the corner, a scene of chaos. The street where the embassy had stood was a wide avenue lined with expensive villas, but the embassy itself was in ruins: half of the building collapsed in a great pile of concrete. A Mercedes, completely intact, sat incongruously on the roof of the neighbouring villa, where it had been blown by the force of the blast. A crowd of onlookers had gathered, and there were American soldiers everywhere. They had parked a long line of tanks down the middle of the street, outside the smouldering ruins of the embassy, and Mahmoud had to reverse quickly back around the corner to park. As he did, Zoe caught sight of a third group of people, the journalists, several of whom she recognised from the night before, wandering amid the wreckage with television cameras. She and Ali left Mahmoud in a side road and headed back to the scene on foot. As they turned into the main street, Zoe could see more: twisted shreds of cars that had been blown apart by the bomb lay scattered across the road, an engine here, half a door there. There were other things on that road too, things that looked like pieces of people torn apart by the blast. Zoe tried not to look too closely, but she couldn't help catching sight of a severed head. The face was badly burned, but she could make out where the eyes had been.

The Iraqi crowd was getting restive, and the American soldiers trying to secure the area were clearly on edge. They were shouting from the tops of the tanks at the Iraqis to get back. Zoe realised she was trapped between the soldiers and the Iraqis, and she wasn't sure which group looked more nervous or liable to sudden violence. All it would take would be one rock thrown at the Americans, or for one soldier to lose his nerve and fire a single shot, and she would have nowhere to run. A dense pack of journalists was moving through the crowd; they were bunched around someone she couldn't see, all seemingly shouting questions at once. The man in the middle was trying to get away, but the pack kept moving with him. Photographers at the edges were holding their cameras high in the air to get a clear view over the heads of the others, with the result that they must have had very little idea of the picture they were taking. Reporters were trying to walk and scribble quotes in their notebooks at the same time; others were using dictaphones, thrusting them blindly into the mass of bodies. The journalists were pushing and shoving each other aggressively, jostling for a better position. Worst off seemed to be the television crews with their heavy cameras; accordingly they were the most aggressive of all—Zoe saw one with his teeth bared as he tried to push his way in. They were in the middle of a potential riot between angry locals and heavily armed soldiers, and all the journalists were worried about was getting their story from this unfortunate man.

Zoe realised that she too would need the quotes from the man in the midst of the press and hurried over to the group. But it was no use; she could not see over the heads of the men or hear anything but the shouts of the other journalists' questions. Between their shoulders, she could vaguely make out the man at the centre of the mêlée. He looked Iraqi, had a blood-stained bandage on his head, and seemed to be wearing some sort of uniform. He looked confused and was desperately trying to get away from all the journalists. She saw Peter Shore in the crowd with his cameraman; he smiled over and nodded.

"Who is this guy?" she shouted across to him. He held up a hand to her as if to say he'd be with her in a minute. At that moment she felt a heavy arm on her shoulder and turned to see a large television cameraman who simply pushed her out of his way. She despaired of getting anything she could use and stood back. Now, to her consternation, she couldn't see Ali: she had been separated from him by the rush of the press, which had moved her some way up the street away from the smouldering embassy. The acrid smell of smoke hung in the air.

"Zoe Temple. How are you?" She looked round in surprise. Jack Wolfe was sitting against a low wall in front of one of the neighbouring villas, looking on as the other journalists jostled each other with what seemed like amusement. To her surprise, he was wearing a loud Iraqi short-sleeved shirt, similar to Ali's and Mahmoud's—quite different from the simple white shirt he had worn the previous night. "Not trying to get a quote along with the rest of our colleagues, then?"

"No, I...well," she stammered, somewhat embarrassed by her failure. "Neither are you."

"No," he smiled. "Everything that unfortunate man has to say on the matter will be on television screens all over the world in less than half an hour. Long before my deadline or yours. I'll take down what he has to say in the comfort of my room. Our colleagues are doing an adequate job of torturing him on their own, don't you think?" She glanced back at the crowd of journalists and at the figure of Peter Shore with his notebook aloft amid the chaos. The journalists were finally dispersing now, leaving the wounded man to wander off in a daze, alone but for a few stragglers who pursued him, trying to get the story they had missed. Zoe thought for a moment she should follow, but it seemed the man had had enough of the world press's attentions: he stared doggedly ahead and said nothing. Blood was seeping out from under the bandage around his head.

"So what do you think?" Jack asked.

"About what?"

"All this."

"It's…I mean, it's horrendous," she said, instantly regretting the emotional response. She expected him to mock, but for once he didn't.

"Yes, it is," he said.

She could hear one of the television cameramen talking loudly. "Got great footage of the severed head," he was saying, "not that those bastards will use it." The American soldiers were getting aggressive. They were trying to clear everyone away from the scene, and one was walking right towards them, shouting and gesturing for them to move back.

"Time to go," said Jack. Not knowing what else to do, Zoe followed him into the side streets. She was looking around for Ali, but she still couldn't see him. She tried to remember where they had left the car, but they were off the main street and she couldn't make out the geography. She realised she might have to ask Jack for a lift. Then she spotted Ali emerging from a crowd that was being shooed towards them. He came over and to her surprise greeted Jack warmly, both men touching their hands to their hearts in the local manner. Then Ali turned to her.

"I got the quotes from that man who was wounded," he said. "He is a policeman who was guarding the embassy when the blast happened. He says many people were killed, perhaps ten. The bomb was hidden in a pick-up truck."

"I told you he was good," said Jack. Zoe hurriedly scribbled down the details from Ali in her notebook. Looking up, she saw Randell approaching, with Peter Shore and his cameraman not far behind. Jack had seen them too, it seemed.

"Still convinced things are going well?" he called out to Randell with a smile. He sounded as if he were amused, rather than being nasty, but Zoe could see from Randell's and Peter's expressions that they took it as a taunt.

"Well, Jack, it's a setback, I have to admit," Randell said. Jack smiled as he walked off, saying over his shoulder to Zoe, "See you later."

"That guy is an arsehole," Peter said after he had left. "Pretty dramatic stuff, though," he said to Zoe after Randell had moved on. "We got some great shots of the street and the soldiers all panicky. And that security guard should play well. You?"

"I got the security guard. I'll have to see what they want in London."

"Oh, I expect they'll go pretty big on this one. Looks like it could have been a suicide bombing. We're heading to the hospitals to see if we can talk to the wounded."

Zoe decided to do the same, but before leaving, she called London. As she read out the hastily written notes she had taken from Ali, she realised she had her first story from a war zone.

Chapter Five

Secrets

7 August 2003

THE BATTERED RED Mercedes was nosing through the Baghdad
streets again, but this time Zoe was not inside: the back seat was
empty, as was the front passenger seat, and Mahmoud sat alone
behind the wheel. There was something furtive in the way he
drove, glancing quickly this way and that, as if he were afraid to
be witnessed. He had kept his sunglasses on even though it was
evening, and the light was fading. He was in the back streets,
where there was little traffic, and he could have sped through,
but he was driving almost wilfully slowly, like a man in two
minds about his journey, who is half convinced he should turn
back, but goes on all the same. The streets were heavy with the
anticipation twilight brings to big cities, the feeling that something is about to happen.

Mahmoud looked up nervously at the passers-by who were
on their way to prayers at the mosque, but none betrayed any
sign they recognised him. The streetlamps were beginning to
show their jaundiced light against the darkening sky, but still
Mahmoud did not turn on the headlights of the Mercedes. The
area he was moving through was a dusty neighbourhood of run-
down private houses, the people who inhabited these streets,
with their grime-stained buildings and rusting window frames,
were not Mahmoud's people: they were his countrymen, yes, but
not his society, and even if he considered them his inferiors, he
felt uncomfortable, an intruder in their world.

This was the season of betrayal. Trust no one, he and his father
and brothers told each other, trust no one but the family, not even
old friends and neighbours—and the people in this neighbourhood were not people Mahmoud would trust in quieter times,

except for the occupants of one house, the place where he was heading. He trusted them, though he knew that if his parents even thought he were here, they would be frightened and angry. And so his visit here was a secret, tacked onto the end of the working day so his family would think he was still driving the foreign journalist around, and Ali would think that Mahmoud had gone straight home. Trust no one, not even Ali.

In the old days, under Saddam, his family had kept a piece of paper next to the telephone that said, "Be careful: the enemy is listening." It was a clever warning that could be easily explained away to any visiting police or security men as a reference to the intelligence services of the Iranians in the old days, or more recently those of the Americans, enemies of the state. But in truth "the enemy" it referred to was Saddam's own intelligence service listening on the line, who could burst into your house in the dead of night and drag you away for a careless joke. You might not be seen again for seven years, like Mahmoud's cousin, who finally came home one day unrecognisably thin, with painful scars and a limp, a broken man in more ways than one. Or you might not come back at all. The enemy was the security apparatus of your own country, and it was always listening: everyone was a potential informer. Mahmoud had a school friend whose name was Saddam; in restaurants and public places, they had all called him by his father's name, Ahmad, in case someone overheard and mistook a joke or derogatory remark about their friend Saddam for a reference to *the* Saddam, the man who could make you disappear, who could make it that you had never been born.

But the enemy was still listening; only now he was everywhere, and he had many faces. He was your country, and the others. Now "the enemy" meant the American soldiers, who could drag you from your bed in the night as easily as Saddam's men once did and who had torturers of their own. But it also meant the Iraqi resistance fighters, ex-army men who considered anyone who worked for the Americans a "collaborator" to be taken down a dead-end street with a bag over his head and left for the dogs to fight over. "The enemy" encompassed the religious extremists who had come from Saudi Arabia and Yemen to fight the Americans, who also carried out executions of collaborators and were rumoured to prefer the knife. And it included the Shia militias who were springing up in Sadr City, who had designs on seizing power in Iraq and their own ideas of what to do with the old Sunni elite, families like Mahmoud's who had supposedly done well under Saddam, although as far as he could remember they had always been terrified. Trust no one, not even Ali, because even though Ali came from the same elite as Mahmoud and had more relatives in the army than Mahmoud did, even though Ali was a friend, in the end Ali was a Shia, and the Shia were the enemy.

Mahmoud peered down the street for the signal and, when he spotted it, turned into a back alley and drove some way up before parking the Mercedes out of sight. Before he got out, he looked furtively up and down the street to make sure no one was watching. It was too dark to keep the sunglasses on without looking ridiculous, and he reluctantly threw them on the dashboard. He locked the car and tried the door handle to make sure, then set off down the street, his heart sounding in his ears as he walked down to the corner, treading again the familiar path of betrayal.

He had met Ali when the tall Shia came looking for a driver for the foreign journalist. Mahmoud had driven for another journalist during the war, but he had gone home and Mahmoud was out of work. A friend had recommended him to Ali, who came to call at his family home. But for his name, you would never have known then that the polite, well-spoken man who sat in the room for guests and drank tea was a Shia. He spoke and gestured like the Iraqis Mahmoud had grown up with all his life. He was well educated, he spoke English and he had a degree in engineering. In front of Mahmoud's father, he was all respect; later, once they were in the car, he and Mahmoud joked easily together and told stories about girls. Ali was one of the Shia who came from a military family and had been able to attend the best schools and universities, growing up with the Sunni elite. In the old days, there would have been no ambiguity, they came from the same background, but now Ali was the enemy, though he was also Mahmoud's best friend.

And Mahmoud knew the house he was on his way to visit now was the house of the enemy. He paused at the end of the street as if reconsidering, lingered a moment in the shadow away from the streetlight and then went on.

They had spent the afternoon driving from hospital to hospital to find the survivors of the bombing at the Jordanian Embassy. The new foreigner, the beautiful young woman, had been very excited, just as Mr Martin would have been, talking quickly to Ali in English, too quickly for Mahmoud to keep up with. But he liked this new foreigner; she seemed kinder, more friendly than Mr Martin—and she was a lot better to snatch glances at in the rear-view mirror. Mahmoud had cared little when he saw the smoking ruins of the Jordanian embassy—the Jordanians were no friends of Iraq; they had helped the Americans to invade, they had bowed down before the Americans and Israel for years, and now they were exulting that Iraq had been brought low. But when they went to the hospitals and Ali emerged from inside to tell Mahmoud what he had seen in there, the innocent Iraqis who had been security guards, or just unlucky enough to be in the area when the bomb went off, one with both his legs gone, another with one of his eyes gouged out, Mahmoud had felt angry. Who was the enemy, the Jordanians or the men behind the bomb?

He came to a door and rang the bell. He ducked in close to the building while he waited for someone to answer. After a few minutes the door opened, and Mahmoud stepped in. A young girl showed him into the reception room with a conspiratorial gleam in her eye. She spoke little, just murmured the customary greetings, but her eyes said enough. She left him there, in the familiar room where he had waited so many times. He glanced over the furniture, cheap and badly made, but lovingly cared for and kept clean, the big brown sofa and the armchairs that did not match, the dining table that was always covered with a fresh white cloth so no one would see the plywood beneath. He looked over the bookshelves, weighed down with foreign books, the titles in English and in another alphabet he could make nothing of, and he felt afraid: books like these could get you killed. And he turned to the shelf above the television, to where it stood beside the framed photographs in pride of place, the sign of the enemy: the cross.

And then the door opened and she was there, Saara, his love, the enemy, with her face like sunlight and her midnight eyes made for dreaming. Her long, dark hair was gathered up but uncovered, and she was dressed in loose, baggy clothes to hide the shape of her firm body, but he could make it out when she moved, and when she deliberately stood provocatively for him so that the folds fell back across her breasts and hips—the body he longed to touch and hold, but knew he could not, not here, in her home, where her mother could walk through the door at any moment. Around her neck hung a little silver crucifix, that flimsy piece of metal that was such a wall between them.

"Hello," he said softly. He could not even embrace her, but held back at a respectable distance.

"Hello, Mahmoud," she said with a smile. Then, as if she had just remembered she didn't mean to smile at him, her face abruptly changed to a pout. "Where have you been? I haven't seen you for days."

"I know," he said. "It's difficult. I have to work when the foreigners want, and there is the curfew."

They sat side by side on the sofa, with a decorous distance between them, always a distance. She leaned forward, all wide eyes, as if she had just remembered something, "Were you at the bombing today? At the Jordanian Embassy?"

"Yes."

"I watched for you on the TV, but I didn't see you. I was worried about you: you be careful; this job of yours isn't safe."

"Don't worry, Ali and I are very careful—"

"But that foreigner, that Martin, he sounds crazy, always rushing into danger."

"He's gone. We've got a new journalist now."

"What's he like?"

"This one is a woman."

"A woman!" She frowned, and Mahmoud wondered if it had been wise to tell her. "Is she pretty?"

"She's not so bad," he said. Then when her brows contracted,

68

he quickly added, "I'm joking! She's a foreigner, not attractive at all. Too thin."

"The Western women all *want* to be thin," she said.

"They're crazy," he said dismissively. Then, "Is your father—?"

"Don't worry, he won't be back for an hour. And Maryam is keeping watch."

"And your brother?"

"He's out too, but anyway he likes you."

"Yes, but—"

"He won't tell anyone."

Mahmoud reached out to touch her, but she drew back.

"Not here," she said sharply, but when she looked up her eyes were laughing. "I want to too, but we can't here," she said.

"Then where? There is nowhere."

"We have to wait for the situation to change," she said. "When it's calmer." Mahmoud didn't think it was going to get any calmer; he thought it was going to get worse, but he didn't tell her that.

"It's all right for you," she said, "driving around all day with the foreigners in your fancy car, while I'm stuck here."

"You think I wouldn't rather be here with you?"

"I don't know," she pouted again. "Maybe you have another girlfriend; maybe you have lots of girlfriends."

He wanted to say he lived only for these stolen minutes with her, that every second she was in his mind, that Saara was the clock he set his hours by, the rhythm to which his heart beat. He wanted to tell her that, but he laughed and said, "Yes, half the city: I go to three different houses every day. All the fathers are chasing me across Baghdad."

She smiled at that.

"You don't know what it's like," she said. "You're out there, hanging around with the foreigners, seeing everything that's happening. I just sit here and watch on TV, cut off from the world. This is what I studied for, to sit in here and watch TV."

He had met Saara at university. From the first moment he saw her, he had been beguiled by the confident girl with the mocking eyes who made fools of all the men who tried to flirt with her. Mahmoud used to watch her with her women friends, passing sly glances at the young men and laughing. He worried what they might be saying when they looked in his direction. And then had come the day when he was studying late in a library that was all but empty to make up for time lost on a trip out of town with his friends, and she was beside him, just three seats away. He sat in silence a long time, agonising, yearning to speak to her, but too shy. He kept glancing up at her, and more than once she met his eyes. Eventually it became intolerable, saying nothing became more embarrassing than speaking, and he murmured, "Hello."

For a long time there was silence. He had dreaded the sort of putdown he had heard her give so many of the men, but this silence was worse. Humiliated, he turned his head back to his books and pretended to read. Then he heard from her direction a soft "Hello" as nervous and uncertain as his. And so it had started. Her diffidence did not last long; within no time she was mocking him.

"The one who likes to pretend he doesn't look at the girls," she laughed. "I thought you'd never say 'Hello'." But she said it playfully, not the way she spoke to other men, and he replied, "You took your time too. I was beginning to think you were deaf."

Soon they were dating in secret. But in a world where young men and women weren't even supposed to look at each other, still less talk, she was an unattainable dream. If she had been a Muslim, he would have asked his mother to sound her family out on the possibility of an arranged marriage, but with a Christian his parents would be against it. He didn't even dare to ask. And so all they could do was snatch a few moments together in a cafe over a Pepsi. To this day, he still hadn't kissed her, though he had imagined it a thousand times. The most they had done was secretly hold hands. She was intelligent—much more so than he was, Mahmoud knew. She spoke English and watched foreign films. She took top honours at university and got a good job in an office. And then the war came and her world fell apart: under Saddam, she had been able to walk to work, now it was dangerous for her inside the company offices, let alone walking the streets.

Her parents wouldn't let her work, and despite her fury, Mahmoud knew they were right. It wasn't just the danger of being groped or worse by some man on the lawless streets. She didn't know how dangerous it had become outside, where men were shot dead behind the wheels of their cars while they waited at traffic lights, and there were reports of mysterious disappearances every day. There were rumours of kidnapping for money, and for a Christian, who didn't have a tribe to protect her as he did, it was even more dangerous. The Christians had a reputation for being rich that made them tempting targets, although in her family's case it was undeserved. But for Saara, he knew, it was torture to sit inside all day, helping her mother with the cleaning, sewing, watching the television all the time for a sense of the world outside. Her mother let her watch the foreign news, but it had to be switched over to respectable television when her father came home—until late at night, when the women were all banished from the room and he could watch the skimpily dressed models on Fashion TV, an open secret in the house, though no one ever admitted to it.

And for Mahmoud the war had been a disaster too. Now all his tentative plans for how they could be together, the dreams of bringing his parents round, the plans in his wilder moments to elope with her and leave the country, seemed impossible. Before, she had been a good Iraqi with a different religion, but now difference was becoming everything. Already he had overheard people muttering against the Christians, that they shared their religion with the Americans, were collaborators, and he feared soon they too would be the enemy. At first he thought he would not be able to see her, but in the end it was her mother who was their benefactor: Saara sent a message to him that he could come and visit when her father was out; her mother would pretend not to notice he was there. She would leave a ribbon beside her window when her father was out. If anything went wrong and her father was there, he was to say he had come to visit her brother Yusuf—Mahmoud got on well with the easy-going, modern Yusuf, who had a girlfriend of his own the family did not know about.

Now Mahmoud was inwardly berating himself for telling her the new journalist was a woman: it would be torture for her, to think he was working with a foreign woman who could roam the streets as she wanted while Saara had to stay locked up safely inside.

The worst thought was that her parents might decide to marry her off. He knew her parents were liberal and had been open to the idea of her having a say in the choice of her husband, but he also knew they would want a Christian so her children could be brought up in the same faith. And there was less chance than ever that his parents would let him offer to marry her in the current uncertainty. And so his nights were haunted by the fear that her parents would decide on a husband for her against her will, and she would be lost to him forever, bundled off into some other man's house, into his bed. His own mother had been pushing him recently to marry, suggesting the daughters of various friends, and he was finding it hard to fend her off. His best hope was that their silent co-conspirator, Saara's mother, who pretended not to know he was there so long as nothing improper took place, would go as far as to protect her daughter from an unhappy marriage. Yet he knew it could not last, however much he willed it, and in his darker moments he was in agony over what to do about it.

But he mentioned none of that now; they had little enough time together. He told her about the scene at the Jordanian Embassy and the crazy foreign journalists all but kicking and punching each other to get an interview with some old security guard who was dazed and probably didn't know what he was saying anyway. And about the trip to the hospitals, though he left out the gory details of the injuries Ali had told him about. And she told him about the little dramas of her life inside the house, of the fight when her mother discovered her sister Maryam, who was only fifteen, putting on make-up and had demanded to know where she had got it. Then Maryam was in the room, breathless, to announce their time was up: she had seen their father's car approaching from the upstairs window. And so Mahmoud quickly took his leave, looking deep into his love's eyes.

"Come back soon," he heard her whisper as he slipped out of the door, up the street and around the corner, just out of the beam of the headlights in time, and back to his red Mercedes. And then, after waiting long enough for Saara's father to be safely inside the house so he would not spot the Mercedes turning, he slowly drove off, away from the home of his love, the enemy.

⸺◦⟦◉⟧◦⸺

Across the city, the cafe in Adhamiya is plunged in gloom. All the wires and cables stretched across the little square cannot bring it light, because the power is out on both sides of the square. But even at this late hour, in the darkness, the cafe is still open, and it is lit with a few candles that throw a twitching light across the walls. No romantic scene this: the candles are old and dirty, and dark stains are visible where they have stood against the walls many times before. When someone opens the door, the draught sends the candlelight jumping across the walls. The red glowing ends of cigarettes are visible too. There are not many people inside the cafe, since it is close to curfew, and most Baghdadis are hurrying home by now, but the few who are still here are smoking. No stranger, knowing the reputation of Adhamiya and of this cafe in particular, would venture inside uninvited at this late hour. But from outside, through the dirty windows, it is possible to make out that all that is being served is tea, the ubiquitous glasses of Iraqi tea, strong and dark.

At one table, two old men are hunched over a game of backgammon. At another, a pair of younger men sit and talk idly. But it is a table among the shadows towards the back of the room that catches the eye. Four men are sitting around it, hunched forward so that their heads lean close together, conspiratorially. No backgammon board here; their glasses of tea stand neglected, steaming. This is not the slow, bored talk of men tired at the end of the day's work, putting off the inevitable return home. These men are deep in conversation, their attention fixed on each other. Three are young men, the fourth approaching late middle age; it is hard to make out much more through the grease stains on the window and the nervous candlelight. The middle-aged man and one of the younger men are familiar faces to anyone who knows the cafe, but the other two are strangers. One of them is clearly

Iraqi, but something about the other suggests he is not. It is not his physical appearance: he is dressed much like the others, and in the candlelight, his dark hair and features could be Iraqi. It is something about the way he sits, his feet resting on his toes, not flat on the ground, the way his hands move as he talks, the quick glances he takes about the room. He seems slightly on edge. The two strangers speak less than the others; they seem to be listening mostly. It appears that the Iraqi stranger has to explain much of what the others say to the foreigner; he could be translating. The middle-aged man says something, and the foreigner turns to face him across the table, and as he does his face briefly catches the candlelight, revealing the features of Jack Wolfe.

Chapter Six

Sex and Saddam City

11 August 2003

ZOE LOOKED AT Peter Shore and wondered. They were sitting at a table with Kate and Mervyn Pile by the pool at the al-Hamra, and Peter was retelling a story from the invasion: in the final days before the fall of Baghdad, all the staff had run away from the Palestine Hotel, where the journalists had been forced to stay by the old Iraqi regime, and in the grip of hunger he and some others had staged a raid on the hotel kitchens to salvage what food they could. But Zoe wasn't really paying that much attention to his words; she had been in Baghdad almost a week and she had begun to experience a familiar feeling. Every night, beside the pool, she watched the journalists slip away to their rooms in pairs. As she lay alone in her bed, she knew that elsewhere in the hotel, in the rooms beside hers, above and below, they were making love—no, not love but lust. And an old feeling had come back, that somewhere a wonderful party was in full swing, and everyone had been invited except her. A few nights before, Janet Sweeney had disappeared with one of the security guards who worked for a big American television network. Only the previous night, Kate and Mervyn had finally headed upstairs together, a development that had seemed inevitable for days. Even journalists who had husbands and wives waiting at home were at it.

The only two journalists at the al-Hamra who conspicuously seemed to avoid the whole issue of pairing off were Alain Martin, the Journonator, and Jack Wolfe. Alain, it seemed, was too wrapped up in his work to find time for seduction. As for Jack, it just seemed part of the distance between him and the other journalists, another facet of the contempt he seemed to feel for them. She hadn't seen him for days—apparently he had gone off on a trip to Basra in the south.

"By then none of the shops were open, there was nowhere to get food," Peter was saying, "so we decided to try to get in the kitchen. It was locked, but Alain managed to get it open somehow. There was a guy from the police who tried to stop us, but he couldn't really be bothered, so we got in and there was nothing, just eggs. So there we were in the middle of the night, with the sound of the bombs falling all around us and the whole building shaking, frying eggs. But by then we were so hungry all we cared about was getting some food."

Zoe could see the sweat glistening in the heat where his neck met his chest at his open collar. It was two months since Zoe had woken up with a man beside her. Now she looked at Peter Shore and wondered if he was going to move on her tonight and what she would do if he asked her up to his room, if he leaned in to kiss her. She looked at him and wondered, but she knew there was nothing to wonder about, because she had already decided.

It was four days since the attack on the Jordanian Embassy, and Zoe was feeling more confident, the bombing and its aftermath had given her several large pieces in the paper. She had got to know more of the reporters: there was Dan Statten, from the *Chicago Report*; Mike Rodham, of Reuters news agency, who seemed to be writing so often he could barely leave the hotel and had to rely on other reporters to call in with the information to feed the agency's unending appetite; Rob Berwick, the cameraman who worked with Peter, an unpretentious type who had little patience with some of his colleagues' more flamboyant behaviour; Louise Merchant, the MTN producer, who seemed constantly harried and spent a lot of time acting as peacemaker between Peter and Rob; and Paul Thorn, a South African who was making a documentary about American soldiers on the frontlines, and seemed more like an old-time adventurer than anything else—with his long limbs stretched out by the pool, he would tell stories of being smuggled out of Haiti across the border in the boot of the British consul's car or being threatened by African diamond smugglers.

She was learning about some of the other guests in the hotel besides the journalists, too. The heavily muscled men who sat separately were private security contractors, former soldiers who worked as mercenaries, guarding Western businesses in Baghdad or the convoys of trucks that brought supplies through the desert. Some worked for the TV companies as security advisers, but most of them were less than friendly towards the reporters. Once Zoe found herself in the lift with one of them; he was carrying a gun and he said to her, "Better keep back, this thing could go off."

She asked Kate about the strange man with long hair and enigmatic eyes who was always hanging around the hotel.

"That's the pianist," Kate said, to her surprise. "Used to be the most famous concert pianist in Iraq, now he plays for us in the restaurant of the Hamra, courtesy of the American invasion. Except no one goes in the restaurant in summer. We all sit out here, so there's nothing for him to do."

Zoe's one regret was that she had been unable to convince Nigel to run the story of Zaynab and her family. He said it was too similar to other stories that had already been published, but Zoe was confident she'd get it through on a slow news day, when Nigel was in a panic with nothing to offer the Editor. All she had to do was return to Zaynab's with a photographer.

"It's getting late," Kate said, pushing back her chair and standing up. Across the table from her, Mervyn did the same. "I think we'll leave you two to it." She gave Zoe a significant look. Zoe smiled but kept the answer to herself.

"Good night," she said.

"Another beer?" Peter asked her.

"Why not?"

"So tell me about yourself."

"What do you want to know?"

"Well, you just sit there all the time listening while everyone else tells their war stories. I want to know a bit about you."

Zoe blushed; she didn't like to admit that she never told stories because she didn't have any. "What's there to tell?"

"How did you get into journalism?"

"Well, I pretty much always wanted to, I suppose. Since I was a kid. When I left uni, I got a job on a local paper."

"And wars?"

"Well, I always wanted to do that too, I suppose. When I got a job at the *Informer* I told them I was up for it." The drinks arrived. "Your turn now, since we're telling about ourselves."

"My turn?"

"It's only fair. I tell you something, you tell me something."

"OK. So what do you want to know?"

"Is it true about you and the princess?"

"Oh," he said, grinning rakishly, "a gentleman never tells."

"So it is true then."

"Your turn."

"No," she shook her head. "You didn't tell me."

"I gave you an answer," he laughed. "It's not my fault if you didn't like it. So where are you from originally?"

"Devon."

"And now? Let me guess. Ladbroke Grove?"

"On my salary? You must be joking."

"Hoxton?"

"Bethnal Green," she laughed. "And that's two questions. Your turn."

"OK."

"How did you become a war correspondent?"

"Oh, back when I started out at the BBC—that was before MTN even existed—I wanted to be a political correspondent. I thought that's where the glamour was, following the prime minister about, keeping tabs on Number Ten. But they had different ideas, shipped me off to Africa, and I fell in love with the whole way of life. Haven't stopped since. Your turn. This your first war?"

Zoe blushed and quickly looked down. "Is it that obvious?"

"No," he laughed. "I just haven't seen you around before, that's all. It's usually the same bunch of people who turn up to these things."

"What was your first war?"

"Lebanon. The civil war. It was completely crazy. I remember my first day we got to a checkpoint and I gave them the wrong ID—the ID the other side had given us. Nearly got shot on my first day." The beers were finished, and they were the only people left by the pool. He pushed his beer can to one side and smiled to himself. "Looks like they're shutting up shop down here. Want to come up for a nightcap? I've got a decent single malt I brought in from London."

The moment when Zoe had been wondering what she would do had come, and she did what she had known she would do all along.

"Sure," she said, and as she got up unsteadily she realised how much the alcohol had gone to her head. She followed him into the main building, and they took the lift up to the sixth floor. He ushered her into a suite similar to hers. While he poured her a whisky, she slipped into the bathroom to make sure she was dressed to be undressed. When she walked back into the sitting room he was on the sofa, and the two armchairs had books and clothes conveniently piled on them. She took a seat next to him.

"It was your turn to answer a question," he said with a smile.

"No, it's your turn, I think," she said.

"OK, ask away."

"How come you never married?" she asked and instantly regretted it, aware of how drunk she had become. "Or do you have some secret wife stashed away no one knows about?" she added quickly.

He laughed. "No secret wife. I guess I just haven't met the right woman yet." It sounded well rehearsed, an answer he had given many times, to many women.

"Your turn," she murmured, and he leaned in and kissed her.

‹–›═‹–›

Benes woke up in the night, sweating, his fingers scrabbling against empty air. He was forcing himself awake, surging desperately up out of sleep, clawing at consciousness. He had seen a young girl with half her face torn away and a blank red space of glistening flesh where her eyes should have been. A nightmare, that was all. Relieved, he strained for the reassuring sound of his wife breathing—but it wasn't there; instead there was a sound of groaning. Unnerved, he groped for Maria, but his hands fell into empty space. There was no sheet or covering over him, but the heat was unbearable; it felt like a presence pushing down on his chest. Straining to open his eyes, he saw the room was bathed in a ghastly yellow light. His body was soaked in sweat, the air was hot even to breathe, and instead of the familiar scent of Maria's body there was a choking smell, a mixture of his own sweat and—it couldn't be, his mind recoiled—sulphur fumes. People were groaning all around him, like souls in torment. And his whole body was burning. Benes was beginning to panic, surely he couldn't be—

Surfacing finally from sleep, he shook himself out of confusion. The sulphur was the smell of oil that hung over Baghdad, the yellow glare the camp light shining in through the fabric of the tent, as it did all night, the groaning the sound of soldiers who could not sleep, and the heat was just Hell City.

He mopped the sweat from his face with his bare hands, and the beginnings of stubble scratched at them. Rubbing the sleep from his eyes, he looked across the tiny tent: the other cot was empty. Rodriguez was out on patrol somewhere. Benes could hear volleys of gunfire in the distance. He needed to piss, and felt the sweat running down his legs as he swung them off the damp cot. Cursing, he felt around for his boots. The small electric fan he and Rodriguez had managed to get hold of buzzed ineffectively in the corner, stirring the heat around. He glanced at his watch: 3 a.m. It was a long time since Benes had suffered nightmares, not since he was a child. This, though, was different. No half-glimpsed images of terror, it had been vivid. He could still see the girl with her eyes torn away, and then it came rushing back to him, all too real, how he had stood over her that night at the checkpoint, how her father had sat behind the wheel of his car and stared in amazement at the dark blood pumping out of his chest, and then looked up at Benes, a look that held no anger, not even a plea for help, just astonishment. And her brother, dead already, with the neat red bullet-hole right between his eyes and the fear frozen on his face for all eternity.

Benes pulled on his boots and tried to put the images out of his mind as he stumbled out and made his way through the narrow path between the tents to the latrine. The groaning went on all around him as the soldiers thrashed in their cots, trying desperately not to think about the heat. It was even worse for the regular soldiers, crammed in nine to a tent. They were supposed to have been housed in an old Iraqi army barracks, but Benes's battalion had arrived after all the space had gone, so they had to live in the sprawling and ever-growing tent camp outside. The latrines were inside the building. Those who got to sleep inside weren't much better off; the building had been gutted by fire before they arrived, and they lived in bare rooms with no glass in the windows. There was no air conditioning and the heat sat in the corridors. Rats moved about the building at night, and you had to be careful where you trod. There were people moving about too, even at this hour of the night: there always were, soldiers coming and going from patrols. The place had a restless air; you had to snatch what sleep you could. Benes reached the latrines and entered a familiar, overpowering reek of human waste. The Iraqi plumbing wasn't much to begin with, and it hadn't been designed for this much use. Benes tried to breathe as little as possible. He felt sweet relief as he stood and pissed, watching the stream disappear, and hurried back outside to the cleaner air.

As he made his way back to the tent, the image of the girl with her eyes torn out came back unbidden to his mind, an unwelcome guest. He could see the flesh glistening, wet where the eyes should have been. He ducked inside the tent and sat on his cot, the fan buzzing away pointlessly in the corner. He could hear the whimpering of the survivors in the car, the mother in the back who had shielded her last child with her own body and somehow kept her alive—though strangely it was the daughter who was injured, while the mother had barely been scratched. It was a desperate sound, inhuman, but there must have been something primal in it because it cut right through him.

He shook his head and tried to think of something else. He thought of the conversation out on patrol the day before: usually they told each other jokes and dirty stories, but something must have got to them that afternoon, because they had talked about their wives and girlfriends. All the married men had their untold secret, the unspoken doubt whether their wives were faithful while they were in Iraq. He thought of his own phone conversations with Maria, with so much left unsaid because he had no way of saying it. She held the telephone to Juan in his crib, and though the baby was too young to speak, Benes heard his son gurgle down a phone line from half a world away, and it filled his heart with more emotion than he had thought it possible to feel. He remembered Maria the night before he had left for Iraq, how she had held onto him the way she had when they first met, as if she wanted to crush them together into a single body—yet still the doubts came, like hungry worms, to feed on his stomach. Perhaps anyone would have doubts out here, so far from home. Benes had been in Iraq three months, deployed just as the president declared major combat operations over and the men who stormed their way in through Kuwait and captured Baghdad were returning home to heroes' welcomes. He had arrived disappointed that he had missed the war, but that had all changed on his first night in the city, when a patrol had come under fire and he had been sent out with his platoon to find the attackers, hunting them through the dark, hostile streets.

His mouth was dry. So soon after pissing, he was thirsty again and he reached beneath the cot for his water bottle. It was almost empty, and he tipped what was left into his mouth. The water was warm and tasted vile. Cursing, he got up to get more from the cooler just inside the building. From somewhere he could hear the tinny sound of music playing through headphones. He filled his water bottle up from the cooler and drank. A squad came in, fresh from patrol, their conversation stifling as they saw him. They looked exhausted; they had probably been on duty for ten hours. Benes was tired too; the platoon had been operating at the limit for weeks, but they had kept going, and he was proud of that. The face of the girl with her eyes torn out came into his mind again. Why did this one horror of all the horrors he had seen haunt him? He had watched Americans die, like the nineteen-year-old who had suddenly fallen to the ground on patrol, whose head had come apart in their hands when they had pulled his helmet off. He had dealt out his share of death too, and he knew how it felt to kill a man. And yet this Iraqi family, a handful of deaths in the night, troubled him. It was the death of one of the platoon he had always feared, the thought of watching the life go out of Moon or Hernandez, as he had watched soldiers from other platoons die, and of sending the pieces of them home in a box. He never thought the deaths of some Iraqi family would trouble him, some dumb fucking Hajjis who didn't know better than to be out driving late at night in a bad part of town.

He filled the water bottle again, went back to his room and lay down on the cot. The noise of the gunfire at the checkpoint filled his mind, the deafening silence that followed, and then the whimpering. He had decided they had to get the survivors out of the car, because the fuel tank might go up at any moment. Doc Martinez, the platoon combat medic, had come over from the house—they couldn't wait for a full team of medics. The boy in the front seat and the girl with her eyes torn out were dead. The driver, the father, was still alive, but Martinez said there was nothing they could do for him, so they concentrated on the mother and daughter in the back. It was dangerous work, not just because of the risk the fuel tank would explode, but because the men were having a hard time keeping back the crowd of angry Iraqis. Most Iraqis kept a gun at home, and the platoon was heavily outnumbered. Benes had called for the Quick Reaction Force, but he was afraid things would get out of hand before it arrived.

Shattered glass fell from the mother's body as Martinez and Steele pulled her out; she still wouldn't let go of the child she had shielded with her body, and they had to prise her fingers off by force. When they did, she broke free and ran back to the car, lunging for the dead bodies of her two other children, as if she could save them too, and some men from the crowd had to drag her away, speaking softly to her in Arabic. Blood poured from cuts and scratches in her face, but she seemed oblivious to her own pain. Hernandez carried out the girl she had protected, bleeding from shrapnel injuries in her head and her foot, in shock and completely passive. From the front of the car, the driver stared out at Benes, his mouth moving, and he seemed to be trying to say something. After a while it moved less, and the flutterings of his chest grew further apart.

Benes had called for a medevac, but an Iraqi ambulance got

there first, and he let the Iraqi crew through to the two survivors while the soldiers held back the crowd. Benes told them to take the mother and daughter to an American medical facility, where they'd get the best treatment, but of course he learned later they had disappeared into the night, presumably to an Iraqi hospital. When the American medics arrived, they said there was nothing to be done for the father. The Quick Reaction Team brought rubber gloves with them and, cursing, set about the grisly task of cleaning the remains of the rest of the family out of the shattered Mercedes.

Benes knew the reason these deaths bothered him so much, though he didn't want to admit it. He told himself the family should not have been out so late at night, but he knew he had made a mistake, had put his men in the wrong place. He had put his snipers on the rooftop right in the line of fire of his own checkpoint. It was a rudimentary error, and he wondered why Hawkes had not called him on it. He could have asked the experienced sergeant for advice on where to put them, but Benes had been determined to prove himself, and he had got it wrong. He had been lucky to get away with it—if members of the platoon had been killed, instead of an Iraqi family, there would have been an investigation. As it was, the incident would probably be forgotten, although he shuddered at what Hawkes must think of him now.

He drifted into troubled sleep, watched over by a young girl with her face torn away where her eyes should have been.

-->≡◎ ◎≡<--

Adel was crouched on a rooftop not unlike the one Benes had chosen as his sniper position. He was keeping low, so he could not be seen above the concrete parapet, although the precaution was probably unnecessary because there was no one below to see him at this time of the night. It was long after curfew, the streets were deserted and no one was sleeping on the adjacent rooftops. They had all been told to stay indoors. The danger to Adel came from American helicopters: when he heard one coming, he would slip under the water tank by his side, where there was just enough space for him, though he had to lie with his face in the dust. By his knees he had a home video camera, a large old-fashioned walkie-talkie and a Kalashnikov rifle. The building he was on was at the edge of Adhamiya; behind and below him lay its narrow lanes; in front of him was a broad road, one of the main routes through the city, which was often used by American patrols at night. It was for one of these patrols that Adel waited. He could make out the concrete bridge where Abu Mustafa and his two sons were waiting, hidden by the dark, armed with two rocket-propelled grenade launchers. The walkie-talkie was old Iraqi army issue. Abu Mustafa had given Adel strict instructions to use it only if he saw a patrol—any more and the Americans might pick him up, and they would all be in danger.

Adel had been elated the day he met Abu Khalid; within an hour of their meeting, the Jordanian Embassy had been bombed. That night, he had returned home to the news that a foreigner, a British journalist, had been in his house even as he was watching the video of the beheading, had been sitting in his father's old chair while Abu Khalid was telling him they wanted to kidnap foreigners. Keeping his reasons from his mother, he had questioned her at length and made her promise to let him know if she heard from the journalist again. But since then he had grown impatient, as the days passed and the foreign woman did not return, and he heard nothing from Abu Khalid. Selim had no news. So when one of his father's old officer comrades from the army, Abu Mustafa, had turned up to ask him to consider joining the resistance—not Abu Khalid's foreigners, but the resistance that was being organised by former army officers—Adel had agreed.

He still thought the officers' strategy of slow attrition was too cautious, but it was better than sitting at home doing nothing. Abu Mustafa had served with his father in the war against Iran and had known Adel since he was a boy. All the same, Adel decided it would be wiser to mention nothing of his meeting with Abu Khalid to the army man. The strange thing was that no one seemed to know who was behind the bombing of the Jordanian Embassy: Abu Mustafa and the other officers said it had come as a surprise to them, and Selim said Abu Khalid had known nothing about it. One of them must have been lying.

Adel decided he would wait to hear from the Saudi, and in the meantime, rather than do nothing, he would join Abu Mustafa and his men. The cell they operated in was small and close-knit: Abu Mustafa and his two sons, both of them ex-soldiers, and a few other army men.

Adel heard a sound of something approaching, and, shaken from his thoughts, he saw a vehicle in the distance. It was loud; it sounded like something armoured. He strained his eyes: it was one of the small half-tanks the Americans drove around the city. He picked up the walkie-talkie and whispered, "The donkeys are moving."

Silence, then the reply crackled back. Adel scrabbled for the video camera and made sure it was on, training it at the tank, which was deafening as it passed below. Abu Khalid was not the only one who wanted to make his own videos in Iraq: Abu Mustafa wanted a film of the attack for propaganda. The flyover was in view through the camera now, but Adel could make out nothing in the darkness. The tank was almost at the bridge. Adel tensed. Surely it was close enough: had something gone wrong? He saw a flash streak through the night and hit the Americans, and then the sound of the explosion came like a hammer hitting hollow metal. The tank was in flames, and the sound of shooting came from the bridge. He concentrated on keeping the camera steady, exhilaration flooding through him. Through the flames he could see the silhouette of an American struggling to get out of the burning vehicle before he was cut down by the bullets.

⊷┉◉☉◉┉⊶

Zoe lay beside Peter. She could see his chest rise and fall as he breathed in his sleep. It had been good—she had told herself she shouldn't compare him to her last lover, that the fumbling of an unfamiliar partner couldn't match the touch of someone who knew every inch of her, but it had been good. She stretched out happily. Outside the gunfire had started up again, the song of the city. She was in occupied Baghdad, at the centre of events, and she had just slept with a famous war correspondent. Zoe looked at Peter Shore and wondered.

Chapter Seven

The Innocent

12 August 2003

THE SIGN OUTSIDE the former Saddam Hussein Central Children's Hospital did not read "Abandon all hope ye who enter here": if it had, it would have been superfluous, a statement of the obvious. Like everything else connected with the former president, the name of the hospital had been changed, and the sign carried a new name, al-Iskan Central Children's Teaching Hospital. The bright new metal sign was almost comically at odds with the wretched buildings that stood beyond it, huddled close together for protection like orphaned children. The real misery of the hospital, though, lay within, hidden from the world's gaze. At the door, the gloom was so uninviting you hesitated to step in, and once you did, there was something wrong from the moment you were inside, though it took a while to realise what it was: there was no hospital smell, no comforting reek of disinfectant. Instead, an air of dust and decay, sickness and sewage, hung over the whole place.

You entered a bare, empty lobby, devoid of furniture, separated by a greasy glass partition from the corridors in the back. Despite the blazing sun outside, there was no air conditioning, and even in the murk the building seemed thick with heat. It was when you stepped into the corridors that the descent into squalor truly began. Puddles of dark, slimy water lay on the bare concrete floor, and the walls were lined with white tiles that wore years of neglected grime. Everywhere the corridors were piled high with rubbish: in one corner, broken bits of old furniture, tables and chairs, stacked up to the ceiling, the dust on them so thick it had formed little clouds of fluff; in another, white toilet bowls strewn across the floor that looked as if they had been new when they were flung there—there were no signs that water had ever flowed through them—but were grey with dust and cracked; in another, rusting metal babies' cots filled with heavy piles of old doctors' notes, the pages crusted brown with grime. There were more yellowing notes littering the stairwell, as if someone had casually thrown them down the steps, and to climb the stairs you had to tread on the records of some child who had died many years before from tuberculosis, leukaemia, or an infection that was never properly diagnosed.

But the corridors were nothing to the wards that lay beyond, where you found the true dark secret of the former Saddam Hussein Central Children's Hospital: the children. They lay, pitifully thin sticks of bodies, crammed in two to each of the old sagging metal beds. In the wards, there were some signs of an attempt at cleaning, but the hospital still intruded: in the sewage pipes that dripped overhead, forming little puddles of dark, foul water in between the beds; in the gruesome smell that hovered at the entrances to bathrooms that were beyond nightmare, layered green and brown with filth and slime; in the remorseless heat that hung over everything, curling around the beds and the tiny bodies inside them; and in the odour of human bodies. Doctors came and went, long inured to the dirt and squalor, their eyes dark and heavy with lack of sleep, wiping the sweat from their faces, struggling to keep their patients safe from the disease the hospital was breeding all around them, let alone whatever conditions they had arrived with. Parents had set up camp around their children's beds, and lines of washing hung in the corners to dry. There were barely any nurses to be seen, and the children's mothers seemed to be doing most of the nursing work: they stood over their children's beds—often a mother on each side for each child—dabbing their foreheads with damp cloths or fanning the air to keep them cool. Dirty curtains were drawn across the windows, and electric fans stirred the air, but the heat was suffocating.

Then there was the sound, an ominous, inhuman metallic sound that haunted the hospital. It would begin in the distance and put your nerves on edge all at once, then rise steadily in volume until it became a metal thunder, before an orderly would appear around the corner, rolling an oxygen cylinder before him. The first time you saw it, you recoiled in shock, waiting for the cylinder to explode, but you quickly became used to seeing them roll past. Sometimes the sound would stop abruptly with a loud ringing, as the cylinder collided perilously with something, only to start up again. When you looked closely you could see that the cylinders were pitted with countless small dents. Sometimes there would be more than one orderly, rolling five or six cylinders between them, knocking them together as they went.

It was through these scenes of misery that Benes was walking. He wondered how anyone could send their children to a place like this, how Iraqis could let the biggest children's hospital in their country be such a pit of squalor, filth and disease. With just two platoons, he thought, he could have had the place clean, hygienic and properly organised within a week. As another orderly came rolling an oxygen cylinder before him, Benes's patience snapped and he turned angrily to the small, balding doctor who was leading them through the hospital.

"Why in hell are they doing that?" he asked angrily. "Don't you realise how dangerous that is?" The small doctor looked up in surprise.

"We know, yes," he said mildly. "But how else can we move them? We have no trolleys. Sometimes the children need oxygen: without it, they can die." Benes could see that the doctor's white coat and the checked shirt he had on underneath it were damp with sweat. Beads of it had gathered under his moustache.

The battalion commander had sent Benes to secure the hospital. Benes wasn't entirely sure what the threat was from a children's hospital and why it was necessary to secure it, but Colonel Jackson said his orders were to secure the city and the hospital fell within their sector. It was possible, Benes supposed, that the insurgents might use the hospital as cover to mount attacks on the Americans, although there had been little activity in the area. He had with him Hawkes, Moon and Hernandez. The small doctor was leading them to the hospital director's office. There was no need for a translator—even in Iraq, doctors could be relied on to speak English. Benes did not relish the prospect of an awkward interview with the hospital director: the negotiations, he knew, would be drawn out and tedious—the more mind-numbing because Benes knew that he was going to set up the patrols exactly as ordered, regardless of what the hospital director said, and that the meeting was just a formality that had to be endured, a facade of consultation with the civilian population. It wasn't as if he were interested in what the people responsible for this nightmare of a hospital had to say; they would probably tell him the soldiers would frighten the children, but he thought there wasn't much left that could frighten a child who had spent time in the former Saddam Hussein Central Children's Hospital. Besides the looming meeting with the director, something else was troubling Benes, though he did not like to admit it to himself. It had been less than two weeks since the incident with the family, and an unwelcome thought kept coming to his mind as he stared at the filthy wards: perhaps this is where they brought her that night, the child who survived.

Doctors and patients alike eyed the American soldiers with hostile, frightened glances as they passed them in the corridors. Those who were talking fell silent when they saw Benes and his men. The children looked up nervously from their beds, and the mothers tried to distract them, all the while glancing warily back at the Americans.

The small doctor stopped and knocked at a door with a sign on it in Arabic. Someone spoke from inside and he pushed the door open. Inside was a huge desk scattered with a disorder of papers, and behind it sat a grey-haired doctor in a neatly pressed white coat and tie, presumably the director. He was holding a meeting with three other doctors. Benes barely noticed two of them because his eyes lingered on the third, a woman, her hair and neck hidden under a headscarf, white to match the coat. The small oval of face that remained visible was enough, the dark-bright eyes, the long lashes, the lips a little parted, and below, the loose white coat that didn't quite mask the shape of her body. The director beckoned him in and shooed the younger doctors from their seats to make way. Benes and Hawkes stepped inside, while Moon and Hernandez pulled security outside the door.

"Come in! Come in!" the director was saying enthusiastically from behind his desk. "Please come in!" He was beaming all over his face, and to Benes's surprise all the other doctors were smiling, including the woman, who looked down when he caught her eye.

"We have been waiting your visit!" the director said, leaning forward and shaking Benes warmly by the hand. He had a look Benes knew well enough from the soldiers, black stains under both his eyes from lack of sleep, his eyelids drooping. He introduced himself and the other doctors. The woman's name was Dr Afaf. Distracted by her, Benes failed to take in the other names and was grateful to see a bombastic gold plaque on the desk with the director's name in English and Arabic, Dr Kamal Aziz, followed by an alphabet of qualifications. He introduced himself and Hawkes, and the director gestured them to the chairs in front of his desk. The three younger doctors stood in a row behind the chairs, and Benes felt as if he were at some sort of prize-giving ceremony.

"You the director here, sir?" Benes asked, taking a seat.

"That is my, ah," Dr Aziz smiled, "responsibility, yes."

"Sir, we're part of the US forces in this sector," Benes began. "As you know, US forces are in the process of securing Baghdad city, and we're here to secure this hospital." The director nodded enthusiastically. "What we basically need to do is ensure this hospital is safe from any attack by insurgents or any law-and-order situations, so we can provide your staff with a secure environment to continue their work." He paused to let Dr Aziz, who appeared to be bursting to say something, respond.

"Yes, yes," he said excitedly. "We have been waiting for you. We have many needs. You have already seen the state of the wards, I think? We tried to keep the hospital open since the war, but we are in great need of assistance. The situation is very bad. We have shortages of medicine, disinfectants, equipment. We need nebulisers for our asthma patients," he said, counting off a series of items on his fingers, "oxygen, trolleys to carry the oxygen, a generator…you noticed the heat? The air conditioning does not work, because the power is out and we do not have a proper generator. Only a small generator, it is meant for a house. It does not provide enough power." He checked himself and paused. "I am sorry to give you this, ah, shopping list so soon.

But it is good you have come. We have been waiting for you, we have so many needs, but now you are here."

The director seemed to be under the misapprehension they had come to resupply the hospital. Benes wondered how to explain.

"Yes, I can see you've got some serious, uh, problems here, sir," he started tentatively. "But see, we're here to secure the area, not to resupply the hospital. We're going to be putting a regular patrol outside, to keep you and your patients safe."

Dr Aziz didn't appear to be listening; he was nodding happily, and as soon as Benes paused to breathe, he started up again: "Medicines. We need medicines. Morphine, for pain. Ciprox for dysentery." He was counting off on his fingers again, running through a bewildering list of drugs Benes had never heard of. This was turning out to be altogether more difficult than he had anticipated: he had expected obstruction and complaints, but not this. "Penicillin," the director was saying, "we are even short of penicillin."

He paused for a moment, and Benes took the opportunity to interrupt: "Sir, I can see you have some serious issues here, but as I said, we're not here to help with supplies. We're only here to secure the hospital area."

"We also have a big problem with the sewage pipes. They leak into the wards. Many of the toilets are permanently blocked. I have asked the ministry many times to send someone, but they do not. And the cleaning staff, we need some money to hire more cleaning staff." Benes exchanged a look with Hawkes and tried again.

"Dr Aziz, sir—"

"Please, ah, Dr Kamal." The director smiled awkwardly. "Aziz was my father's name." Benes's eyes strayed back to the plaque on the desk. He shifted uncomfortably in his seat.

"I'm sorry, sir, Dr Kamal. Please understand me: we're not here to fix these things you're talking about. We're just here to secure the hospital, to ensure your safety." The director looked at him in surprise.

"Secure the hospital?" he said. "But we don't need this, there is no fighting here. We need medicines, generators, trolleys—we need to fix the pipes…"

Benes began to feel his patience sapping away. He was tired; he didn't have the energy for this discussion.

"Sir, I understand that," he said firmly. "I can see you've got problems here, but you need to address those to the civilian authorities at the CPA. We're just here to secure the hospital, and that's all we're going to do."

The director stared at him in astonishment; then he crumpled and fell back in his chair. He looked visibly older, as if something that had been keeping him going had been taken away. Benes could feel the disappointment in the room, could feel the eyes of the three other doctors on his back.

"So you will not give us equipment."

"I'm sorry, sir, but that's not an area under my control. We're just here to ensure the safety of the hospital."

"But our patients are dying. They need medicine, not soldiers with guns."

"Sir, it's not a military matter," he said. "You need to speak to the CPA."

"You think we haven't spoken to them?" Dr Kamal said. He picked up a sheaf of papers from his desk. "Every day I send them urgent requests. Every day they tell me they will send someone, but they never do. Here," he held up a piece of paper, "here is the latest promise. I thought they had sent you, but no. Do you think we want to keep children like this? What am I supposed to do without money or equipment, without medicine? Every day I send requests, and I get nothing. Look at these doctors: they are exhausted, they are working twenty hours a day trying to keep these children alive, and for the last two months they have not even been paid. We have a dysentery epidemic inside the hospital, Lieutenant. Children come here with a simple problem and they die of dysentery. And when I need to give them medicine we do not have it, and I have to send the children's parents out to the market to buy the medicine, where the prices are high, and they have to borrow from their relatives to afford one bottle of tablets, and when they come back I find they have been sold the medicine that was supposed to be here, medicine from government stocks, because some corrupt person there has sold it to the market and kept the money for himself."

"Sir, I appreciate what you're saying," Benes said, forcing himself to remain patient. "But see, the thing is, supplying the hospital comes under the authority of the CPA and there's not a lot I can do about that. I just don't have the authority to bring in the supplies you need."

Dr Kamal leaned forward. "Do you have children, Lieutenant?"

"Yes, sir. One son."

"And if he was sick, you would want him to come to a hospital like this?"

"No, sir."

The director eyed him for a while; then he seemed to come to a decision.

"Will you help us, Lieutenant?" he asked.

Benes wasn't sure how to answer; he needed to keep the hospital staff friendly so the platoon wouldn't be in danger. "If I can," he said.

"They will not listen to us. Maybe they will listen to you. Please tell them the conditions we are facing."

"I'll be glad to make a full report on the situation here—"

"Tell them we need medicines. Tell them the children are dying."

"I'll pass on your concerns."

Dr Kamal nodded and sat back.

"How can we help you, Lieutenant?"

"Sir, we need to set up patrols outside the hospital, to ensure your safety. They won't interfere with your work; the soldiers will be under orders—"

"I cannot stop you, Lieutenant. Set up your patrol. Anything else?"

Benes hesitated.

"We'd like to take a quick look around the hospital, just so we know the terrain we're operating in," he said.

"You want to see the hospital? Of course, you are welcome." The director stood up. "You can tell your commanders the conditions. I will show you. Please come." He ushered them to the door, speaking to the other three doctors in Arabic. Benes turned to Hawkes.

"Better bring up the rear, Sergeant," he said, "just in case."

Moon and Hernandez joined them. The two male doctors left, but Dr Afaf was coming along on their tour, to Benes's pleasure. He would have liked to spend the time looking at her—he didn't get to look at many women in Iraq—but as the director led him from ward to ward, he couldn't keep his eyes off the children. Some were twisted with pain; others stared up at him in incomprehension of what was happening to them. In one place where they stopped to look at the fire exit, Benes found it blocked with razor wire. Beyond the wire was a pile of blankets stained black with what looked like dried blood. Screams echoed from a ward ahead—not the screams of children, but those of a grown man. Dr Kamal led them forward, and Benes saw a man thrashing on a hospital bed while doctors and nurses worked around him. Blood was pouring from the man's leg, and several of the nurses had their hands full just trying to hold him down.

"This is our emergency room," said Dr Kamal. "We are not supposed to have an emergency room, but we had to open it because of the situation in the city. This hospital is supposed to be only for children but we have so many emergency cases we cannot turn them away." The beds were crammed in very close, and a foul, rotting odour hung in the air, like bad teeth. If they had brought the girl from the car here that night, he thought, it would have been to this room.

"Who is he?" Benes asked, pointing at the man on the bed. Dr Kamal spoke to the doctors around the bed in Arabic; one of them answered him quickly, working on the man all the while.

"He has a gunshot wound," Dr Kamal explained. "It has shattered the bone. It is very painful, but he will be all right."

"How did he get the wound?"

The director spoke to the doctor working on the patient's leg again.

"Two men brought him in half an hour ago," he translated to Benes. "They said he was driving near here and someone stole his car. They got in next to him and shot him and then pushed him on the road. These men picked him up."

"You believe that story?" Hawkes asked.

"Why not?" shrugged Dr Kamal. "It happens like this every day in Baghdad."

"How do we know he's not an insurgent?" Hawkes persisted.

The director looked puzzled. "Insurgent? Why should he be an insurgent?"

"He has a gunshot wound."

"Lots of people are shot in Baghdad, not all are insurgents."

"So how do you guys know if the people you're treating here are insurgents?"

Dr Kamal smiled awkwardly. "They do not tell us if they are insurgents," he said.

Benes exchanged looks with Hawkes: they would have to keep a close eye on who was admitted to the emergency room.

Dr Kamal led them on through the corridors to a large ward of children, where a pool of dark liquid with the unmistakable smell of shit overflowed from the bathroom, spreading its way between the beds. Nurses and the children's mothers were working together, trying to mop it up. Benes felt sick from the odour rising from the floor.

"This is our leukaemia ward," Dr Kamal said. "Leukaemia is very treatable in children. But here, we lose five or six every week."

Benes looked at the nearest bed—there were two children in it. One, a girl of about thirteen, was contorted in agony, her toes curled with pain, her face locked in a silent scream.

Her mother kept dabbing gently at her forehead with a damp cloth. Next to her was a smaller girl who seemed to be having some sort of fit, her face twitching uncontrollably.

"But what's going on with this stuff?" Benes asked, pointing at the foul water spilling out of the bathroom.

"The drains are blocked. It happens one or two times a week. It is very dangerous for these children. I have told the CPA, but there is no money." A doctor came up to Dr Kamal and spoke to him urgently in Arabic.

"Excuse me, one moment please," he said to Benes and walked across to the small office opposite. Dr Afaf, standing next to Benes, reached over to the small child and gently stroked her face as it twitched.

"What's up with her?" Benes asked. Dr Afaf looked up, surprised.

"The disease has spread to her central nervous system," she said.

"Is that bad?" asked Benes. Dr Afaf nodded. She didn't let it show on her face, but smiled down at the child. The older girl's mother spoke, and Dr Afaf answered her questions in Arabic.

"Why did they let this hospital get like this?" he asked.

"Don't you know?" Dr Afaf said. "Saddam kept it like this to show the world what American sanctions had done to Iraq. He wanted to say the hospital was like this because of the sanctions." Benes looked around the room, at the children, and the pool of filthy water spreading between the beds.

"What's his name, your son?" Dr Afaf asked, her eyes still on the two girls in the bed.

"My son?"

"You told Dr Kamal you have a son."

"Yes. His name's Juan."

"That's a nice name. This is Aisha," Dr Afaf said, gently stroking the older girl on her foot, which was still twisted in agony. "And the small one is Fatma. How old is your son?"

"He'll be one next month."

"And your wife is in America?"

"Yes."

"She must miss you."

"Yes. I miss her too. You married?"

"Yes," she said with a smile.

"Any children?" She shook her head. "Will she be OK?" he said, looking down at Aisha.

"She is tired," Dr Afaf answered. But the way she said it had an air of finality about it.

Chapter Eight

Callaghan & Carlisle

13 August 2003

CHARLIE CALLAGHAN WAS bored. He sat, contrary to orders, with one leg dangling out of the open door of the helicopter. Beneath him, the buildings of Baghdad rushed past at dizzying speed, so close he felt he could lean out of the cockpit and grab a piece of laundry drying on the nearest rooftop and disappear with it into the distance. He often grinned at the thought: Charlie Callaghan, panty thief, swooping out of the sky to make off with some Iraqi lady's lacy lingerie while her husband shook his fist at the departing helicopter from below. Hot air blew in through the open door like a furnace blast, so hard it knocked the breath out of you. It was hard to breathe at first—that is, if you were new to it, but Callaghan had been riding the wind for months and knew how to let it fill his lungs without panicking. The first two months it had been a trip, sweeping over the city with the hot wind pummelling his face and the rooftops skimming below, but he had been doing it for too long now and it had become routine. In the middle of a war, riding in a helicopter over occupied Baghdad, Charlie Callaghan was bored. There was nothing interesting about this flight, no insurgents to track through the streets, as they had last week, Carlisle keeping the helicopter on their trail over the maze of streets as they ducked into a residential neighbourhood to escape. Today was just another routine surveillance flight, and Carlisle at the controls looked as bored as Callaghan felt. The second helicopter followed close behind, with Malone at the controls. They always flew in pairs: that way if one was shot down, the other could pick up the survivors.

You could see the story of Baghdad from up here. If Callaghan looked out of his open door, to the west, he could see smoke slowly rising into the sky from an attack on an American patrol or an Iraqi police vehicle or perhaps a police station. If he craned his neck round and looked back the way they had come, he could see a similar column of smoke. Beneath them now, as they passed over a street, he saw an American Humvee stopped in the middle of the road with the gunner training his weapon on an unmarked white car while the other traffic swerved out of the way.

Automatically, without even thinking about it, he radioed this latest snapshot of violence in. He was supposed to keep track of every column of smoke, every incident they saw from up here, and they saw plenty. He was on the radio almost constantly as they flew, providing live commentary on the war that was going on below. One thing to be said for riding the helicopters: it left you in no doubt. The president might think the war was over, but Callaghan had no such illusions—he watched it flash by beneath his feet every day. And every now and then it came a little too close to his feet for comfort. More than once, the insurgents had fired up at them with a Kalashnikov. Back at base, Callaghan laughed with the others at the idea of some dumb Hajji trying to take out an armoured helicopter with a rifle, like an ignorant tribesman firing a bow and arrow at a tank, but up here he knew that Kalashnikovs could damage helicopters and the people inside them. Sometimes the insurgents fired rocket-propelled grenades, and though as far as Callaghan knew no helicopter had been hit by one, he shuddered to think he might be in the first. If he didn't mention these fears to the others, not even to Carlisle, it was because he tried not to think about them.

He preferred to be one half of Callaghan and Carlisle, known throughout the battalion as all-American rebels—or at least that was how he liked to think they were known. They had been disciplined four times, as a unit, the pair of them, since they arrived in Baghdad, and the executive officer had threatened to split them up—not that he was likely to go through with it, Callaghan reckoned. Carlisle was one of those steady, confident types who would ride his helicopter into hell on a dare. Callaghan had liked Jim Carlisle from the moment they met, and knew his time in Iraq would be the better for knowing him. Carlisle loved to fly his helicopter—he always referred to her as "his," and as a she, not an it. He took great delight in flying even lower and closer to the buildings than they were supposed to, so the rooftops would almost graze the soles of Callaghan's boots, and they would have to jerk sharply up when an obstacle came into view ahead. It was Carlisle's calm reck-lessness that had got Callaghan through the last four months in the sandbox without sex or drink—except for the time they had spotted Iraqis drinking illicit hooch outside the base, driven out without permission and bluffed the Iraqis into handing it over at gunpoint, claiming they were confiscating it, and ended up blind drunk on duty and in front of the colonel with a screaming hangover the next day.

But that had been more than three weeks back and Charlie Callaghan was bored, riding the dust-carrying winds over Baghdad. Up ahead he could see a black flag flying from a communication tower. Callaghan had seen strange flags flying over this sector before, always one solid colour, black, red or green, without any design. He wondered what they were and why the Iraqis bothered to put them there. They weren't Iraqi national flags, nor the flags of any group or faction he'd heard of. As the helicopter flashed past, he idly stretched out to see if he could touch the flag. It whipped by, inches from his fingers. He turned his head to watch it fade into the distance, flapping frantically in the draught from the helicopter.

"Hey, Carlisle," he said. "Take us back—I want to see if I can get a hold of that flag."

"What the fuck you want the flag for?" But Carlisle was already smiling.

"Trophy, man. That thing would look neat on our tent."

Carlisle laughed and lurched the helicopter around on its axis. The flag was just a speck in the distance; they'd gone far past it while they were talking. He heard Malone over the radio, asking what they were doing, and Carlisle replying they just wanted to check something back at the tower. Malone turned and followed. Carlisle pointed the nose of the helicopter down and raced in low and fast towards the communication tower. As they came in close, he slowed the helicopter, so they were hovering just a few inches from the flag. Malone held back and came over the radio again asking why they were hovering there.

"Just checking this out," Carlisle deadpanned. Callaghan leaned out towards the flag, but it was still just out of reach.

"Fuck," he said. "Take us in a bit nearer." Carlisle eased the helicopter slowly in. They were very close to the communication tower now, and though Carlisle betrayed no sign of it, they both knew that if the rotors hit it they could seriously damage the helicopter—they might even crash the damn thing. Malone was back on the radio sounding tense; he'd worked out what they were doing. Callaghan strained to reach the flag, but it flapped out of his grasp. They weren't supposed to hover over one spot like this; it left them exposed, and Malone wasn't happy about it. Callaghan slipped open his harness, and with one hand holding onto the helicopter and his feet braced against the door sill, he hung out over the void to reach the flag. The helicopter swayed with his weight before Carlisle corrected it. Callaghan grabbed at the flag, but his hand closed on empty air. Below, he could see people were beginning to look up at the helicopter and point. He reached for the flag again, and it was in his hand. He pulled, but it refused to budge. It was securely tied, and he realised it was going to be harder to dislodge from the communication tower than he had thought. But he was in no mood to give up now, and he began to pull.

⟶▬◉▬⟵

To Callaghan and Carlisle, the streets below were just another sector of the city they flew over day and night, one of the quieter ones where there were few attacks on American patrols. But to the inhabitants, these particular streets of dust-coloured buildings were Sadr City, which had once been Saddam City, forced to bear the name of its oppressor. People began to gather in the streets to watch the curious spectacle unfolding above. At first there was confusion as to what the American helicopters were doing, hovering so close to the communication tower. One man suggested they had come to repair it, so the telephones would start working again, but the others laughed and told him the tower had nothing to do with the phone lines. Another thought the Americans were putting in a satellite so they could beam American television in. A third, more suspicious, said they were taking down the communication tower to prevent Sadr City from receiving any television or radio. And then a fourth, a younger man who until then had not dared raise his voice and argue with the others, pointed and exclaimed, "They're taking down the flag!"

There was shock as the crowd stared, a long and horrified silence, and then the shouting began.

"How dare they?"

"Kill them!"

And then another young man—the situation had changed now and it was time for the actions of the young—stooped to the ground, straightened up and hurled something up at the helicopter. There was a metallic thud as the stone made contact. The American who was leaning out looked down in surprise, and the helicopter moved up and away. As it did so, the flag the American had been trying without success to dislodge came free in his hand, and the crowd erupted. More stones were hurled, and as both helicopters moved out of range of such primitive missiles, several of the men who lived nearby ran home to get their guns. By the time they had returned, however, the helicopters were gone, and so the crowd surged through the streets in search of Americans.

Because what to Callaghan and Carlisle was just an old bit of black cloth tied to a communication mast was to the Shia of Sadr City a symbol of the martyr Hussein—and by tearing it down, Charlie Callaghan had managed profoundly to offend every man, woman and child for miles around.

He and Carlisle were safely out of their reach. Instead, a group of soldiers driving in an unarmoured Humvee through a sector where they had encountered little trouble before found themselves face to face with an angry crowd. And it was Charlie Callaghan, watching from above with the torn black flag at his feet, who radioed in that there was trouble in the sector and an American patrol in need of reinforcements.

The Hotel al-Hamra was changing colour. Ali had told Zoe that the name wasn't really accurate anyway, since *hamra* meant red and the hotel was a dusty brown colour, like most of the buildings in Baghdad. But over the last few days, planks had appeared suspended on ropes from the roof outside the building, and now, as Zoe watched, painters were sitting precariously on them, repainting the hotel a white so bright that it hurt her eyes in the sun. She was sitting in the small Internet cafe she had discovered across the street from the hotel. There was no Internet in the rooms at the al-Hamra, and the business centre had just four computers, which were almost always busy. Zoe had been connecting to the Internet with her satellite phone, a painfully slow business, until she found the small cafe crammed with antiquated computers on the ground floor of one of the cheaper hotels where the freelancers stayed. Electronic alarms would go off every so often, when the power failed and the backup batteries took over, until one of the staff could start up the generator just outside, which sent clouds of choking smoke inside every time someone opened the door. Zoe watched through the window as the painters slowly descended the exterior of the al-Hamra.

The occupation wasn't bad for everyone: the hotel's owners had received such an unexpected influx of cash that they had decided to spend some of it on a new coat of paint. They had briefly experimented with highlighting some of the balconies in red, which had led to grim jokes from the journalists about the intention being to hide the blood of those who were shot while trying to get a signal for their satellite phones, but they had given up the idea in favour of painting the hotel white all over. Ali, who was sitting a couple of computers down from her, was not impressed: he said the white would soon turn filthy in the Baghdad dust.

It had been a quiet day, and Zoe had been casting around the Internet for ideas for a story when she had come upon Jack Wolfe's latest piece for the *Daily Post*. She was surprised, reading it, that it was written by the man she knew from the al-Hamra. It was the story of an Iraqi child who had lost his leg in the war.

For Selim Abdullah, the world ended at 11.30 a.m. on 3 April. That was when an American rocket came through the side of the pick-up truck the ten-year-old boy was riding in and tore off his leg below the knee. Since then, his life has been one of agony, forced to hobble around on wooden crutches. There has been much debate over whether the American invasion has improved life for ordinary Iraqis. For Selim, an ordinary Iraqi, there is no debate: the Americans have ruined his life.

"Why did George Bush cut off my leg?" he asks. "I never did anything to him." His future is bleak, his family are farmers, but he will not be able to work the fields. With little formal education, he will probably have to spend his adult life relying on the charity of relatives. Without an income, it is unlikely he will be able to marry.

If he were British or American, he could get a state-of-the-art prosthetic leg and be able to walk again. Even in Iraq, artificial legs are available if you have money. But his family cannot afford such things.

While Ali Ismail Abbas, the twelve-year-old boy who lost his arms in a US air strike, was flown to London to be fitted with prosthetic arms, Selim is one of the thousands who got left behind, who did not make it to the television cameras and capture a rich nation's heart.

He was in the wrong place at the wrong time. He was out with his father, who was working in the family rice paddies just outside Baghdad, when the American invasion force came through. The family tried to flee in their pick-up, but they were too late.

The door opened, with the usual burst of choking generator smoke, and Mahmoud came in. He spoke urgently to Ali in Arabic, and Ali turned to Zoe.

"There's something going on in Sadr City," he said. "Some people there have attacked the Americans and there is a fight going on. Lots of the journalists are going."

"OK," she said. "Let's go."

She wondered for a moment whether to go back to the hotel

room for her flak jacket, but decided the humiliation would be too much if none of the other journalists were wearing one.

⟶⟨●⟩⟨●⟩⟵

Benes was lying in his tent, in the relentless heat, when Captain Parks came to the open flap in a hurry.

"There's something major going down in Sadr," he said breathlessly. "The whole company's moving out. Time: now."

Benes sat up and started pulling on clothes. Sadr City was out of his usual area, so whatever was going down must be pretty big for them to send for backup from outside. By the time he found Hawkes, the sergeant already had the platoon ready to move. They headed through Baghdad in a column of unarmoured Humvees—the company didn't have a single armoured vehicle between them.

⟶⟨●⟩⟨●⟩⟵

Callaghan and Carlisle flew high over the city, out of reach of the chaos and violence they had caused. At Callaghan's feet was the trophy he had been so determined to secure, the little square of black cloth that had caused a riot on the streets beneath.

"Fuck, man, it's really kicking off down there," he said, peering down at the crowd in the street below, which was being held back by a line of armoured vehicles blocking the road. Young men were hurling rocks that thudded metallically off the roofs of the Bradleys and Humvees. More threateningly, several of those in the crowd were armed, and gunfire rang out. The soldiers were in full defensive posture, and the helicopters had to keep flying quick unpredictable passes above.

"Why'd you have to take that fucking flag, man?" Carlisle asked.

"Shit, I don't know. How was I to know they'd go crazy? I mean, it's just a fucking flag."

⟶⟨●⟩⟨●⟩⟵

What had happened after they took the flag was that the crowd, deprived of a helicopter on which to vent its anger, had attacked the first American patrol it found. The patrol, taken unaware, had found itself pinned down and, unable to escape, called for backup. But by the time reinforcements had arrived the crowd had swelled, with the result that the reinforcements were too few in number and too lightly armed, and the protestors turned on them as well. The soldiers, under fire and with no easy way out, had fired back at the gunmen who were firing at them out of the mass of people. Pretty soon, things got out of hand.

→—⊙—⊙—←

Zoe was crouched in a narrow alley, backed up against the wall, wishing she had worn her flak jacket. At the end of the alley, she could see an American soldier in the main street, down on one knee, firing from the shoulder. Behind the American was an armoured vehicle with several other soldiers positioned around it, all of them firing. She couldn't see who they were shooting at, but she could hear the din of an angry crowd. Every so often helicopters would circle overhead, very low and very fast, the noise of the rotors so loud it made her flinch. It was a scene straight out of the movies.

Peter was beside her, and Rob was filming further up the street, inching ever closer to the Americans. She had run into them on the way, and they had come up the alley together. If she'd been alone, she wouldn't have come so close to the firing, but Peter and Rob had wanted to and she didn't want to let them know she was afraid. Peter was wearing a flak jacket—as a TV reporter he had to use one on camera because of the insurance, but Rob hadn't bothered with his. When she asked him, he told her his editors couldn't see he wasn't wearing one, so he didn't see the point. A clutch of journalists appeared at the other end of the alley and began moving up the opposite wall. Among them, Zoe recognised Randell and the Journonator, his equipment strapped to his body. Zoe found herself nodding a greeting to them across the alley, as if she had run into them at some social function.

Rob came back down the alley towards them, crouched over and moving backwards so he could keep filming. When he was level, Peter leaned over and yelled into his ear, above the din, "What's going on?"

"Can't really see," Rob yelled back. "Americans are facing off against a big crowd. Looks pretty ugly. Want to do a quick piece to camera?"

"Yeah, might as well get one in. Let's do it close up; adds to the drama."

Zoe watched as Peter shuffled out in front of Rob and, hunched over the camera, began to speak loudly.

"As you can see behind me now," he said, "American troops are facing off against an angry crowd of protestors. This is Sadr City, an area populated mainly by Shia, who up till now have been welcoming to the Americans." As if on cue, the American soldier behind fired off a volley. "Today, that seems to have changed," Peter continued. "We're getting reports that the violence may have begun when an American helicopter removed a religious flag from a building. How's that?" he asked Rob in his normal voice.

"Fine. One more to make sure?"

"All right," Peter said, and he began reciting the same monologue to the camera. A helicopter swept overhead and drowned him out; as soon as it was gone, he started from the beginning again. Behind him Zoe could make out an American soldier gesturing angrily at the journalists. Rob put the camera down, with Peter mid-sentence.

"Looks like we need to get out of here," he said, nodding back down the street at the American. Peter looked back over his shoulder.

"Press," someone shouted from the other side of the street, but the soldier kept gesturing.

"Better get going," Peter said, and they all began to back down the alley, keeping close to the buildings. At the other end of the alley, they could see more American soldiers waiting for them. Zoe remembered the story of Peter and his combat knife in the Balkans, and she hoped he didn't have anything like that with him now. Across the street, Alain had fished a large white handkerchief out of his pocket and was holding it up in his hand like a white flag. Because Peter had TV written across his flak jacket in large letters made from masking tape, the others made him go first as a sort of walking billboard to announce their identity to the soldiers.

"American press," Randell called out loudly. The soldiers at the end of the street seemed relaxed as they drew level; their guns were lowered and pointing at the ground.

"You guys press?" one of them asked.

"Bernard Randell, *Washington Report*."

"Peter Shore, MTN."

"OK," the soldier said, "you people are going to need to move back from here." There was a loud metallic clang. Zoe flinched as the soldiers wheeled round, their rifles raised. Something made of metal was rolling at Peter's feet, glinting in the sun. A grenade? Zoe tensed, waiting for it to go off.

"Sorry, guys," Rob said, "it's just the leading lady's hairspray." Peter was looking sheepish. Looking down, Zoe could see that it was the can of hairspray he had used to fix his hair in the car, ready to go on camera. The soldiers laughed.

"Get Miss England outta here," one of them said as Peter stooped down to gather up his hairspray.

⸻

Benes crouched at the end of another street with Hawkes beside him. In front of them, Gutierrez and Jackson were at the guns of the Humvees, while the others crouched on the ground on either side, their rifles drawn. Beyond them was the crowd.

"This shit is getting out of hand," Hawkes said. As he spoke, a rock sailed through the air, missed Benes's head by a few inches and landed on the ground behind him. Hunt and Ramirez looked round. They were waiting for him to give the order.

"Not yet, Sergeant," he said.

"We're highly exposed, sir." Benes looked across at Jackson—he was exposed all right, on top of the Humvee. Another rock came in and bounced noisily off the roof of Gutierrez's Humvee. A couple more of the men glanced round. Still, Benes hesitated. From somewhere, a gunshot rang out.

"OK," he said, "light them up." All around him, the platoon opened fire.

—▪◉▪—

After some hours, the soldiers managed to contain the crowd and calm the situation. Within an hour or so after the streets had cleared, what had seemed at the time like a major clash had become a relatively minor fracas. There were no casualties among the Americans, and though reports were not clear, it seemed there had not been many among the Iraqis either. To Zoe's surprise, but not to that of more experienced correspondents, the newspapers and television networks of the world were not much interested in the small-scale unrest that they had taken such risks to witness: it only merited a few paragraphs tacked onto the end of a political story in the *Informer*. Talks were under way between the Americans and the Shia leadership in Sadr City to defuse the cause of the violence, and the Americans had promised a full investigation into the flag incident.

—▪◉▪—

As Callaghan and Carlisle flew back towards base, Carlisle noticed the flag still at Callaghan's feet.

"Lose that fucking flag," he said. "Last thing we want is to get back with the evidence at our fucking feet."

So Callaghan picked up the flag and flung it out of the helicopter. He didn't look back to see it slowly flutter down over the empty rooftops.

Chapter Nine

Divided Nations

ZOE WAS IN the waiting room at the offices of the United Nations, which were housed in a disused hotel in a nondescript corner of the city, among the usual dust-coloured buildings and broad, open highways. Expecting lengthy security checks, Zoe had arrived in plenty of time, but she had been waved straight into the building, with the result that she was early for her appointment. The waiting room where she sat had been decorated in desultory style: hard plastic chairs, a few unloved potted plants and a framed picture of the UN headquarters in New York.

She was getting nervous, it was getting towards the time of the afternoon when she needed a story to offer Nigel Langham, and the interview she had scheduled with the UN spokesman, Mehmet Ozdemir, was all she had. Even if he didn't say anything newsworthy, she was going to have to pull a story together from it. The spokesman's assistant, a British woman, put her head around the door to tell Zoe he would be with her in a moment. Zoe glanced out of the window. Outside an American soldier was sitting, bored, in the sun.

"Zoe Temple. And how are you?" She looked up to see Jack Wolfe standing over her.

"Hello Jack, I…how are you?"

"Fine, fine," he said, sitting down beside her. "You here to see Ozdemir?"

"Yes."

"I've just been with him. He's good. How's Baghdad treating you?"

"It's going well, yes. Haven't seen you in a while."

"I was in Mosul. How was your jaunt up to Sadr City the other day?"

"Intense," she said. "We were pretty close to the action. Were you there?"

"No, didn't bother," he shrugged. "It was never going to make the front, and I didn't fancy getting my head blown off for a couple of paragraphs on page twenty-three. I hear Peter dropped a bit of a clanger."

Zoe winced; the story of Peter's hairspray had been the talk of the al-Hamra.

"Well, I must be getting on," Jack said. "Keep your head down."

As he left, Zoe saw Ozdemir's assistant approaching with a smile. She had just got up when she felt the world come apart: something invisible hit her hard in the chest and knocked the breath out of her, the floor turned to liquid and seemed to give way in every direction at once, the assistant was flying towards her through the air with a startled look on her face, the lights went out, and there was a deafening noise and then screaming in her ears and darkness and pain. She tried to breathe but she couldn't; her lungs were empty and she began to panic. After what seemed an age she managed to get some air into her lungs and scrambled up from the floor. People were pushing past her in the darkness; she could hear voices but she couldn't make out what they were saying through the screaming in her ears. She tried to call out, but she could barely hear her own voice.

"Zoe?" Someone was moving against the flow of people, pushing back towards her. She heard her name, quiet but distinct: he must have been shouting. As her eyes adjusted, she made out Jack Wolfe, shouldering his way back through the crowd.

"You OK?" he said, or maybe shouted.

"Yes."

"We've got to get out."

As she stepped forward, Zoe tripped over something. Peering down, she could see Ozdemir's assistant lying on the floor and knelt down to try to help her. There was blood in her perfect blonde hair.

"She's dead," she heard Jack saying above her. But she could see the imploring in the woman's eyes looking up at her. Zoe reached out and touched her gently on the shoulder; as she did, the back of the woman's head came away.

Zoe decided she must be dreaming; she couldn't have just seen a woman's head come apart, so she just stood there and waited to wake.

"Come on." Jack pulled roughly at her arm, and she followed. There was light ahead, and they walked towards it, but the corridor ended in open air, over a two-storey drop to the ground. The building had been torn away, and a sign reading "Humanitarian Information Centre for Iraq" pointed at the empty sky. A huddle of people were standing there, deciding whether to jump, when someone shouted, "There's a stairway this way."

They followed the others back, feeling their way in the dark. Zoe thought she could feel the building moving again and worried what was left of it might collapse at any moment. Someone in front pushed open a door that gave onto a stairwell, and she ran down it, somehow managing to avoid the bits of broken plaster and glass that littered the stairs, out through an empty doorway and into the sunlight. There were American soldiers all around, shouting to go this way or that.

"We've got to get out of here before they get organised," Jack said. "If we get stuck in here, they'll have us locked down for hours."

As they stumbled away over rough ground, Zoe looked back and saw the building, a whole corner of it collapsed in rubble and a great dirty brown cloud that looked like smoke rising in a column from the wreckage. Ahead, she could see a small knot of reporters already gathered, and American soldiers keeping them back.

"We're press," she said to the soldiers, who turned in surprise to see them coming from behind, but let them through. The other reporters crowded round.

"Jesus, what happened to you?"

"Were you inside?"

"Are you all right?"

She saw Mervyn Pile, Randell, Mike Rodham and, of course, Alain the Journonator among the crowd. Zoe realised she must look rather dramatic, with bits of plaster in her hair and stuck to her clothes.

"Zoe, are you all right? Your head's bleeding!" Paul Thorn pushed his way through to her.

"I'm fine," she said, but putting her hand to her head she felt something damp, and when she looked at her hand, she saw blood. Alain was beside her, pulling out a sealed packet of chemical wipes, the sort young mothers carry around for babies. Paul took one and dabbed at Zoe's head.

"You're all right, it's just a surface scratch," he said. "What happened?"

"There was an explosion; I think it must have been a bomb."

She looked for Jack, but he had slipped away and was talking to some of the other journalists. Paul had cleaned her forehead now, and Alain had produced a plaster, which he was sticking to it.

"It's OK, Zo, take it easy," Paul said.

"You'll be fine, hon," said an American woman Zoe didn't recognise.

"Here, come and sit down," said Randell, leading her to the grass verge. She sat down on the ground while the others crowded around.

"Must have been pretty bad in there," the American woman said.

"Half the building's gone," Zoe said, "just collapsed. I saw this woman; I spoke with her and now she's dead. She was walking towards me and then..." Looking up, she noticed that two or three of the reporters crowded around had surreptitiously got their notebooks out and were taking notes. They held their notebooks low, as if they were ashamed of them or didn't want her to see them, and wrote without looking down, all the while fixing her with sympathetic looks. Randell had his notebook out, so did Mervyn.

Zoe wanted to be professional and give them a calm, detailed account of what she had seen, but her ears were screaming, and part of her wished they would go away and leave her to think. For some reason, she had an overwhelming feeling her mother must never know what had happened. She kept seeing Ozdemir's assistant, blood in her perfect hair.

"Zo, are you all right?" She looked up with relief to see Peter pushing his way through the crowd. "What happened? Were you inside?" She got up to meet him as he came level, the other journalists parting slightly, reluctantly, to let him through.

"God, Peter, it was…half the fucking building's come down."

"Yeah, I heard. Where were you? How'd you get out?"

"I was waiting to see Ozdemir. There was this…explosion and it was just chaos in there. There was this woman, I was talking to her and the next minute she was dead, right in front of me."

"Jesus, Zo, sounds pretty fucking close."

Then she noticed. Like the others, Peter had taken his notebook from his pocket and was jotting down the details. When she stopped speaking, he looked up, and he must have noticed the rebuke in her eyes, because he said, "You don't mind, do you?"

"No, of course not," she said, and she wanted it to be true.

"Listen, Zo, do you think you could say a few words for the camera?" he asked.

"Sure, why not?" She forced herself to be professional in front of the camera; she told herself it would be good for her career. When she had finished, some of the journalists who had been at the back pressed forward and asked her to go through the details again.

"They're saying de Mello's still trapped in there," Mervyn said. Zoe was thinking she should call her mother, before the television pictures went out.

"Listen, Zo, are you going to be OK here if I go and get some more info on what's going on?" Peter asked.

"Yes, of course."

"You'll be all right?"

"I'll be fine." If he couldn't understand without asking, there was no point in telling him. She didn't want to call the paper; she wanted some time to herself. Then she realised she had forgotten Ali and Mahmoud. She had left them waiting for her in the UN car park, and they were probably desperately looking for her—or worse, they could have been killed when the building collapsed. She tried to remember on which side of the building they had parked. There was no way of getting back to the car park; the Americans were all over the place, and they had put up a rope to keep the journalists back. She pulled the satellite phone from her pocket, but there was no way of calling them—they didn't have a phone. She saw she had nine missed calls, all from the *Informer*. When she called back, Nigel answered and broke in furiously as soon as he heard her voice.

"Zoe, where the hell have you been? I don't know if you're aware," he said, his voice heavy with irony, "but there's been a massive explosion at the UN and we are *desperate* for details here." He was so stressed he sounded almost demented. "I know you're under pressure over there but you *cannot* go disappearing like this. The Editor is demanding to know what you can give us. The wires are saying suicide bomb. What can you tell me?"

Zoe waited for him to subside.

"I was inside," she said.

"What? Inside *where*?"

"Inside the UN building. I was there when the bomb went off."

There was a pause. Then Nigel's voice came back transformed.

"That's fantastic! Well done, Zoe. Can you do us an eyewitness piece? The Editor will love this." She heard him take his mouth away from the receiver and shout across the newsroom, "Zoe was inside the UN building. Do you want it for the front?" She couldn't make out the reply. Nigel came back to her. "You're all right and all that, aren't you?" he said.

"Yes, yes, I'm fine."

"No injuries?"

"No, I'm OK."

"Great. Well, we want—" he broke off, and she could make out someone else saying something indistinct. Nigel was back: "Just put down everything, Zoe. A first-person account. You're going all over the front. Write as much as you like. You'd better get going."

She needed to get back to the hotel and her computer—but first she had to find Ali and Mahmoud. She looked around and saw Kate standing at the rope, watching the efforts to dig through the wreckage.

"Kate!"

"Hey, Zo! Is it true you were in there?"

"Yes."

"Merv told me. You OK?"

"I'm fine. Bit shaken up but fine."

"What happened?"

"Listen, I'll tell you later. But I need to find Ali and Mahmoud."

"Didn't Ali find you?"

"No, have you seen him? Is he OK?"

"They're both fine. They've been looking for you. They're over there," she said, pointing to the other side of the road. Zoe thanked her and set off. When she saw Ali he rushed towards her.

"Miss Zoe. Alhamdulillah. Are you all right? We looked everywhere. What happened? We were afraid you were in there." As he went on, telling her how worried he and Mahmoud had been, Zoe realised how good it felt to find someone who only wanted to know she was safe, not a story for the front page or a quick interview for the camera.

In the car on the way, she called her mother and told her not to worry about what she saw on the television, lying to her that it was all being exaggerated and she hadn't been in any danger. When they reached the hotel, she went to the Internet cafe to read the news wires. The bomb had been inside a truck that was driven up to the building by a suicide bomber. Several people were feared dead, including Sergio Vieira de Mello, the head of the UN mission, but there was little further information.

Back in her room, she hunched over her laptop and tried to write down what she had seen. She had been at the centre of events, but she couldn't convey it; what she wrote seemed more a self-serving account of her own brush with death, with her cast as intrepid reporter, than a real account of what it had been like. She tried to describe Ozdemir's assistant, but the words seemed inadequate. Her satellite phone rang; the deadline was nearing, and Nigel was getting nervous. Zoe knew what she had written wasn't good enough, she wanted more time, but Nigel told her to send it anyway. Reluctantly, she walked back across to the

Internet cafe to email it to London. When she had sent it, she went back to the hotel, sat by the pool and ordered a beer. As she sat in the courtyard, which was beginning to fill with weary journalists, she realised that she was not particularly eager for her friends to join her or to relive her experiences of the afternoon for them again. The ring of the satellite phone cut through her thoughts: she answered it and heard Nigel's voice.

"Zoe, that is one of the best pieces any of us have read here in a long time. I just thought you should know you're all over the front with a picture byline. Well done, now go and get yourself a drink." Zoe lifted the beer can to her lips. She should have felt elated: the paper thought what she had written was so good they had put her photograph on the front page. And she should have felt devastated: she had watched a woman die in front of her. But she felt neither, only flat and empty.

⇥⊨⊜⊨⇤

Adel sat and watched the television pictures of the smoking UN building, refusing to listen to his father's voice saying, *These were not soldiers; they were civilians. They should not have died.* As far as Adel was concerned, the UN was the same as the Americans; for years they had ground down the Iraqi people with their sanctions, with their weapons inspectors they had helped prepare the way for the American invasion. They had come unwanted, and now they had paid the price.

But he was no nearer discovering who was behind the bombing than he had been with the Jordanian Embassy. Abu Mustafa had told the cell that even if the ex-army resistance groups were behind it, he could tell them nothing, because he himself knew nothing. None of the cells knew what any of the others were doing: that way, it was harder for the Americans to get any reliable intelligence on the next attack. Adel wasn't sure if there was any centralised command or coordination at all; certainly Abu Mustafa seemed to be making his own decisions about attacks. As for the foreigners, if Selim knew anything, he wasn't saying, and Adel was beginning to doubt Selim was as close to them as he pretended: Adel had heard nothing more from him about Abu Khalid since their meeting. The word in the cafes and on the streets was that there were many different groups of foreign fighters operating inside Iraq, all with their own aims and ideas. The Americans had so many enemies in Iraq it was impossible to tell who was behind the bombings, Adel thought with satisfaction.

Chapter Ten

Iraq and a Hard Place

21–22 August 2003

Mahmoud sat by Saara's side and listened to the sounds of the house he knew so well. He could hear Saara's mother moving around; she was upstairs now, above them. A short time before, she had been on the other side of the door. He had heard the stillness when she stopped to eavesdrop, and picked his words carefully. He could hear Saara's sister Maryam—he was so used to the sounds of the house he could tell the footsteps of the young girl and her mother apart. Maryam had given him a smile of complicity when she answered the door. She was getting older and more knowing, and he wondered if that might become a problem. The way things were in Baghdad, all it would take would be for her to tell a friend, schoolgirls playing conspirators. He thought of mentioning it to Saara, but she seemed distracted, her mind only half on the conversation. At first he thought she was annoyed because he hadn't come over straight after the bombing at the UN. He had known she would be worried, but the journalist had kept him waiting at the hotel until it was too late, and when he finally got to the house, the ribbon was not by the window.

But now he wasn't so sure that was what was bothering her. She had brushed aside his apologies, and even when he described the bombing, and how he and Ali had seen the building collapse, her mind seemed elsewhere. He looked at her, her eyes focused on some trouble he could not see, and she was more beautiful than ever. He tried to ask what was on her mind, but she didn't answer, and he knew he would have to wait. They sat and worked their way through the usual exchange of news, the aftermath of the bombing, how he and Ali had searched for the journalist and thought she had died in the explosion, then found her alive; how Saara's mother had heard that Maryam had been flirting with a boy outside the school and had flown into a rage with her; and how her father and Yusuf had argued about politics the night before.

"I've never seen them fight like that," she said. "It was all right when they had calmed down, but for a moment I was scared Yusuf might leave, or that my father might throw him out. I think…things are getting to them." For a moment it seemed she was about to go on, but she stopped herself. "How's Ali?" she asked.

"He's fine," Mahmoud answered, surprised.

"He is still a good friend?"

"Yes." Mahmoud wondered where she was going. "He's one of the best."

"Good," she murmured, looking down at her hands and twisting her ring absent-mindedly. "It's just the way things are going, I wondered if you could stay friends with…with a Shia." She was more aware of what was going on outside the confines of the house than he had thought: you could lock her up in here all day long, but you couldn't cage her mind.

"To me he's not a Shia; he's one of us, an Iraqi," he said. "And he's a good guy."

"And what about a Christian?" She looked up at him. "Can you stay friends with her?"

"Of course." She looked so fragile at that moment, staring at him. "What's wrong?"

She stood up and crossed to the bookcase. Reaching behind one of the books with the strange foreign writing on it, she pulled out a piece of paper.

"You must never tell any of the others I showed you this," she said, "not Yusuf, not Maryam, definitely not my father. You mustn't tell anybody."

"What is it?" he asked. She passed him the paper. It was a simple hand-scrawled note.

"To the Jews and Crusaders, this is not your land," it read. "We know that you are spies among us, working for the occupiers, and we are warning you that you should leave and go to your own people. Otherwise your fate is known ahead of time and your punishment will be just. We will take justice into our own hands in order to defend our people, who reject the traitor even more than the occupier. May the curse of God be on all those who extend a helping hand to the aggressors."

There was no signature. Mahmoud stared in shock.

"We never helped the Americans," Saara said quietly. "We are Iraqis. This is our land."

"Where did this come from?" Mahmoud had often heard the Americans described as crusaders, but never Iraqi Christians.

"It came under the door two days ago," she said. "I found it. My father made me promise not to tell my mother or Maryam about it."

"It's probably just some local idiot taking advantage of the situation, trying to scare you," he said, though he didn't believe it. "Or someone who thinks if you leave he can come and steal your house. No one will do anything, I…" He looked up and saw that she had tears in her eyes.

"What should we do?" she said. It broke his heart to see her like this. He crossed the uncrossable line, stepped over the invisible distance between them, and took her in his arms. For once she did not resist but let herself press against him; he kissed her—then there was a sound from behind the door and they leapt apart.

⊸⊷⊛⊷⊶

Benes moved through the corridors of the al-Iskan Central Children's Teaching Hospital. The wards stretched to either side of him, in semi-darkness, so the children could try to sleep. Somewhere in the distance he could hear a child crying; nearer there was the sound of someone moaning in pain. From the end of the corridor came the clanging of an orderly rolling an oxygen cylinder; beyond, in the Baghdad night, the gunfire had already started up. As he walked, Benes couldn't help glancing at the children. A lot of them were still awake and looked back at him with eyes filled with confusion at their own suffering. Others twisted uncomfortably in their sleep or shook with fever. And in every face Benes saw the girl they took out of the car alive that night, and he wondered what had become of her, if she was in a hospital somewhere, or if she was one more among the dead that nobody, it seemed, was counting.

"Lieutenant Benes?" He snapped out of his reverie and saw Dr Afaf before him, unmistakable despite being covered from head to toe in loose white clothes and a headscarf. She had just come out of one of the wards to the side and looked surprised to see him. "You are back?" He thought he detected a hint of pleasure in her eyes, but perhaps it was just his vanity. "Can we help you?"

"Dr Afaf, how're you doing? We had a bit of a problem earlier on, and I wanted to speak with Dr Kamal."

"You mean your soldier and Dr Hussein? It is nothing. You know the situation: the doctors are under a lot of stress; sometimes they lose their tempers." There had been an altercation between Zivkovich and one of the doctors, nothing serious, but Benes wanted to smooth things over with the director all the same.

"I just wanted to speak with Dr Kamal to make sure everything's OK."

"He is operating; you can't see him now. He'll be out in maybe half an hour." She kept glancing up at him as she spoke, her eyes flicking back to the children. "Can you wait?" Did she sound hopeful? He wondered why it mattered to him; they were both married, and he had no intention of being unfaithful to Maria, and yet he liked speaking to Dr Afaf. It must have been the absence of female company.

"Half an hour, you say?"

"Maybe. Perhaps less, or more."

"We'll wait for a bit. What sort of operation is it?" he asked to keep the conversation going.

"A boy with a broken leg. It is not serious. Dr Kamal will pin it and it should heal completely. Dr Kamal is our best orthopaedic surgeon."

"Really? I guess I thought his hands were too full running the hospital to do much else."

"We're too short of doctors for anyone not to work," she said. "What about you, Lieutenant? You seem tired."

"Yeah, long day."

"And how's the situation outside? Is it getting better?"

"Well, obviously as the hold-outs and dead-enders from the old regime get weaker, they're getting more desperate…" Benes started to give her the official line, but seeing her eyes upon him, he felt cheap: this was the closest he had come to a real conversation with an Iraqi. So he found himself telling her the truth: "No, it's not getting any better. To be honest with you, it's getting worse."

"And what will become of us?"

"I don't know," he replied, feeling relieved to speak honestly. "I don't think anybody knows."

She nodded and there was a silence between them—an easy silence, where neither felt the need to speak.

"What about you, Dr Afaf?" he asked. "Do you agree with Dr Kamal? Are you angry we haven't done more for the hospital?"

"Dr Kamal is a good man; he is fighting to keep the hospital going, and sometimes he gets…frustrated. But I…" She hesitated. "I don't think we should sit and wait for the Americans or the Arabs or anyone else to solve our problems…I think it is for Iraqis to solve our problems. But please, I'm not criticising Dr Kamal," she added hurriedly, as if afraid she had been too frank. "He knows the situation much better than I do."

"Don't worry, I won't tell him," he grinned, and she smiled back.

"You must miss your son, such a long way from home," she said. "And your wife too."

"Yeah, I realised today I haven't seen Juan in three months. I don't know what he looks like any more."

A cloud crossed her face.

"Children grow so quickly," she said.

"You'll have your own soon."

"Yes…" she said and trailed off. Then abruptly she added, "We had a daughter. Her name was Amira, but she…was sick. I couldn't do anything. She died."

"I'm sorry."

"It was a long time ago, two years. She was only a few weeks old. She was sick; there was nothing anyone could do."

The corridor and the hospital beds had receded until Benes was barely aware of them; for the first time in months, he forgot he was in Baghdad. He could have been anywhere. He was talking to an Iraqi as if he and she were the same, and it felt like a burden lifted.

The doors at the end of the corridor opened and Dr Kamal came out in a surgeon's smock.

"They told me you were waiting for me, Lieutenant," he called loudly. "Please, wait in my office. I will be one minute." Benes nodded. He turned to Dr Afaf.

"I guess I'll see you again. I'm…I'm sorry about your daughter."

"Thank you."

⊷⊶

Night fell across Baghdad. Not darkness, which had already covered the city some hours previously, nor silence, which the city's haunted streets never knew amid the skeleton dance of the guns. No, night came to Baghdad with the curfew, the true division of night and day, when the streets emptied of life and the last stragglers hurried back to the safety of their homes, abandoning the city. When they were gone, fear seemed to huddle in the darkened corners, waiting to ambush anyone who ventured out, as if the shadows were populated by the ghosts of those who had died, unable to rest or find peace until their deaths had been avenged. And the dust of the desert crept in silent and unobserved on the wind as it had for millennia, settling on the roads and the buildings, as temporary as occupying armies, as little noticed as each individual death. In the dust were the bones of old occupiers and insurgents who fought here long ago, ground fine by the desert winds. The city is fallen, as she has fallen through the centuries, and now the occupiers are beginning to fall, stumbling in her dust of ancient bones. Babylon is fallen, is fallen; and all the graven images of her gods he hath broken unto the ground.

⊷⊶

Zoe was in Peter's room on the sixth floor of the al-Hamra, gazing out of the window at the empty streets as the gunfire echoed in the distance. She was tired and wanted to go to sleep, but Peter had poured her a glass of whisky she didn't want and was sitting eagerly waiting by the television, which was tuned to MTN. His report would be on any moment, and Zoe knew he not only wanted to sit and watch it, he wanted her to watch it with him. That was why her untouched glass of whisky sat on the table in front of the empty seat next to him on the sofa, the ice slowly melting. Her head pounded; she had been out in the sun too long. He would want to make love, and she didn't want to, not tonight.

"Zo," he called, "it's on."

Reluctantly she turned, crossed to the sofa and sat down next to him. He put his arm around her shoulder but she didn't move in close. She took the glass and sipped half-heartedly from it.

"Meanwhile, in Baghdad today…" The report began, and Peter was walking through the rubble of the UN building, talking about the hunt for those responsible and what the bombing meant for Iraq. Zoe watched as he walked around the ruined section of the building, where she had stood in an open doorway on the top floor two days before and looked out into emptiness. She thought uncomfortably of her own front-page piece. She had received almost universal praise from the other reporters, but she couldn't help feeling faintly embarrassed by it. She had described her own experiences inside the building as if she had done something remarkable and brave, rather than just been in the wrong place at the right time. On the screen Peter was recounting the official line from the Americans, that the bombing was the work of Saddam loyalists who refused to accept that his regime was finished, possibly with the help of Islamic militants from other Arab countries.

"While many observers fear this horrific attack may signal the start of a more sustained campaign of violence, the Americans are saying it is a sign of the growing desperation of the insurgents," he told the camera. "With fewer and fewer places left to run, and too weak to take on the Americans, they have turned on soft targets like the United Nations. Last night the Americans were insisting this"—he gestured behind him to the ruins of the building—"was the insurgents' last stand. Across Iraq, people are hoping they are right. Peter Shore, MTN, at the UN building in Baghdad."

As the report finished Peter switched off the sound. She knew that meant he would want to go to bed and felt his arm tighten around her shoulders, his hand beginning to caress her breast. She shifted away slightly in her seat, but he leaned in closer, so she could smell the whisky on his breath. She broke free of him and sat forward, drawing a cigarette from the packet on the table.

"What's wrong?" he asked. She tried to light the cigarette and fumbled at the lighter.

"I don't know," she said.

"You OK, Zo? You still freaked out by the bombing? I mean, anyone would be."

"Yes. No. It's not that. I don't know."

"Hey, take it easy, Zo." He put an arm comfortingly around her shoulders. "It's normal to feel like this; you were in a bad spot there." She let herself rest against his arm. Later, she lay awake in bed beside him and watched him breathing in his sleep. Soon, she knew, she would have to end it.

->-><-<-

Mahmoud lay awake in his bed, thinking of Saara. He had kissed her at last, his beloved, he had felt her body against his; he had felt her heart beating. But the letter came back into his mind. He had tried to tell her that he, Mahmoud, would protect her, would not let anything happen, but there was little he could do. He couldn't admit their love to anyone, not even to his best friend Ali. If they came for her in the night, if they came for his Saara—the fear ran through him so hard he sat bolt upright in bed. He lay back down, and wondered if he should throw caution aside, drive there now and take her away in the car. But where would they go? He couldn't get visas for them to travel together outside the country, and there was nowhere safe for them inside Iraq. The Christians had no tribe to protect them. If his family got a letter like that, his father would go to the sheikh, and it would be settled between tribes, but Saara's family had no tribe. He heard a sound beyond the door.

"Mahmoud?" came his father's voice. "I heard a sound. Are you OK?"

"It's nothing, I'm sorry," he called out. "I had a bad dream, that's all."

⇥⊷⊷⊶⊶

Zoe decided to face Peter the next afternoon. All day, the thought that she had to get out of it had been gnawing at her, but she was reluctant to go through the scene itself, to watch his face crumple in self-pity or listen to him wheedle with her to stay. She found him in the extra room the MTN team had taken to use as an office, across the corridor from his suite, going over some footage.

"Got a minute?" she asked.

"Yeah, sure, I could do with a break."

"Can we go to your room?" she said, glancing over at Louise, the producer.

"Sure. Back in a minute," he said to Louise.

"Look," she said when they reached the room, "we need to talk."

"Oh. That bad, huh?" he said, sitting down and gesturing her to a chair. She stayed standing.

"Yes," she tried to smile. "Look, Peter, this just isn't working out for me. I mean, you're a great guy and all that, and I know I must be crazy to do this, but I just think it's run its course for me."

"OK." He shrugged nonchalantly and leaned back in his seat.

"It's just," she went on with her rehearsed speech, "things happened a bit fast."

"I understand."

"I mean, I probably got more involved than I meant to—"

"Yeah, it's easily done, isn't it?" he said with a smile. She stood, unsure what to say next. "Hey," he said, "it's not as if we were

127

serious or anything." He looked up at her, not a trace of disappointment in his eyes. "I mean, I wasn't, and I didn't think you were?"

"No," she said quickly.

"So no worries," he said. "I hope we can still be friends."

"Yes. Absolutely." She stood there awkwardly for a while. "Well, I'd better—"

"Sure." He got up and kissed her on the cheek. "See you, Zo."

As she walked down the stairs, she realised she had wanted him to react with self-pity because it would have made her feel desired, and because it is easy to walk away from someone you have lost respect for. It is not so easy to walk away from someone who has no respect for you.

Chapter Eleven

Zoned Out

30–31 August 2003

ZOE SAT IN the Mercedes as they drove south, tense with the journey ahead. It was her last day in Iraq. David Wilson was on his way back to take over, and she had expected to be on the road to Jordan by now, but Iraq had conspired to produce one last convulsion of violence before she left. She had been in her room the previous afternoon when Kate had come knocking at the door, breathless, to tell her there had been a massive car bomb in the Shia holy city of Najaf, south of Baghdad. Ayatollah Mohammed Bakr al-Hakim, one of the most powerful of the Shia leaders, had been assassinated as he left the mosque after prayers, and scores of bystanders had been killed in the explosion. Nigel Langham, who called minutes later, had wanted her to go to Najaf immediately, but the police had closed the city off, and there was no getting in that day, so he had asked her to stay and keep trying until David could take over. Today the word was that the road was open. They had set off early in the morning and were passing through a flat, dusty landscape dotted with groves of palm trees, the heat already beating through the windscreen despite the air conditioning and the early hour. Najaf was the spiritual capital of the Shia in Iraq, and Zoe had been curious to see it, but now she was feeling apprehensive, not least because Ali had been reluctant to go—and over the weeks in Baghdad she had learned to trust his sense of what was safe and what was not.

"We should wait for a few days," he had said. "It will be very tense in Najaf now. Believe me, you have not seen the people in Najaf; they are not like the people here in Baghdad. They are very…passionate."

Najaf was Shia territory, and Ali was a Shia, and above all he knew how to stay alive in Iraq. But Zoe knew that, as a journalist, she couldn't avoid going. She had seen the other reporters leaving the al-Hamra for Najaf that morning: if they were there and she wasn't, the *Informer* would not be forgiving.

"We have to go," she had told Ali. "It goes with the job."

"All right," he had nodded, "but we must be careful."

Zoe had mixed feelings about leaving Iraq. After four weeks without a day off, she was exhausted and longed for a world without suicide bombers and ambushes, a world where she didn't have to think about staying alive every moment. She would be glad to get out of the relentless heat and to be away from Peter. Since they had broken up, he had not been shy of her company, sitting at the usual table by the pool and joking with the others. But all the same she was going to miss Iraq; she had made good friends—Kate, Mervyn, Dan, even the prickly Janet and Alain, the Journonator—she loved the camaraderie by the pool in the evenings. More than that, Iraq was the most interesting work she had ever done, and it was hard to face the thought of returning to the news desk in London.

But there was no time to think of all that now; she had to put it from her mind and concentrate on the dangerous journey ahead, and the need to think of her personal safety again had made her realise that, to an extent, she had been basking in the deceptive satisfaction of a job done. She didn't want to die today, just hours before she was supposed to be heading home.

--→■◎■←--

Benes was moving through manicured lawns and open spaces. The scent of freshly cut grass lingered in the air and trees shaded the road, their leaves picking out patterns in the sunlight on the asphalt. Ahead, through the branches, Benes caught glimpses of a broad, imposing stone building; he could have been in the pleasure gardens of some European palace, but for the makeshift speed bump the Humvee had just lurched over, which had been improvised from an old set of tank tracks, and the speed limit signs that looked like something straight out of suburban

America. And there was something of the suburbs about the place; if you ignored the vast palaces, there was a sense of sleepy contentment, of propriety, of safety. What little traffic there was moved slowly, with none of the frenetic fear of Baghdad's streets. He scanned the lawns to either side from habit, but no one would be waiting in ambush here. When a metallic crashing cut across the calm, Benes winced automatically, bracing for the blast, and gripped the side of the Humvee, ready to jump down and take cover, but it was just the sound of iron girders being unloaded from the back of a truck. The second Humvee followed as always, but Benes realised they were the only ones moving in a convoy. Everyone else was driving normally, in single vehicles. It had been so long, Benes realised, that he had forgotten what safety felt like: the odd mortar might land here from time to time, but the suicide bombers and the grenade launchers and the improvised explosive devices couldn't get in.

And yet he could hear Baghdad, just a few blocks away, the helicopters, distant gunfire, surging traffic. He was in the heart of Baghdad, but he was somewhere else entirely, a world of mown lawns and speed bumps. He was inside the walls of the Green Zone, the citadel the Americans had made for themselves in the centre of the city, suburban America within, a medieval fortress from the outside. The ten-foot walls might have been made of cinder blocks, the watchtowers might be concrete pillboxes, and the entrances garlanded with razor wire, but this was a medieval fortress all the same, from whose safety the rulers issued laws and edicts for the teeming streets without. It had been the old citadel of Saddam Hussein; the grand buildings strewn about were his pleasure palaces, but he had needed no walls to keep the people out; fear was his wall and his watchman.

And what did these walls mean? Benes thought bitterly. They were hardly an emblem of a liberated Iraq, these walls that divided ruler and ruled, conqueror and conquered. As they had crossed the open parade ground, with its sculptures of crossed swords held aloft by arms said to have been modelled on Saddam's own, the symbol of the pride and power of the former dictator, the thought came to Benes that if this were America, the open space would now belong to the people, and children would clamber over those monumental arms, or at least crowd round and gaze at them. But the Iraqi people had not been allowed to take possession; they had been walled out. Up ahead, he could see the palace, its four corners topped by giant carved heads that Benes had heard were supposed to represent the warrior Saladin, but whose features looked suspiciously like Saddam's. He wondered how the Iraqis saw the Americans inside.

"Shit, why couldn't we be posted in here?" Moon said from the back. "Look at this place."

"Tell me about it," Gibbs agreed from behind the wheel.

"I heard they even got air conditioning," Gutierrez said, sitting relaxed beside Moon: for once, there was no need to man the gun. "That right, sir?"

"How the fuck would I know?" Benes replied. "You think I drop by here for a drink when you're all asleep?"

"Back home ain't even this good," said Moon, gazing out, his features more boyish than ever.

"You shitting me?" Gutierrez said.

"Not where I'm from," Moon replied.

"At least it ain't fuckin' Iraq," Gibbs said languidly.

Benes saw Green Zone civilians strolling across the road from one palace to the next, dressed in bizarre mixtures of clothing he could only think of as occupation chic: button-down collar shirts and trousers modelled on military fatigues, or formal trousers worn over combat boots, sometimes a gun in a side holster. But they were all dressed coolly in the heat, none of them wearing flak jackets.

Benes was here to visit the Coalition Provisional Authority, the CPA, the American civilians who were the occupation government in all but name. He had brought the Humvee and Gibbs, Moon and Gutierrez, on the pretence that he needed to liaise with the CPA about securing the children's hospital, but the truth was that the hospital was secure—as secure as anything could be in Baghdad. He had come to the Green Zone to try to get something done about the state of the hospital. With Captain Parks's quiet blessing, he had secured fuel for the hospital's generators, small and inadequate as they were. He wanted to do more, but hospitals were CPA: he could do nothing without orders from them. He wrote a report on the hospital: it disappeared into silence. He followed it with a memo to the CPA Health Ministry: it disappeared too, and he was sure by now it had ended up on a great pile of official papers somewhere marked "To be ignored". He probably should have left it at that, he thought. If his continued insistence annoyed the civilians at the Health Ministry, they might make an official complaint against him, and for a moment he wondered about abandoning his visit and turning back, but he had come too far.

All the same, it was proving difficult to find the Health Ministry. Nobody in the Green Zone seemed to know where it was. A few brief telephone enquiries back at camp had established that the people he needed to speak to were at the CPA Health Ministry—not to be confused with the Iraqi Health Ministry, which was an entirely separate government department, though it answered to the CPA. The CPA Health Ministry was a small group of Americans inside the Green Zone who had the real power. He got a telephone number for them—strangely, they had an American phone number, a Washington code, so to call them across the same city he had to make an international call to the US—and made an appointment to meet a Richard Webb, one of the officials there.

But nobody knew where the CPA Health Ministry was. Not the soldier at the entrance to the Green Zone and not the civilians he had stopped to ask since then, who looked into the Humvee blinking with that curious mixture of respect and condescension civilians in authority have for the military. He was sent to one building, where they had never heard of Richard Webb, nor even that the CPA had a Health Ministry; to another, where they knew of Mr Webb, but not where his office was; to a third, where they were convinced Richard Webb had nothing to do with the Health Ministry and that his office was not in the Green Zone at all. Worst of all, at the main Republican Palace, which was the CPA headquarters, where he thought the Health Ministry was most likely to be, he couldn't even get in the door. The guards were adamant: no one could get in without an escort from inside, not even a US officer.

It was around nine in the morning when Zoe reached Najaf. The turning from the road was deserted, no police, no traffic. As they drove into the city, the streets were empty, but for the odd car that moved quickly through, not stopping at traffic lights and swerving fast around corners. Zoe was surprised at how scruffy the holy city seemed; it appeared to be made up of low, ramshackle buildings. Ali insisted they stop at a police station to ask about the situation before going any further, but he came back having learned little: the police told him the road was open and they were welcome to proceed, but nothing about the safety of doing so. The shops were all closed, metal shutters down as if the owners were expecting trouble; some had even been boarded up with planks of wood. As they moved on, they began to see people on the streets, and Zoe was grateful for the headscarf—Ali had brought her an Iraqi-style floor-length coat to wear as well. People stared angrily into the car, as if they were looking for someone. They came to a metal police barrier, and Ali spoke to the police officers at it, the heat pouring into the car from the open window, then Mahmoud turned the car and they moved out of earshot before Ali spoke in English. The road was closed, but they could proceed on foot.

"But I do not think we should go. He says there is a huge crowd inside and they are angry." Zoe thought for a moment. He was probably right, but there was no way she could leave Najaf without looking further.

"We have to go on, Ali," she said. "We have to find something to write."

"OK, but don't say anything. Because you are a woman, no one will expect you to speak. Let me talk to the people. I will tell you what they say when we return. And don't bring your notebook."

Mahmoud parked the car in a side street, and they got out. Zoe had a strange feeling as she stepped out of the car, as if the air were thick and she were forcing her body forward through it, as if wading through deep water. She pulled the headscarf tight, and they began walking towards the centre. Zoe was reminded how unnerving wearing the scarf could be; it blocked her from seeing what was going on to either side. As they got further in, it was obvious the mood was ugly: groups of young men stood around, casting suspicious glances at everyone who passed. There were no women in the streets, and even under the headscarf Zoe felt horribly conspicuous. The narrow streets gave way to a wide open space, at the centre of which was a huge mosque—and right in front of it, a deep crater blown in the road. Zoe couldn't believe the scale of the crater; bits of charred and twisted metal still lay scattered about. People were shouting loudly. She turned her head to the source of the sound and saw two men arguing. One pushed the other and Ali took her shoulder, quickly steering her back the way they had come.

Someone stepped forward and said something to Ali, gesturing towards Zoe. Her stomach lurched, and she felt her heart pounding. Ali murmured something, as if in agreement with the man, and pulled her behind him. To Zoe's relief, they were heading back the way they had come. But as they turned a corner, they came upon another group of men shouting, and Ali pulled her down a side street. There were two small shops open, and he ducked inside one that appeared to sell pickles and spoke to the shopkeeper. They spoke for a while, then another customer came in and Ali stepped back to let the shopkeeper serve him, speaking very softly into Zoe's ear, the way a man might speak to his wife.

"Some people in the street told me I should not bring a woman here," he said. "This man has agreed to tell me what happened. Then we must go." Zoe nodded her agreement. The customer left with only a cursory glance towards them. Once he was out of the shop, Ali and the man behind the counter started speaking again. After a brief conversation, the man handed Ali a large plastic box full of pickles, and Ali handed him some money. They shook hands, and Ali led Zoe from the shop, back the way they had come. They rounded a corner, and the way ahead was blocked. There was a group of foreign journalists on the street, a television crew with a camera, making no effort to hide their presence, and they seemed to be getting into an argument with the Iraqis crowded around them.

"Go back! Go back!" an Iraqi was shouting at them in English, while the others spoke in Arabic. But instead of backing away, the television crew argued.

"We're press! Press!" one was shouting. "Not American. French." Ali gripped Zoe's arm and tried to turn back, but already they were being jostled by more Iraqis arriving from behind. Zoe looked at Ali and could see fear in his eyes. He turned to try to push their way out, but whichever way they turned the crowd jostled up against them. One of the Iraqi men, the one who was shouting in English, pulled something out of his pocket and brandished it in the faces of the French camera crew. The man who had been arguing looked frightened.

"Go back! Go back!" the Iraqi screamed, his voice cracking.

"OK, OK, we go," said the lead journalist, backing away and stumbling against his own cameraman. Zoe peered through the crowd to see what the Iraqi was holding and felt a chill as she made out a hand grenade. Others in the crowd must have seen it as well, because people were surging back, pushing and elbowing others out of their way, and in the mêlée Zoe was separated from Ali. She looked around desperately as she was carried in the tide of people, but she could not see him. She felt her headscarf being pulled as she was jostled against someone and reached up in fear that it might come off, exposing her as a foreigner. To get out of the crowd, she ducked into a side street and stood there, looking for any sight of Ali. With a rising sense of panic, she realised she had no idea of the way back to the car.

-->=⊙=⊙=<--

What Benes needed, he realised, was a phone so he could call Richard Webb, but the guards outside the palace had no idea where he could find one. Frustrated and worried that he was late for his appointment, he told Gibbs to drive back to a palatial villa they had passed once already, where he had seen soldiers standing outside. They pulled up at the villa, and Benes dismounted, motioning to Moon to follow him. When they saw Benes, the soldiers outside quickly straightened.

"I'm looking for the CPA Health Ministry, but no one around

here seems to know where it is," Benes said. "You got a phone I can borrow?"

"You want to speak to Sergeant Ross, sir. He's out back. It's chow time for the lions." Benes barely registered the "lions", he assumed it must be the private slang of the unit. "Through the door, turn left, all the way to the end of the corridor, sir."

Benes walked in, Moon by his side, and felt the chill of air conditioning. The room they entered was vast; the floor under his feet was marble, the walls panelled with some sort of wood that looked like silk. Across the room, a group of junior officers were sitting on chairs that looked as if they came from a movie set. Not wanting to get tangled up in conversation with them, Benes quickly veered left and followed the directions into a long corridor. Beyond heavy wooden doors, the handles gleaming gold, Benes saw rooms strewn with desks and chairs. He pushed open a door at the end of the corridor to emerge blinking into sunlight again, into some sort of walled garden. This was no chow hall; he must have got the directions wrong. As he was about to turn and go back, he heard a deep animal growl, and his eyes adjusting to the light, caught sight of a black cage in the centre of the garden, and inside it, unmistakable, a lion, crouching low and glaring at him, unblinking. There were others in the cage beside it, one of them a big male with a shaggy mane.

"Jesus! Fuckin' lions!" Moon said beside him. A group of three soldiers stood close by the cage, and they turned at his words and laughed.

"Welcome to the zoo!" one called, then noticing Benes, quickly called the others to attention.

"I'm looking for a Sergeant Ross," Benes said.

"That's me, sir."

"You running a zoo here, Sergeant?" Benes asked.

"No, sir," Ross smiled. "These're Uday's lions. Someone's got to look after them."

"Uday's lions?" Benes had heard the rumours that Saddam's son Uday had kept a private zoo, but he was bemused to find American soldiers keeping it running.

"Yeah, dude had cheetahs, leopards, you name it. We shifted them all to the city zoo except these lions. They're man-eaters.

Fucking psycho used to feed people to them. These're going in a few days now. I'm going to miss them."

"You're gonna miss the man-eaters?"

"Ain't their fault, sir, they just do what they do. They're lions."

"I guess so. I'm lost, Sergeant, wondered if you could help. Got a meeting with the CPA Health Ministry and no one seems to know where it is. I was wondering if I could borrow a phone?"

"Civilians in this place," Ross said, fishing, to Benes's amazement, a cell phone out of his pocket, "half of them don't know where their own office is."

"You got cell phones in here?"

"They only work in the Green Zone, sir. Don't work outside the gate."

Benes dialled the number. As he listened to the ringing tone, he watched Moon walk close to the cage and crouch down, staring at the lions like a child on a visit to the zoo, much to the amusement of the other soldiers. The male had come up close to Moon now and was staring back at him. A woman's voice answered the phone.

"Richard Webb, please," Benes asked.

"Hold on."

The soldiers were watching Moon expectantly, waiting for something to happen. Suddenly, the big lion leapt forward against the bars of the cage as if it were about to tear Moon's throat out. To the amazement of the watching men, Moon didn't flinch, just crouched there, looking calmly back at the lion. One of the two soldiers let out a low whistle.

Richard Webb came on the line. It turned out his office was in the main palace, and he was waiting for a call to let him know Benes was there, though how he was expecting Benes to call was a mystery. He agreed to wait at the entrance.

"Stop playing with the kitties, Moon," Benes said, hanging up and handing the phone back to Sergeant Ross. "Thank you, Sergeant," he said.

"Any time, sir."

When they were back in the Humvee and heading for the palace, Benes asked Moon, "How'd you do that?"

"Do what, sir?" Moon asked, unable to hold back his smile of satisfaction.

"You know what."

"I knew he was going to do that, sir. Used to work in a zoo, before I joined up. Summer job. I worked with the lions. They do that." Benes let Moon tell the other two and enjoy his moment of triumph.

-->=◎ ◎=<--

Zoe looked around for Ali, but she couldn't see him. She wanted to call his name, but she couldn't risk giving herself away. Someone was speaking Arabic near her. She cursed herself for not thinking to remember the way they had come; she had left it to Ali so she could concentrate on the scene to write about it later. She realised the voice she heard speaking Arabic was talking to her and turned to see a man looking at her in a puzzled way. He must have been trying to help a woman in distress and couldn't understand why she wasn't answering him. As their eyes met, she saw his gaze harden: he was getting suspicious. She should say something—but she knew no Arabic. She scanned the street desperately for Ali. The man spoke again, in harsher tones.

It had attracted the attention of others, and the man stepped towards her. Zoe felt an arm on her shoulder and looked around for Ali, but saw instead an Iraqi who spoke angrily to the man who had been questioning her and then pulled her along with him into the street. In panic, she tried to pull away, but he steered her towards another Iraqi, who stepped forward to speak to her. As the second man leaned towards her face, she recognised Jack Wolfe—like her, dressed in Iraqi clothes to avoid attracting attention. With his dark colouring, he had fooled her for a moment. He gestured with his eyes to her to come, and she followed him through the crowd. The man who had taken her by the arm led the way. She realised it was Adnan, Jack's translator. As they made their way through the narrow lanes she felt a touch at her arm and turned to see Ali, who murmured a greeting to Adnan and quietly accompanied them. Zoe felt a wave of relief when she saw the car, with Mahmoud standing beside it, looking concerned. Without speaking, she and Ali got inside. She nodded to Jack, who gave her a quick smile. She remained silent as Mahmoud backed out of the street. She didn't want to say a word of English until they were clear of the crowds and on the way out of Najaf.

⊰⊱◆⊰⊱

Benes had, at last, found Richard Webb, a tall young Californian in a blue button-down shirt, who this time was waiting for him at the entrance to the main Republican Palace. He shook Benes's hand firmly and thanked him for "everything you guys are doing". Benes left the others waiting outside and followed Webb through a vast entrance hall and even bigger central rotunda. Webb led him up a grand staircase, along a corridor so wide partitions had been put up to create more office space in it, and into a high-ceilinged room that had been filled with makeshift plastic chairs and desks. Papers spilled over the tables, around the computers, and in some cases overflowed into piles on the floor. There were coffee rings on the documents and empty mugs everywhere. Most of the people in the room were surprisingly young: a few were gathered around a large television that was showing the highlights of a basketball game back home, but most were hunched over their desks, poring over their screens, or talking into phones. The room hummed with computers. Several cots were pushed up against the wall on which some of those working here slept at night—the beds only half made, Benes noted. This was definitely a civilian camp.

"Welcome to the Health Ministry," Webb said enthusiastically, leading Benes to his own desk. He offered Benes a mug of coffee and, after a few pleasantries, asked, "So what can I do to help?"

"Well, sir, we have a position at the al-Iskan children's hospital—"

"Al-Iskan? Is that in Baghdad?"

"Yes, sir," Benes replied, "that's the main children's hospital in Baghdad."

"OK."

"Yeah, well, we've got a position there, and, uh," Benes paused, weighing up the ways he had considered introducing the subject, "well, I sent your office an email on this situation about a week back."

"Let me see if I've got that," Webb said, turning to his computer and scrolling down through his emails. Benes hesitated a moment, then went on.

"It's just that we've come into contact with the hospital staff and patients, and we just wanted to make sure you were aware of the situation there."

"Uh-huh?" Webb replied still scanning through his emails. "What situation would that be?"

"Well, it's, uh," Benes stumbled, painfully aware his composure deserted him when he had to deal with civilian officialdom. The lines of command, so clear in the military, were all blurred. "The situation is not good, sir. The hospital is in pretty bad shape. The place is filthy. They don't have enough power. They're short on oxygen, short on medicine—"

"Oh, the medicines, right," Webb interrupted, turning back to Benes. "Well, see, that's a problem we've been addressing. See, the thing is, we're in the process of drawing up a new formulary. We need to make sure the medicines the Iraqis are giving out to their patients are appropriate. There's a whole lot of medicines they use that we wouldn't necessarily be using in the States. They've got about forty-five hundred different drugs on their approved formulary, which is too many to be handing out for free—did you know they've got a free healthcare system here? They don't pay a thing. So we've got some guys coming in from the US to draw up a new formulary. It'll be done in a couple months; then we can start restocking the hospitals."

"But they need medicine now. These kids I've seen, they're sick—"

"Yes. The problem is, Lieutenant, the government is out of drugs, which means we've got to buy new supplies. Iraq used to buy all these medicines from places like Syria, Iran, Russia. Obviously we can't go buying them from places like that—we've got to switch over. But the same drugs aren't necessarily available. And that means we need to agree on a new formulary." He was talking in a slow, faintly patronising way, as if taking the time to explain complexities Benes's blunt military mind would have difficulty grasping.

"But what about the meantime, sir?" he interrupted. "These kids, some of them are dying."

"We're taking care of that, Lieutenant. No Iraqi is going to die for want of basic healthcare."

"Well, they've got some other pretty major problems there, sir. They're pretty short on power; the air conditioning doesn't work too well."

"We've got the same problem across Baghdad, Lieutenant," Webb said, smiling. In the background, the office air conditioning hummed gently. "You'd have to speak to the Energy Ministry down the corridor, but I think they're doing everything they can. Can I get you a refill?" he gestured to Benes's coffee cup.

"Ah, sure, yeah. Well," Benes kept trying, "the place is pretty filthy, and they don't have the money to get it cleaned up."

"It's the same across the board, Lieutenant," Webb said, pouring Benes a fresh cup. "You don't know how many hospitals I've been to across the city—they're all filthy. After a while they all blur into each other. We're doing what we can, but it's a major task."

"Their sewage system is busted; they've got raw sewage overflowing in the leukaemia ward."

Webb, who was about to take a sip from his coffee, grimaced and put the cup down.

"Do you know how much money the US government is pumping into healthcare here, Lieutenant?" he smiled.

"No, sir."

"Seven hundred and ninety-three million dollars. More than three-quarters of a billion. But it's not just the hospitals. See, the people here have the mentality that if you want healthcare, you've got to go to a hospital. We're trying to set up outpatient clinics to deal with everyday health problems that don't require hospitalisation, but we're starting from scratch. You know, in the rural areas, most women still give birth at home?" The conversation was drifting away from the hospital, and Benes needed to steer it back.

"I can see you've got your work cut out for you," he said, "but the problems of this hospital would be relatively easy to fix. I know if we had the authority, my guys could have it fixed up in no time."

"Ah, if only I could do that with all my problems, Lieutenant," Webb said, still smiling, "just pass them on down the line to you guys. But we can't go taking up your time with that sort of thing; we've got private contractors for that. But thanks for letting us know what's going on—we'll be sure to look into it. Now, look, if that's all, I'd better get to sorting out this damn health system." He was standing up, the meeting was coming to an end, and Benes found himself standing as well. He felt impotent; a military meeting he could have handled, but he didn't know how to deal with this civilian.

"You'll look into it?"

"Yes, of course." Webb held out his hand. "Let us know anything else we can help your guys with. And let me say again," he said, as he led Benes towards the exit, "thank you for everything you and your guys are doing for our country...and for Iraq."

→⊶⊷←

"That was serious," Ali said.

"Yes." Zoe nodded. They were in the outskirts of Najaf now, clear of the centre and the crowds, and she felt safe enough to speak.

"The people are blaming the Americans for what happened."

"Why? This was the last thing the Americans wanted."

"The people are angry," Ali shrugged. "They're looking for someone to blame. It is best to stay away from situations like this." Zoe said nothing. "You know Ridwan, the translator of Mr Paul?"

"Ridwan?"

"The man with long hair and a beard."

"Oh, the hippie, sure." Zoe had seen him hanging around the Internet cafe.

"The hippie, yes." Ali laughed. "That's what we call him. How did you know?"

"No, it's just his hair."

"But the people here thought he was from Al-Qa'ida and they attacked him."

"What? Why?"

"Sometimes, the Wahabis...you know Wahabis?"

"Sure." Zoe didn't, but thought it best to hide her ignorance.

"Sometimes they grow their hair long, so they thought he was one of them. But Ridwan is not a Wahabi; he has long hair because he likes rock music."

"Was he OK?"

"Yes, he escaped."

Zoe found herself laughing, more out of relief than anything. They were clear of Najaf now, on the open road back to Baghdad, and she felt safer. Ahead, she noticed a car pulled to the side of the road, with an obvious flat tyre, and the driver standing alongside trying to flag down a passing car. Mahmoud accelerated to get clear, but as they passed, Zoe recognised the man waving hopefully for them to stop: it was Adnan, the translator who a short while before had taken her by the arm. Mahmoud must have recognised him too, because he braked hard and pulled the car into the verge, then reversed back up the road towards the car.

"It is Mr Jack's car," Ali said.

"How did they get ahead of us?" ·

"They passed us a few miles ago, you didn't see? Marwan, Mr Jack's driver, is very fast."

"Crazy man," said Mahmoud. "That is why he break tyre."

As they drew level, Zoe saw Jack getting out of the car to meet them and opened her window to call out to him.

"Need rescuing?" she asked.

"Thanks," he said, leaning in. "Not much of a getaway, is it? Turns out we don't even have a spare tyre."

"Well, I reckon it's time I paid you back. You seem to be trying to make a habit of rescuing me."

He looked puzzled.

"When was that?"

"Just now, in Najaf."

"Who said *you* needed rescuing?" he said, smiling. "Adnan

and I reckoned you were our ticket out of there. And anyway, that hardly makes a habit."

"What about the UN?" For the first time, Zoe thought she detected a hint of embarrassment in Jack: he looked away, but when he looked back he was smiling again.

"The UN? I don't remember doing any rescuing there."

While they were talking, Ali and Mahmoud had got out the spare tyre to see if it would fit Jack's car. While the two drivers worked on it, Ali came over, looking concerned.

"This is not such a good place for foreigners. Perhaps it would be better if we went ahead with Mr Jack. Adnan and Marwan will fix the wheel and follow us."

"If that's OK by you?" Jack asked Zoe.

"Sure," she said, making room for him on the back seat.

"I like your disguise," he said once they were under way.

"The headscarf?"

"Yeah. Suits you."

"Yours too," she countered. He was wearing the same sort of brightly coloured shirt Ali and Mahmoud usually wore.

"This?" he asked. "What makes you think this isn't my regular summer wardrobe?"

"Is it?"

"No," he laughed. "Helps not to stand out, though."

"Cigarette?" she offered.

"Thanks," he accepted, pulling a lighter out of his pocket. He held the flame out for her.

"How's Peter?"

"That…didn't work out."

"I'm sorry."

"Yeah, well, you know…" She trailed off, unsure what to say. He nodded. "You don't like him much, do you?" she asked.

"Me? I barely know the guy, I'm sure he's great." Zoe noticed that Ali and Mahmoud were giving them privacy, staring ahead and speaking together in Arabic.

"Pretty intense back there," Zoe said.

"Mmm." Jack nodded. "Did you see the Journonator? I hope he's all right."

"No. What happened to him?"

"They were chasing him down the street. I saw him go by, running for his life. With an Iraqi behind him, kicking him in the arse as he ran. There are few sights as amusing as an international newsman in full flight with an enraged local kicking him in the arse to spur him on. But I hope he's OK."

"God, so do I," Zoe said, worried for Alain.

"He's very experienced; he should be all right. But it's going to cause trouble, this. I mean, it's far bigger than the UN, though I doubt many of our colleagues will see it that way."

"How do you mean?"

"It'll just be dead Iraqis to them, but that's the point. To the Iraqi audience, the UN was just dead foreigners. Whoever did this deliberately killed Iraqis."

"They were after Hakim, weren't they?"

"The way they did it, with a car bomb right outside the mosque, just after prayers, they were bound to kill a lot of people. I think they wanted to."

"Who do you think did it?"

"I don't know," he said, shaking his head. "There were plenty of people who wanted Hakim dead. Isn't that right, Ali?"

"I'm sorry?" Ali leaned over the back of the seat pretending, unconvincingly, that he hadn't been listening.

"I was saying Hakim had lots of enemies. People who might've killed him."

"Hakim? A lot of people will be celebrating today."

"There's a queue of suspects for assassinating him," Jack went on. "But the way they did it, I don't know. Someone wanted mass casualties. Someone is trying to stir Iraqis up, Sunni against Shia."

"It is not possible, Mr Jack," Ali said. "Iraqis are united. We do not think of Sunni and Shia." They fell silent. Zoe sat and smoked, thinking the story was getting more interesting just as she left.

"But what were you doing in the middle of all that?" Jack broke across her chain of thought. "I thought you were supposed to be out of here last night."

"I was, but the paper asked me to stay an extra day and cover this. David…do you know David Wilson?" He nodded. "He's coming to take over, but he wasn't due in till this afternoon, and they didn't want to miss it."

"Don't you know you should never take a risk on your last day?"

"I didn't think you'd be the superstitious type."

"It's not superstition. You make mistakes on your last day. You tell yourself it's one last job before you get home to safety, and you take stupid risks."

"I didn't know I was breaking the rules," she said lightly.

"Oh, that's not a rule. There are only two rules of being a war correspondent."

"And they are?"

"Never be the first to go anywhere."

"Surely journalists always want to be first?"

"The first person to get somewhere is the most likely to get killed. Let someone else be a hero. If they survive, follow them."

"And the other rule?"

"Never miss lunch."

She laughed.

"Well, what about you? *You* were in Najaf just now."

"It wasn't my last day. And it wasn't really the sort of thing you could afford to duck out of—I think the paper would have had me out of here pretty fast if I'd sat that one out at the hotel."

"Otherwise you would have done?"

"Well, maybe not," he conceded.

"So how does an Irishman end up as a war correspondent for a British paper anyway?" she asked.

"Just followed the work," he shrugged. "There are more papers in the UK." She looked across at him for a moment and wondered, then decided to probe a little.

"I liked your piece about Selim Abdullah," she ventured.

"Who?"

"The child who lost his leg, on the farm outside Baghdad."

"Oh, that kid. What about him?"

"No, I mean—I think it's great, what you're doing for him."

"What I'm doing for him?" He looked confused. "What am I doing for him?"

"Well, highlighting his case. So he gets help."

"Oh." He seemed surprised. "Well, yeah, that would be nice." It was Zoe's turn to be confused; she wasn't sure what she had expected from him, but it wasn't this complete lack of interest.

"Come on," she tried, "you're hoping someone's going to read that and do something for him."

"What? No. I mean, I'd be happy if that happened, but that wasn't the plan. It was a good story, that's all."

"So that's it?"

He shrugged. Zoe watched the barren landscape passing the window.

"I liked your piece on the UN bombing," he said.

"Thanks," she said, embarrassed but pleased.

They lapsed into silence again. Zoe couldn't decide if she couldn't get past Jack's guard, or if he really was as cynical as he made out. As they came into the Baghdad suburbs and found themselves in the inevitable traffic, he asked, "So when are you next in town?"

"I don't know. Depends if they want to send me back. I was only here to cover a gap."

"Oh, I think they'll send you back."

"I hope so. I mean, I'll be glad to get a rest and get out of this heat, but I really want to get back."

"Yeah, never turn down a chance for a break—shit, look at those idiots," he said, pointing across the road. A couple of American Humvees had got tired of waiting in the traffic, or perhaps nervous at the thought they might be attacked, and were driving up on the pavement at high speed. "And they wonder why people don't like them," Jack said.

They were pulling into the hotel now, and Zoe realised she had been so involved in the conversation she hadn't even called London to let them know how her trip to Najaf had gone. Jack held out his hand.

"Thanks for the ride," he said. "I owe you one."

"No, I think I still owe you," she said, and when he looked back puzzled she added, "The UN, and today."

"Let's call it even. Have a safe journey home, Zoe Temple, and I'll see you next time you're in town."

As he walked away, Zoe felt dissatisfied. She had talked with him all the way back from Najaf, but she felt no closer to unravelling him. Perhaps the others were right; perhaps there was nothing to unravel.

Across the city, across her hot streets burning with fear and intrigue, Adel sat watching the news on television, distracted by the sound of his mother noisily preparing the evening meal. *I warned you,* he heard his father's voice say. On the screen in front of him were the injured of Najaf in their hospital beds. Adel stared at the picture of a man whose face had been ripped apart: one eye was missing, and blackened blood was smeared down his cheek and smudged on the pillow. Adel did not like the Shia, he didn't trust them, and he didn't like the way they pretended they had accepted the Americans, all the while watching and waiting to seize power. All the same, they were Iraqis, and Adel did not feel comfortable with what he saw. He wondered idly if the rumour on the streets might be true, after all, that the Americans had planted the car bomb to stir up anger between Sunni and Shia so they would have an excuse to stay in Iraq, saying they were here to prevent a civil war. Adel wanted to believe it, but in his heart he knew it wasn't true. He watched uncomfortably as the television showed more of the wounded. *I warned you,* the voice came in his head, *I warned you.*

Zoe sat in the four-wheel drive as it raced through the empty streets. The city was transformed at this time of night; she had never seen it without its usual traffic jams. Somehow it seemed smaller, diminished. They had slipped out of the hotel in the dark, just as the curfew was lifted at 4 a.m., and there was no one else about. Bits of paper and other rubbish skittered across the road, blown by a wind she had never noticed before. The driver, not Sa'ad this time but another Jordanian just as red-eyed with exhaustion, pushed the car fast through the empty junctions, and Zoe looked on tensely as they turned each corner, afraid they might come upon a nervous American patrol or, worse, insurgents. But there was no one; the city was silent, except for the sound of distant gunfire somewhere else, in another street, in someone else's life. Sitting in the four-wheel drive, facing a journey back along the route she had come in on, through the desert to Jordan, she realised the life of a war correspondent was nothing like she had imagined, but she wanted more of it. As soon as she was back in the office, she would pester Nigel Langham, telling him she wanted another stint in Baghdad. She had only been sent as a one-off, to cover a gap, now she had to convince Nigel to send her on a regular basis, or at least on a second trip. She looked back at the straggling edges of Baghdad as the city retreated into the night and told herself she would be back.

As the four-wheel drive slipped into the desert, the wind picked up behind it, sending the dust scurrying after it, stretching out like fingers from the fallen city.

PART TWO

Winter 2003–04

Chapter Twelve

Who's Your Baghdaddy?

27 November 2003

BENES WALKED GINGERLY through the night, knowing each step could be his last. It was so quiet he could hear the sound of his own breathing and the drumming of his own blood, and the whisper of the undergrowth bending beneath his feet. Every unexpected noise set fear racing: a crack—just the sound of a loose stick breaking under his boot; a whirring—just the sound of a startled bird taking flight. He shivered in the cold. Up ahead, through the unworldly green of his night vision goggles, he could see the big frame of Zivkovich picking his way through the undergrowth. The lights of Baghdad burned in the distance. Benes took care to place his feet where Zivkovich had stood; he knew the big man was matching his steps to those of Hernandez in front of him, and Hernandez in turn was following the footsteps of Jackson. If they all trod on the same patch of ground, there was less chance of stepping on an improvised explosive device buried under the soft earth, but it was no guarantee: this was not a simple minefield. The Iraqi insurgents kept watch and detonated their IEDs by remote control. There were plenty of places for them to hide among the palm groves; often they used the darkened farmhouses. Sometimes they waited until the first men had crossed, then cut the patrol in half. They said you saw the light first, before you heard the sound or felt the blast. And so they walked on, a column of men heading into the night that knew what they did not: whether they would all be coming back alive. And today was Thanksgiving.

The line snaked on: Gutierrez, Jackson, Gibbs, Matthews, Harvell, Kerry, Drake, Martinez, Doyle, and on back to Zivkovich and then Benes himself, and on behind, Chavez,

Horton, Bateman, Jones, and on to Miles bringing up the rear. They moved silently and avoided talking on the radio. This was not how Benes had wanted the platoon to spend Thanksgiving; he would have rather they were back on base, where there would at least be some celebrations. Conditions on the forward operating base had improved: instead of tents the platoon now had specially built accommodations, basic but comfortable, with air conditioning. The food was better too—they had eaten Thanksgiving dinner before they came out, but it had been a muted occasion with the prospect of the patrol ahead. Benes suspected from some of the men's furtive behaviour that they had got hold of some beer on the black market and were planning to celebrate in their own way later, but as long as they waited till after the patrol he had decided not to notice.

There was a rumble and he tensed, but it was just thunder in the distance. Rain was the last thing they wanted, with a long walk ahead of them, five klicks in all, in the cold. Benes was feeling it despite his flak jacket and helmet, and the layers he had on under his battle dress. He still found it hard to believe that the furnace heat that had seemed inescapable a few months before could have given way to such cold. When they came to Iraq, he had thought they would be home long before November, but the months had stretched on and the violence had grown worse, and the deployment had been extended, and then extended again.

The lights of Baghdad were a cruel reminder of how far away help would be if they were ambushed. Technically, they were still in Baghdad, at least according to the intricate map of operations pinned up back on base, where these fields were neatly shaded in as if they were another built-up area, but out here the map seemed like a fantasy, drawn by someone who had never set foot outside the city streets. Baghdad thinned out long before you reached this scruffy collection of farms on the city's edge, a rural nowhere that nobody would have cared about but for the fact that it lay within easy reach of the main road—and because there had been a spate of ambushes on American convoys passing through. Some higher-up had decided what was needed was a "presence operation" in the area, which meant Benes and the platoon out here on foot, night after night.

Benes waited every moment for the flash of light that would mean Gutierrez or Jackson, Gibbs or Zivkovich, was dead. It was easier to deal with the possibility of his own death. The long months in Iraq had hardened him, and he knew he could take every precaution, do everything right, and still a footstep on the wrong patch of dust could kill him. You learned to be fatalistic about it, but he could not be fatalistic about the others, because they were his responsibility. They were his friends, his brothers; some of them he had become closer to than almost anyone he had ever known, but he was also their commander, and he had to get them home alive.

Right at the front, stepping into the black unknown, was Gutierrez. Going first was the most dangerous position of all: each of the platoon took his own attitude to going first; some wanted to get it out of the way and volunteered, knowing that once it was done, they wouldn't have to do it again; others kept quiet and hoped the mission would be over before their turn came up. Gutierrez had volunteered. He had just got back from leave, and Benes wondered if he should have let him go first. Maybe Gutierrez felt guilty that he had been home with his girl-friend, drinking beer and making love, while the rest of them were out here, but Benes worried whether his senses would be sharp enough after two weeks at home. Would he notice the slight mound of earth, the disturbed undergrowth, the tiny detail out of place? But he had volunteered, and it was best to let someone volunteer.

As they were changing to head out, Gutierrez had shown off the T-shirt he had bought at the PX in Kuwait on his way back in: it had a picture of a Joe lounging against a Humvee, with the words "Who's your Baghdaddy?" printed around him. Within a couple of weeks, Benes knew, they would all have one. All evening, as they got ready to come out on patrol, the men had been wedging the phrase into conversation.

"Hey, Gibbs, can you pass me the ammo?"

"Who's your Baghdaddy?"

"Yo, Jackson, you rig up that iPod?"

"Who's your Baghdaddy?"

And when Benes had asked before they set out if anyone

wanted to go first tonight, Gutierrez had stepped forward to volunteer, before turning to the others with a grin and asking, "Who's your Baghdaddy?"

⊷⊶⊙⊷⊶

All was darkness. Cautiously, Nouri inched his head from side to side to see if there were any holes he could look through, but there was only darkness. Even the slight movement sent pain stabbing through his body, but that was not the reason for his hesitancy. Nouri's fear was that by moving he might attract their attention. It was impossible to see out of the hood they had put over his head, so he listened, studying the noises of the room carefully: moaning coming from somewhere to his right, men breathing, heavy boots on the concrete floor. He felt his muscles tauten painfully as the footsteps came closer. His body was in agony, stretched out where they had chained him to the cold metal bars, a little too high so that, although his feet touched the ground, his arms had to bear almost all his weight. Every breath brought pain; his arms and shoulders had gone through different agonies, each worse than the last, and now they were throbbing so hard he thought the bones would finally snap and let him fall, limp, from the bars.

Yet even that was nothing to the pain from his chest, where one of them had hit him so hard he had fallen to the ground, unable to breathe as they screamed at him and the translator shouted at him to get up before they hurt him more. And he was cold. At first, when they made him strip, it was the humiliation of being naked in front of the woman that had troubled him, the sight of her pointing at his groin and laughing. Even when they pulled the hood down over his head, he could still hear her laughing, but now it was just about the cold. The metal bars were wet—they had thrown cold water over them before they chained him—so they burned into his naked back like blocks of ice. The cold had numbed everything but the pain; his arms and chest screamed, but he couldn't feel his feet, and was dimly aware of his legs as weights hanging from his body.

The dark inside the hood was harder to endure because he

knew that beyond it, the lights were still on. They could see him, pinned naked to the wall of bars, unable to move, unable to protect himself, helpless. The big one with the moustache had leaned close to his ear, so close he could smell the man's foul breath, and whispered something. The translator had told him the man said that when he had finished with him, Nouri would wish he was dead. At the time he hadn't thought it possible; it was a sin for a man to wish to be dead. But now, as he hung in the darkness, all he wished for was death.

⊷⊶⊷

Benes walked on through the night, picturing his son in his mind to reassure himself he could still remember what he looked like—not just how Juan looked in the pictures he kept under his uniform, but how he looked when he was moving, smiling, laughing in his mother's arms. The first drops of rain were falling; he felt a couple trickle inside his collar and run cold down his back, and he hunched his shoulders. It was seven months since he had seen Juan or Maria. He knew it was better not to think of them on patrol—it could get to you, distract you so you weren't ready when things went wrong, but he couldn't help it. That was the problem with these patrols, too much time to think. They had left too early for him to call Maria; he would call when they got back, and she would probably put Juan on as she often did, so he could hear his son gurgle and laugh down the line from thousands of miles away. He tried to think of something else.

It was when he thought of Juan and Maria that the idea of dying troubled him: a man can face his own death; it is the thought of those he leaves behind that undoes him. He knew his wife would probably know before an officer turned up, solemn-faced, on the doorstep: she would already have heard from the unofficial network of wives and families. One of them would have had a call from someone in the platoon. He knew, too, that when the military was done with its flags and ceremonies, she would be left to face it alone. For Juan, Benes would be the father he had never known, a story mingled with his mother's tears.

He snapped out of it and back to the present; it was that kind of drifting that got you killed. The thing was to stay alive, not worry about dying. The rain was falling hard now, soaking through his battle dress and the layers beneath, icy against his skin, so cold that his entire body was numb and in pain at the same time. He peered through his night vision goggles into the surrounding countryside. Up ahead, a dog started barking, and Benes held his breath. When the dogs started was the most dangerous time; they gave away the patrols to the insurgents. The dog quickly set off others, barking from all sides into the night.

⊷⊶◉⊷⊶

Nouri heard a metal clanging. One of them was running something hard and heavy along the bars of the cells, and it was getting closer to him. The sound reached its harsh crescendo right behind him—he felt the club, or whatever it was, brush against the back of his head—then it passed, and the sound died down again. He realised he was trembling. But he had not broken down; he had not given them that. Nouri's life had been taken away from him: nobody knew where he was; his family knew the Americans had taken him, but after that, nothing. As far as they were concerned, he must have disappeared off the face of the earth. But Nouri knew where he was; he had recognised the place when they drew up outside the walls: Abu Ghraib, Saddam's prison, where people disappeared never to be seen again, and where, they said, if you were unwise enough to linger outside, from time to time you might hear the screams. The Americans had brought him here, and he still had no idea why.

Nouri had been at home when they came. The power had been off, so there was no television, and he was sitting talking with his father. It was after curfew, and his mother and sisters were in the kitchen, clearing up after dinner. He would have opened the door to them, but the Americans broke it down without knocking and came into the room so fast Nouri didn't know what was happening, seven or eight of them, all with their guns pointing at him, screaming in a language he didn't understand.

He had put his arms in the air, but one of them lunged forward and threw him to the ground, face first, and put his boot on Nouri's neck. Then he saw the Americans make his father, old and frail as he was, lie down on the ground beside him, his body trembling with the effort. He avoided his father's eyes. Some of the Americans went through to the private part of the house, where his mother and sisters were. More Americans came in, and an Iraqi who was working as their translator.

"If you cooperate you will not be hurt," the translator said. Nouri tried to make eye contact with him, to see what sort of Iraqi could do this to them, but the man was not looking at him. "Where are the guns?" he asked. Nouri couldn't collect his thoughts to speak. The American who had his boot on Nouri's neck shouted something and then lifted his foot and kicked him in the ribs.

"Tell him where the guns are," the translator said. "Tell them what they want to know. Believe me, it will be better for you that way. I have seen what they do."

"Guns? I don't know about any guns." Nouri wondered if he should mention his father's old Kalashnikov, but he was afraid they would misunderstand. His mother and sisters were brought in; the women were allowed to stand, but they could see him and his father lying there on the ground. One of his sisters was crying.

"Where are the guns?" the translator asked again, this time to his father.

"There are no guns here," Nouri said. "We don't know what you're talking about."

A soldier came into the room holding the Kalashnikov.

"You said you had no guns," the translator said. "Where are the others?"

"But that's just an AK," Nouri said, "to protect us from looters."

They were made to lie on the floor while the soldiers searched the house, casually throwing things out of drawers and cupboards and onto the floor. One of the soldiers dropped a plate and it smashed. They tied Nouri's hands behind his back with a length of plastic that dug into his wrists.

"We're not insurgents," he said, "we're Shia." He tried to appeal to the translator. "Every house in Iraq has a Kalashnikov, you know that. Tell them it's just for our own protection." The translator ignored him.

When they found nothing except the AK, Nouri hoped they would release him and his father, but one of the soldiers pulled him to his feet and the translator told him he was being arrested.

"Why? What has he done?" his mother said.

"He is a Baathist," the translator said.

"Baathist!" his father exclaimed. "The Baathists killed his brother. How can we even think of being Baathists?"

But it was no use protesting. Nouri looked his father in the eyes as they dragged him from the room, and he took leave of his father like a man. He was the only one they took. They ordered him into the back of one of their strange-shaped jeeps. The translator did not come with them; the Americans spoke to him often during the journey but he didn't understand what they said. He was driven across the city and put in a small prison cell overnight. Nouri had no idea why their house had been singled out to be searched, or why they thought he was a Baathist: he had never had anything to do with the Baath Party, and the Americans could have found a Kalashnikov in any house in the neighbourhood—in any house in Baghdad for that matter. Now, Nouri reflected, the Americans would take it and leave his sisters and parents with no protection.

A few years before, under Saddam, it had been the police who had come in the dead of night and taken away his elder brother, accusing him of being anti-Baathist. As far as Nouri knew, his brother had not been involved in politics, but the family had never seen him again. They had searched for him at every prison in the city, but no one knew anything about him. That was how it was under Saddam.

In the grey light before dawn, other Americans came and put him in a jeep. They drove him out of the city, and before they reached the walls, Nouri knew where they were heading. He had driven that road before, when he came with his father to try to find information about his brother. They were taking him to the place where the family had always believed his brother died, Abu Ghraib.

He had been led inside and taken from room to room, finger-printed, photographed, asked his name and where he came from. They took him to a place deep inside the prison and put him in a cell with other prisoners. Some were common criminals; some were Baathists and other resistance fighters; most, like him, had no idea why they were here. They all told him the terror would come. The American guards paid the prisoners little attention, and he lost track of time as the day passed, sitting on a small patch of floor. It must have been night when the new guards arrived. They ordered the prisoners to take their clothes off. One of the guards was a woman, but when Nouri hesitated, the big guard hit him. And it began. They made the men stand naked in a line and put bags over their heads. He heard laughter. There was an Iraqi translator, passing on the orders, but through the torture and humiliation, they didn't ask any questions.

Nouri heard a sound that struck new fear into him, a low, threatening growl, the sound of a dog. He heard himself sob. They had brought dogs to set on him. He twisted his head, desperate to see, though he knew it was hopeless. The dog sounded huge and savage, and it was coming for him.

Improvised explosive device. IED. Benes thought, as he walked, how the army managed to give the enemy's weapons names that were belittling, as if they were amateurish little things, cobbled together. People at home probably thought these improvised weapons were relatively harmless, not much of a threat to the heavily armed US military, but they were powerful enough to blow craters in the road, effective even against armoured vehicles. Against the platoon's unarmoured vehicles they were lethal: the battalion had tried putting sandbags in the floors of the Humvees to shield the passengers from blasts, but the IEDs ripped straight through them. So Benes had started impro-vising armour, getting the men to hook spare flak vests over the sides and laying them on the floor. On foot, you were even more vulnerable: when someone was hit, Benes had heard, the others usually couldn't find all the pieces of him. The Iraqis hid the IEDs everywhere; they put them in the carcasses of dead dogs by the roadside and detonated them when a convoy passed. Once, they strapped them to live donkeys they then goaded into running towards a group of Americans. Out among the farms, the insurgents didn't need to be so inventive—it was easy to hide IEDs in the soft ground.

The dogs had quieted down, and they didn't seem to have attracted any attention, although you couldn't be sure of it. The rain had stopped, and Benes could hear the big drops falling off the fronds of the palm trees into the soft ground. He was cold and soaked, but there wasn't much further to go: they were well past halfway and on the return leg. They were passing close by a couple of farmhouses again, and Benes ran his eyes across them for any sign of activity. Why couldn't they just send in a proper mission to flush the area clean of insurgents, so they didn't have to endure this nightly shit? Zivkovich had grumbled earlier as they got ready to come out on patrol. Benes had told him to shut the fuck up and get on with it, because privately he agreed with him. The problem, he knew, was telling who the insurgents were, scattered among the general population. The official line was that most of the attacks were the work of foreigners coming in across the border, but Benes knew the people they had captured laying IEDs were local farmers. The same man you passed working in the fields, the man who smiled and waved to you by day, could be up there at night, on the roof of a farmhouse with a Kalashnikov, ready to detonate an IED with a touch of a single button. You only knew who the enemy was at the moment he turned to kill you. The patrols were as much bait as hunters, sent on foot to draw the enemy out. At times Benes felt as if the Iraqis were all the enemy, that it didn't matter which one of them pulled the trigger, but then he remembered a girl in the back of a car, blood and broken glass all around her, her eyes ripped away from her face, and he thought there were children in these houses too, sleeping the fitful sleep of fear. The innocent were among the enemy, the enemy among the innocent, each population invisible within the other. In those houses, behind those walls, were the people they had come to Iraq to liberate, and the enemy, sleeping side by side, brother and sister, husband and wife, parent and child, they had loyalties to each other you could not hope to penetrate; they were inextricably involved with each other, and would be, long after the Americans had left.

⋆⊷⊶⋆

They had brought the dog for the man in the cell next to his, not for him, and to his shame Nouri had been grateful as he heard the man's screams. But then it had stopped, and he heard his own cell door opening. He could hear the dog breathing, thick and heavy, they were bringing it for him. He could smell it. He heard a low growl and felt rough hands behind his back, unchaining him. He slid to the ground, too weak to get up, and tried to scrabble away from the dog across the floor. Someone tore the hood from his head, sharp light hurt his eyes, and there was the dog, even bigger than he had imagined, drool hanging from its teeth. It was being held back on a leash by an American he hadn't seen before, and a little behind stood the big American, the one who had hit him. Nouri was backed up against the bars with nowhere to turn. He tried to shield his body with his hands and looked up imploringly at the Americans. The dog was so close he could feel the warmth of its breath on his skin—in a moment it would start to maul him, and there was nothing he could do.

"Please!" he cried out, "Please!"

He couldn't think what else to say, but the Americans laughed, and the dog kept growling, straining at the leash that the American kept just tight enough that it couldn't quite reach him, though he was sure with every new lunge that it would. The big American leaned forward and whispered something in his ear, in Arabic, mispronounced, but Nouri understood it.

"I'm going to kill you," he said.

Just as Nouri gave up hope, it was over. They took the dog away and pulled the hood back over his head, but they didn't chain him up again; they left him on the cold floor of the cell. And still they hadn't asked him a single question.

Benes was grateful when he saw the patrol base ahead. A few more paces and they would have survived another night. The patrol base was a farmhouse whose owners had been caught laying IEDs and packed off to the prison at Abu Ghraib. The army had taken over the rudimentary house, and another platoon was living there, pulling guard duty. Benes did not envy them their cold Thanksgiving; they would still be there when he and the platoon were back on base in Baghdad. When he got to the door, he found Gutierrez and the others waiting for him. He sent them on inside and waited by the entrance in his cold, wet uniform to count every man in. As they gathered for the drive back to Baghdad, he sought out Gutierrez, and told him, "Good job."

"Roger that, sir," said Gutierrez, then turned to the others with a grin, saying, "Hey, who's your Baghdaddy?"

Chapter Thirteen

Down the Plughole

24 January 2004

ZOE LOOKED DOWN from the window of the airliner at the desert below her. The journey from Amman to Baghdad that had taken eight hours by road would be just an hour by air, but the atmosphere on board was tense. The Iraqi sitting beside Zoe looked like a condemned man contemplating the last minutes of life in his cell before they came to drag him reluctant to the gallows, a man who has realised that everything is fleeting, and that his own time is almost done. The passenger across the aisle from him, a soldier or security contractor from the look of him, was staring fixedly at the back of the seat in front of him, as if studying the fraying grey cloth minutely. Even the stewardess looked on edge and kept glancing out of the windows. Most unsettling was the silence. Zoe had never before been on a flight where none of the passengers spoke. The plane was almost full, yet nobody said a word: all she could hear was the steady sound of the engines and the beating of her own heart. It was not just that they were heading to Baghdad, with its ambushes and carjackings. Everyone on the flight, Zoe knew, was thinking one thing: that as they came in to land at Baghdad airport, someone would be trying to shoot them out of the sky. A couple of months before, a cargo plane on its way out of Baghdad had been hit by a surface-to-air missile as it climbed from the airport. The plane had been badly damaged and the pilots had lost all control—it was only by a remarkable feat of flying that they managed to get back on the ground safely, using only the engines to steer.

After that, Baghdad airport had been closed to civilian flights for some time. It had been reopened for just two weeks: security had been tightened, and officially at least, it was safe. Flights had landed and taken off without incident, but all the same, when the announcement to board had come, Zoe had thought of changing her mind and not getting on the plane, of taking a taxi back into Amman and arranging a car to drive her across the border and back to Baghdad. She had known, though, that everyone on the *Informer* would find out, that her friends in Baghdad would probably find out too, and she could not face them knowing she had lost her nerve, so she had gathered her hand luggage and her courage and walked onto the plane. She had let herself be talked into taking the flight in part by Nigel Langham—as confident of its safety as you would expect from a man who was not contemplating taking it himself—in part by David Wilson, who had taken the same flight out the day before and told her it was "the only way into Baggers", and most of all by Kate, who had emailed her from the al-Hamra to say she thought it was the best option, that the road journey had been getting more dangerous of late.

They had boarded in the usual way at Queen Alia International Airport in Amman, Baghdad listed on the old-fashioned mechanical departures board between London and Dubai. The captain had made the familiar reassuring announcement before they took off, the stewardesses had been past with a trolley to serve soft drinks, there was even a curtained-off business class section at the front: it was a routine short-haul hop into a war zone. Although the flight was officially operated by a Jordanian airline, the plane was white and unmarked, and most of the crew, judging by the accents, were South Africans. The whole thing tended to give the impression that the flight was a sort of performance, as if someone were trying to pretend that all was well in Iraq and regular commercial airlines were flying in.

She looked out over the desert and tried not to think of the landing. From up here, she could see the strange abstract patterns of different colours where the soil changed or where rock formations broke through to the surface. It was utterly empty; you could see how Iraq was cut off from the world by the desert. All the major towns and cities, almost all the people, lay beyond this sea of dust: from the west at least, Iraq was an island. The note of the engines changed slightly, but they continued flying level. The man beside her was still fixed on his own thoughts, staring down at his hands. David had told her about the landing over dinner in Amman the night before—the "last supper", he had called it with a dark smile, which had not improved her state of mind. The plane would make something called a "corkscrew descent", in order to avoid the threat of being shot down. It would fly until they were directly above the runway, high enough to be out of missile range, then descend in a tight spiral so they did not stray beyond the perimeter of the airport below. In theory at least, that should keep them safe from any insurgent with a missile launcher on his shoulder: the US military had secured the area around the airport far enough back that the runway was out of range.

Zoe tried to think beyond the landing, to reaching the al-Hamra and her friends. It had been a long, hard journey back. When she returned to London in the summer, it had been to congratulations and recognition. The Editor himself, Henry Haight, who had never so much as noticed her before, went out of his way to welcome her back. Nigel Langham had taken her out to lunch to thank her and tell her she had a bright future as far as the foreign desk was concerned—but he had also made it clear that with David and Martin Dalton covering Iraq, the present was not so bright, and for the moment he didn't need her. She had hung around the foreign desk, emailed Nigel with story ideas, but without success. She was particularly depressed the day the Americans found Saddam, hiding in a small hole in the ground, and she was forced to watch it on the news like everyone else while her friends were covering the story in Iraq. Zoe began to give up hope of getting back. But all the while, events were quietly conspiring, and the fallen city was reaching out for her. Martin Dalton accepted an offer of more money to move to a rival newspaper, and Nigel called her across to the foreign desk to ask if she'd go to Iraq again. The Editor hadn't made up his mind yet, but if she performed well, she could even get the permanent job of alternating six-week stints with David in Baghdad.

The engine note changed again. She could see a change in the landscape where the vegetation around the Euphrates River began, not exactly lush green, more a darker shade of brown, but it meant they were closing on Baghdad. She felt dizzy and slightly sick. The man beside her looked terribly pale, his mouth was working and he was clutching at his chest, and Zoe worried he might be about to have a heart attack. Across the aisle, the muscle man was trying to sit nonchalantly, but the sweat stains were visible creeping out from under his armpits. She could see the city beneath them now. The plane tilted to one side and stayed there, as if it were standing on end in the air, and began to turn. Zoe felt gravity clutching at her stomach as they descended. Out of the window, she could see straight down to the ground and the runway of the airport beneath; across the aisle, through the other window, there was nothing but blue sky. They would be low enough to be in missile range soon. She willed the pilot to keep them in the tight spiral, even though it felt as if the plane was straining at its limits—an illusion, she knew, yet it was hard to rid herself of the thought that at any moment they might lose control and tumble spinning out of the sky. She wondered if you could see the missile that hit you, spot it rushing upwards, and tried to scan the horizon, but there was no horizon, only the runway turning and turning beneath them. Zoe felt the tight downward spiral tugging at her, and for some reason the thought came to her that this must be how water felt going down a plughole. The sweat was running down her back. Down the plughole into Baghdad. And then they were levelling off, the wings snapping back to the horizontal, and she heard the pilot push the engines up and looked out of the window to see they were flying away from the runway low over the desert scrub, the last dart away to set up the final approach. The plane tipped onto its wings again, turned, then levelled off, and they were coming in to land. As they touched the runway, all Zoe felt was relief and exhaustion, and when she leaned forward her soaked shirt peeled off the seat.

"Welcome to hell," she heard an American voice say from somewhere across the aisle, and a few nervous laughs came in reply. The plane came to a halt just beside the terminal building, and gathering her belongings, Zoe followed the other passengers out to a Baghdad afternoon that was mercifully free of the heat of the previous summer. She walked down the rusting old iron steps and across the concrete to the terminal building, glancing back at the plane that had brought her safely to Baghdad, gleaming in the weak sunlight. The arrivals hall had none of the romance of the desert outpost of her last arrival in Iraq, just long queues and passport officials, and as the euphoria of surviving the landing dissipated, Zoe remembered David's words of the evening before: "It's not the landing you've got to worry about; it's the drive into Baghdad." The airport road had become one of the most dangerous stretches in the country, with more insurgent attacks than anywhere else. Zoe reached the head of the queue and a bored-looking official stamped her passport. She found her bag on the carousel, but there were no luggage trolleys around and she found herself struggling with the heavy bag. David had told her Ali and Mahmoud would be waiting in the airport car park—all she had to do was find her way there.

"Need some help?" She looked up to see an American soldier reach across her and pick up the bag effortlessly.

"Thanks," she smiled. "Do you know where the car park is?"

"Can't say I do," he shrugged. "Don't know my way around here myself, but I'll try to find out." He strode ahead of her with the bag, out into sunlight that made her blink after the dark of the terminal, and walked over to ask an Iraqi in uniform the way. The American looked Hispanic. He wasn't enormous, as many of the soldiers were, and he moved lightly. From his insignia she could tell he was some sort of officer.

"This guy says there's some sort of shuttle bus stops by here that'll take you to the parking lot," he said, turning back to her.

"Thanks," she said again. He stood with the bag still in his hands, not putting it down despite the weight.

"Planning on staying long?" he asked.

"About a month."

"Yeah? I've been here a year and I can't wait to get out. You with the CPA or something?"

"No, press," she said.

"Well, beats the CPA." Several of the other passengers gathering at the bus stop gave disapproving looks, and she wondered if they were CPA officials.

"You based here at the airport?" she asked. "Or am I not allowed to ask?"

"Oh, you can ask," he grinned. "I wish. No, I'm just here chasing up…something. I'm based back in town. Who d'you work for?"

"The *Informer*—it's a London paper."

"Uh huh? You out here on an embed?"

"No, but I wouldn't mind getting on one."

"Based in the Green Zone?"

"No, at the al-Hamra Hotel."

"Where's that?"

"Jadriyah." He looked none the wiser. "On the east side of the river," she added.

"Oh, that's real Baghdad. Well, good for you. A lot of the journalists seem to spend most of their time in the Green Zone: you don't see much of Iraq in there."

"No."

"So what sort of thing do you report on? Insurgent attacks and all that?"

"Yes, when it happens."

"No positive stories about all the good we're doing out here?"

"Sure, when I see some of it."

He laughed.

"You know a story you should check out?" he said. She could see the bus approaching. "The al-Iskan Children's Teaching Hospital. Go ask them what the CPA's been doing for them."

"What has the CPA been doing for them?"

"Nothing."

"Nothing?"

"They're letting the children die while they argue about buying medicine." The bus had pulled up and he lifted her bag on.

"Seriously?"

"Check it out. Ask for Dr Afaf if they won't let you in. She'll help you. And the director, Kamal."

"I will…I mean, thanks." Zoe couldn't believe her luck—she'd been back in Iraq twenty minutes and already she had a story. Even Nigel Langham should be happy with that. The driver was revving the engine of the bus, and the other passengers were looking on impatiently.

"Sorry, I didn't get your name," Zoe said.

"Uh, you didn't hear it from me," he laughed. But as the bus pulled away she caught a glimpse of his nametag: Benes.

◦—◦ ◉ ◦—◦

Benes turned back to the airport terminal, and the weary job ahead. The executive officer had sent him to find out what had happened to some new armour they were supposed to have received. It wasn't part of Benes's regular duties, but there had been several injuries when a couple of mortars hit the base the previous evening, and they were short of manpower. When he had no luck at the military airfield, he had come across to the civilian terminal to see if they had been sent there by mistake. He didn't know why he had decided to tell the journalist about the children's hospital—it had been months since the battalion commander had decided it was secure and discontinued the patrols, saying he needed the platoon elsewhere. Benes hadn't thought about the hospital for weeks. The journalist was attractive, blonde hair falling across her face: perhaps, Benes thought, he had wanted to impress her with a good tip for a story. Or maybe something about her had reminded him of his conversations with Dr Afaf. He hadn't seen Afaf since his visits to the hospital ended: she was always on the ward he had to pass through to get to the director's office, and after he ran into her several times, he began to suspect she looked forward to their conversations as much as he did. He had noticed the looks the others exchanged when he spoke to her, but they were wrong: he wouldn't have tried anything with her even if it weren't for the danger. He had no desire to be unfaithful to Maria. Afaf had been his one human contact with the Iraqis, and he had treasured it. As they became easier with each other, he learned she was married to a lawyer ten years her senior, named Fuad. It had been an arranged marriage, but she spoke of him with affection.

Apart from Afaf, he didn't miss the hospital. Dr Kamal had not got any easier to deal with, and nothing more had come of his visit to Richard Webb in the Green Zone. Benes had just been relieved he hadn't got in any trouble over the visit: either

Webb hadn't complained, or the higher-ups hadn't seen fit to take any complaint seriously. The months had passed and the platoon had been involved in other, more dangerous missions, but for some reason that morning, speaking with the journalist, the hospital had come into his mind.

⊷⊶⊙⊷⊶

When Zoe found Ali and Mahmoud waiting in the car park, they seemed so genuinely glad to see her that for a moment she forgot the dangerous journey on the airport road ahead, until Ali reminded her. In any event, they negotiated the road without incident: Mahmoud driving fast, he and Ali quiet with concentration, Zoe darting nervous looks out of the windows into the scrubby verges for waiting gunmen. There were few other cars on the road, and they were driving fast too: they passed one battered old orange and white taxi that was shuddering with the strain. They reached the al-Hamra to find it much as Zoe had left it, except that the white paint was now dirty, as Ali had predicted. As always in the middle of the afternoon, it was deserted: the journalists were out working in the city. One welcome change was that a mobile phone network had been set up. David had left a phone with Ali for her, the ringtone, she discovered, set to play the *Ride of the Valkyries*, and she used it to call the paper and let them know she had arrived safely, and then she decided to take a nap.

When she emerged from the room that evening in search of Kate and the others, the courtyard by the pool was deserted. Now that night had fallen it was chilly, and she wasn't surprised no one wanted to sit out in the cold. Across the courtyard, she could see lights glowing from the windows of a room she had never been in, and as she walked over she made out people sitting at tables and heard the sound of a piano. She followed it into what she discovered was the main restaurant—no one had used it in the heat of summer—thronged with the usual crowd of journalists and security contractors. There were newcomers among the journalists she didn't recognise, but she saw Kate, smiling and waving to her from a table with Mervyn, Janet Sweeney,

Mike Rodham from Reuters, and Paul Thorn, the South African documentary maker.

"Zo! Welcome back!" Kate said.

"Hey, Zo!"

"When did you get back in?"

"Good to see you!"

Zoe took the seat Mervyn pulled across for her and glanced around the room. It was as dated as the rest of the hotel, with dark-red walls and the paper worn through to tatters in a few places. In the corner, the pianist with enigmatic eyes was hunched over a piano, a cigarette hanging from his mouth. Zoe felt as if she were in a scene from *Casablanca*, and at any moment Humphrey Bogart would walk through the door, except this was a *Casablanca* with classical music.

"So how was the flight?" Kate asked.

"Ah, you know, it was fine. So who's in town?"

"Oh, most of the same crowd."

"Except Randell," Janet said with glee from across the table. "No one's seen much of him since things started to turn bad. I heard he's gone off the Iraqis now they have had the audacity to prove him wrong by not showering the Americans with love and flowers."

"Don't worry," Kate said. "Peter's not in town. He was here a couple of weeks ago; probably won't be through again for a bit."

"Oh, that's all long done with," Zoe said, secretly pleased. "So how are things here?"

"Not great. The official line is it's all quieting down now they got Saddam, but I reckon things're not looking so hot."

"How do you mean?"

"It's getting heavy out there. You should hear what happened to Paul in Fallujah—Paul, tell Zo about your trip to Fallujah."

"What, the crazy kid with the RPG?" he asked with a grin. "I was in an embed down there with the Americans, and they decided, as part of their hearts and minds campaign, they would put up a new sign that said 'Welcome to Fallujah' at the entrance to the town. Only some of the insurgents must have had a sense of humour, because they kept hiding their explosives inside the sign and blowing it up whenever an American convoy went past." As he spoke, conversation around the rest of the table died down: Paul's stories had something of a reputation. "They'd try to take out the Americans, and if that failed, at the very least they'd shred the sign. But the Americans weren't giving in, and every time the Iraqis blew the sign up, they'd go out there and put another one up. It was crazy, all the Iraqis had to do was blow the sign up and they knew the Americans would be there the next day. So the Americans said to me, 'We're going to fix this sign, are you coming?'" He grimaced, and they all laughed. "I thought, well, fuck, this is stupid, we're going to get shot. But I didn't have the guts to say no to them, when they were all heading out there to face the danger, so I just grabbed the camera and went along, like a fucking idiot. So we're out there, and we're sitting ducks in the middle of this huge road at the entrance to Fallujah, and the whole place is deserted because as soon as anyone sees the Americans coming they clear out. And there's no cover at all. Sure enough, we haven't been there twenty minutes when the shooting starts, and we're pinned down in the middle of the road." Everyone was leaning forward to listen now. "So the Americans all take up positions and start shooting, and I'm stuck in the middle of it all with nothing but a camera and a flimsy fucking flak jacket. I didn't even have a helmet on. And this American turns to me and says, 'Fucking Hajjis are all cowards; they hide in the buildings and shoot at us, but none of them will come out and show his face like a man.' And at that point, at that exact moment, this kid, he can't have been more than sixteen, dressed in a long white dishdasha thing, no body armour or anything, comes walking into the middle of the road carrying a fucking RPG, cool as you like, points the thing at us, fires and walks off. Somehow the fucker misses. The Americans are so stunned no one even shoots at him. Fuck knows how he missed at that range, but thank fuck he did."

Janet broke the silence.

"That's nothing," she said. "I was in Ramadi last week and..." She veered off into a story of her own exploits. Nothing had changed in the months Zoe had been away: it might be cold and they might be inside rather than by the pool, but Janet still had to outdo everyone else, the beer was still flowing, the sound of gunfire still echoed outside, the journalists still laughed and drank late into the night. No one really knew quite how bad it would get, but they were here, doing the job they loved, telling the story, and Zoe was glad she was back.

Chapter Fourteen

Resistances

25–29 January 2004

To a CASUAL observer, there was nothing particularly noteworthy about the car making its way through the darkened city streets. The power was out, but in the headlamps of passing cars it was possible to make out a battered American Oldsmobile, years out of date, its creased and crumpled sides telling a history of minor scrapes and collisions. There was some time to go before the curfew began, and several cars were still on the roads, though the traffic was beginning to thin. But more acute eyes might have noticed that there was something out of the ordinary about the way the car was being driven so carefully for a Baghdad driver—so much so that other drivers quickly grew impatient and overtook. The Oldsmobile slowed well ahead of turns in the road and then coasted round them smoothly. Where there was damage in the road surface made by the tracks of an American tank, it came almost to a stop, and then made its way gingerly around, but when another car pulled out in front, it did not brake but swerved wildly around it into the path of oncoming traffic, narrowly avoiding a head-on collision. It was as if there was something especially fragile inside the car, and the driver wanted to avoid any sharp turn or braking that might damage it. The driver was shrouded in the darkness inside the car, but as the lights of a passing car briefly lit up the interior and sent his shadow stretching across the building behind, it was possible to make out the features of Adel.

He drove nervously, scanning the road ahead for any sign of the Americans or the Iraqi police. Although he knew it might attract the attention of a passing patrol, he thought it best to drive cautiously: in the boot of the car were hidden enough mortar shells and rocket-propelled grenades to blow up half the street, together with several boxes of Kalashnikov ammunition. In theory, they were safe to transport, but these were old stocks the resistance had picked up from ammunition dumps across Baghdad, and Abu Mustafa had warned Adel to be careful with them. The others had been over this route many times to make sure it was clear, and there were look-outs posted ahead who would call Adel on his mobile phone if they saw any sign of a checkpoint. Even though the night was cold, he had the window open to listen for any warning sound.

And then he saw it, clear in the headlights of the car as he turned a blind corner, a checkpoint. Iraqi police, not Americans. Why hadn't the others warned him? He thought quickly: there was room to turn the car, but the police had seen him—one was already waving a torch for him to stop—and if he ran they'd know he had something to hide. They might open fire. If only they were Americans: he didn't want to die for Iraqi police.

He hesitated a moment too long and coasted up to the checkpoint. Under the seat beside him Adel had a handgun, and he knew he would have to use it before they could search the car. The Iraqi police officer was shouting something at him. Adel stared out at him, wondering when to reach for the gun. The officer was shouting that Adel had forgotten to turn off his headlights so they didn't dazzle the men on the checkpoint. He switched them off. The policeman leaned in at the window and asked for Adel's papers. For a moment his hand hesitated between the glove box and the gun under the seat, but it chose the glove box, reached inside for the papers and handed them over. *He couldn't delay it much longer.* As the officer looked the papers over, another wandered across and peered through the windows into the back of the car. *He would have to do it now.* Adel leaned his body slightly across, so he could reach the gun easily.

"OK, you can go."

Adel froze in surprise. He forced himself to relax and turn back to the policeman, who was holding his papers out for him. He made himself take them slowly and not snatch at them, glancing at the second officer and trying not to look relieved. Then he put his foot down gently and slowly moved off. They had been too bored to check the car thoroughly. He was so relieved he laughed out loud, and it was some time before he realised he had forgotten to put his lights back on.

⋆⇢⊨⊜⊣⋆

Nouri lay awake in his cell. He could feel the bodies of the other prisoners on either side, could feel the swell of them as they breathed. But Nouri was not uncomfortable; he was treasuring his little patch of freedom in the cell, no larger than the floor beneath his body. He was not blindfolded or chained any more, he was fully clothed, there were no dogs, and most importantly, there was no fear stalking him in the darkness. Nouri knew for the first time what it meant to be free, the very beginning of freedom—power over his own body. Though his ribs were still sore, he could feel his wounds slowly healing. Some weeks before, the torture had stopped. New Americans had come and moved him and the other prisoners from the torture cells into another part of the prison. They had given him a sort of orange suit to wear, a prisoner's uniform, but better than the only thing the other Americans had given him to wear, some women's underwear the big one had flung at him and ordered him to pull on, while the woman stood by and laughed.

Nouri had no idea why the torture had stopped. When they came to move him, he thought the interrogation would finally begin, but they brought him to the large cell with the other prisoners and left him there with no explanation. For some time, maybe a week, that had been all. At first, he had flinched whenever an American came near; he hadn't believed the other prisoners when they told him there was little violence in this part of the prison. Slowly, as he realised no one was coming to bring pain, Nouri began to let his guard down, but he still knew they would come back for him. And they had come, two Americans with a translator who told him he was wanted for an "interview". His interrogation had come at last.

At first his legs refused to move, but the American soldiers were strangely patient, and they didn't drag him out by force, but waited until he was ready, and when he reached the room where they took him, it was stranger still. There were two Americans in the room, officers, one of them apparently very senior from the deferential way the others behaved towards him. Yet these two treated Nouri politely, even with respect, and he began to think it was all an elaborate joke, and at any moment they would knock him to the ground and make him strip again or attach electrodes to him, but there was no hint of violence. Strangest of all were the questions. They didn't seem interested in whether he had committed any crime or opposed the Americans in any way. All they wanted to know was how he had been treated in the prison. At first he said nothing about the torture, afraid that if he mentioned it they would punish him.

They began to ask him directly if he had been abused, but Nouri remained silent: it was a trap, he was sure; one word of complaint and he would be sent back to that place. Finally the chief American, the one who had stars on his shoulders, laid down his pen and spoke earnestly to the translator, who turned to Nouri and explained that he must not be afraid to tell the truth, that those men in the other wing of the prison, where he had been before, were not supposed to torture the prisoners. All these two officers wanted from him was the truth. Still suspecting a trap, but feeling he had no choice, Nouri haltingly detailed what had happened to him. When he finished, they said nothing; the senior one signed a piece of paper and held it out to him. That was why they had no more questions. They had a confession ready for him to sign; they would make him sign it and he would spend the rest of his life in Abu Ghraib. He turned despondently to the translator.

"I have no pen," he said.

"No, this is for you," the translator said. "Take it. It is important." Nouri looked at the piece of paper: it was in some foreign language. He took it hesitantly.

"I am innocent," he said, looking at the senior officer. "It is a mistake. Please." The officer smiled and spoke to the translator.

"That is not for these men to decide," the translator said. "Your case will be decided later."

"But they have not asked—no one has asked me," Nouri protested. "I am innocent."

He did not try to resist when the Americans led him gently from the room, but looked back over his shoulder at the officers. Their heads were down, studying their notes.

Since then there had been nothing. He had heard rumours from the other prisoners that the Americans who had tortured him were in serious trouble and had been taken away from the prison, but he wasn't ready to believe them. It could all be a trick, and the moment he started to believe, they might come for him again.

He didn't know how long he had been there. He had meant to count the days and nights—others who had been in prison had always told him they counted them—but he had lost track when he was in the other place. He had tried to count the visits of the big man, the one who had said he would kill him, but he had passed out from pain a couple of times. He wondered if his family knew where he was, or if they were still looking for him, as they had once gone from prison to prison to look for his brother. He thought of his father, forced to relive the nightmare of searching; he thought of his mother and sisters in the house without protection, without even the Kalashnikov, at the mercy of anyone who cared to steal what little they had or, worse, wanted to have his way with them.

Most of his fellow prisoners in the cell had been rounded up by the Americans on suspicion of being resistance fighters or storing weapons caches, like him, and almost all protested their innocence. One man said he had heard that people would give false information against you to the Americans to settle a grudge or to get the men out of a house. A few were criminals, and Nouri kept his distance from them. But one man, Abbas, who at first insisted he was innocent, one day quietly told Nouri he was a member of one of the Shia militias. He told Nouri very discreetly, so the Sunni prisoners and the guards would not overhear. He had not been arrested for belonging to the militia, but for having a gun in his house. The militias were not resistance, like the Sunni fighters, but they weren't entirely pro-American either. They were determined to make sure the Shia got their freedom this time. Before he came to Abu Ghraib, Nouri and his father had been against the militias, but now as he listened to Abbas, he began to think the Shia needed someone to fight for them.

Nouri had given up trying to tell the others what had happened to him in the torture cells, but Abbas listened. There were parts of it he didn't want to tell; he didn't want anyone to know about his humiliation, about the time he was forced to lie down naked in a pile with the other prisoners, all of them naked too, their bodies touching his; or the time another man was made to lie down with his mouth close to Nouri's naked genitals; or the time they were made to stand naked in a row, with the bags over their heads, while they could hear the Americans taking pictures and laughing. Still less did he want to tell them about the time the big American had made him touch himself in front of the woman. At first he had refused, until the translator told him what the big American was threatening to do. He hated the thought that anyone might ever find out that he had done these things, even though he had been forced to do them. They had made him do what he could not bear—they had proved they had dominion over him. The scars of battle can be worn with pride, but the scars of torture are kept hidden, because they show that the wearer has lost his own body.

Each day without torture brought Nouri back to life. Even in prison, even in a crowded cell, he was in control a little. He decided when to stretch and when to curl his legs, when to stand and when to sit, when to open his eyes and when to close them. It was a little, a very little, but it was a kingdom to a man who had had everything taken from him. But as his life returned to him, it brought with it growing anxiety for his family and the need to ensure they were safe. He asked Abbas how often prisoners were released, but he just shrugged. Abbas hadn't seen anyone let out. And so Nouri sat and waited. He felt as if he had always been there. In fact, he had been in Abu Ghraib two months.

⋯⊷⊶⋯

The square outside the cafe in Adhamiya was dark when Adel turned into it, the power out on both sides. Despite the chill winter night, a number of men were standing around, stamping their feet against the cold, hands stuffed in their pockets, their faces wrapped in red-check headscarves. Among them he recognised Daoud, Selim's friend from the meeting with Abu Khalid. Their eyes met, but Daoud said nothing. Adel opened the boot of the car, and the men quickly began distributing the contents among themselves: mortar shells, rocket-propelled grenades, Kalashnikov ammunition.

"There was a checkpoint," he told Abu Mustafa. "Iraqi police."

"They let you through?"

"Idiots didn't check the boot. But they might next time."

Abu Mustafa nodded and walked away to make a call on his mobile phone. There was a flood of light across the square and the men looked up, but it was just the power coming back on. The lights shone out of the cafe and the curtained windows of the houses. Inside the cafe someone turned them off, and as if getting the hint, one by one the lights in the houses went out, and the square returned to darkness. A second car pulled up. As the driver opened the boot, Adel caught a glimpse of the contents: tightly wrapped little bundles, not as impressive to look at as RPG launchers or a machine gun, but deadlier. These were the bombs, cannibalised parts of more sophisticated weapons, armour-piercing shells, heavy explosives, remote control detonators, all wrapped in little bundles ready to bury on the roadside, in a drain, in the body of a dead animal, ready to rip through American jeeps and punch holes in their armoured cars. The men handled them cautiously. Anwar, the man who had delivered the bombs, said they couldn't go off accidentally, but it was better to be careful.

What would the Americans think if they could see this square? Adel wondered. What would the "masters" of Iraq think if they could see the people they thought they had conquered handing out weapons to kill them with? The Americans had been so triumphant when they found Saddam, parading him on television with his long grey beard, like a helpless old man. Adel had no love for Saddam. As a schoolboy, he had learned to feel terror whenever Saddam's name was mentioned: you never spoke of him, you never dared to notice his palaces as you drove past;

noticing a building could get you killed. Saddam had sent Adel's father to fight in two wars, against Iran and Kuwait. His father rarely spoke of Iran, and when he did shadows fell across his face: he had lost three fingers there, and everyone agreed he had got off lightly. Adel had been glad when Saddam was defeated, but when the Americans brought him on television, when they humiliated him by parading him before the cameras, Adel felt as if the humiliation was his own. Saddam was an Iraqi, the president of Iraq, and foreigners were treating him like a slave. If they treated Saddam like a slave, what did that make the ordinary Iraqis who had feared him?

The boot was empty, and Adel got back in the car for the drive back. He still had time to make it before the curfew began, and this time he could pass through the checkpoint without worrying, except about the handgun under the seat, and only an American checkpoint would care about that. He watched the men disappear back into the night with the mortars and RPGs; many would be used in attacks that night. He had been scornful of Abu Mustafa and the army officers at first, but he had grown to respect them. In October, they had managed to hit the al-Rashid Hotel when the American Wolfowitz was inside, and they were hitting American patrols every day, but Adel yearned for another big attack, like the bombing of the UN. He kept in contact with Selim, but he heard little from the foreigners. He was beginning to think whoever had been behind the attack on the Shia political parties in Najaf might have been right: the more demands the Shia made, the more they clamoured for power, the more he worried about their intentions. They were demanding elections because there were more of them than there were Sunnis, and they thought they could take over. The police on the checkpoint, working for the Americans, were probably Shia: it would explain why they were working for the enemy.

When Mahmoud found a parking space, it was some way from the Higher Education Ministry building, and he had to walk back along the street. It was early morning, and the air was already warming in the sun. He glanced at his watch: allowing for traffic, he had half an hour before he had to leave for the al-Hamra to pick up the journalist. The road outside the ministry was, as ever, crowded with supplicants, young men and women pleading with the indifferent guards to let them in, older people, looking slightly confused, clutching little bits of paper as if they were talismans. Under Saddam, people had been wary of government buildings, now they came in their hundreds to petition a ministry that was powerless, since the real decisions were being made across town, by Americans inside the Green Zone, where the people could not go.

Mahmoud pushed his way through the crowd and up to the guard, who recognised him and let him in. Inside it was the same: people lined the corridors and crowded into the doorways of ill-tempered officials who were trying to wave them away. This building was a new, temporary home for the ministry—the old building had been looted and torched in the first weeks after the fall of Baghdad—and everything had a makeshift appearance about it. Mahmoud picked his way through, past the offices of junior bureaucrats, towards a small office at the far end. He saw some of the waiting crowd start to follow him, as if they believed he knew something they didn't and that the office might contain someone who could help them. In fact, it was just the typists' room and contained nothing of interest to them, but to Mahmoud it was the most important office in Baghdad. He could see her through the door, behind a desk groaning with official documents, his Saara. Some official he didn't know was with her, going over a document, so Mahmoud waited outside. Saara lifted her eyes to him once and smiled. She was wearing a headscarf; she had never worn one before.

Mahmoud had mixed feelings about Saara coming to work at the ministry. Baghdad had not grown any safer since her family's original decision that she should stay in the house—on the contrary, it was getting worse—but her job here meant he could see her more often, and outside the stifling house, with her mother always just beyond the door. The family line was that she had been allowed out to work because they needed the money, but Mahmoud knew it was a lie they were telling themselves.

The truth was that they had given into Saara's persistence. She had managed to get herself a job offer without even setting foot outside the house, by sending messages via her brother Yusuf: first to her old faculty at the university, then to a contact at the Higher Education Ministry. It was just temporary work as a typist, but it got her out of the house. Yusuf dropped her at the ministry each morning on his way to work and picked her up in the evening, so she never travelled the streets alone.

Mahmoud was glad, at least, she had chosen a job here, in the Iraqi ministry, rather than going to work for the Americans in the Green Zone. Just a few days before, a suicide bomber had driven a truck full of explosives up to one of the entrances to the Green Zone and killed twenty people as they queued to get in, most of them Iraqis trying to get to work—the Iraqis had to wait in long lines for security checks, while the Americans drove straight through. The danger was not only at the gates to the Green Zone. It could follow you home. There would be a knock at the door one night, and when you opened it, a gunman would shoot you dead on the spot. If you stopped answering the door, he'd be there the next morning, waiting by your car to shoot you down in broad daylight. So far it was those who worked directly for the Americans who had been targeted, but Mahmoud was concerned it could spread to the ministry. He took considerable precautions to prevent anyone from his neighbourhood knowing he worked as a driver for the foreigners—even for a journalist. He took different routes to work every day and stopped off in other places, to drink tea with a friend, or to get the car checked. As far as his neighbours were concerned, he ran a private car service, and all his clients were Iraqis.

He looked impatiently at his watch. The official was taking too long going over his document with Saara. He was using up their time together.

"What difference does it make?" Saara had said when he told her he was worried about her working at the ministry. "If I stay in the house, they say they'll come and kill me there. If I'm going to be killed, I'd rather be out living than sitting here and waiting for it."

There had been no more letters threatening the family as

Christians. As the weeks passed and the initial shock faded, Saara told him the family had decided it was just some neighbour with a grudge. All the same, her father had got hold of a Kalashnikov to go with the old handgun he kept. It wasn't just the threat of political violence—there were kidnappings too. Mahmoud had heard of one family whose nine-year-old son had been abducted: when the father couldn't get the money together quickly enough, the kidnappers sent him one of the boy's fingers. After that he sold everything and got his son back alive.

Mahmoud had started carrying a gun in the Mercedes, a handgun he kept under the passenger seat, in defiance of Mr David's instructions. He and Ali had discussed it, but they had agreed to keep the gun secret from the journalists. Mr David didn't know Iraq as well as he thought he did. He said they could be arrested by the Americans for carrying a gun, which was true, but being arrested by the Americans was not as bad as being murdered in your own car while you waited at a red traffic light, shot and left for dead while your attackers dragged the foreign journalist out of the back. Mahmoud had told Saara that he agreed the threatening letter was probably from a neighbour, but privately he had his doubts. He had heard of similar letters appearing in other parts of the city, and had decided that if he heard of any attacks, he would get Saara out of the house and hide her somewhere, though he had no idea where. For a while he had toyed with the idea of getting her a room at the al-Hamra, until he realised that even with the money he was making from driving, he could afford only a week at the prices they were charging.

The bureaucrat finished and left the small office without glancing at Mahmoud, just another supplicant waiting in the corridor. Mahmoud waited until he was sure the official had gone, then went into the small office. Saara shared it with another secretary, an older woman, but she worked different hours and usually wasn't there in the mornings when Mahmoud visited, so they had a little time to themselves.

"Mahmoud! How are you?" Saara looked up at him smiling, but stayed behind the desk. They couldn't risk anything more than talking here. There had been no repeat of the kiss; Saara had been too nervous to let him touch her again in the house. "What have you been doing while I'm stuck in this office all day?" she asked.

"I've been in another ministry," he smiled.

"Another ministry?" She frowned.

"The Health Ministry. That journalist wanted permission to go in a hospital."

"The woman journalist?" She arched her eyebrows mockingly. "So you can spend your entire day in the Health Ministry for her, but you can only come to my ministry for a few minutes?" In fact, it was only because of the strange hours the journalist worked that he was able to come—he was supposed to be at the hotel by ten, but she often wouldn't be down until half past.

"But the Health Ministry is so much more exciting," he replied. "The crowds, the grey walls, the officials saying no." She laughed. "So how's your family?" he asked.

"Oh, Yusuf has been practising with the Kalashnikov. I'm afraid if anyone attacks the house he'll shoot his own feet instead of them."

"He knows what he's doing."

"And how would you know? When did you see him shooting?"

"He's an Iraqi. All Iraqis know how to shoot."

"So what are you doing today?"

"Going back to this hospital, with the permission. Ali is miserable; he has to walk through all the wards full of sick children. He's worried he'll catch something, and this journalist acts as if she is immune to disease. It's the same with Mr David. He behaves as if bullets will not hit him but will see that he is a British journalist and turn around and hit someone else instead. They're all crazy."

"And you? Are you going in with the sick people?"

"No, I'll stay in the car."

"What will you do?"

"Sit in the car all day and think of you."

"Won't it get boring for you?"

"No," he laughed. "I can think of you for one, maybe even two hours without getting bored."

"Wouldn't you rather be doing something, instead of thinking?"

He heard footsteps behind him and quickly straightened. By the time the official came through the door, he was standing quite correctly, well back from Saara's desk, thanking her for telling him which room he needed, and taking his leave. She looked up briefly from her typing as he left, a small smile on her lips.

⇀⇁◉ ◉↼↽

Zoe found the children's hospital exactly as the American soldier had told her. She had to engage in a degree of subterfuge to get inside—the Iraqi security guards refused to let her enter, insisting that no foreigners were allowed, so Ali went in alone, pretending he was visiting relatives, and found Dr Afaf, who told the guards Zoe was an official guest. Zoe liked Dr Afaf, with her quiet, calm manner. When she mentioned that she had heard about the hospital from an American called Benes, she noticed the doctor colour and wondered what her connection with the officer was. Zoe could see the newspaper would love the hospital story, and more importantly, that by publishing it she might be able to get something done about the conditions here. It was the sort of journalism Zoe believed in, the sort that could force those in authority to put things right, and as far as she could see it was a scoop.

The only problem was photographs. It was one thing to show Zoe around discreetly, Dr Afaf said, but there was no way a photographer would be allowed in the wards without permission from the ministry, and the *Informer*, Zoe knew, wouldn't run the story without pictures. At first she thought that was the end of it; there was no way the Americans would give her permission, but then she discovered it was the Iraqi ministry she needed permission from, not the CPA, and she gambled that amid the chaos of Baghdad the Iraqis wouldn't realise why she was interested in the hospital, so together with Ali she fought through the crowds at the Health Ministry to a weary-looking official, besieged by doctors demanding salaries that hadn't been paid for months, who gave her permission partly, Zoe suspected, just to get her out of the office. The *Informer* ran the story across a double-page spread.

"Well done," Nigel said. "We've parked our tanks all over the *Guardian*'s front lawn with this one. The Editor *himself* was praising your piece at conference. Keep 'em coming."

Zoe wished she could track down Lieutenant Benes to thank him for the tip-off, but she found there was no easy way to track down an individual officer in Baghdad. She did drop into the hospital to let Dr Afaf know about the piece and promised to get her a copy of the paper. While she was there, Dr Afaf told her one other piece of information. Zoe had mentioned Jack Wolfe's piece about the boy who lost his leg in the war, thinking it would be of interest to a children's doctor, and Dr Afaf told her there was a specialist centre in Baghdad that could fit him with a prosthetic limb.

Chapter Fifteen

Unfinished Business

1–5 February 2004

FOR A FEW days, Zoe enjoyed the success of her story on the children's hospital. For the first time in Iraq, other journalists sought her out to ask for contacts so they could follow up the story—not the British, who couldn't be seen to be copying their rival, but reporters from other countries. The story's moment was short-lived, though. Within a couple of days came much more dramatic news: coordinated suicide bombings at the offices of the two main Kurdish parties had killed more than a hundred people. Zoe left for the scene the next day, driving north across the featureless desert with Ali and Mahmoud, stuck for long hours behind American convoys while the soldiers warned them off trying to pass by waving their guns.

Night had already fallen by the time they reached Arbil, a city in the area that had been under Kurdish control before the war. On the dusty plain not far away, Alexander the Great had routed the ancient Persians in a collision between west and east, the after-shocks of which were still trembling through the world thousands of years later, but Zoe found modern Arbil much like the rest of Iraq, except that the people had a different look about them. She visited the scene of the attacks and interviewed the survivors in hospital. Suicide bombings were becoming routine. She knew most of what she would see and hear; it was just the local details she had to fill in. The wounded lay in the same uncomprehending pain, their eyes questioning, as if to ask what they had done to deserve this, their lives shattered, their bodies broken, their loved ones dead. The local authorities had security camera footage of one of the bombers. They said his face looked Arab, not Kurdish, but the image was too blurred for Zoe to tell.

Back at the hotel she had checked into for the night, Zoe found a number of things missing from her room; nothing of value, just a T-shirt, some moisturiser and a spare notebook. She also found a man's shirt that looked like Ali's hanging in her wardrobe. Crossing the hotel corridor, she knocked on the door of the room Ali and Mahmoud were sharing. Ali answered, but before she could ask if the shirt was his, he held up her missing T-shirt. Her notebook was in their room, as well as her moisturiser.

"I think I know what has happened," Ali said, laughing. "Maybe the Kurdish intelligence people have searched our rooms. Only a Kurd could put the things back in the wrong rooms."

In the lift on her way down to dinner, Zoe ran into a familiar acquaintance.

"Zoe Temple! So you're back in Iraq." Jack Wolfe was wearing a black leather jacket that suited him as little as the bright shirts he had worn in the summer.

"Jack, how are you?"

"Couldn't be better."

"Haven't seen you around."

"I was in Basra, seeing how the Brits were getting on." He must have moved fast to reach Arbil from Basra, Zoe thought, it was the other end of Iraq. "How're you enjoying our little excursion to the north? All our colleagues are tripping over themselves with theories about who's responsible this time: Baathist dead-enders, Al-Qa'ida."

"And what do you think?"

"I've got no idea," he said, smiling. "And I don't think they have either. I loved your piece on the kids' hospital."

"Thanks. Well, it's nice to do a story that can do some good."

He gave her a sceptical look, and Zoe felt a flash of irritation. It reminded her of his reaction when she had asked about the boy who had lost his leg, and she wanted to tell him about the clinic Dr Afaf had mentioned. The lift doors opened, and she saw Kate waving her over to a table in the restaurant.

"Join us?" she asked. Jack nodded. As he had predicted, the others were discussing who was responsible for the bombings, putting forward different theories. It was some time before Zoe could break free of the conversation to lean across to Jack.

"Listen, I learned something interesting at the hospital."

"Yes?"

"There's a prosthetic limb clinic in Baghdad."

"There is?" He looked disappointed.

"So that boy you wrote about, Selim, they could give him an artificial leg."

"Oh, him again." He didn't sound enthusiastic; in fact, he looked embarrassed she had brought the subject up.

"You could do a follow-up on the boy getting his leg."

"And this clinic's going to do it for free?"

"No." Dr Afaf had told her the clinic was expensive. "But your paper could pay. The *Post*'s got plenty of money."

"No chance."

"Isn't it worth a try?"

"They won't do it."

"You could get your readers to sponsor it."

"The paper would never run it."

"Surely it's worth a try?"

"If you think it's such a great idea, why don't you do it?" She was confused by his reaction. She had thought he might be reluctant, but she hadn't expected outright hostility.

"Well, it's your story, I wouldn't want to—"

"I'm finished with it. You're welcome to it."

"No, I mean, I wasn't saying—"

"Really, if you feel so strongly about it."

"OK. Where does the boy live?"

"In a farm outside Mahmudiya."

"Fine, I'll go and check it out."

There was an uncomfortable pause.

"I don't think that's such a great idea," Jack said.

"Look, if you don't want me to do it—"

"No, it's not that. I don't think you should go there."

"It's your story—"

"It's just that area isn't really all that safe any more. I wouldn't go wandering around there if I were you." It sounded like an excuse.

"Mahmudiya's fine. It's on the main road."

"Mahmudiya's not fine. It was OK when I went, but it's not safe now."

"What's the problem? I haven't heard of anything going on there."

"Believe me, it's not safe."

Kate prevented the conversation going any further by leaning across and asking Zoe if she had seen the video of the suicide bomber. By the time she turned back, she saw that Jack had slipped away unnoticed. Later, in bed, the silence of Arbil eerie after the nightly gunfire of Baghdad, she thought of his strange warning about Mahmudiya. The town lay on the main road south from Baghdad to Najaf, one she and the other journalists frequently drove. She wondered if he had said it to try to stop her taking his story, but there was no way she could do that. She had only spoken in anger; the *Informer* wouldn't run a story that had already been in a rival paper. Surely Jack knew that? Or did he have something to hide, she wondered: had he lied about the story, perhaps even made it up?

※

Benes was playing basketball with some of the men on base when he saw Captain Parks beckon him over.

"Benes, you're the expert on that children's hospital, right, al-Iskan?"

"Roger that, sir," he said, trying to mask his concern. The journalist he had sent to the hospital had run a long and highly critical piece. He'd read it on the Internet and knew there would be trouble if it were ever traced back to him.

"Some fucking journalist has done a number on it, going off on how the place sucks and is filthy and all and we've done shit to help. So now CPA is pissed and CPIC is pissed and for all I know Donald fucking Rumsfeld's wife is pissed. So we got to deal with it, as if we haven't got enough fires to piss out. You think, since you know the place, you can handle this?"

Benes took care to reply in the same weary tones as the captain. He knew Parks was doing more to get the sector cleaned up and services running than anyone at the CPA, but he was exhausted from the task: the Iraqis treated him as some sort of arbiter, and he spent his days sorting out disputes over the price of petrol and who was responsible for getting the sewers unblocked.

"Don't get too involved," Parks said. "Just identify the basics we can do. The simple stuff, lights, water. Leave the medical shit to the CPA."

It wasn't until Parks had gone that he realised this meant he would see Afaf again.

⋯⊶⊷⋯

Nouri lay on his simple mattress on the floor in the inner room. He couldn't believe he was home. At first, when he woke in the mornings, his eyes would seek out his fellow prisoners, and when they were not there, panic would rise in him, and he would think he had been taken back to his lonely cell in the torture wing. Then, when he made out the shapes of his parents and sisters sleeping, he would be confused, even though he was in the room, on the mattress, where he had slept for almost all his life. Everything looked different now: the shapes of the room, once so familiar, were alien. His father's snores were those of a stranger. He felt as if he had never been in this room before, as if his past belonged to someone else, and he, the Nouri who now existed, was seeing this world for the first time. Though he woke before the rest of the family, he would stay in bed long after they were up, watching silently from his mattress as they went about the rituals of life, folding blankets, rolling mattresses. His mother would come and offer him breakfast, and he would eat it in his bed like an invalid—his ribs still ached where they had been broken—eat a quarter of what he used to and feel full, and then his mother would look worried and ask him to eat more, and he would try until she went into the other room. All he had energy for was to eat, then sleep the hours away. It was strange to think that he could, if he wanted, get up and walk out of the house, down the street, get a ride into central Baghdad, even out of the city, into all that impossible space. It was too much. This room was enough freedom for now, and he stretched out on his mattress and felt bliss for a moment. All Saddam's palaces could not have given him such luxury as that little room gave Nouri.

The events of the last three days had come fast. When the Americans came to the cell for him again, at first Nouri had not been alarmed; he had thought they wanted to ask more questions about the torture, or to ask him about his own case. But when they took him to another room, threw him an old dishdasha and ordered him to change, he was afraid they were dressing him in normal clothes because they needed him out of prison uniform for what was about to happen, as if it was something they wanted to be able to deny had anything to do with them. There were other men changing in the room, silent, fear in their faces.

"But…but these are not my clothes," he protested.

"Put them on, you're being released," the translator said.

Nouri's mind reeled: they were letting him go. He changed quickly. He was handed another piece of paper and told to keep it. Then, without warning, the Americans put a hood over his head. For a moment, Nouri was paralysed, dread crawled up his spine, he was going back there…but then he realised it was worse than that. They were going to make him disappear. He was a witness, he should never have spoken to those officers, they were going to kill him and dump the body and that was why they needed him out of the prison uniform. He began struggling with the Americans, pulling at the hood, fighting for his life.

"Take it easy, you're being released," the translator said.

Released, cruel joke, the final release. Help, help me please. But they were too strong, and they had his hands tied behind his back. They ordered him to walk, and he could hear the other prisoners walking alongside him, their footsteps echoing in the corridors. Then the sound changed, and he knew he was outside for the first time in weeks: even through the hood he was aware of an unaccustomed brightness and felt the warmth of the winter sun on his body. He was ordered to step up, and he climbed onto what felt like the back of a truck. He could hear other men around him, but he was too afraid to speak to them. The truck started, and Nouri knew it was the final journey of his life: they were taking him to die for being a witness to their crimes. From time to time, he heard other prisoners cry out in fear.

The truck stopped, and Nouri felt the hood being tugged from his head. He tried to look round, but he was blinded by the sun. Someone was untying his arms and pushing him off the truck. He stumbled and fell, then scrabbled to his feet. He saw that he was on the main highway that ran past Abu Ghraib into Baghdad: they couldn't do it here; there were too many witnesses. They were emptying the truck, ordering everyone off, untying them and taking off the hoods. Nouri didn't recognise any of the other prisoners; they were from other cells. He wondered if he should make a run for it, but the Americans had guns and they would shoot him down. The last prisoner was off, and to Nouri's surprise, the Americans got back in the truck and drove off. Could it be true, then, that he was being released? That he was free? For a moment, in the sun, it made no sense. He pulled out the piece of paper they had given him, but it was in English. He looked at the other prisoners; several were already walking away.

"What do we do?" he asked one. The man shrugged, he looked as confused as Nouri.

"Go home," said another. "Get out of here before they realise they made a mistake."

"But I've got no money," said Nouri.

"Walk."

"But I've got to get to Sadr City." The other man whistled and shrugged.

"Come with me," said another. "I know a taxi driver who'll take you. Your family can pay him when you get home."

And so Nouri had walked to the other prisoner's home, and even though he had never been to Sadr City, the taxi driver had taken him on trust that his family would pay when he got back. Nouri worried his family might have moved, and he would have no way of paying the driver or of finding them, but when he got home and staggered to the door, there was his father shuffling sleepily to answer it, then crying like a child and holding him in his arms, while his mother and sisters came running from inside the house, and all the while Nouri felt the stubble of his father's beard scratching at his skin and stood in the unfamiliar sun wondering what to do. Even when his mother's joy gave way to sorrow at the thin, limping shell he had become, still Nouri could not find any tears of his own. He stood there silent, embarrassed because he found he could feel nothing.

It turned out his family had known where he was. The day after he was arrested, his father had gone to the Iraqi police, who had helped them find out where he was being held. While Nouri had been in Abu Ghraib wondering if they even knew he was alive, his father had been visiting regularly, trying to get news of him—but the Americans never told him anything.

He lay on his thin mattress, luxuriating in the sense of freedom. No one would come and take him back to the torture cells now. In a short time, his mother would come with his lunch. He knew she would chide him for lying in bed all day and urge him to get up, go out, see his friends. But he would spend one more day in bed, he would take his time, he had earned it, and he needed it. Maybe in the evening, when it was late enough, he would get up and sit for a while with his father and smoke.

⇥⟨●⟩⇤

Adel was looking through some old papers of his father's when he saw it. His mother had asked him to find some paperwork which the family laywer needed, and he had just started on the second drawer in the old chest in the living room, when he saw the small business card lying on top of the other papers. It was white and new, and stood out against the yellowing papers beneath, and the writing on it was in English, not Arabic. He picked it up and glanced at it out of idle curiosity, and was about to put it to one side when something about the words written on it caught his attention. The company name the *Informer* was emblazoned across the top of that card and, beneath it, "Zoe Temple: news reporter". He wondered how this foreigner's card came to be with his father's papers, then he remembered: she must be the journalist who had come to see his mother all those months before, who had sat here, in his father's chair—even as Adel sat and watched the video of the Russian soldier being killed, and Abu Khalid told him they wanted to capture foreigners in Iraq. Adel recalled how frustrated he had been, that the journalist had escaped him by a matter of hours, and how he had thought then that within a few weeks there would be foreign hostages in Iraq. He looked over the business card: there were several phone numbers, all international, and an email address. He slipped it into his pocket.

⇥⊜⊜⇤

When Benes got to the hospital, he found Dr Afaf waiting for him in the corridor outside the director's office, just as she always had. Perhaps she had heard he was coming back, perhaps it was just a coincidence.

"So you came back," she said.

"Yes. Seems we're finally going to do something to help."

"Dr Kamal will be pleased."

"Yeah, he's pretty happy." Benes glanced at Sergeant Hawkes to see if he was watching, but he was standing to one side, pretending to be interested in what was going on in a neighbouring ward, although all that was happening was a couple of nurses changing the sheets on a bed. The first thing Hawkes had said to Benes when he heard they were coming back was "You'll get to see that hot Hajji doctor chick again", and he hadn't stopped mentioning her since. The other men grinned whenever her name came up, and Benes was feeling self-conscious. He was glad to see her all the same.

"We're not going to be able to do everything," he said. "We can't do anything about medicines and all that."

"It is good if you do anything."

"Yeah, I guess." Benes felt embarrassed. Captain Parks had made Benes's limits clear, he wasn't to get involved in anything medical; apparently that was "the CPA's baby". American soldiers were not to get involved in any of the clean-up; they had more important things to do. There was a military fund available for reconstruction in Iraq, and Benes was to hire Iraqis to sort the hospital out. But the fund was small, and expensive equipment was out of the question.

"So how've you been?" he asked Dr Afaf.

"Good, Alhamdulillah," she said. "And you?"

198

"Good, I guess. The guys are getting tired."

"You've been away from home a long time—that's difficult. Do you know how long you'll stay?"

"In Iraq? Or at the hospital?"

Dr Afaf coloured.

"I meant in Iraq," she said.

"We're supposed to head out in April, but we already had our stay extended several times, so I guess the guys'll only believe it when we finally leave."

"April. It's not so long."

"So what have you been doing?"

"The same. We are trying to take care of the children. What about you? Where have you been?"

"All over. We've been doing patrols, some of them in not-so-great places. I think the guys miss the hospital."

"They're coming back?"

"No, actually they were pretty piss...unhappy," he corrected himself, "when they found out I was coming back here and they weren't."

"They like it here?"

"Well, you know, it's kinda safer than a lot of the places they get sent."

She smiled. They stood together awkwardly a moment.

"Well, I must get back to my work," she said.

"Yeah, sure. It's good to see you again."

"Yes. You too."

As she left, Benes felt himself back in the reality of Iraq. One of the hospital porters, who had stopped to rest from pushing an oxygen cylinder along the ground, was giving him a hostile look. The interview with Dr Kamal had been difficult, but then he had expected that. The director thought he was going to get what he wanted, and there had been the inevitable disappointment when he learned the limits of what Benes could do. Not trespassing on the CPA's territory didn't just mean not providing new medicine for the hospital: it meant no oxygen cylinders, no new generators, no medical staff...in fact, no qualified staff at all. The best Benes could offer was cleaners. He could probably get something done about the drains and get more fuel for the existing generators.

"Ungrateful bastard," Hawkes had growled as they left the office. Hawkes had been against their return to the hospital from the start; the idea of being involved, however peripherally, in cleaning it up incensed him. He referred to it as "playing nurse-maid to the fucking Hajjis", and with all the limits on what he could do, Benes was beginning to wonder whether he might be right. It seemed they were here more on a face-saving mission than anything else, so the higher-ups back in Washington could say they were doing something about the hospital. He feared that in the end, having told the journalist about the hospital might do more harm than good by allowing the likes of Richard Webb at the CPA to say the hospital had been taken care of, when all they were doing was fixing a few drains. Still, it was good to see Afaf again.

Chapter Sixteen

Car Chase

7 February 2004

Two FIGURES MADE their way through the narrow back streets of Adhamiya. Though they were not locals, they attracted little attention. It was mid-afternoon, and Adhamiya was not as unwelcoming by day as it could be at night; besides, the two men were clearly Iraqi shabab. They had the careless swagger, swinging their chests as they walked, and from the purposeful way they negotiated the streets, they knew their way around. There was another reason many of those watching avoided asking questions of them: in Adhamiya, young men who had an air of business about them were often resistance fighters, especially young men no one had seen around before—and it wasn't a good idea to go challenging such men, or asking who they were. One of them was wearing a red and white headscarf, innocuous enough—a lot of the shabab wore them in winter—but the resistance were known to favour the same headscarves, which they wore wrapped about their faces as a means of disguise, so no one was keen to peer too closely at the features below it, the dark eyes and stubbly beard.

If they had let their eyes linger for more than a moment over his features, however, they would have noticed that all was not quite as it should be. The colouring might have been right, the close-trimmed beard, but the shape of his face was not quite Iraqi. It might fool a casual glance, but not more severe scrutiny. The clothes were perfect, the formal trousers, the shirt, the leather jacket, but there was something almost studied about the walk, as if it did not come naturally. To the other residents of the al-Hamra Hotel, in the unlikely event any of them had been in Adhamiya that afternoon, he would have been instantly recognisable as Jack Wolfe, and the Iraqi man beside him as his translator, Adnan.

They made their way through the streets to the small square with electric cables stretched across it. Adnan held the door of the cafe open for Jack, then followed him inside. Two or three tables were occupied; the men sitting at them looked up briefly, registered the newcomers and returned to their conversations and their backgammon. A young boy who was serving tea gestured them to a table, then went through a curtain into the back of the building. After a short time he came back out with two glasses of tea and was followed minutes later by a tall, middle-aged man, drying his hands on a long dishdasha that looked hastily pulled on. He seemed surprised to see Jack and Adnan, but he shook each by the hand, touching his other hand to his heart, then pulled up a chair and sat down. He spoke in Arabic, and Adnan leaned forward to translate softly to Jack—but not so softly that one or two of those at the other tables did not look up sharply.

"Mr Arif says welcome," Adnan translated. "He says you are very brave to come here."

"Brave, brave," the tall man repeated in English.

"It's always a pleasure to come here," Jack said.

"No, really," Adnan murmured. "He says it is very risky for you to come here now." Arif began speaking, and Adnan continued to translate *sotto voce*. "He says you are always welcome in his cafe, because you are Irish and you have suffered under the British, like the Iraqis, and your people fought the British, like the Iraqis. He says, do you know that if you were American or British, you would be killed if you came here?"

Jack nodded and shifted uncomfortably in his seat.

"But he says not everyone in Adhamiya will understand that you are Irish," Adnan went on. "The situation is becoming serious. People here are becoming extreme."

Arif gave Jack a grave look, then said something else.

"Mr Arif says there is a video disc that might interest you," Adnan translated, "people have been distributing it here. He says it shows an American soldier being killed. They cut his head." Jack looked up sharply. "Not in Iraq. Somewhere else, maybe Afghanistan. But he hopes soon they will do the same here."

"Where can I get it?" Jack asked.

"Mr Arif says he will give you a copy, because you are brave enough to come here, to Adhamiya, when it is so risky for you. But he asks that in future you do not come. He does not ask this because you are not welcome, you are always welcome, he says, but he is worried you will not be safe. You are safe inside his cafe—"

"Safe!" Arif broke in forcefully, gesturing with his massive arm across the expanse of the cafe and towards the door. The other customers who had looked up suspiciously took note of this display and turned back to their own conversations.

"But he says he does not feel you will be safe in the streets here," Adnan went on. "He will get you this video, but he asks that I come alone to take it for you. He says in future it will be better if you have any questions, if I come alone."

"How is the situation in Adhamiya now?" Jack asked.

"Really, I think it is better if I ask these questions later, when I come for the disc," Adnan said. "It is better if we go now."

Jack nodded, glancing around the room nervously.

"Is it—" he began to ask.

"It should be safe for us, if we go now," Adnan murmured, but he looked on edge. As they got up to leave, Arif embraced Jack and kissed him on the cheek—a gesture that was not lost on the other customers. As the door closed behind them, Arif cast his eye over his customers. No one got up to follow the foreigner.

⊷━⊚━⊶

Zoe was in the back of the car, on the way back to Baghdad after a fruitless trip to Najaf, regretting the hours wasted on the journey only to return empty-handed. She looked out of the window at the featureless towns as they passed. In the front, Ali and Mahmoud were deep in conversation. A thought came to her.

"Ali," she asked. "Are we anywhere near Mahmudiya?"

"Yes, it's about half an hour from here."

"Ahead, or did we already pass through it?"

"Ahead."

After she returned from the north, Zoe had asked Ali if he and Mahmoud had heard anything about Mahmudiya, but they hadn't, and she had soon found herself preoccupied with other matters and forgotten the story of the boy who had lost his leg. Now, though, finding that by chance she would be passing through the town Jack had seemed so keen to keep her away from, she was curious again.

"Can we stop there?" she asked. "At the local hospital?"

"OK." He looked round at her. "Any particular reason?"

"It's just a story I heard about a kid who was wounded in the war. It won't take long."

Mahmudiya, when they reached it, was a small, nondescript town, dusty like everywhere she had been in Iraq. It took some time to find the hospital, and as they drove through the streets, Mahmoud muttered something to Ali in a tone that caught Zoe's attention.

"What's up?" she asked.

"It's probably nothing," Ali said. "Mahmoud's nervous about that car. He says it has driven past us twice." Zoe looked at the car he was indicating, a battered white BMW moving slowly past them.

"You think it's a problem?" she asked.

"They're probably lost or looking for somewhere, the same as us," Ali said. The white car moved on, and Zoe put it down to excessive caution on Mahmoud's part. They had to stop to ask directions to the hospital, but eventually they found it, a small, low building in a state of disrepair, and Mahmoud pulled up outside the door. As she walked in with Ali, Zoe noticed one or two hostile glances. Ali asked for the hospital director, and they were shown into an office. From the moment she stepped inside, Zoe could tell something was wrong. The director, who introduced himself as Dr Qusay, looked at her as if she was the last person in the world he wanted to walk into his office. Ali began to explain why they had come, but unusually for an Iraqi, the doctor interrupted him.

"Why are you here?" he asked Zoe in English. His tone wasn't hostile, but it was urgent.

"I came about one of your patients, a boy, Selim Abdullah, I think his name is. I don't know if you remember, but a journalist called Jack Wolfe wrote a story about him—"

"Yes, I know him."

"Well, he lost his leg, right, in the—"

"Yes, in the bombing."

"Well, I…" Zoe was unsure what to say next. "I wanted to see, well, if there's any way to get him an artificial leg. There's a clinic in Baghdad—"

"You came to help? But he already has a leg. They came from Baghdad."

"They came? Who?"

"From the clinic."

"When?"

"Some months before. But why have you come to Mahmudiya? Don't you know about the situation?"

"What situation?"

The director turned and spoke to Ali in Arabic. As the two men spoke, Ali's expression changed.

"We should go," he said, turning to Zoe. She hadn't seen him look so worried since the Najaf bombing.

"What?" Feeling nervous, she stuffed her notebook in her bag and stood up ready to leave, but she wanted to know what the danger was. "I don't understand."

"There is a…problem for you here. It's not safe," said the doctor. There was a silence; he looked at her. "They are hunting you." His words hung in the air.

"What?"

"They are hunting for the foreigners here."

"It is best if we leave," Ali repeated.

"But who…who is hunting foreigners?"

"I…cannot say." Dr Qusay was trying to move them towards the door. "But it is not safe for you. And it is not safe for the hospital if you are seen here. Please."

"OK, I…I…" Zoe stammered.

"I am sorry," Dr Qusay said. "Please, put your scarf to hide your face as you leave. Try to look Iraqi." He spoke rapidly to Ali in Arabic, and then turned back to Zoe. "And take care of a white BMW car."

Zoe looked at Ali. They walked quickly out of the office, Zoe pulling the headscarf tight around her face and keeping her eyes on the ground to avoid making eye contact with anyone. Mahmoud was waiting outside and there was, thankfully, no sign of the white BMW. As they got in, Ali spoke quickly to Mahmoud, and he drove off fast, without waiting even for her to finish closing the door.

"What was all that about?" Zoe asked Ali when they were clear of the town.

"I think it is not safe in Mahmudiya," he said. "This is something new."

"But what was that about someone *hunting* us?"

"He told me there are foreigners in the town, from the Arab countries. They are Wahabis, I don't say they are Al-Qa'ida, but they are like Al-Qa'ida. They have threatened the hospital."

So Jack's warning was not a lie to keep her away from Mahmudiya. There was something unnerving about the words Dr Qusay had used; somehow the idea of being *hunted* was worse than the other dangers she had encountered in Iraq. Zoe noticed that they were accelerating hard and looked up, surprised. Ali and Mahmoud were speaking in Arabic.

"What's up?" she asked. "Why are we—"

"White BMW," Ali said. Zoe looked behind and saw it, so close she could see the driver's nose and mouth below his sunglasses. There were three of them in the car, two in the front and one in the back. The BMW's lights flashed, signalling them to stop, but Mahmoud drove faster, weaving from lane to lane. He and Ali were quiet, concentrating. She glanced over Mahmoud's shoulder at the speedometer. It read 200 km/h: that was over 120 miles an hour. They were swerving hard around other traffic, missing cars by inches, but the BMW was still close behind. 220 km/h. Cars were coming at the windscreen fast, but Mahmoud slowed for nothing, finding ways round, squeezing through gaps in the traffic. The white car was sounding its horn now, close behind them and trying to pull in front. Two trucks loomed ahead, no way between them. At the last minute, Mahmoud pulled through a gap in the central divider, into the lane of oncoming traffic. The BMW followed, but it was dropping back. 240 km/h. Mahmoud ducked the car back to the other side of the road. The white car was fading now, but Mahmoud kept driving fast to put distance between them. He didn't slow until they came into the suburbs of Baghdad, where he dropped down to his usual speed, laughing with nervous relief.

"That was close," Ali said. He was not laughing. Zoe realised her hands were shaking and dropped back in the seat, exhausted. Her head was soaked with sweat, and she pulled the scarf off.

"Thanks, Mahmoud," she said.

"Mercedes good car."

That night at the hotel, Dr Qusay's words echoed in her mind: *They are hunting you.* She had been in danger before in Iraq, but it was something else to be tracked through the streets as prey, to feel the hunters closing in, to know even in the moment of escape that they were still out there, watching and waiting. She had a story for the paper out of the trip to Mahmudiya after all: there were militants an hour's drive from Baghdad, looking for foreigners to kill under the Americans' noses.

But she felt guilty that she had led Ali and Mahmoud into danger because she hadn't believed Jack's warning. She wondered how he had known about Mahmudiya when none of the other journalists had, when even Ali, who spoke to all the drivers and translators who went up and down the road daily, hadn't known. Not many of them had reason to stop in Mahmudiya, and Jack could have heard about it when he was there for the story about the boy, she supposed, or from contacts he made then—but in that case why hadn't he published a story about it?

She would have to warn the others to stay away—but then she realised that spreading a warning around the hotel would pre-empt her story about Mahmudiya. If she told the others, they might run the story too, and she could lose a scoop. It was one day, she reasoned; anyone who was going that way would already have left, and she could safely wait until the story was published the next day. All the same, she hoped nothing happened to anyone in Mahmudiya in the meantime.

With the drama of the chase on her mind, it was some time before she remembered the story that had taken her to Mahmudiya in the first place. It seemed Jack's account of the boy had been true, and what was more, that he had already been given a prosthetic leg. That could be proof Jack's scepticism was wrong, that his story had made a difference—but then, she thought, Dr Qusay could have been lying about it, just to get her out of his hospital.

Chapter Seventeen

The Road to Hell

10–13 February 2004

IT WAS NOT long before Zoe had to travel through Mahmudiya again, despite her best intentions. She woke to the news that a suicide bombing in Iskandariya, a town just south of Mahmudiya, had killed more than fifty people. The other journalists in the al-Hamra were getting ready to drive south, and Zoe knew she had no choice but to join them. Over Ali's protests, they headed south again, Zoe keeping her headscarf on throughout the journey, her heart pumping, and Mahmoud driving fast, determined to stop for nothing. When they reached Iskandariya, the journey had been for nothing, the Americans had cordoned off the town and there was no way in to witness the scene of the attack.

Not for the first time, Zoe realised how easy it was to risk her life for nothing. The journalists were crowded up close to the American military cordon, the cameramen trying to film over their shoulders, though there was nothing to see but the outlines of buildings in the distance. Among them she could see Peter Shore, who had arrived back in Baghdad a couple of days before—and whom she had so far succeeded in avoiding. A pair of American helicopters flew overhead. A few young men had come out of the town and crossed the American cordon to talk to the journalists, explaining what had happened. It was the second day of a police recruitment drive, and a car full of explosives had been driven into a crowd of men gathered at the local police station to sign up.

"Americans do this," one of the Iraqis said angrily, gesturing at the helicopters overhead. "They make bomb on Iraqis." It wasn't clear whether he thought that the helicopters had fired into the crowd, or that the Americans were behind the suicide bomber in the car, but improbable as his accusation was, it clearly resonated with the other Iraqis, who began to denounce the Americans, despite the soldiers standing nearby. It was more likely, Zoe thought, that the bombing had been the work of the same insurgent group that had chased her a few miles up the road in Mahmudiya.

"We found the bodies burned and broken into pieces," one of the young men from the town was telling the journalists. "We found pieces of flesh on the roof, we found body parts that we couldn't tell who they belonged to. There were pieces of women."

Zoe wandered a little away from the others. The black line of the road stretched on in the unforgiving light. There were palm trees in the background, their feathery leaves stirring in a slight breeze. The air was free of the sulphurous smell that always hung over Baghdad, and for a moment the place seemed beautiful to Zoe, despite what had happened there. They would be waking up now in London. If they heard about what had happened here at all, it would be a news announcement on the television, over-heard in the background while they were making breakfast or catching their attention for a moment on the radio in the traffic on the way to work. They would barely register these deaths in a country far away, in a town called Iskandariya. And her own report the next day would be read only by a few readers hiding their hangovers behind the newspaper on the bus or the Tube. Everyone was tied up in the cares of their own lives, and it all seemed somehow irrelevant to Zoe, fifty people cut to pieces trying to get a job, and the press corps jostling and pushing each other for a view of nothing because they couldn't get in to see the bloody mess where they had died.

"Back on Highway 8?" a voice said behind her. Zoe looked round. Jack was there, with a grave look in his eyes, as if he had been struck by the same thought as her. An illusion, she put it from her mind.

"Hey, Jack, how are you?"

"I've been worse…" The helicopters swung overhead, drowning his voice for a moment. "Miserable business," she heard him say. "So you made it to Mahmudiya then?"

"Yes."

"That was a good piece," he said, "very good. But be careful." He didn't seem bothered that she had ignored his advice to stay away from the town. "Looks like your friends in the white BMW have struck again," he said, gesturing towards the cordoned-off road. "Gives us a little more idea who's behind these attacks."

"Yes," she said. "Not that it'll be much comfort to the people here. They were only trying to get a job."

"Clever, though," he said. "They were trying to get a job with the police. The insurgents are letting Iraqis know they'll target anyone who works for the Americans. They're trying to make it impossible for the Americans to govern Iraq."

"The people here seem to think the Americans did it."

"Yes," he smiled. "Well, I suppose that'll suit them even better. More than they planned for. There's something else. Know what's interesting about this town, apart from the fact it's just down the road from your beloved Mahmudiya?"

"Iskandariya? No."

"It's mixed. Shia and Sunni. Mahmudiya is a Sunni town, but this is practically the dividing line between Sunni and Shia, Sunni to the north, Shia to the south. I think they're trying to whip up a civil war."

The American soldiers were getting nervous. More locals had gathered, and they were beginning to shout slogans. Jack suggested it might be wise to head off, and they walked back towards where the cars were parked.

"How come you never did a story on Mahmudiya?" Zoe asked as they walked.

"What story?"

"About the men in the white car? Hunting foreigners?"

"I didn't know about it. That was your scoop."

"Then how did you know Mahmudiya was dangerous?" She stopped in the road.

"What?" He stopped too.

"You warned me not to go."

"Oh, well, there was the ambush on the Spanish. And the Iraqis last month. I didn't think it was the sort of place to be nosing around too much."

"The attack on the Spanish?"

"Didn't you know? Seven Spanish intelligence agents were killed there in November. And a couple of Iraqis working for one of the American networks last month. I thought you knew."

They walked on in silence. It was only when he was climbing into the back of his car that she thought to say, "Oh, I found out some news about Selim."

"Who?"

"The child who lost his leg."

"Oh, him. What about him?"

"The doctor said he got an artificial leg. Someone paid for it."

"Great." Jack shrugged. "See you in Baghdad."

Mahmoud woke to the news there had been another suicide bombing, this time in Baghdad at an Iraqi army base. New recruits had been reporting for duty when a suicide bomber drove into them in a car full of explosives, just like the day before in Iskandariya. The crowds were spilling out of the well-defended barracks onto the street, where they were easy to hit, and more than forty were killed. Mahmoud's immediate thought was of Saara; it was clear they were going after anyone they saw as collaborating. He rushed to her office but could only get a few minutes with her between all the officials who needed typing done.

"Don't worry," she told him, "they're attacking the police and army, those are armed men. They aren't going to come here; this is just the Higher Education Ministry. What are we going to do? Refuse to give the insurgents degrees?"

"They'll see you as working for the Americans," he said.

"What about you? Won't they see you the same way?"

"I can take care of myself."

"What? And I can't?"

"It's not that, it's…I'm driving around all day, they don't know where I am. Here they can come for you whenever they please."

"So what do you want me to do? Go back to the house and let

211

them win? Then they've already defeated us. I want to live a life, Mahmoud. Besides, if I go back to the house, we won't be able to meet every day."

Mahmoud had no answer to that. He knew she was right, if she stopped coming to work at the ministry, they would be back to tiptoeing around her father, only able to meet when he was away from the house. He was torn between his desire to see her and his fear, but he couldn't stay to argue. He knew Zoe would want to go and visit the site of the bombing as soon as she woke up, and he couldn't afford to be late for work.

"Don't worry," Saara told him as he left.

But he was worried. The visit to the blast site did nothing to alleviate his fears: the crater in the road, the pieces of bodies being collected, the red smears of blood that would have to be hosed and scrubbed away. Nor did the stories Ali brought back of the wounded they had seen in hospital. That night, in his dreams, Mahmoud saw men packing a car with explosives. When it was full, one of them turned to the others and said, "Where is this one for?"

"The Higher Education Ministry," one of the others replied.

He woke up to find he had turned so much in his bed he had twisted the bedclothes into a rope around his body. When he reached the ministry, she wasn't there. He asked about her, but the other secretaries said she hadn't come to work that day. At first he thought she had seen the danger and decided to stay away, but as the day wore on he began to worry that she had been kidnapped on her way to the ministry. He longed to get away from work so he could visit her brother Yusuf to ask about her, but Zoe had him driving around Baghdad all day. In the evening, he drove to the house and looked at the upstairs window, but the signal was not there. He waited for a long time outside, in case her brother passed by, or one of her friends, but no one came, and still there was no signal. He drove home, telling himself there was nothing to worry about. That night, in his dreams, he saw the same men packing explosives into the car.

"Change of plan," one of them said. Then the car was driving through the city, but this time it was taking a different route. Mahmoud watched in confusion, then he realised where it was going, following his familiar route, heading to her home. There was no way to stop them, no way to keep her safe.

The next day she was again not at the ministry, and no one there seemed to have any information on whether she was coming back. Again, Zoe kept him driving all day. Distracted by thoughts of Saara, he nearly drove into an American convoy, and Ali had to shout at him to stop. He slammed the brakes on at the last minute, looking up to see an American soldier aiming his gun straight at them from the top of the Humvee. Mahmoud smiled up at him apologetically, but the American did not smile, just stared down the barrel of the gun. The journalist started screaming at him from the back of the car in a way she had not done before. She was shouting in English, and Mahmoud could not make out most of what she was saying.

"Do you understand?" she was asking him. "Mahmoud, do you understand? Ali, ask him. Does he understand?"

"Yes, yes, understand," he said. "Sorry."

"What's up with you?" Ali said when they were under way again.

"Nothing. Just problems at home."

"Be careful. Please. We could have been killed."

"Sorry."

That evening he went to her house again, and to his relief, the ribbon was there. When her sister opened the door, and he saw Saara sitting beyond her unharmed, his heart leapt. He rushed into the room, forgetting himself and talking loudly until he heard a sound like someone dropping something above, and Saara gestured to him angrily to be quiet.

"Are you all right?" he asked. "I was worried when you didn't come to the ministry. Has anything happened?"

"Only my father has become as paranoid as you, and he won't let me go back to work," she said. "What do they think will happen? Do they think it is safer here, where someone can come any time they like? At the ministry there are guards, what is there here?"

"At least you're safe."

"Safe? How am I safe? Here, where they put notes under the door and threaten to kill us? You call this safe? None of us is safe in Baghdad any more. But when we hide in here, we let these people win. They want me to hide away here and not dare to go to work. But I was not made for such a world. I want to *live* a life, Mahmoud. I do not want just to have a life, to hide in the shadows and protect it at all costs as if that is all there is, just to eat and breathe, sleep and wake. Life is worth nothing unless we can *live* it." Her eyes were blazing, her head tipped back.

"But what can we do, with the situation like this?" Mahmoud said. "Do you think I like this, to come here like a thief, hide from your father, only get to see you for a few minutes at the ministry?"

Saara was crying, tears running silently from her eyes, and she was trying to hide it, turning away and blinking. Mahmoud heard a door creak above and ignored it; he stepped forward and took her in his arms and felt her heart beating against his.

"I'm all right," she said, her voice muffled against his shoulder.

"I know."

⇥▷■◉■◁⇤

At first, Dr Afaf was there each day, waiting in the corridor outside Dr Kamal's office, just as she had always been. But on Benes's third visit, to his disappointment there was no sign of her. He thought little of it, assuming she had been called away on hospital business or held up by a case. But when, the next time he visited, she was again absent, he wondered if he had said something that had offended her. He walked through some of the wards where she usually worked, but she was not there either. She did not reappear the whole time he was back at the hospital. Without their conversations, the hospital became tedious and frustrating. It took days of negotiation and bargaining to get Iraqis to do what he could have got soldiers to finish in a single afternoon, but eventually he got the worst of the sewage pipes fixed and a half-hearted clean-up operation under way. He got hold of more generator fuel and even managed to buy some oxygen cylinders on the black market, though he had to swear Dr Kamal to secrecy for fear he would be reprimanded for straying into CPA territory. As he looked up and down the corridors on his last day, Benes felt disillusioned. He had wanted the hospital properly cleaned up, but all he had achieved was a facelift. He was on his way to Dr Kamal's office for a final meeting when a young woman doctor he had not spoken to before stopped him.

"Excuse me, Captain," she said.

"Lieutenant," Benes said.

"Yes, I…I was wondering, do you know what has happened to Dr Afaf?"

"Happened? No. What happened?"

"I don't know. No one does. But she hasn't been to work for a week."

"Maybe she's sick."

"I went to her home—please don't tell the director. I went but her family wouldn't speak to me. They said she wasn't there… they seemed scared. I didn't know them before, so maybe…" She trailed off uncertainly. "Dr Afaf is my friend, and I'm worried. We thought maybe…maybe you could find out about her."

"Do you have any idea what might have happened?"

"Maybe the director knows. He will not tell us, but maybe he will tell you."

"I'll ask him."

"But…" she hesitated. "But there's something else."

"Yes?"

She stood in silence for a moment, then seemed to force herself to go on.

"I'm worried—we all are—that, well, she spent a lot of time talking to you. It's not that you did anything bad, but in Baghdad now…it can be…I'm sorry…it can be dangerous to be seen with an American."

Benes felt his blood thicken and stop in his veins.

"I didn't—I mean I—didn't realise," he said. "I should have… I'll find out about her, I promise. I didn't catch your name."

"Please don't tell the director," she said. She looked frightened.

"No, of course, I mean, I just wanted to be able to let you know what I find out."

"I'll wait for you here."

"Isn't it bad for you to be seen with me?"

"I have to find out about her."

Benes went on to Dr Kamal's office. Why hadn't he thought, all those times when they stood talking in the corridor for anyone to see, of the danger to her?

"Lieutenant," Dr Kamal said, smiling up from behind his desk and gesturing Benes and Hawkes to seats, "and Sergeant. You have come to tell me you are finished."

"Afraid so," Benes said, but his mind was on Dr Afaf.

"But there is so much still to do."

Hawkes stared rigidly ahead.

"I know that, sir, and I wish I could do it for you," Benes said, forcing himself to go on with the pleasantries. "But I've done just about everything I was authorised to do, and some I wasn't."

"Will you have tea?"

Benes nodded, and Dr Kamal spoke into an intercom. Benes glanced across at Hawkes, worried what the sergeant would think when he asked about Dr Afaf. Would he think Benes had gone soft? Or blame him for her disappearance, as Benes was blaming himself? He would probably just think Benes was wasting their time as usual, chasing after his Hajji chick.

"We thank you for what you have done, Lieutenant," Dr Kamal was saying. "Of course, there is much more to do, but you have done what you could for us, and we are grateful."

"I wish we could have done more."

"We will keep trying, Lieutenant. Maybe we will see you here again."

Benes felt Hawkes stiffen beside him. There was a knock at the door and a boy came in with the tea.

"There was one other thing," Benes said, glancing at Hawkes as he spoke. Hawkes was studying the wall, carefully ignoring him. "I was wondering what happened to Dr Afaf."

Dr Kamal looked up sharply. For a long time he said nothing. He stared at Benes, then looked down at his tea. He dropped sugar in it and watched it slowly dissolve. Then he looked up again and sighed through his nose.

"I don't know," he said finally. "I don't know what has happened. She hasn't been to work in a week. When I send messages to her home, I hear nothing. I'm...I'm very worried."

Benes's skin felt clammy. "What do you think might have happened to her?" he asked.

"I don't want to think," the director said, looking at Benes evenly. Benes could see the flecks in his irises. "There is no point to guessing. We must wait for news."

"And if there isn't any?"

Dr Kamal said nothing and looked down at his papers.

"Maybe we could look into it?" Benes suggested.

"That may not be...helpful for her," Dr Kamal said. "She hasn't been...wise to be seen with you so much. Forgive me, but it is not good to be seen with an American in Baghdad these days."

Benes felt a flash of anger. If they had all known it was dangerous for her to be seen talking to him, they should have warned him.

"There must be something we can do," he said.

"I'm sure it is nothing," Dr Kamal said unconvincingly. "Maybe one of her relatives is sick. If I find anything, I'll let you know."

Benes shook the director's hand and left. He had unwittingly endangered the only Iraqi he had managed to have any sort of friendship with. He wanted to do something, to run somewhere, to take some action, but he didn't know what. He saw the young woman doctor who had approached him waiting.

"The director says he doesn't know," he told her. "He's worried too." Her face fell. He glanced over at Hawkes and hesitated for a moment. Hawkes would be against putting the men in danger hunting for some Hajji chick who'd got herself in trouble, he knew. "Look, give me her address," he said. "We'll go check it out."

"I don't know."

"We'll be careful."

The doctor hesitated, but reluctantly she pulled out a piece of paper and scribbled down an address on it, both in English and in Arabic. As she wrote, Benes contemplated the argument he was about to have with Hawkes.

"Please, don't make any problem for her," she said. Benes nodded and walked off too quickly for Hawkes to protest. He knew anger was overcoming the fear now, anger at anyone who might have done something to her just for talking to an American, but he knew too as a soldier it was dangerous when anger took command.

"Motherfucking country," Hawkes said to him when he caught up. "If they've fucked around with the only person who's shown us any decency or respect since we came in the damn place…" Benes looked over in surprise. Hawkes's face had turned pale and he was clenching his fists. "I hope she's OK," said the sergeant. "But if she isn't, if she isn't…"

Chapter Eighteen

Valentines

14 February 2004

ZOE WAS HEADING down the front steps of the al-Hamra to the Internet cafe when she saw Jack coming in the other direction.

"Zoe," he called out, "have you heard about Fallujah?"

"No. What's happened?"

"They've attacked the police and the army. Not just a car bombing this time—they've gone in and raided the police head-quarters. Stormed the Iraqi army garrison too."

Her first reaction was one of relief that she had something to write about for the day—the exhaustion of Iraq was beginning to tell on her once more, and she had not been looking forward to telling Nigel Langham she had nothing and hearing his blood pressure rise down the phone. But she quickly checked those thoughts: people had almost certainly died in the morning's raids, and they were more bad news for the Iraqis' hopes of peace and stability. She had noticed of late that Ali and Mahmoud, who at first had seemed to revel gleefully in every setback for the Americans, had begun to look increasingly concerned at each new attack, as if they had realised that, whatever their feelings about being invaded and occupied, the failure of the Americans, which seemed more likely every day, could plunge their country into anarchy and, although neither of them admitted it, civil war.

"Are there many dead?" she asked Jack.

"No news yet, but it seems likely. They went in there with heavy machine guns and rockets. Want to head over and see what's happening?"

As he spoke, a car pulled up beside them, and Peter Shore emerged, followed by Rob and Louise. Zoe had managed to avoid Peter since he got back to Baghdad, apart from a few polite words. As he got out of the car, his eyes flicked from her to Jack, taking them in together in a way she didn't like.

"Hey," he said, "how's it going?"

"Not bad," said Zoe. "You?"

"Just got back from Fallujah."

"It's pretty tense over there," Louise added.

"Yeah, we were just thinking of heading that way—"

"Oh, I wouldn't if I were you," Peter interrupted. "We had to cut and run. It was looking pretty ropey. The locals weren't too keen on having us around."

"Right," Zoe said, dispirited. "What did you see?"

"Oh, the usual, tension on the streets, young guys hanging around." He spoke as if he was trying not to say too much and flashed Louise and Rob a warning look. "No sign of the Americans."

"Well, I suppose I'll try to make a couple of phone calls then," Zoe said.

"I would," he said, heading up the steps to the hotel. "Don't go sticking your neck out there. It's not worth it." Zoe watched as he breezed into the hotel, followed by Rob and Louise.

"So want to head over to Fallujah then?" she heard over her shoulder.

"Well, I think, I mean you heard what Peter said. It's probably not—"

"You and I can keep a lower profile than Mr Shore and his camera," Jack said with a grin, pulling his red-check Arab head-scarf out of his pocket.

"I don't know." She wanted to go, in part because she resented Peter's air of superiority, but also because the excitement of being at the centre of events was pulling at her again.

"Well, I'm going."

Zoe stood undecided for a moment. Jack had been right about Mahmudiya, and he seemed confident it was safe to go to Fallujah, but she knew too that there was no love lost between him and Peter, and she feared he could be trying to prove a point. On the other hand, it wasn't beyond Peter to exaggerate the danger to keep them from Fallujah so he'd have the story to himself. She could see Ali approaching, talking with one of the other translators. Jack was already calling his car over. As soon as he saw her, Ali hurried to tell her the news from Fallujah.

"I'm thinking of going," she interrupted him. "What do you think?"

"You want to go?"

"Only if it's safe."

He thought for a while.

"It's risky, but if we stay in the car and you wear your scarf and coat, I think we can go," he said. "Only we must be prepared to turn back if necessary."

"OK," Zoe said, and the decision seemed to be made. They were calling Mahmoud over, and she was telling Jack they'd follow his car.

Zoe had expected an American presence at the turn-off to Fallujah and half hoped they wouldn't be allowed in, but when they reached it, the turn-off was open and unguarded, the road deserted. Ahead, Jack's car turned towards the town. Zoe caught Ali's eye in the rear-view mirror as they followed—he looked as apprehensive as she felt. On the outskirts, the streets were empty, but as they got closer to the centre they began to see cars and people. There was no sign of the Americans.

"It's better if we don't go together," Ali said, turning round in his seat. "Two cars will look suspicious."

Reluctantly, Zoe agreed, and Mahmoud turned off down a side street. They were alone now, without even the flimsy sense of security the other car provided. There were more people around, and they were attracting searching looks.

"Let's stop here and I'll ask someone," Ali said. They pulled up, and he got out, motioning Zoe to stay where she was. She felt herself crouching down under the headscarf, trying to hide herself away. Now that they were here, it seemed reckless to have risked their lives for a story she could easily have covered from Baghdad.

"Miss Zoe," Ali said, leaning in at the other window and making her jump. "Sorry," he said. "This gentleman will speak to us. He has invited you for tea." Zoe looked over Ali's shoulder. Behind him a man with a scarred face and hard eyes stood in the entrance to a small, darkened shop. Zoe wondered if she would come out alive.

"Tea? Is it safe?"

"I think so. It's not good to say no." She felt the eyes of the street on her as she crossed to the shop. Ali introduced the man as Mr Murtaza, and he showed them into a tiny shop crammed full of electronic goods, mobile phones, alarm clocks, fax machines, digital scales, all piled up to the ceiling. Zoe and Ali sat in two cramped chairs either side of a tiny glass-topped counter that contained more mobile phones and calculators. There was no room for Mr Murtaza to squeeze in himself, so he stood in the doorway. It all looked very natural, but Zoe realised he had carefully arranged the scene so no one could see her from outside, blocking the view with his own frame—and the only exit.

"So," Ali said, "what do you want to ask?"

Zoe realised she was so unnerved by the situation that she had been sitting in silence, and Mr Murtaza was looking at her curiously.

"Uh, I…did he see what happened earlier? At the police headquarters?" Ali and the shopkeeper spoke in Arabic.

"He says he didn't see; he was here. But he heard from his friends that many police were killed. He says the people here are happy. They don't like the Americans, and they don't like any Iraqi who works with them."

Zoe looked up and saw the shopkeeper's eyes on her. She didn't like the way he was looking at her.

"Does, um, does he know who it was who attacked the police? I mean, not the people themselves," she added quickly, realising the question had made her sound like a spy, "but were they Iraqis or foreigners?"

At first Mr Murtaza said nothing; he gave an ugly, unfriendly smile. Then he said something brief.

"They are with us," Ali translated.

"Just that?"

Mr Murtaza spoke again.

"If they are Iraqi or not, they are one with the Iraqi people because of what they have done," Ali translated. There was movement at the door, and the shopkeeper stood aside to let someone in. Zoe flinched. It was just a young man with glasses of tea, and the shopkeeper laughed.

"He says you are afraid," Ali said. "He says you are right to be afraid." Mr Murtaza stepped outside to speak to someone.

"Should we go?" Zoe whispered to Ali. He shook his head.

"I think it is OK," he said. Before they could speak more, the shopkeeper returned, accompanied by a younger man.

"This is Mr Fahmi," Ali translated. "He was at the police headquarters."

Zoe wasn't sure she wanted to meet one of those who had attacked the police station.

"He is a lieutenant in the police," Ali continued, "a survivor of the attack." Zoe was confused: Mr Murtaza had just said he was against the police.

"But he's not wearing any uniform," she said. The two men laughed.

"It's not good to be seen in a uniform today," Ali explained.

"So what happened?"

Ali and the police officer spoke for some time. Zoe noticed Mr Murtaza was giving her a conspiratorial look from over the police officer's shoulder. Was he warning her not to give away what he had said about the police, or was he watching her?

"It happened at half past eight in the morning," Ali translated. "Lieutenant Fahmi could not see what was happening: he was trapped inside. He could hear shooting. After only fifteen minutes, they took control of the station and started killing the police inside and throwing grenades in the rooms. Lieutenant Fahmi escaped. As he ran from the room, the attackers threw a grenade at him, but by chance it fell at his feet and he was able to kick it away before it went off."

"Did he see who the attackers were? I mean, if they were Iraqi?"

"He says he could not see, but he does not believe Iraqis would attack their brother Iraqis like this." Behind him, Mr Murtaza's eyes gleamed. "Is it all the questions for him?" Ali said. "He has to go."

As Lieutenant Fahmi left, he shook hands with the shopkeeper.

"Is it enough?" Ali asked. "I think we should leave too."

"Sure," Zoe said, standing up uncertainly. Mr Murtaza stood back to let them out, smiling and nodding, and he showed them across the road to the car. Ali asked if they had enough and could go back to Baghdad, and Zoe quickly agreed, feeling she had pushed her luck far enough.

"Do you think he was really there, at the police headquarters?" she asked as they drove.

"Yes, why not?"

"Only Mr Murtaza seemed to support the attackers."

"Yes, he did."

"But they were friends?"

"Not friends. They knew each other."

"So Lieutenant Fahmi doesn't know that Mr Murtaza supports the men who attacked him?"

"Maybe he knows, but he doesn't say anything."

By now they were close to the main road. Ahead, Jack's car was waiting for them. Mahmoud drove close, and Zoe wound down the window, so she could speak to Jack without getting out. He was wearing his headscarf.

"You OK?" he said.

"Yeah, no problems."

"See you in Baghdad."

When she got back to the hotel, he was waiting at the little stand that sold gifts just inside the hotel entrance, looking at a particularly hideous cigarette lighter shaped like a heart. It had a picture of Saddam on the front and an American bomber swooping overhead. When you opened it, red and blue lights started flashing as if the plane had dropped its bombs.

"Buying a gift for someone special?" Zoe asked.

"No, I was just thinking, it's a strange way to spend Valentine's Day." He put the lighter back down. "Well, I'd better go and write this up."

"See you at dinner?"

"Oh yes," he smiled, "mustn't miss Paul telling everyone how he escaped from Amazonian drug lords in a canoe made from a hollowed out tree trunk."

"Or Janet saying 'That's nothing' and then telling everyone

how she escaped down the same river in an umbrella?" Zoe laughed.

"Or the Journonator leaping up from the table and searching all his pockets to see which of his phones is ringing."

"Don't forget to watch out for Peter's report from Fallujah," she said, then, in an imitation of Peter's dramatic television voice, added, "This is Peter Shore, MTN, Hell."

When Jack had wandered off, Zoe checked her watch. He was right, it was the fourteenth of February; she'd been so involved in Iraq she hadn't realised. Strange that she should have run into Peter on this of all days. She shrugged and went to call the *Informer* and tell them about Fallujah.

<hr>

Adel looked back at the business card to make sure he had copied the email address right. He hunched over the computer screen, worried someone might read what he had written, ill at ease in the unfamiliar Internet cafe. The manager had looked him over warily when he came in, and Adel could feel the man's eyes on his back now. He would have preferred to send the message from his regular Internet cafe, but it was safer somewhere he was unknown, just in case the email was ever traced back. The customer on his left was engrossed in a computer game, but Adel felt sure the man on his right was stealing glances over his shoulder. He forced himself to remain calm, reminded himself there was no reason for them to be interested in what he had written. He read through the message again. It was important there was nothing in it to arouse the journalist's suspicions, or alert her in any way. He didn't want to frighten her off—and if she took the message to the Americans it could be disastrous.

Dear Zoe, do you remember me? I am Zaynab. You come to my house to ask about my husband and children, who were killed by Americans. Do you publish your article? I looked for it on the internet, but I can't find it.

I ask my friend, who is speak English, to write this message. I am so happy there are foreigners like you who tell the truth about Iraq. If there is some help we can give you in your work please tell us. Life is very bad for us, and we are asking your help to tell the world how we are suffering in Iraq.

Adel felt guilty about using his mother's name without her knowledge, but he was sure if he used his own name the foreigner wouldn't trust him. He was exposing his mother to danger, but even the Americans could not suspect an old widow. And at any rate, he reminded himself, he had done nothing more than send a message trying to find out what the journalist had written about his father: if the Americans came asking questions, that was no crime.

He had told no one of his plans, because he wasn't sure what they were, or how far he intended to go. At times, he dreamed that he would be the first Iraqi resistance fighter to take a foreigner hostage, and thought how that would stun Abu Khalid, who wasn't even interested in Adel's help, and just sent back messages through Selim telling him to wait. He thought how Abu Mustafa, who just used Adel as a look-out and delivery boy for ammunition, would react. But at other times the reality of it came to him, and he wondered what he would do with her once he had captured her, where he would hold her, how he would guard her. And sometimes he heard his father's voice—he could even see the look of disapproval on his face. He didn't need his father to tell him that a woman journalist was a poor substitute for an American soldier, but perhaps she could lead him to someone more interesting. At any rate, he decided sending the first message couldn't do any harm. First he'd establish the line of communication, then he'd decide what to do.

It had been easy enough to turn the conversation to hostage-taking and ask Selim what he knew about it: Selim loved to boast. Adel hated the way he gave himself airs, as if he were an expert, but what he had to say was useful all the same. The thing was never to sound too keen, Selim said, you had to let them come to you. "Like a lover," he had said. Press them too hard and they'd get suspicious: you just opened the way to them and they would come to you. The journalists were the easiest, because they were always hungry for new stories and information.

Adel had set up a new free hotmail account with an innocuous-sounding name that could never be traced back to him or his mother. He pressed send, logged out of the account and went to pay. He would not come back to this Internet cafe again, but would find another. It was important not to leave a trail.

⋯⋯⋯

The address Benes had been given for Dr Afaf led to a simple, pleasant house in a quiet neighbourhood. There was a small patch of garden in front; the flowers were well tended and the path to the door was spotless. When he had calmed from his initial anger, Benes had debated for some time whether it was wise to come: it was not, strictly speaking, a proper use of army resources, and he would need to bring two Humvees full of men and a translator. But when Hawkes came and asked him when they were going to find out what had happened to the "doctor chick", he decided that following up the possible endangerment of a civilian contact who had helped their work at the hospital was a reasonable use of resources and, more importantly, that with the platoon sergeant's backing, he would get away with it. The house was fairly close to where the platoon was pulling a checkpoint, which made it easier. As the Humvees drew up in front of the house, he reflected this was not the best entrance to make, in numbers and heavily armed, but with the situation as it was in Baghdad, and standing orders on how he could travel through the city, there was no avoiding it. He decided to take only Hawkes and the translator to the door, in order not to frighten the family. The translator, a nervous young Iraqi who had replaced the last one after Captain Parks discovered he was taking bribes, knocked at the door. After a while a man in his early middle age appeared—probably the husband, Fuad, Benes thought. When he saw Hawkes and Benes, he drew back inside with a look of fright.

"Tell him not to worry; we're not here to cause anyone any trouble," Benes said. "We're just trying to find some information." The man looked on fearfully as the translator spoke. "We're looking for a Dr Afaf. Does she live here?"

"She...she is not here," the man stammered in English, to Benes's surprise.

"But this is her house?"

The man nodded reluctantly, then looked as if he wished he had lied.

"But she is not here," he repeated.

"Are you her husband?"

He didn't reply. He looked confused, as if he hadn't understood.

"Ask him if he's her husband," Benes told the translator.

"He says no."

"Tell him there's nothing to be afraid of," Benes said. "We just want to make sure she's OK. She hasn't been at work for a while, and the hospital asked us to check up on her."

"He says he doesn't know where she is. He hasn't seen her."

"Ask him who he is."

"He says he's a relative."

"Can we speak with her husband?"

"He says he's not here."

"Can you ask him what his name is?"

The man hesitated.

"Abdullah," he said. His voice sounded a little choked off, and Benes wasn't sure he was telling the truth.

"Can we come in?" Benes asked.

"She is not here," Abdullah said in English. Hawkes, who looked to be losing patience, took a step forward, and the man immediately backed away. "But you can come," he said.

"Get Moon and Gutierrez to look the place over," Benes said to Hawkes. Inside, the house looked clean and well cared for. Benes detected signs of Dr Afaf everywhere: in the colours she had chosen for the furniture, in the careful arrangement of ornaments on the shelves, in the vase of flowers on the table—but the flowers were dead and needed changing. There was a picture of a baby on a side table, and Benes remembered Afaf telling him that her child had died.

"Don't go tearing the place apart," he told Moon and Gutierrez. "This isn't a raid." The soldiers went cautiously from room to room, weapons ready, but didn't disturb anything.

"Anyone else living here?" Benes asked.

"Just Dr Afaf and her husband," the translator said. "Mr Abdullah says he is only visiting."

Benes looked at the clean, tidy rooms and wondered if they would be so well cared for if the woman of the house had been missing for a week. The flowers were the only sign of neglect.

"Place is empty, sir," Gutierrez said. "No sign of anyone. Only way to check further is to start tearing it up."

Benes shook his head.

"I've had enough," Hawkes broke in, stepping up to Abdullah menacingly. "You tell us what the fuck's happened to her or we're going to fuck with you."

Abdullah backed away fearfully.

"I don't know, I don't know," he said.

"What have you done to her?" Hawkes growled.

"Me? I not do anything to her. I look for her, but I cannot find her," he stammered. "Please. Believe me. I never hurt her. Please, you find her."

"Where should we look?" Benes asked. "Where could she be?"

"I don't know."

"Any idea, anything at all?"

But Abdullah said nothing, just spread his hands in a gesture of helplessness.

"We're getting nowhere," Benes said to Hawkes. "Let's get out of here."

Hawkes gave Abdullah one last menacing glare then followed him out of the room. A thought came to Benes as he stepped into the sunlight, and he turned back towards the house.

"Mr Fuad?" he called.

"Yes," the man who had said his name was Abdullah replied, looking up. Benes could tell from the cornered look in his eyes that he realised he had been caught. He was her husband.

"We're just trying to find your wife and make sure she's OK, sir," he said.

Fuad came forward nervously to the door and nodded.

"Is there anything you can tell us that might help us find her?"
He wanted to tell Fuad not to worry about anything he might

have heard, that there was nothing between him and Afaf—but then Fuad might not have heard anything, and anyway Benes didn't know how to say it.

Fuad shook his head. He looked at Benes, a strange sort of pleading in his eyes. "Well, OK, I guess we'll keep looking," Benes said, though he had no idea where to look.

"Please," Fuad said as they turned to leave. "Please if you find anything…" his voice tailed off.

Benes looked back at him.

"Sure," he said. He turned to the Humvee.

⁌ ⁍

When Zoe saw the message from Zaynab, she felt guilty and embarrassed. Here was a woman who had lost her children and her husband, asking to see the story Zoe had written about it—and she hadn't even been able to get it in the paper. "I am so happy there are foreigners like you who tell the truth about Iraq," Zaynab said, and Zoe burned with shame. She remembered how she had felt that day in Zaynab's house, how she thought she would tell the world Zaynab's suffering—journalism that mattered. And she remembered how quickly she had forgotten about Zaynab, swept along in the headlong rush of events. At first she wanted to close the message and put off replying to another day, but she knew she couldn't. She had to answer this poor bereaved woman who had trawled through the Internet, searching for her dead husband's name, looking for a piece Zoe had never written. She wondered how to reply without wounding Zaynab further: she could lie and say that the piece had appeared in the paper but not on the website, but she thought Zaynab might ask her for a cutting or a photocopy, or worse, simply see through the lie, and she couldn't bring herself to do it. She wrote:

Dear Zaynab, thanks for your message, it's good to hear from you. How is your daughter? Is she recovered from her injuries? I hope you and she are okay.

I'm sorry you couldn't find the piece about you. I wrote it but I'm afraid my editors haven't used it yet. I'm still hoping

230

to persuade them to, because it's an important story and I believe it should be told. I'm so sorry to have to tell you this, but I am still trying and I will let you know if the story is published.

Please let me know if you need anything or if I can help in any way.

Zoe read the message over and debated the last line: it sounded a little too much like adding insult to injury, after she had already failed to do the one thing she could to help Zaynab. She deleted it, and sent the rest of the message, promising herself she would try to find a way of getting Zaynab's story in the paper. Perhaps there would be a slow news day, when Nigel was desperate for something. And now she had Zaynab's email address, so it would be easy to arrange photos, and update her story.

Nouri was still lying in bed when his mother said he had a visitor. At first he lied that he was too unwell to get up, hoping she would send whoever it was away: he didn't want his old friends to see what had become of him. But when she said the man's name was Abbas, and that he said he had been in prison with Nouri, he sat up and told her he would be there in a minute, and then went to wash his face.

Abbas was waiting in the front room, sitting easily like a man who had never been forced to lie in the dirt in a prison cell. He was transformed from the man Nouri remembered from Abu Ghraib: his beard neatly trimmed, his hair newly cut, dressed in pressed black shirt and trousers, the uniform of the militia. Nouri was conscious of his own dishevelled appearance, his long hair and beard, and the dirty old dishdasha he had pulled on. His sense of embarrassment only grew when he learned that Abbas had been released some time after him and had only been out of Abu Ghraib for a few days.

"They said they had arrested me by mistake," Abbas said. "They said they got the wrong man, and I wasn't going to argue with them."

Nouri hadn't expected to see any of his fellow prisoners again; he had thought they would want only to forget their time inside, as he did. But Abbas was full of concern for him and kept addressing him as "my friend". He said he had tracked Nouri down after he got out of Abu Ghraib, that it hadn't been difficult to find him, just a matter of a few questions here and there. He didn't reveal the full purpose behind his visit until he had talked Nouri into leaving the house and walking to a nearby cafe— "You need to get out," he said, and Nouri's father agreed. Nouri tried to avoid the eyes of everyone they passed on the way there and kept his own on his feet except when someone greeted him and he was obliged to look up. Once they were sitting in the cafe and had their glasses of tea, Abbas told him why he had come: he wanted Nouri to join the militia.

"The Shia need to act," he said. "The Sunnis have their insurgents, who do we have to fight for us? The Americans? You know they will not help…they are only interested in themselves. They will do nothing for us unless we force them. Already the Sunni have attacked our people in Najaf, and there will be more."

Nouri hesitated. When the Americans first arrived in Baghdad, and the militias began to emerge, he had kept his distance from them. Many of those who joined were unemployed, young men who hung around street corners and in cafes, and all of a sudden they were taking over and telling others how to live, what was allowed and what was not. Like most of his friends, Nouri had preferred to wait and see what the Americans would do and keep up the demand for elections, which the Shia would be certain to win because of their numbers. But after his time in Abu Ghraib, he believed most of what Abbas said was true: that the Americans had no intention of giving up control of Iraq, that they wanted the country's oil and wealth, would set up permanent military bases, and install Iraqis who were loyal to them in a puppet government. And besides, Abbas was not like the other militia members he knew—he was a serious man.

"Don't think the militia needs you," Abbas said. "We have thousands already. I came to you because I want to help you."

⇥⊷⊶⇤

Adel was incensed when he read Zoe's reply to his email. His father, his brother, his sister, all murdered in their car, and this woman would not even put it in her newspaper? She didn't even bother to pretend, to make up some lie or excuse; she just told his mother directly that their deaths weren't important enough for her editors. The foreigners were all the same: there was no difference between the Americans who fired the bullets and this British journalist who pretended to care only to throw it back in his mother's face. In his fury, he forgot that he had sent the message to trap the journalist, and was about to write a reply when he stopped himself. He was glad, at least, his mother would never read her message.

But, despite his anger, a part of him was relieved: the more he had thought about it, the less sure he was he wanted to take it any further. It was one thing to dream of being the first to capture a foreign hostage, it was something else actually to do it. He signed out of the hotmail account.

Chapter Nineteen

Mercenaries

20–27 February 2004

BENES THOUGHT HE must have come to the wrong place. The building ahead looked nothing like he had expected. It was almost a relief: if they couldn't find the hotel, then he could turn round and change his mind, fail to keep the appointment and avoid the mistake he feared he was making.

"You sure you got the right address?" he asked the translator in the back of the Humvee over his shoulder.

"Yes, sir," the translator replied. "Al-Hamra Hotel."

Benes looked back at the tall concrete building as they approached, and wondered if this could possibly be where the journalists stayed. It looked like a hotel, but he could see at a glance that it wasn't secure: before they even reached the entrance, he could already see multiple ways of taking the building. There was a cinder block blast wall, but it was too close to the hotel to be of much use against a serious attack, and would just trap those inside. No one was standing watch, and there was nothing to stop someone firing a rocket straight over the wall and into the upper floors: in fact, you could stroll up the street here, fire your rocket and walk away before the journalists even knew what hit them. There was no checkpoint at the entrance, just a gap in the wall with a flimsy metal barrier and a couple of scrawny-looking Iraqi guards with Kalashnikovs. Benes had seen enough of the Iraqis to know the guards were probably brave, but they'd be of little use if someone decided to drive a car bomb over them and through the entrance. He shuddered.

The guards looked nervous as soon as they saw the Americans coming. Gibbs signalled them to raise the barrier, and they looked at each other, as if unsure what to do. One started talking into a radio. As the lead Humvee drew level, the other guard came over and peered in.

"US army," Benes said, unnecessarily. "I got a meeting with a guest at the hotel here. Open up."

"Meeting?" the guard said.

"We're not waiting around exposed here," Benes said. "Raise the barrier and we'll talk inside." The guard hesitated. "Open up," Benes repeated.

The guard ducked back and opened the barrier. His colleague started to argue, gesturing with his radio, but Gibbs drove in before he could stop them, and the second Humvee followed. There was a small forecourt enclosed by the wall, the hotel on one side and some smaller buildings on the other, with people milling around, a mix of Iraqis and Westerners. Benes got out of the Humvee, noting the effect the soldiers' arrival had: everyone stopped what they were doing and stared with wary expressions on their faces. Another Iraqi with a radio was hurrying towards them, shouting at the guards who had let them in. Benes felt a flash of irritation, and started up the steps, calling to Hawkes, "Let's go, Sergeant." Hawkes and Jackson followed him, leaving the others waiting with the Humvees.

"Excuse me," the Iraqi with the radio was saying, "excuse me, sir, is there a problem?"

"No problem," Benes said, walking past him. "I got a meeting with a guest, is all." The Iraqi hurried after him and pushed in front again.

"I am Ahmad, head of security for the hotel."

"Good to meet you, Ahmad."

"We weren't told you were coming."

Benes had wanted to slip in and out quietly, but that was impossible when he had to travel around the city in force, with two Humvees full of heavily armed men. More people were milling around and staring now; they were coming out of the building opposite to see what was happening. The last thing he wanted was all this attention. He forced himself to remain patient.

"It's no big deal, Ahmad," he said. "I'm just here to meet with a journalist who's staying at the hotel. Nothing to worry about. You know where I can find a Zoe Temple?"

"Zoe Temple?"

"Yeah, from the *Informer*."

"One moment, I'll ask."

Ahmad ducked in through the hotel entrance, and Benes followed him into the lobby, where he found himself blinking in the gloom. This wasn't what he'd expected at all: he thought he'd find the journalists somewhere safe and comfortable like the Green Zone; instead, the hotel was a sitting target for an insurgent attack, and the lobby was straight out of the Seventies, complete with peeling wallpaper and a few old brown chairs.

It had been easy enough to find Zoe Temple. He'd forgotten her name from their meeting at the airport, and where she'd said she was staying, but he'd found her article on the hospital online, and emailed the paper she worked for. He got a reply direct from her within an hour, agreeing to meet. Benes would have preferred to call her into the base than meet here, where it could arouse the curiosity of other journalists, but getting permission for reporters to come on base was complicated, and he was fairly sure the XO wouldn't approve of what he was about to do. He knew it was risky: the journalist could easily make a story that could be damaging for the military out of what he was about to tell her—and get him in serious trouble. That, he knew, was why he was so short of patience for the hotel security man, who now seemed to be having an animated discussion with the clerk at the reception desk. Benes walked up and cut straight across it.

"I'm here to meet with Zoe Temple, from the *Informer*," he said.

"Yes, sir," the clerk said, "she is in the second building, across the courtyard." He pointed to a door that led outside. The security man started arguing again but Benes ignored him and crossed to the door. He knew it wasn't safe to blunder around an unsecured building like this, but Benes didn't see what else he could do. He emerged into a "courtyard" that was more like what he had expected to find: a large swimming pool in whose inviting blue waters a young woman in a bathing suit was doing slow, languid lengths, while people sat in small groups at tables beside it, drinking beer. Benes could see the condensation running down the outside of the beer cans, and tried not to think about it. The people at the tables looked like journalists, most of them badly out of shape, and dressed in scruffy approximations of military clothes, cheap "combat" trousers and desert boots. In one corner was a man who appeared to have three different cell phones strapped to his body for some reason. So they did live in some style after all, Benes thought, watching the swimmer turn gracefully at the end of the pool, they just kept it well hidden— though not, he noted, from the neighbours. The windows of the surrounding buildings overlooked the pool: a single sniper up there could take out half the people here before they had a chance to run for cover.

A tall man cut across in front of him, his hand outstretched.

"Peter Shore, MTN," he said, in a way that implied he expected Benes to have heard of him. He was wearing some ridiculous blue silk scarf draped around his neck, and his blond hair looked like he'd just blow-dried it. The man looked as if he thought he was on a film set.

"I'm looking for a Zoe Temple," Benes said, not taking his hand.

"Zoe? She's over in the second building. I'll show you," Mr Shore said, leading the way. "So what brings you guys over here?"

"Just got a meeting with Ms Temple," Benes said.

"You doing an interview? Because, if you are, we'd love something too. Wouldn't interfere with what Zoe's got planned at all; we're television you see. MTN," he said again, as if he thought Benes knew what it was.

"No, we're not here for an interview," Benes said. "Just a meeting. You want anything like that, you'll have to go through CPIC."

"You based in the Green Zone, Lieutenant?" Mr Shore tried again. They were close to the edge of the pool and Benes thought for a moment of the satisfaction it would give him to tip Mr Shore in, blue scarf and all, but forced himself to remain calm.

"You know, I'm not authorised to speak with the press in general," he said, "I'm just here to see Ms Temple."

As they came up to the second building, the door opened and two large bearded men came out, M-16 rifles slung across their backs, heading straight for him. Benes's stomach lurched—had he led Hawkes and Jackson into an ambush? He heard their weapons go up either side of him, and realised his own was in his hand before he'd even thought about it. Mr Shore, he noticed, had got out of the way in a hurry; Benes couldn't help but be impressed by the speed with which he'd separated himself from the soldiers.

"Easy, guys," the first of the two gunmen said, in what sounded like a South African accent, "we're on your side."

Benes looked him over, unsure. He was a bear of a man, clearly strong but grotesquely overweight, his sweat-stained T-shirt straining at his belly. The second was in better shape, similarly dressed in camouflage trousers and a black T-shirt. They didn't look much like Iraqis, and neither had made a move for his rifle. But to Benes, anyone with a gun and a beard was the enemy.

"Who are you?" he said.

"We're with Makepeace Security; we're working with you guys over here," the South African replied.

"You got some papers?"

"Uh-huh." The giant went for his pocket, and Benes watched his hand all the way. He pulled out his documents and handed them over. "We're contractors, working with your guys on the convoys." Benes knew there were private security contractors working with the military in Iraq: mercenaries in all but name, they guarded supply convoys and some bases to free up troops for combat operations. He looked through their papers: they seemed in order, though he wasn't really sure what he was looking for.

"You?" he asked the second.

"The same." He had a British accent. "We're together."

"What unit you with?"

"I told you, we're with Makepeace," said the South African.

"No, who's your contact in the military?"

"Major West at CJTF-7"

"Where's he based at?"

"He's in the Green Zone. Listen, what's the problem, guy?" the big South African said. There was an arrogance about him, a man not used to being challenged. "We're on your side."

"What are you doing carrying weapons around the hotel like that?"

"Got to get them to the car somehow."

"Uh-huh." Benes nodded. If any of the men in the platoon carried weapons casually like that, Hawkes would lay into them. "What's with the beards?"

"Trying to blend in. With the locals."

"Yeah? Well, you're doing too good a job of it. Gave us a scare."

The South African grinned in a way Benes didn't like. He noticed everyone was now staring at them; even the woman who'd been swimming lengths had stopped and was resting at the end of the pool, looking across. So much for slipping in unnoticed.

"If you're gonna carry weapons through the hotel they should be secured," he said. "Lot of civilians here."

"OK, Lieutenant," the mercenary said. "I'll be sure to mention our meeting to Major West."

"You mention it to anyone you like," Benes said. It would have been better to let it go, but the shock they had given him was spilling over into anger.

"Listen, we're on the same side, guy," the South African said. "I'm ex-military myself. We're the same as you."

"With respect, sir, you are not the same as us," Benes said. "We're fighting for our country. What are you fighting for?"

The South African stared at him a moment, then walked out, trailed by his silent British companion.

"Lieutenant Benes?"

He turned and saw the journalist he'd come to see. She looked exactly as she had the day he met her at the airport, sunlight in her blonde hair.

"Ms Temple."

"Please, call me Zoe." She gestured him over to a table, while Jackson pulled guard and Hawkes scowled over the scene. Mr Shore seemed to be hovering near them again.

"Excuse me," Benes said to him. "I want to talk to Ms Temple." Mr Shore nodded and looked awkward.

"Right. Well, see you later, Zo," he said, and moved away reluctantly.

"Sorry about the, uh, entrance," Benes said to Zoe.

"Oh, don't worry, Lieutenant," she said, pronouncing it the British way, leftenant, "I think you just made yourself very popular with the press corps."

"Yeah? How's that?"

"Well, no one really likes those guys. They're a bit arrogant. They're always walking around the hotel with guns. And they act like they're the big military experts, and we're just in the way all the time. So I think quite a few of us were rather pleased to see them put in their place by a real soldier."

Benes grinned in spite of himself.

"Do your guys want to join us?" she asked.

"They're fine."

"Can I get you a drink? Some beer?"

"Water would be great, if you got it, ma'am."

She signalled a waiter over, and while she asked for a bottle of water, Benes looked around. He forced himself not to think of the cold beer—it was torture to sit and watch others enjoy it while he couldn't. It was early evening and the place wasn't full, but some of those around the pool already seemed to have drunk a lot. He shuddered to think what would happen if the hotel came under attack later, when they'd had time to drink a few more beers.

"Thank you for agreeing to see me, ma'am," he began.

"Oh no, it's a pleasure. I haven't had a chance to thank you for tipping me off about the children's hospital, by the way. It was a great story, and hopefully we were able to do some good with it."

The waiter returned with a bottle of cold water, and Benes noticed that Zoe had sent some across to Hawkes and Jackson as well. He looked her over, remembering their meeting at the airport, and how she had reminded him of Afaf, though they looked nothing like each other. There was something about her he liked, the way she was direct in a place where everyone seemed to have something to hide. Under different circumstances he could have been attracted to her. But he had to be careful, he reminded himself: there was no knowing what she might do with what he was about to tell her.

"Yeah, well, you did a great job with the story," he said, and was amused to see her blush. She still had no idea of the consequences of that meeting at the airport: a chance encounter, a few minutes' conversation waiting for a bus, that had sent him back to the hospital, into Afaf's path—and had got her killed, or kidnapped, or sent her into hiding in fear for her life. Or perhaps it had done nothing, and she had disappeared for some other reason. Perhaps it had nothing to do with him after all, and he was flaying himself with guilt for no reason. "Must have really pis—ticked off someone in Washington, because my guys got sent back in there to straighten the place out."

"That's great!"

"Yeah, well, we did what we could."

"Perhaps I could do a follow-up piece? On how you've cleaned the place up?"

"Yeah, well, I guess you could." Benes realised he had better get off the subject before he said too much—if she wrote another story saying the military had been prevented from cleaning up the hospital properly, the higher-ups would know where it came from. "But that's not what I came to talk about." He hesitated. The problem with journalists was that you never knew what they might publish. This one might seem genuine, but he barely knew her. "The problem is, well, something else happened. *May* have happened."

Zoe looked puzzled. "I'm sorry, I don't—"

"Did you meet Dr Afaf at the hospital?"

"Yes, she was the contact you gave me. Really helpful—I couldn't have written the story without her."

Benes looked across at her. She was still so happy, so convinced that between them, they had done good at the hospital.

"Listen, this isn't—I mean, this is not for publication. What I'm about to tell you."

She looked confused. "OK," she said.

"I need you to give me your word. Because it could…could put someone's life in danger."

"OK," she repeated. "Look, the last thing I want to do is endanger anyone. What's happened?"

"She's disappeared."

"What?"

"Dr Afaf. She's disappeared. Nobody knows where she's gone."

"Jesus!"

"We wondered if you might have heard anything."

"Me? No, this is the first I've heard of it. I haven't been back to al-Iskan since I did the story."

"No stories going around? Something you might have heard as a reporter?"

"No, nothing. But then you don't. I mean, people disappear all the time in Baghdad..." She trailed off, as if unwilling to finish the sentence.

"Do you think you could ask around about it, see if you can find anything?"

"I...sure...of course I'd be happy to. But what happened?"

"She was helping us as well, with our work at the hospital, and, well, we're concerned that somebody may have seen her spending too much time around American soldiers for their liking."

Benes felt Hawkes's eyes on him, but the sergeant said nothing. Benes wasn't about to tell the journalist he was worried Afaf had been spending too much time with *him*—it was dangerous enough talking to her without taking the risk she might write a story about the Iraqi doctor killed for an affair with an American officer, or something like that. He looked at her again, wondering if he was a fool even to trust her with what he was telling her.

"God, that's terrible," she said." Do you...I mean, did anyone say something to suggest—"

"No, it's just that no one knows where she is, and the other doctors think that might be the reason. But you really mustn't publish anything about this. It's possible she may have gone into hiding: she could have heard she was in danger and decided to stay away from the hospital. So, you see, it's important you don't write about it."

"No, absolutely."

"And another thing: it would be better if you didn't say it came from us in any way. The military, I mean. If anyone was trying to do something to her because she was helping American soldiers, it's probably better if they don't know we're looking for her."

"Yes, I can see that."

"So you'll ask around...carefully?"

"Yes. I mean, I'll try. Though I don't know that I'll be able to find anything you guys can't."

Benes told her about his conversations with the hospital director and the other doctor, how there was no sign of Afaf at her home and her husband seemed frightened. He didn't mention his own visit to the house, but made it sound as if this information had come from the doctors—he didn't want to mention any more of his own involvement than he had to, just in case Zoe did write something about it.

"And let me know if you find anything?" he said.

"Yes, of course. I've got your email," Zoe said.

"Thanks," he said. "It's good to meet one of you guys who actually want to help for a change instead of just criticising."

As he walked out of the hotel, he wondered if he had done the right thing. All his efforts to find out what had happened to Dr Afaf had ended in failure. It was difficult, with the patrols and other duties the platoon had, to find time to continue his search, but he'd been to the Iraqi police to ask if they knew anything. No one had reported her missing, and no case had been filed. The officer he met, eager to please an American, had been all too ready to open a case and begin investigations at once, and Benes wondered if he was so diligent when Iraqis came in with stories of their missing relatives. But he could not be sure she had not decided to disappear herself, because of the danger he had put her in, in which case the last thing he wanted was to track her down, and he had visions of the police bursting into her home and tearing it apart, so he told them to leave it. She might even have been there that day, at her house, hiding from the soldiers in some secret place only she and her husband knew about, watching through a crack in the door as Benes stood on her carpets, in the room she had decorated, by the photograph of her dead child, willing him to leave without discovering her. Or she might have been safely somewhere else, at a friend's house or a relative's. If she was in danger, it was the right thing to do, to disappear without a trace from the hospital where her enemies could find her, and it was only natural she should not risk contacting him.

But other fears came to him, that her husband, who had seemed an innocent victim, was somehow involved in the disappearance, that he had decided to remove her from temptation, taken her away from the hospital where her work was and locked her up in some house—or, worse, that he had heard she was spending a lot of time at the hospital talking to an American soldier and killed her in a fit of jealous rage. Or Fuad could be the innocent man he seemed, searching for his wife, and she could have been abducted or killed by local extremists.

At any rate, he had reached the limit of what he could do, and he couldn't divert any more of the platoon's time to it. He'd even been to speak with Captain Parks about her, and told him that one of the doctors who had helped them at the hospital had disappeared.

"Hajjis are disappearing all the time, Lieutenant," Parks had said. "We can't have the US army sending out search parties every time one of them doesn't turn up to work. What can I do? Place is fucked up."

Then the idea of the journalist had come to him. Perhaps she might have heard something—and even if she hadn't, she could investigate it. Wasn't that what journalists did, investigate? She probably had a much better idea than he did of how to go about something like this, she'd frighten people less than two Humvees full of armed men, and the fact she'd written about the hospital and met with Afaf gave her every reason to be looking for her. There was a risk she'd write about the doctor's disappearance, but so long as she kept Benes and the military out of it, he didn't see that it would cause a problem. In fact, an article might even help.

All the same, he couldn't help returning to the thought that if he had not run into Zoe at the airport and mentioned al-Iskan to her, and if she had not written her well-intentioned article trying to get conditions improved there, Afaf would probably still be at work on the leukaemia ward today, wondering what had become of the American officer who briefly passed through the hospital to set up a patrol.

⊷⊷⊷⊷

Zoe watched as Benes left. She had been looking forward to seeing the American again, and thanking him for the tip about the hospital story. And she had been amused to find him in the courtyard, facing off with the mercenaries. She had arrived just in time to witness Peter duck ignominiously out of the way, and was struck by the contrast between his behaviour and Benes's calm self-assurance as he put the mercenaries in their place. The large South African had ordered her out of his way just a few days before, so Benes could hardly have done more to ingratiate himself with her, and then to crown it all he had dismissed Peter from their table like a nosy schoolboy.

But she had been devastated to hear about Dr Afaf. She had liked the calm, serious doctor, and was horrified to think that her story might have put Afaf in danger. She wondered, though, about Benes. She thought she had detected something when Afaf spoke about Benes at the hospital, and he seemed to be taking an unusual interest in what was, in the end, just one more disappeared Iraqi among thousands. And he did seem very keen to keep himself out of the story. Had the doctors' concern been about Afaf spending too much time helping the Americans—or one American in particular? She knew she would have to avoid mentioning any of this to Nigel Langham. The merest suggestion that an Iraqi doctor at the hospital she had written about—"our hospital", Nigel had taken to calling it—had disappeared after a secret affair with an American officer, and Nigel would want it all over the front page. And that, Zoe thought, would write Afaf's death sentence, if she was still alive. If Afaf was alive—Zoe winced at the thought. She would do what she could to find out what had happened to Afaf, and keep it from Nigel and the paper. If she found out that Afaf was all right and a story couldn't do her any harm, then perhaps she would write about it. And if Afaf was dead—but Zoe didn't like to think about that.

Peter inevitably came asking questions about what the American officer had wanted to talk to her about, but it was easy enough to send him away saying it was "something she was working on", and implying it was an exclusive she didn't want to share. After all, it was what he would have done if he had a story: the previous week, it turned out he had only got as far as the outskirts of Fallujah, and his report consisted of a few shots of empty streets.

The problem was that there wasn't much Zoe could find out. Benes had made the mistake she found a lot of people made, of thinking that journalists had some special channels of information, or ability to uncover things others couldn't. In fact, most of the best stories came from people like him, as the children's hospital did. She went back to al-Iskan, and spoke with the director, Dr Kamal, and the young woman doctor who had sought out Benes. Neither of them knew any more, and Dr Kamal urged her not to enquire further.

"It could make things worse for her if they know you are looking for her," he said.

"They?" Zoe said. "Who? If who knows?"

"I don't know," Dr Kamal shrugged. "Her enemies. I don't even know if they exist, but if they do—"

"But you think she's alive?"

Dr Kamal held up his hands.

"I don't know," he said.

Zoe had been to Afaf's house, but her husband wouldn't let her inside, and refused to speak to her. He was clearly very frightened of something, but it was impossible to tell what. Ali spoke to his friends, and Mahmoud asked the drivers, who were always a potent source of information, but no one had heard anything. Eventually, Ali made the grim suggestion that they try the morgue, and Zoe reluctantly agreed, but to her relief it had received no unidentified bodies that answered Afaf's description.

"It is very difficult," Ali said. "Every day, someone goes missing in Iraq, and most of them are not found. And if she does not want us to find her, then I think we will not."

"Then you think she's alive?"

Ali did not answer for a moment.

"I hope," he said.

Chapter Twenty

Karbala

2 March 2004

ZOE WOKE WITH a sense of foreboding. For a moment, she didn't know where she was and sat up in a panic. She saw the familiar room at the al-Hamra, sunlight spilling in through the thin curtains, everything as it should be, but she had the feeling there was some danger looming over her. She glanced across at the clock, and it came rushing back to her: today was the day of Ashura, and she was going to Karbala. She lay back in bed for a moment and toyed with the idea of not going, of staying in Baghdad and watching on television, but she knew she couldn't do that. The *Informer* would recall her to London, and she would be taken off the story. At the very least, she would lose the respect of the other journalists. There was no way out of it.

The first time the journalists had been aware of the coming Ashura was when it intruded into the cosy world they had made for themselves behind the hotel's blast walls. It had been late evening in the restaurant, the last food served and serious drinking in flow, the pianist finished for the night, when someone started playing dance music on the hotel stereo. It was something they'd done many times before, but on that night the manager had come hurrying into the room to ask them to turn it off. He had practically implored them, and there had been real fear on his face.

"Please," he said. "Shia people will make problems for us. This is an important time for them."

When the music was switched off, Zoe had heard them in the distance, chanting to the sound of drums. The next day she had seen them out on the streets of Baghdad, a column of men dressed all in black, holding up the traffic as they marched to the beat of a drum and swinging silver chains, whipping themselves in time to the beat. It was a Shia ritual, Ali explained, to mark the martyrdom of one of their most important saints. But these were just the preliminaries; they were leading up to the day of Ashura, when hundreds of thousands of Shia would flock to the city of Karbala, where the saint was buried. The rituals had been banned under Saddam, and this was the first time they were taking place for decades. It was a major story, and under normal circumstances the journalists would have been falling over each other to be there. The problem, as far as Zoe was concerned, was that hundreds of thousands of Shia massed together in the same place on a fixed date was likely to prove too tempting a target for the insurgents to ignore. They had, after all, already attacked the other Shia holy city of Najaf. Ali said the public displays of mourning were already causing tension between Baghdad's Shia and Sunnis, and for the last few nights, the sole topic of conversation at the al-Hamra had been Ashura, and the journalists' fears that Karbala was going to be attacked.

Karbala was a long drive, and in order to reach the city they had to leave early. Outside, it was already warm, despite the hour: the season was turning, and it was going to be a hot day. Most of the journalists were already out loading their cars. Zoe found Ali and Mahmoud waiting, both of them looking sleepy. She had talked over the dangers with them several times, but even Ali, who was usually against taking unnecessary risks, seemed to feel it was a story they couldn't miss. The authorities were promising tight security, he said.

The Baghdad traffic was worse than usual, the roads jammed with cars and buses making their way to Karbala. As they left the city, they were joined by a long column of people on foot, stretching into the horizon ahead like some scene out of the Middle Ages, pilgrims walking the dusty road all the way to Karbala. It would take them hours, but they seemed untroubled. The road led through Mahmudiya, but Ali said he didn't believe the insurgents would risk anything with the sheer numbers heading through today, and there was a heavy American presence around the town. They turned onto a road Zoe had not been on before, where the traffic thinned considerably. Apparently, there was a choice of routes to Karbala, and most of the pilgrims had taken the other one. The road led through dense groves of palm trees, the greenest country Zoe had seen in Iraq. As they rounded a corner, Zoe saw what looked like a checkpoint ahead, except that the armed men were not wearing any uniform she recognised, but were dressed all in black. Ali muttered something; he sounded concerned.

"What is it?" Zoe said.

"I don't know."

"Should we go back?"

But the men at the checkpoint had already seen them and were waving down the car. Ali got out to speak with them, while Zoe watched nervously from the back seat. After a few minutes, he returned and one of the men in black waved the car through.

"That was very interesting," Ali said. "They're the Mahdi Army. You know? One of the Shia militias, their leader is Moqtada al-Sadr. They've made their own security to check who is coming to Karbala."

"And the Americans let them?"

"It seems. When I told them you're a journalist, they were OK. But I don't think it's wise to let them set up checkposts like this."

As they got closer to Karbala, they came upon the line of pilgrims again, and the traffic slowed to a crawl. Zoe could see men in black whipping themselves with chains, and others, dressed in white, who were striking themselves on the forehead with swords until blood ran down their faces. Several had large open wounds. There was a parking area, which was as far as cars were allowed to go, and Ali said they would have to continue on foot. As Zoe got out, she saw Jack Wolfe's car pull up alongside and he came over, wearing his headscarf, and suggested they go in together. Mahmoud wanted to see the rituals, so they all went: Zoe, Ali, Mahmoud, Jack, and his translator Adnan.

As they joined the press of people, Zoe thought she had never seen a crowd so large; it went on as far as she could see in every direction, women hidden beneath headscarves and abayas, men in long black dishdashas, Afghans in round woollen caps, Iranians in green silk scarves, and locals pushing wooden barrows laden with food for the pilgrims. The tide of the crowd pulled them towards the city. They came to a human chain, men in civilian clothes with their hands linked, holding back the masses while others frisked people before letting them in. There would be little chance if a suicide bomber struck at the cordon, where thousands of people were pushing forward, and Zoe felt safer once they were through. On the other side, the crowd grew even denser. They were being funnelled into a broad street, and Zoe could see nothing but people and the tops of buildings.

"I don't like this," Jack said. "We're too exposed. We need to get out of this street."

"I think we're all right," Zoe said. She was feeling reasonably safe after the security checks, and she didn't want to miss anything after going to so much trouble to get here.

"No, it's too crowded."

"Well, where do you want to go then?"

"Up one of those side streets." He pointed at a narrow alley that led off to one side: it would be hell fighting through the crowd to get there.

"The security looked pretty good to me. I think it's OK."

"I don't like it."

"OK, you go then," she said, irritated at his insistence. "I'm going to hang around here." He hesitated a moment, and then he was gone in the crowd. She pressed on, craning her head to see what was going on. The sound of drums came from ahead, and people were setting up wooden barrows along the path and handing out food. As Zoe passed, a woman smiled at her from under her black abaya. There was a strange muffled sound from ahead, as if something very heavy had just crashed to the ground, the sort of sound you hear at construction sites. Zoe looked up, but no one else seemed troubled.

"What was that?" she asked Ali.

"I don't know," he said. "Maybe someone is letting off fireworks."

They walked on a little, and then Zoe heard the screaming. She turned and saw the fear in Ali's eyes before he was abruptly swept away from her. The crowd seemed to buckle as if a great wave of people was rolling back through it, and then it broke over her and she was being pushed and pulled along with it, she was being dragged and something knocked the breath out of her; there was a second sound, like the first but louder, and another wave of people came, moving in the opposite direction. She was tossed and turned by the two waves breaking on each other; no sign of Ali or Mahmoud, only arms, faces, eyes, fear, blood; she stumbled; she knew she must not fall, for if she fell there was no hope; she was carried by the crowd, her feet lifted from under her; there was another of those sounds, more screaming; something knocked into her, and she tried desperately to keep her balance, but she was going down, down to certain death among the whirl of feet.

Someone caught her as she fell, and she was being pulled through the crowd. She tried to look, but she couldn't see who it was; the only hope was to go with them. Another of the crashing sounds. All around was panic, people shouting, hitting and scrabbling at each other in their desperation. Her unseen guide was cutting across the tide of people diagonally, like a swimmer crossing a current, towards the side of the street. When they got there, he pulled her into a narrow alley, and she saw it was Jack, of course, as it always was. She saw Adnan, but there was no sign of Ali or Mahmoud. The alley was less crowded, but people were beginning to spill into it, and Zoe decided it was too dangerous to speak; she didn't know how the people would react to hearing English. They kept walking away from the main street, turning from alley to alley as another of the strange crashing sounds came from behind them. It was hopeless to go back for Ali and Mahmoud; she would never find them amid the confusion, and Zoe only hoped they did not linger searching for her. Two more crashes. She realised she was thinking with a strange clarity; after her initial confusion in the crowd, she didn't feel at all panicked or even afraid. It felt as if time had slowed down. Another crash—that made seven. She didn't know why she was counting them. Adnan was leading them, guessing the way out. They had reached an alley that was almost deserted, but she could still hear shouting and screaming in the distance. There was a new sound, closer, one Zoe knew. Adnan stopped and ducked behind the cover of a wall, motioning them to do the same.

"Shooting," he breathed.

Zoe saw a group of men run past the end of the alley, firing rifles at some unseen target. She pressed herself against the wall; she could see ants running across the peeling paint.

"It's safe," Adnan said, and they went on. Zoe looked to see who the gunmen had been shooting at, but the street was empty.

"Who were they shooting at?" she asked.

"No one," said Adnan, "ghosts. It's panic."

The sounds of screaming were getting further away, and Zoe felt as if they were moving towards safety. They were out of the narrow alleys and on a wide main road; there was a howling of sirens and Zoe saw a line of ambulances, seven or eight of them in a row, driving as fast as they could, the back doors hanging open.

"How do we get to the car?" Jack asked.

"I don't know," Adnan said.

They wandered around aimlessly for some time, trying to get their bearings, but it was impossible in the unfamiliar city. Several more ambulances passed. Zoe felt numb. There had been an attack, just as everyone had feared, but she still couldn't make out what had happened. She didn't even know if the crashing noises were bombs or something else. All she knew was that people had died, people who had been standing by her in the crowd just a few moments before.

Eventually, Adnan found a taxi driver who agreed to take them back to the car park. They sat in silence, not risking conversation. When they got there, to her relief Zoe saw Ali and Mahmoud waiting by the car with the same look of shock she had seen on the faces of Jack and Adnan. When he caught sight of her, Mahmoud called out and pointed, until Ali dug him sharply in the ribs and told him not to attract attention. Ali told her a lot of the people in the crowd were turning on foreign reporters and blaming them for what had happened. She spoke with Jack, and they decided to leave for Baghdad immediately, the two cars travelling in convoy for safety. As they left the city, they saw the great column of faithful was still streaming in, undeterred. Winding down the window, Ali asked them if they had heard what had happened and warned them not to go on, but they kept walking towards the city.

"They say they trust in their fate," he said.

The traffic was light heading back to Baghdad; they were some of the first to leave, and Zoe called the *Informer* from the road. Nigel told her it was a "massive story", and she would be "all over the front". When they came to the Mahdi Army checkpoint, there were many more armed men than before, and the mood had changed. They had clearly heard what had happened in Karbala, and ordered Zoe out of the car while they searched it. They looked over her press credentials and passport for some time. Jack was getting an even harder time behind; they were shouting at him in Arabic.

"They say we can leave," Ali said, but Zoe hung back. They were dragging Jack away from his car. Adnan was trying to intervene, but the militiamen were ignoring him.

"I think they're suspicious because he's wearing an Iraqi headscarf," Ali said. One of the gunmen interrupted him. "They say we must go now."

"Tell them we're together, we can't leave without the others."

Ali spoke with the gunman, who looked at her mistrustfully. She watched as Ali went over to help Jack; twice, she saw him gesture back towards her.

"Get in car," Mahmoud said, but she shook her head, so he got out and stood beside her. She watched as one of the black-clad men made a mobile phone call. He spoke for some time, and then appeared to soften. They allowed Jack to get back in his car.

"It's OK," Ali said, walking back to her. "Let's go."

She didn't let Mahmoud start until Jack's car had passed. He had come back for her, so she would wait for him.

"They wanted to arrest him," Ali said. "I asked their leader to call a man I know, who is one of their commanders. If he hadn't spoken with them, they would have taken Mr Jack."

After that, it was just the long drive back to Baghdad. Zoe didn't even notice when they passed through Mahmudiya. The sound of screaming kept coming back to her, and people's faces, their mouths wide open, their eyes pleading. When they reached Baghdad, Jack came over.

"Thanks," he said. "For the checkpoint. Thought I was in trouble for a bit there."

"No, I mean, it was the least I...thank you, for, for...you know, in the crowd."

"I just saw you and grabbed you, that's all. Maybe this thing isn't so clever after all," he said ruefully, holding up his headscarf. He was trying to act calm, but he was clearly shaken. They stood in silence; there was so much she wanted to say.

"I'll see you later," he said. She went to the Internet cafe to try to find out more about what had happened in Karbala. The details weren't clear, but the wire reports said there had been nine blasts in all, and the Americans thought they had been a combination of suicide bombs and mortars fired into the city from the surrounding countryside. There were unconfirmed reports of squads of armed men firing into the crowds. There had been a near simultaneous attack on a Shia shrine in Baghdad. No one knew how many people had died; some were talking of hundreds. Zoe read it all in a daze; the words on the screen seemed detached from what she had experienced, as if they were about somewhere else—or rather, as if they were rewriting the reality of what she had experienced, replacing the unbearable with something that could be contained in words, understood.

Back in the room, exhausted, she could barely bring herself to type, but she knew all she needed to do was write her story and then she could rest. When it was done and she had emailed it to London, she tried lying on her bed, but she couldn't sleep and the images came back to her, so she went down to sit in the restaurant, even though it was too early for dinner. She needed some response to the death and pain. Several of the others were there already, but there was none of the usual laughter; the mood was sombre. Almost everyone had been in Karbala; they all had their own stories of what they had seen. Kate had watched a woman die before her eyes and kept staring into space as if she were watching it play out again and again. Paul had been hit in the face by what he thought was human skin, torn away in the blast. Zoe sat and talked to whoever came to the table. Different people arrived and left, moving on once they had told their stories. It was as if everyone felt the need to unburden themselves. Peter came in.

"Were you there?" he asked her.

"Yes," she nodded. "You?"

"Yes. How…how are you?"

"Alive," she said. It was the first thing that came into her head—it seemed the only reasonable answer to the question. He sat and talked a while, then got up to go and do a piece to camera. She wondered how he would look to people watching back in London, with that haunted look in his eyes. Would they know what it meant? She didn't order any food, but sat and smoked. Kate had just got up and left with Mervyn when Jack came in. He walked straight over and sat down opposite her.

"You all right?" he asked. She shook her head and looked at him. "Want a drink?" he said, seeing her glass empty.

"I want to get out of here," she said.

"Come and have a drink in my room."

She nodded and stood up without speaking, followed him from the restaurant and up the stairs, all in silence. When he closed the door of the room behind her, he stood and looked into her eyes for a moment, then leaned in and kissed her. She clung to him.

⊷⊶ ⊙⊷⊷

Later that night, she lay in the darkened room and felt him breathing next to her. She raised herself on one arm and looked down at the outlines of his face in the faint light. It had been desperate love-making at first, the two of them not speaking, just clutching out for life after what they had felt of death. But then the *Informer* had called when they were resting after, and Zoe had to suppress the urge to hysterical laughter as the voice of Nigel Langham came over the line, enthusing about her piece and asking if she was all right. Jack had been struggling to keep silent through the call, and when she hung up he started laughing, and the laughter had lost its desperate edge and it was as if all the distance between them vanished, and they were laughing together, and then they were serious, and then they were making love again, and it had come to Zoe, this strange feeling, that there was no other place she should be but in his arms, in a seedy, run-down hotel in Baghdad, with the sound of the guns outside.

Chapter Twenty-One

Belonging

2–6 March 2004

SINCE THE NIGHT of his father's death, Adel's mother had changed. The woman he had known, who fussed and doted on her children, the beating heart of the household, was gone, leaving in her place, it seemed at times, little more than the empty shell that had once contained her. She would sit for long hours, staring into space, her mouth working as she mumbled silently to herself; at other times he would catch her trembling and leaning against a doorway, unable to stand. When he asked her something, she would give short, vacant replies. The mother who had protected him all his life had become weak and frightened, and every time Adel saw her shrink from a knock at the door or from the sound of gunfire at night, his heart fell away. But after the attacks on Karbala, she had come alive, shouting and raging at the television.

"What is this madness, this evil?" she shouted. "To do this to innocent people trying to pray? Is this what we have become? This?"

In vain, Adel had tried to reason with her.

"The Shia brought this on themselves," he told her. "This is their fault. You haven't seen them, on the streets. You've been in the house; you haven't seen the way they are parading themselves in front of us, closing the streets off so they can hold their processions, as if they want to taunt us. They think they are going to turn Iraq into a Shia country. Well, now they have had their answer."

But his mother would not listen, and though Adel would not admit it, he doubted his own words even as he spoke them. He had argued with Selim about the attacks in the cafe in Adhamiya a few hours earlier, late-afternoon sunlight clinging to the cigarette smoke in the air.

"But they're not the enemy, not the *real* enemy," he had said. "We should be concentrating on fighting the Americans, not killing Iraqis."

"But they *are* the enemy," Selim had said. "They're all the enemy. Can't you see that? This is not just about the Americans. Why do you hang around with those old men from the army? Tell them to join us." Selim went on to boast of the growing strength of the foreign fighters. In Fallujah, he said, they were already fully integrated with the local resistance. And they might be, for all Adel knew, and then again they might not—it was hard enough to know what was happening in Baghdad, let alone another city. It wasn't even clear who was behind the attacks in Karbala. Selim was adamant the foreigners were behind it, but he was vague on the details, and Adel suspected that if Abu Khalid's cell was involved, he had not confided in Selim. Whoever was responsible, Adel feared they were doing the enemy's work for them, helping his father's killers. After these attacks, the Americans would have the excuse they wanted to stay in Iraq, to tell their lies about a civil war and pretend they were there to prevent one.

At least that was what he told himself as his mother raged at the television, but there was something else stirring beneath, though he didn't like to think about it: the thought that his mother was so alive in her anger because the images of shrapnel tearing through the crowd in Karbala were all too close to her own memories of the bullets and fragments tearing through the car, through her husband and her children.

⊸⊶⊙⊷⊰

At first, Nouri didn't want to go to Karbala. It had taken a second visit from Abbas before he had agreed to join the militia, and he still didn't feel entirely at ease. He felt guilty going to Karbala for Ashura while his parents had to stay in Baghdad because of his father's ill health, and though he did not admit it to Abbas, he was afraid he would not be able to handle the crowds. He had only just gathered the courage to leave the house and go out on the streets. But it had been impossible to refuse, and so he had gone, and instead of the expected rituals, he had spent the day carrying the wounded to hospital, using as makeshift stretchers the wooden barrows people had brought food on, pieces of corrugated metal roofing and doors torn from their hinges. And amid the death and blood all around him, Nouri had forgotten his own fears and lost himself in doing what little he could to help, plunging again and again into the crowd while others fled. Some of the militia tried to hunt down the attackers, but Nouri was content helping the wounded. He realised, whatever he had said and agreed to do before, that was the day he truly joined the militia. His own sufferings were small in comparison with those of the people around him, his share of the burden they had to bear in the struggle for freedom. That day he no longer felt helpless, alone; he felt part of a community that could endure all it had to endure, even this, and claim its freedom with its own hands.

--->==@ @==<---

The journalists rid themselves of the horror of Karbala by turning their minds over to theories. They sat late into the night discussing the attacks. Who was behind them, how had they smuggled the explosives in, what was their motivation, what did it all *mean* for Iraq? Some thought those responsible were trying to start a civil war, some that it was a response to Shia political assertiveness, some that they were just trying to create as much chaos as possible. The Americans came up with evidence that the Jordanian terrorist Zarqawi had been behind the attacks: some of the journalists believed it, some didn't, and the two sides grew heated with each other. Unable to come up with satisfactory answers to any of these questions, they fell back on that favourite recourse of the press when it runs out of facts: trying to predict the future, and the words "civil war" were bandied about more than ever.

At first Zoe wanted to keep what had happened between Jack and her from the others. It was not just that it was no trophy seduction—her friends, after all, couldn't stand him—it was that she didn't want it damaged by their disapproval or made into just another liaison of convenience, sex in a war zone. But she couldn't hide it, not when she sat with him in the restaurant and curious eyes sought them out, the way they spoke, their private smiles.

"So what's going on with you?" Kate asked one evening, mischief-eyed. "Hardly seen you in days."

"Oh, I've just been working," Zoe said.

"Really? You seem to be spending a lot of time with *somebody*."

"Well, I—"

"I was wondering when you two were going to get down to it. You two've been making eyes at each other since the day you met. I'm amazed it's taken you this long."

That surprised Zoe. She hadn't really thought of him that way until the night after Karbala—well, maybe a little before—but certainly not as far back as when they first met.

"Look, I know that you don't like him—" she began.

"What's that got to do with it?" Kate waved her aside. "So long as you're happy, Zo. If you can put up with the guy, then I can."

She tried bringing him over to join the others at their table one evening, but it wasn't long before his sense of humour was setting them on edge, and after that she decided not to repeat the experiment. She, though, wanted to know everything about him, and gradually she got it out of him in murmured bedroom conversations, her head nestled on his hip, looking up at him as he spoke: the poor background, the fight to go to university, the parents who had died early, the two younger sisters he had supported, how he got a job on a Dublin newspaper by turning up with his own exclusive on a government contracts scandal, then caught the notice of the London press and moved across the Irish Sea. She had wondered why his paper had sent such an inexperienced correspondent to cover the Iraq invasion, when the other papers were sending well-known names. It turned out the *Post* didn't have much of a foreign news operation, and Jack had used his holiday time on a trip to Baghdad ahead of the invasion.

He had returned with a notebook full of stories and contacts, effectively making himself the Iraq expert on the paper. As she learned more, she saw, as she had always known, that the confidence, the air of unconcerned amusement, the cynical humour, were all a mask, and beneath it he was vulnerable. The doubts that still came to her from time to time—why he didn't care about the child who had lost his leg, how he had known to get out of the crowd in Karbala—she brushed aside as jitters, agents of misinformation.

She received an email from Lieutenant Benes, asking if she had found out anything more about Afaf, and realised that in the turmoil of Karbala she had forgotten all about the missing doctor. She wrote back saying she had found nothing, but was still looking. In truth, though, after talking it over with Ali, she realised she had nowhere left to look, and no one left to ask. She had drawn a complete blank.

A shadow was stretching over her: her time in Iraq was coming to an end, and as the days counted down, she cursed fate that she should have found Jack in Iraq, where her presence was entirely dependent on the *Informer*. David was on his way to take over, and there was no way she could stay on in Baghdad without the paper to pay her bills and justify her presence. Jack, who was permanently based in Baghdad for the *Post*, could no more leave than she could stay. In theory, she was supposed to be back in six weeks, but Henry Haight or Nigel Langham could change their minds on a whim and send someone else instead.

"I don't think there's any chance of that after the job you've done here," Jack said. "There's more chance you'll get home and realise you're sick of Iraq, and I won't be able to drag you back out here."

⊷⊷◉⊶⊷

In the days that followed that one giddy night after Karbala, Saara's mood grew sombre: after watching the carnage, the Christians were worried they might be next, and there was no chance of the family letting her out to work again. Some families had even stopped going to church, worried about an attack, though Saara's father refused to take that step. She said she had never seen him so worried—every day there seemed to be news of another Christian family deciding to leave Iraq, at least for a time while things were bad, and packing up the house where they had lived all their lives. Mahmoud's fear must have shown on his face, because she smiled and said, "Don't worry, there's no chance of us leaving. My father is adamant that no one is chasing him out of his own country."

And so the man who didn't even know that Mahmoud was seeing his daughter became his secret ally. But he worried what he would do if the family did decide to leave: it was easy for Christians to get asylum in the US or other Western countries, but it was not so easy for a Muslim like him to get a visa to join them—and he had no official justification to follow her anywhere. And so he began to live in dread of the day she would tell him she was leaving.

⋅→▷●◁←⋅

The day came, inevitably, when Zoe had to leave. The night before she had lain awake with Jack in bed, drinking red wine he had got hold of from an Iraqi who claimed it came from Saddam's old cellars.

"Zoe Temple. Her body is a…" he had murmured, brushing his lips against her skin, and they had made love and promised they wouldn't let this enforced separation end things for them, before falling asleep tangled in each other's arms.

He drove with her to the airport to see her off, but the security guards wouldn't let him in without a ticket, and they had to bid each other farewell in the car park, not risking a kiss in the open, but looking into each other's eyes. When he was a speck in the distance she felt afraid for him, alone in Iraq, and for a terrible moment thought she wouldn't see him again. She was so preoccupied that she barely noticed the bizarre, opulent architecture Saddam had lavished on the airport that once bore his name, or the long delays that had the other passengers fidgeting and irritable, and it was only on the plane that she was jolted back to her surroundings, when she remembered they had to fly up through the danger zone in a tight spiral again. The other passengers around her were silent as they taxied to the end of the runway, faces sweating in the sunlight that came through the windows. The captain's voice came over the tannoy, "Ladies and gentleman, we've been requested to hold our position because of ongoing hostilities in the area."

Ongoing hostilities? Zoe looked out of the window and craned her neck to see what was going on, but there was nothing on the horizon except low-lying bushes. It was getting hotter inside the plane; she could feel a film of sweat gathering between her back and the seat. This couldn't be the best place to wait, exposed on the runway. There was the sound of an explosion in the distance, and Zoe saw a cloud of smoke rising on the horizon. That seemed to make up the pilot's mind. Without any further announcement, he pushed up the engines and they were rushing down the runway. Zoe stared out of the window as they took off, scanning the ground below. What was that among those low bushes: someone moving, or just the shadows jumping as the plane turned? Then they were turning into the tight cork-screw again, the ground tilted away from her window and all Zoe could see was sky, and she looked across the aisle and could make out a patch of runway through the far window. She was willing the engines on—*rise, damn you, rise!*—and then they were levelling off in the sky, safely out of range, and looking out of the window at the tiny cars on the road below, she wondered where Jack was, amid all the violence and fear down there, and when she would see him again.

PART THREE

Spring 2004

Chapter Twenty-Two

IED

25–28 March 2004

ONE FOOT AFTER the other, in the steps of the man who went before, Benes trudged on, in the monotony of danger. They had made this patrol so many times it was as natural as breathing, hands ready on his gun, eyes scanning the horizon, listening for a sound out of place. Your mind could not be on edge all the time so your body did it for you, took over silently the process of watching. Moon was out in front tonight: he had volunteered, joking that it was a full moon, so it was his night, the Night of the Moon, and then Hernandez had howled like a wolf and they had all laughed. The full moon made it more dangerous—most of the enemy didn't have night vision goggles, but they didn't need them in the moonlight. It was the last time they would walk the patrol, out in the fields on the edge of Baghdad, and Benes was allowing himself the luxury of thinking that each step was one he would never have to take again, through the watching dark, the listening fields, the hunched, conspiratorial farmhouses— even though he knew it meant he was letting down his guard, and he couldn't afford a moment's loss of concentration. The platoon had been back out here a week, walking the patrols no one wanted to walk, but this was their last night in the fields. The next day they would be back in relative safety on base, and they were due to head home from Iraq in a couple of weeks.

Home. He had noticed a strange mood in the men over the last week, a giddiness, a fever, like children at the end of the school year, and he had felt it in himself too. They had been told so many times they were going home only to be denied, but this time they believed it, because their replacements from the 1st Cavalry Division had started to arrive, because helicopters and tanks were being moved out to Kuwait, ahead of being shipped home. He walked on and allowed himself to think he would soon see his wife and son again, hold Juan in his arms, make love to Maria, feel her body against his and breathe in her scent—

But he couldn't let himself dwell on that yet; he was still in Iraq, where a moment's loss of concentration could kill him. He was so tired, so crushingly, grindingly, pulverisingly tired that it was hard to concentrate any more, hard to keep his mind on anything but staying awake, to prevent himself slipping into dreams and half-dreams as he dragged his feet one after the other. Sleep kept trying to draw him back into her maze, clutching soft-fingered at the edges of his mind. He had watched 1st Cavalry officers arriving with the innocence of men who hadn't spent a year in Iraq, and he recognised in them what he had once been. He remembered the hopes he had brought with him to Iraq, how he would serve his country, and he thought that in a couple of weeks he would be dragging himself home, not in glory but glad to survive, and he wondered if it was always like that for a soldier.

Everything he had tried to achieve in Iraq had gone wrong. He had never found out what had happened to Dr Afaf. The hospital, where he thought he might have done some little to help, was much as it had always been: a little cleaner perhaps, but that was all. And, ever with him was the thought of the checkpoint that night, the shattered car and the girl with her eyes torn away.

The lights of the patrol base showed through the trees ahead, and Benes began to feel the tension fall away from him. Just a few more steps. The snipers at the farmhouse were already watching over them, so no one would attack now. As he reached the door and pulled off his helmet, he felt sweet relief run through him: the platoon had survived its last patrol; never again would they walk those fields. While they were out, the platoon who were relieving them had arrived and were making themselves as much at home as the farmhouse's meagre comforts allowed, so the men gratefully gathered their kit and loaded up the Humvees for the short drive back to base. They set out in convoy, the guns swinging overhead. A lot of the officers believed it was riskier to travel at night, but Benes preferred it. There was no traffic and you could drive fast all the way. Benes sat back in the Humvee seat, beside Gibbs at the wheel, feeling the stress of months draining away from him. All that lay ahead were a few weeks on base in Baghdad and then the battalion would be on its way home.

There was a searing white light from ahead and Benes looked up. He felt something hit him, an invisible force that slapped the breath out of him, then he heard the sound and he knew it had happened, the terrible thing he had almost convinced himself wouldn't happen. The platoon had been hit.

IED.

❖

"Someone tried to get in here last night." Mahmoud had barely sat down when Saara told him.

"What? Who?"

"I don't know. We were asleep and there was a noise outside; it woke me up. There was someone out there; I saw him. I looked out my window and he was there, down by the door. I couldn't see what he was doing, but I ran to Yusuf's room and woke him. Yusuf got the gun and went straight to the window. He meant to fire a warning shot over his head, but he had it set wrong, to automatic, and he must have fired twenty bullets, b-r-r-r-r, all over the street."

"Did he hit him?"

"No, Yusuf fired over his head, but when he heard it he ran away."

"Maybe he was just trying to steal your car," Mahmoud said.

"Maybe," Saara paused, as if reluctant to go on. "But it looked like he was doing something to the door, maybe trying to get in."

"He was probably just a thief trying his luck. He could have got the wrong house." There were several houses standing empty in the neighbourhood, easy prey for thieves, but Mahmoud didn't like to mention it, because the reason they were empty was that their Christian owners had fled.

"That's what my father says," Saara nodded, "but..." She hesitated.

"But?"

"What if…what if he comes back?"

"Well, he knows you're armed now and ready to shoot. That may make him think twice."

"What if there are more of them?"

"It was just a thief," Mahmoud said, but his mind was racing. He wanted to reassure her, but he knew it could just as easily have been an extremist. And that next time there might be more of them and a warning shot from the bedroom window might not be enough. He wondered if he should tell her to leave, to get out of the city while she still could, but then they would be apart, and he didn't want that.

"Did you hear what happened to our neighbours?" she asked.

"No. What?"

"Their son disappeared two weeks ago, Yaqub, his name was. At first, they didn't know what had happened; they were beside themselves. His father and brothers went looking for him. They didn't know if he'd been arrested by the Americans or if he'd been in some accident. Then the letter came. He'd been kidnapped, and the people who had him wanted $10,000, or they said they'd kill him. There's no way they could raise $10,000. The father is a doctor—even when he's paid he makes hardly any money. He sent a message to the kidnappers pleading with them to reduce the ransom, but they refused. He tried everything, but he couldn't find the money. Eventually he asked a friend in the police to help him. Two days after he asked, they sent him his son's head in a sack."

Mahmoud felt sick.

"Do they know who the kidnappers were?" he said.

She shook her head. Mahmoud stared at his feet. He knew what he had to say, but it was hard to speak.

"You should go," he said.

"What?"

"You should leave," he said, looking up at her. "Get out of Iraq while the situation is bad. I mean, I don't want…it's just… it's not safe for you. It's better if you go." As he spoke the words he felt as if he were giving up everything he had ever wanted.

"I don't want to leave you," she said simply.

"I don't want to leave you either. But I don't want…something to happen to you."

"I can't go," she said. "My father refuses to leave; he's adamant, he's staying. He said my mother and sister and I can go, and he and Yusuf will stay, but my mother and I agreed we are not leaving him. And I'm not leaving you."

Mahmoud smiled at her, not knowing whether to be relieved or afraid. Outside, the gunfire echoed in the distance.

⋆⋅⊷⊷⊷⋅⋆

Benes wanted to run to the front of the convoy and find out what had happened, but he knew he shouldn't. The insurgents often set one IED off, then waited for the soldiers to come to the aid of their fallen comrades and set off more or ambushed them with gunfire. He spoke into the radio: nothing came back but static. The convoy had slewed to a halt, and he could hear Jackson swinging the gun above his head. Benes scanned the horizon, a bare stretch of road, no bridge or buildings for the insurgents to hide behind.

"Jesus…fuck…no, man…shit shit shit." Moon's voice came over the radio, he was alive at least.

"What happened?" Benes said.

"We've been hit." There was shock in Moon's voice. He had been in the lead Humvee, along with Hernandez on the gun and Gutierrez, who had just switched fire-teams because of his promotion, at the wheel.

"You need medics?"

"No. Maybe. I don't know." There was a silence. "It's Gutierrez, he…" His voice trailed off. That was enough for Benes. He told Gibbs to call for a medevac helicopter, and he was out of the Humvee and running. Ahead of him, he could see Hawkes and Zivkovich running forward too, but beyond them nothing but a cloud of dust where the IED had gone off. Moon appeared out of it, blood smeared on his uniform, and then they were inside the choking dust, and Benes almost ran into the metal shape, a twisted impossible mess that it took him a moment to realise was what was left of the Humvee, and there in the front seat, looking straight at him, was Gutierrez.

"Gutierrez, you OK?"

Gutierrez didn't answer. A few seconds passed before Benes realised that his expression didn't change: he didn't blink; his face was completely still. Moving closer, Benes saw that his legs weren't there, his body was gone below the waist, his left arm too, a red wet patch where it should have been, and for a moment Benes didn't understand, and wondered where they were, and then he knew. He heard moaning and Hernandez was pulling himself out of the wreckage. He went to help, but Hernandez shook his head and said, "I'm OK…Gu…Gutierrez."

Doc Martinez, the medic, came running up behind him, out of breath. Benes pointed him to Gutierrez, but he knew. Martinez bent over Gutierrez and then looked up and shook his head. Somehow Hernandez and Moon only had cuts and scratches. Gutierrez's body had taken the full blast; it was his blood smeared all over Moon. Benes looked at Gutierrez's face, untouched, perfect, as good-looking as he had been earlier in the evening when they were all getting ready to come out. He looked so alive—the look of concentration so fierce in his eyes, the brows drawn down just a little, the lips just apart as if he were catching his breath—that Benes couldn't believe he was dead. He sank to his knees beside the body and held Gutierrez's head in his hands. Hawkes came and stood beside him, looking down at Gutierrez's body.

"Let's find these motherfuckers and take them out," he said. Benes nodded and they spread out into the night. Steele spotted some movement behind a grove of trees and they opened fire until bits of bark and wood came spraying out, but when Hawkes went forward there was no one there, of course, just a dead bird.

They didn't find the insurgents. The explosives had been hidden in a culvert under the road and detonated by remote control. It took them some time to find all the pieces of Gutierrez and gather them up, then they lifted what was left of his body into the back of Benes's Humvee and placed the rest of him on top. Benes and Hawkes sat on either side of him to keep the body from slipping, and they began the long drive back. The weight

Benes felt on his shoulder was no longer Gutierrez, was less and less him the further they drove from the place where he last drew breath, as the warmth went out of him. Gutierrez, who an hour before had been laughing about what he would do when he got home. He shouldn't have been in the lead Humvee: if he hadn't got the promotion he'd been so proud of, he'd still have been in Benes's Humvee.

They went on, a funeral procession, Benes and Hawkes pall-bearers, the platoon Humvees honour guard and mourners, the only salute the barking of the dogs, the only pall the light of the moon. It couldn't be undone—Benes couldn't take the world back, knit the bones he was carrying back together, breathe air into the voice. He had wanted to take all the platoon home alive. He asked himself what he had done wrong, what the mistake had been that had killed Gutierrez. If he hadn't been in the first Humvee, another of the platoon would have been. The route, the time of the journey, were all planned and ordered from above: Gutierrez's arrival on that spot, at that time, had been decided by others before Benes got there, before the platoon even set out. There was no way of knowing the route would be targeted that night, and there was nothing Benes could have done, no decision he could have made, that would have changed it. As they drove, Benes realised that of all that had gone wrong in Iraq, this, the thing he had feared most of all, was the only one that was not remotely his fault. He had endangered Afaf, he had made the mistake that killed the children, but there had been nothing he could have done that would have saved Gutierrez.

In the days that followed, there were times when Benes wanted to take a gun and a Humvee and drive out of the base and shoot the first Iraqi he saw. But he forced those emotions down and tried to keep himself busy thinking of the rest of the platoon, who were going through the same feelings. Gutierrez's body had been taken from them with indecent haste, a helicopter waiting for them when they arrived back at base, the crew with a docket for Benes to sign. And they had left him there, in the night, the eyes of the platoon on him, all waiting for him to say something, to make it right, but no words came. He had to write to Gutierrez's parents and tell them how their son had died. Together, the battalion went through the ceremonies of remembrance, but the words that had stirred Benes at memorials for men he didn't know sounded empty to him now, as if they were play-acting at grief. It was better when the men spoke. Gutierrez's friends each said a few words, Moon's in particular stayed with Benes a long time, and he wished he'd heard them before he wrote the letter to Gutierrez's parents.

"I'm no good at speeches and all," Moon said, "all I know, Gutierrez was my friend. I guess before we came here we all had some messed-up ideas of what combat would be like, and Iraq and all, and it's been a lot tougher than most of us imagined, but, well, the only thing that hasn't been a disappointment is the guys I've served with, and none more than Gutierrez. He was brave and loyal. He never let anyone down. There's no one I'd rather have at my back."

Wrapped in his grief, Benes didn't even notice that some small-time newspaper had been closed down by the CPA, and a few Shia were protesting about it.

Chapter Twenty-Three

Hostages

31 March–9 April 2004

ZOE WAS IN a Paris hotel bed with Jack when she saw the bodies in Fallujah. She was lying back sweetly exhausted, the bedding in a satisfied tumble, their clothes strewn happily about, a bottle of wine, half drunk, neglected on the bedside table, bells from some church spilling in with the spring chill through the open window. Jack was on leave from Iraq, and Zoe had taken a few days' holiday so they could meet in Paris, away from newspaper offices and inquisitive flatmates, but now Iraq was intruding, swimming across Zoe's eyes from the muted television. There was no mistaking those colours, that dust-laden sky, those palm trees in the distance. A crowd was pushing its way across the screen, men jostling each other to get nearest the camera, waving their arms in the air, their mouths open in silent cries. In the middle of the crowd, hanging from a bridge, was something black Zoe couldn't quite make out. Tired, she closed her eyes to block the images out. There were news reports from Iraq every day, crowds celebrating or protesting something or other. She began to drift out to sleep, borne by crowds of celebrating Iraqis, the sun beating down and the sound of a bell, and then she realised what it was, that black thing hanging in the centre of the crowd, and she was wide awake and sitting up and it was there on the television, unmistakable, a human body burned and charred, hanging from an old iron bridge. Not one body but two. She recognised the bridge, too—she had stood just feet from it in Fallujah.

"Jack!"

She scrabbled for the remote control to turn the sound up. Jack sat up in bed, rubbing his eyes in confusion. The sound on the report was, inevitably, in French, and she flicked impatiently through the news channels until she found one in English. She heard the familiar tones of Peter Shore: "Four American civilian security contractors were today killed and dismembered in the Iraqi city of Fallujah. In scenes which some viewers may find disturbing, their mutilated and partially burnt bodies were hung from a bridge and displayed before celebrating crowds. It appears the Americans, who were working for a private security firm, were the victims of a planned ambush. It is believed they were lured to the city centre, where they were attacked by a crowd who set their cars alight, then dragged them from the vehicles and beat them to death. In scenes that are frankly too disturbing to show, the crowd then mutilated the bodies of the dead Americans."

Zoe watched in horror as the scenes played out in streets where, only weeks before, she and Jack had been. The tape was looping round behind Peter's voice, showing the crowd by the bridge again, but it wasn't the bodies in the background that horrified Zoe most, it was the expressions on the faces of the Iraqis around them, expressions of joy.

"The message from Fallujah yesterday was stark. Now every Westerner, whether in uniform or not, is a target in Iraq."

Jack was on his mobile phone, calling Adnan in Baghdad for more information.

"Yes, which channel?" he was saying. "Hang on, I'll see if we've got it." He reached for the remote control and started changing the channel till he came to one of the Arabic news networks.

"Adnan says they're showing more on the Arab stations," he explained.

The screen showed the Americans already dead but not yet hung from the bridge, one of them on the ground, his body burning, the other being dragged out from beneath a car and one of the Iraqis kicking at his head until he kicked it clean off the body.

Later, Zoe lay curled beside Jack. The touch of his body couldn't put it from her mind. Those things, those objects hanging from the bridge, could have been any of the contractors she saw every day at the al-Hamra, men she passed in the lobby or shared the lift with, men she had noticed casting their eyes over her body. For the first time, the thought of returning to Iraq frightened her.

⋅►═◉═◄⋅

Adel watched the television pictures from Fallujah and felt he was one with the crowd. His hands dragged the Americans from under the car, he could feel their blood warm on his skin; he was pouring the petrol, lighting the match; he was swinging the metal pipe and bringing it down again and again; he kicked the American head until it separated from the body; he was shouting with joy and running after the car as it dragged the body of the American through the streets. The Americans were not just killed, they were humiliated: their bodies played with before the world's eyes, taken apart, rearranged, strung up from the bridge like puppets, children's toys. This was what Adel had waited for, and he was impatient for more: for the Americans to try to retaliate, to find what awaited them in Fallujah, for the fighting to spread to Baghdad. As always, it was impossible to find out who was behind the killings, but this time it was not because of a wall of silence, it was because every faction was claiming them. Selim said it was the foreigners; Abu Mustafa said it was the former army cells in Fallujah. The whole country was behind them—the whole country except the Kurds. Even the Shia were sending messages of support.

Adel looked at the television pictures and thought: maybe Abu Khalid's Hollywood videos were coming to Iraq after all.

⋅►═◉═◄⋅

Benes was briefing one of the 1st Cavalry officers who were taking over from the division when they moved out in a few days, explaining the layout of the sector, when Captain Parks looked in through the open door.

"Something going down in Sadr City," he said. "We're rolling. Get your guys together."

"Sadr?" Benes looked up. "You sure?"

They had been on edge all day, expecting to be sent to

Fallujah. Sadr City was the other side of Baghdad, and it was Shia territory.

"That's what they said," Parks replied. "Sadr's crazies are trying to take the place over, cop stations, government offices, the lot. You probably want to roll too," he said to the new officer. "It's your guys getting hit."

"Shit," Benes said. "The marines are about to go into Fallujah, and we're sent to do fucking police work in Sadr."

⇥⊙⊙⇤

Nouri ran fast down the street, clutching his rifle. The sound of shooting came from ahead. He could hear the helicopters moving overhead, and the rumble of the American tanks moving somewhere in the streets nearby. He saw militia fighters running across the open end of the street. A few civilians were still on the streets, trying to get home, running under the cover of the wall and stopping from time to time, looking fearfully around them. Nouri slowed to help an old man, but Abbas shouted at him from behind to keep going.

It had begun in Freedom Square, an irony that was not lost on Nouri. That was where the Americans made their first move against the militia, when they stormed the offices of its newspaper, brandishing a piece of paper signed by Bremer, the American who ruled Iraq, saying the paper had to close for sixty days. Nouri marched with the others to protest in the square: the militia had rescued him from despair after the Americans tortured him, and now they were turning on it as well, but he knew that together they were not helpless, as he had been when he was alone in Abu Ghraib. United, they could stand against the Americans. The leader spoke out against the closure and denounced Bremer. Then the Americans arrested one of the leader's deputies. After that, the order went out: take control of Sadr City. Abbas had called at Nouri's house and told him to get his gun. They had moved swiftly and seized the police stations and government buildings. Now the Americans were responding, pouring into Sadr City in force, and the sound of shooting echoed in the streets where Nouri had grown up.

As he reached the end of the street and rounded the corner, the Americans came into view. He could see the face of the nearest soldier; he looked young and scared. Nouri aimed his rifle and fired.

→≡●≡←

"What the fuck is going on?" The 1st Cavalry lieutenant was crouched low beside Benes in the alleyway. "I thought these were supposed to be Shia."

"They are," Benes replied as a round hit the wall behind him, sending plaster painfully onto his back: it missed by inches.

"Then why are they fucking shooting at us?"

"Does it matter?" Benes said, and he felt a wall of heat in his face as someone fired an RPG from close range. He dived to the ground as the blast went off somewhere behind him. It did matter, though, because it meant the Americans were facing a fight on two fronts, Sunni and Shia at the same time. They were out there, darting around furtively. They thought they could hide in the shadows, but Benes could see them all clearly through his night vision goggles. They had ambushed a 1st Cavalry patrol; there were seven or eight wounded. Not police work after all, then.

→≡●≡←

"The whole thing's an unbelievable mess," Jack's voice came down the line to Zoe from Baghdad, distorting and breaking up from time to time. "The Americans had eight dead yesterday in Sadr City, and one in Najaf. No one knows how many Iraqi casualties there are. And all when they're about to go into Fallujah."

Zoe pictured him sitting in the familiar room at the al-Hamra as he spoke, the television on silently in the background, notebooks strewn around the desk. He had flown back to Baghdad after their few days in Paris, while she returned to London.

"And the crazy thing is, it's got nothing to do with Fallujah," he said. "It's completely unconnected. It's all because Bremer shut down this newspaper that's connected to Moqtada al-Sadr's group, the Mahdi Army. Moqtada wasn't happy about it and denounced Bremer in a sermon a couple of days ago. Bremer responded by sending in troops to arrest one of his closest lieutenants, a guy called Yacoubi."

Zoe was hunched over her desk at the *Informer*: with so much going on in Iraq, Nigel Langham had drafted her in to help with the coverage.

"The Mahdi Army came out in force. The Spanish got it in the neck in Najaf, before the Americans sent in backup. There are soldiers from all over the place, from countries who only sent them because they thought there'd be no trouble in the Shia areas, who've suddenly found themselves on the frontline. Apparently some poor guy got killed with a grenade in the mouth, they just put it in and pulled the pin.

"So the Americans have managed to start a separate fight with the Shia just when they were planning to go in and deal with the Sunnis in Fallujah. And meanwhile—no one will confirm this—the word is that the Iraqi army, the new one, is refusing to go into Fallujah. All the guys the Americans have just trained up so they can take over from them just refused point blank to fight against their fellow Iraqis."

Zoe was impatient to be back in Baghdad and almost resented Jack for being there without her. There was no word from Nigel yet on when the paper was sending her: David had two more weeks to go in his stint, and as he was the more experienced correspondent, the paper would want to keep him there as long as possible while the story was moving so quickly.

"The fighting's still going on in Sadr City today," Jack said. "They've sent in tanks and Apaches. God knows where it's all heading: it's not as if they can back down over Fallujah now. They've got the whole place sealed off. If they don't go in, the Sunni insurgents will treat it as a victory."

"Listen, be careful," she said. "Don't go getting killed before I get back there."

"Don't worry," he laughed, "we can't get anywhere near the action; I'm just cooped up in the hotel all day. The only danger is whether I can survive another of Janet's stories."

Nouri was sitting on the floor. He didn't know the owners of the house, but they had let him and some of the others rest there. Outside he could hear the American tanks. They had been doing well until the Americans sent the tanks in, but there was no way they could hold out against tanks and helicopters. He had seen the American helicopters flying overhead before, but not what they could do when they fired. Nouri knew the militia would not be able to hold onto the police stations, had probably already given them up while he and Abbas were fighting in the streets, but even if they lost all the territory they had captured in the night, they would have won something the Americans couldn't take back. The Shia had stood as one. And now the fighting was spreading: in Najaf, in Basra, in Kut, the Shia were rising.

"Have you seen these?" another fighter who had just come in asked, his face blackened with smoke, as he passed round a piece of paper. The owner of the house had brought in tea and was passing it out to the young men sitting on the floor, their guns beside them. The owner was as old as his father, and Nouri was glad his parents' house was far away from the fighting. Abbas passed him the piece of paper the other fighter had brought in: it was a letter from Fallujah. Incredible. The Sunnis of Fallujah were writing to Sadr City to tell them they supported them in their struggle against the Americans. Nouri wondered how they had got the letters out of Fallujah and felt a reckless glee in his heart.

Exhausted, Benes sat down in the cover of the armoured vehicle and took the water the sergeant was offering. He looked across at Hernandez, his face hidden behind dirt and smoke and sweat, the lines around his eyes a latticework of pale skin. Sadr City was, supposedly, back under control, though it didn't look that way. The smell of gunfire hung in the air, and helicopters came in low overhead. It was the heaviest fighting they had seen in Iraq, and they were supposed to be leaving in a matter of days. It had given him and the men something to think about besides

Gutierrez's death: at least their last memory of Iraq would not be carrying a fallen comrade through the night.

Everyone had been looking the wrong way, he thought, expecting trouble from the Sunnis. Nobody had been paying attention to the Shia. And they were still looking the wrong way, watching Fallujah when the real crisis was where he was, crouched in a smoke-blackened street. The Americans had already lost the struggle for the hearts of the Sunni, but they were losing the Shia right now on the streets of Sadr City. The place was a slum packed with civilians, and more than once he had seen women and children peering anxiously out of the windows at the fighting.

⁂

"It has started in Fallujah," Selim told Adel before he even had time to sit down.

"When?"

"Today. I spoke to our brothers a short time ago." They were in the cafe in Adhamiya, and several men were crowding round the table to hear the news. "The Americans are trying to fight their way in, but we are holding them back, Alhamdulillah." Nobody was touching his tea; all attention was on Selim. "And our brothers launched a surprise attack on them, in Ramadi, where they were not expecting to fight, and killed a dozen of them, maybe more. They will have to send some of their forces from Fallujah to save the rest."

"The Americans are finished," one of the men said. "Even the Shia are fighting them now." Adel glanced at Selim when he heard this, but his friend said nothing.

Adel hung around the cafe all day, hungry for news from Fallujah. He ran into an old friend he hadn't seen since the Americans invaded: Ibrahim had been with his relatives in Mosul, where he said he had been with the local resistance, but he had had to leave after he was identified in an operation. Now, like Adel, he was frustrated to find himself in Baghdad.

This was the moment Adel had longed for, to avenge his father's death, but he was cut off from the stage and could not play his part. He spoke with Abu Mustafa, but the old man told him they had to wait for the fighting to come to Baghdad: a foolish attempt to get into Fallujah and the cell would be uncovered, they would be captured or killed, and no use to anyone. He approached Selim, but the message from Abu Khalid was the same: they needed fighters in Baghdad for the coming battle, and he should wait.

—⊶⊷—

"It's getting worse," Jack said down the line. "The Americans have hit a mosque in Fallujah, and there are reports of forty dead. The Americans say the insurgents were using the mosque as cover to fire at them. They probably were, but hitting it's just going to increase the anger. Sadr City's quieter, but the Shia are coming out everywhere now, practically the entire south has risen up, Nassiriya, Amara, Kut. The Americans are sending reinforcements south: they've cancelled the troop rotation out of Iraq— apparently they're turning soldiers round on their way to the airport and sending them back to fight. They're fire-fighting all over the place, but their commanders still seem to be throwing the fuel on. They just don't get it. They've announced they want to arrest Moqtada. Arrest him! They can't even take control of the streets from his militia."

In the background, Zoe could hear the sound of a helicopter and men shouting. "Where are you?" she asked.

"On the road to Fallujah, but it's hopeless, they won't let us anywhere near. All we can do is interview the convoys coming to deliver aid. They're getting turned away as well."

—⊶⊷—

Benes was in the Internet cafe on base writing an email to Maria about the fighting in Sadr City when he heard the battalion commander was calling a general meeting. Benes's hand hovered over the keyboard for a moment, then, reluctantly, he deleted the line he had just typed in: "I can't wait to see you again." If the colonel wanted to speak to the entire battalion, it could mean only one thing, that the redeployment was cancelled. Benes had just washed the dirt of Sadr City from his tired body. In the auditorium, he could see it in the faces of the other soldiers; many looked so grim it was as if they had already had the news. And when the colonel spoke, he confirmed it. The redeployment was postponed; they were staying in Iraq to deal with the crisis; those who had already left on their way to Kuwait were being called back. The battalion was being sent south to take over from coalition allies who had been overwhelmed by Sadr's militia in the south central zone, the Shia heartlands. They were heading for Kut at dawn.

Benes had never been there, had no idea of the place, except that it was Shia and the Mahdi Army had taken it over from a small force of Ukrainians who had been posted there as part of the international coalition. He felt exhausted. It was only the thought of going home and falling into Maria's arms that had kept him going, but he knew he couldn't show the platoon. All around him were men in shock. He got up and headed back to the Internet cafe to email Maria with the news.

⇒⊶⊙⊷⊸

The images, when they came, even after everything Zoe had seen, were shocking. Silence fell over the newsroom at the *Informer* as they played on the television screens. Three Japanese, two men, a woman, blindfolded and cowering on the floor; behind them masked men, all in black, with rifles and RPG launchers. They forced the Japanese to lie on the floor and held knives at their throats, the prisoners squirming away from the blades. The woman screamed, the sound like something half remembered from a childhood nightmare.

"We offer you two choices: either pull out your forces, or we will burn them alive. We give you three days starting the day this tape is broadcast."

Burn them alive. It was a step on from Fallujah. There they had burned the dead bodies, now they were threatening to burn the prisoners alive. The journalists had talked, many times, around the pool at the al-Hamra, about the danger that insurgents would start taking hostages, and the older reporters had spoken of Lebanon and the years the hostages there spent in captivity, chained up in the darkness. But not for Iraq such gentle terror: three days was all they had, and then the fire. Zoe hoped it was an empty threat. And those masks, a curious echo of the blindfolds, everyone's face hidden, captor and captive, individuality erased, turned into players in the drama, almost as if such horrors would be impossible if they had faces.

"Two of them were volunteers who came to work with street children," Jack said down the line from Baghdad. "The other one was a photographer. Things are changing so fast it's hard to keep up with what's safe and what isn't. They picked up a couple of journalists yesterday; they were going to kill them until the guys explained they were press. They let them go, but one of the Japanese is a photographer. It all depends who picks you up. There are reports of missing people coming in all the time, but with everything going on, no one knows who's been kidnapped and who hasn't. There's a British laundry worker who hasn't been heard from in days. Things are getting out of control. The doctors in Fallujah say the Americans have killed 280 there so far."

There was the sound of an explosion in the background.

"What was that?" Zoe asked.

"I don't know."

"Where are you?"

"In the hotel. They've been going off all day. No one seems to know what they are."

⊷⊶

Benes sat in the stillness of the night, waiting to go into battle. The order was for silence, yet he could hear all around him the sounds of men preparing, checking their weapons, going over their equipment, murmuring prayers. All he could hear from Gibbs at the wheel of the Humvee was the sound of his breathing. Ahead, visible in the darkness through his night vision goggles, lay the empty bridge, and beyond it, the enemy. Ahead, too, lay the waiting until they would cross onto the bridge and into the line of fire.

283

Benes had known they would have to fight in Kut. Even when they had arrived in the city and children had run into the streets to wave at the long column of American tanks and Humvees as the helicopters passed overhead, he had known this was no victory procession. The city lay amid palms on either side of a lazy Tigris River: the side they arrived on was under control, but the other side, across the river, had been taken over by the Mahdi Army.

There were two bridges, and neither looked as if it would take tanks, so the colonel had sent them round the long way, to cross at a bridge to the north that was secure, and then double-back under cover of darkness. They had retaken the CPA headquarters and one of the bridges, and for a while it had looked as if the platoon might not have to fight after all, but the Mahdi Army had dug in at a police station that overlooked the other bridge. Benes and the platoon were drawn up across from them, waiting to attack in Humvees because the bridge was too weak to take tanks. The Humvees were supposed to have been up-armoured, but Benes knew that would offer little protection if they came under RPG fire. Stretching ahead of him now, the bridge looked like a shooting alley. He thought of the Mahdi Army fighters on the other side, staring back at him across the empty span.

The order came, and they moved forward. Benes's rifle was clammy in his hands; he could hear Zivkovich swinging the well-oiled gun over their heads. Silence from the other side. The sound of the wheels changed, and they were on the bridge, hemmed in, suspended over the drop to the river beneath. Silence from the other side. They advanced. The sound from below changed again; they were across the bridge and on solid ground, and Benes breathed in relief. And then the Mahdi Army broke their silence. There were RPGs coming in. Gibbs veered the Humvee to one side, while Benes shot back with his rifle and Zivkovich fired the gun overhead. Benes could see the fighters on the roof of the police station, clear in his night vision. There was the flash of an explosion, except the dazzling white light went on and on, and Benes thought he had been blinded until he tore off his night goggles and realised it wasn't an explosion; the Mahdi Army had turned on floodlights.

"Take those lights out," he shouted. Without the advantage of night vision, the platoon was a sitting target under the flood-lights. The snipers took aim, and the lights went out. Just as Benes got his goggles back on, new lights came on: the Mahdi Army had spares. Benes crouched low and fired into the blinding light. Exposed like this, they were going to be cut down. They were too close to the enemy to call in air support; they needed to fall back, but there was no order from behind. He cradled the hot rifle in his arms and fired into the night as the spent ammunition littered around his feet and the incoming fire moved the air around his face. The order came: they drew back to the middle of the bridge, and Benes could see the Mahdi Army fighters celebrating. They thought they had driven the Americans back, but Benes could hear the AC-130 coming in. There was another bright light from the police station, but this time he felt the heat and the blast of the air strike, and the guns from the other side fell silent.

Later, they went forward again. All that was left of the enemy were the smears of blood where they had dragged away their wounded.

Adel sat in the front passenger seat of the car as they made slow progress along the narrow road. The back seat was piled with food and supplies, so high that all you could see in the rear-view mirror were packs of fruit juice and milk, and Adel's seat was pushed uncomfortably forward to make room. Ahead, he could see a truck piled with more supplies: blankets, baby clothes, packets of biscuits, tins of vegetables and still more fruit juice, and on top of them all, volunteers waving Iraqi flags and chanting excitedly, thrusting their fists into the air as people ran out of the houses on either side of the road to cheer the convoy on.

"Fallujah!" they were shouting, "Fallujah!"

His friend Ibrahim, at the wheel of the car, seemed borne by the same euphoria. He kept turning to Adel and grinning, nodding his head out towards the crowds, but Adel was regretting his decision to join the convoy.

When he had seen the pictures of the Japanese hostages on the television, Adel had remembered how he'd dreamed of being the first to take a foreigner hostage, and for a moment even felt as if the masked resistance fighters behind them had stolen his idea. He had been brooding on it when Ibrahim called to say some of the residents of Adhamiya were planning to try to take food and supplies to the besieged people of Fallujah, and suggest they joined the convoy. They might be able to get inside the city and join the fight against the Americans, Ibrahim said, and Adel had agreed, but when they joined the others in Baghdad in the early morning, he saw there was little chance of that. Most of the men on the convoy were not fighters at all; they seemed to think it was a remarkable act of defiance against the Americans just to drive trucks of food towards Fallujah, where they would almost certainly be turned away. Most of them appeared to be unarmed. Several had objected when Adel had arrived with a Kalashnikov and refused to let him bring it along. Ibrahim had taken him to one side and persuaded him to leave the Kalashnikov and bring a handgun instead, which they could easily hide in the car—Ibrahim said he already had one under the seat—and Adel had run home and tucked a handgun in the waistband of his jeans, under his shirt.

They hadn't even been allowed to use the main road out of Baghdad—that had been sealed off with tanks and razor wire by the Americans—so they had bumped their way down interminable back roads through the suburbs, most of which were barely more than villages, before finally being allowed back onto the main highway. Now, though, Adel feared that all that lay ahead was a long and tedious day of driving, only to be turned away from Fallujah. Coming down the highway in the opposite direction was a convoy of Americans, armoured vehicles in the lead and behind them petrol tankers. Adel sighed. His rag-tag relief convoy would be forced off the road to make way for the Americans—

The sound of gunfire cut across the sky. Adel looked to see where it was coming from. The Americans were wheeling their guns around, and the bullets were slapping low overhead; the tankers could go up at any moment. There was an explosion as a rocket-propelled grenade came in.

"Get off the road!" Adel shouted, but Ibrahim was already spinning the wheel, lurching off the highway and onto the waste ground beside. He misjudged the turn and the wheels of the car span furiously in the dirt as he tried to back up. The car gave a lurch and stalled. Adel silently cursed Ibrahim as a fool, ducking involuntarily in the car as more bullets came in. All around, the convoy was scattering, turning and heading back towards Baghdad. The starter motor was whining, but the car wouldn't start, and Adel wondered if Ibrahim would ask him to get out and push. He could see the sweat pouring from Ibrahim's face as he tried to get the car to start. There was a new sound; bullets were coming from the other direction as well now. The attackers were firing on the Americans from both sides, and Adel was trapped in the middle of an ambush. He wondered whether he ought to get out of the car and lie down flat, out of the bullets' way. Ibrahim finally got the car to start, backed quickly out of the ditch and turned towards Baghdad. They raced back along the dirt roads, the gunfight lost behind them in the dust kicked up by the wheels.

Adel realised he was shaking. He had been so close to them, to his father's killers, and he had turned and run. He felt the handgun digging into his midriff. Ibrahim was heading back to Baghdad, all thought of reaching Fallujah abandoned.

"Turn back," Adel said.

"Back there?" Ibrahim said. "Are you crazy?"

"We have to go back. We have to fight."

"What can we do in the middle of the road, on our own? We'll just get killed. You want to fight, you've got to be part of the ambush—you can't just pull out a gun and start shooting."

Ibrahim refused to turn around, and Adel spent the journey back to Baghdad staring out of the window, brooding on his lost opportunity.

⟶▸◉◂⟵

"They're saying they've taken six more hostages: two Americans and four Italians." It was David's voice down the line from Baghdad, with a distracting echo. Zoe hadn't been able to get hold of Jack all day, and she was worried.

"Jesus," she said.

"Yeah, they're saying they got them on the road between Baghdad and Fallujah. There's no confirmation here. Are you hearing anything?"

"The Italians are denying it, saying all their people are safe."

"One of the reporters here says he saw a couple of guys who shouted out 'Italians' being taken into a mosque."

"Sounds bad."

"Doesn't it just? The Americans have got back control of Kut, but Sadr's guys are looking dug in in Najaf...Listen, do you think you could take over a bit earlier than planned, perhaps in a couple of days?"

"Of course. When shall I come in?"

"Soon as you can? I know you're not due back in Baggers for a week or so, but it's just that I'm getting a bit tired. Probably best to swap over. No one knows how long this could all go on, and you need to have your wits about you here."

"Absolutely. I'll speak to Nigel."

Chapter Twenty-Four

The Trap

12–24 April 2004

THERE WAS NO one waiting at the airport for Zoe when she arrived in Baghdad. A few days before, Alain Martin's driver had almost been arrested in the car park, with the result that none of the translators and drivers wanted to wait. David had told Zoe over the phone that she could take the airport shuttle bus into town: it didn't usually go to the al-Hamra, but if she paid the driver extra he would make a detour and drop her there. She would not meet David this time; he was leaving on the same plane she had come in on and would probably be boarding by now. The bus was not difficult to find, ancient and battered looking, drawn up outside the terminal building in the harsh sunlight and empty except for the driver, who was sitting, bored, behind the wheel. Zoe climbed on board, struggling with the weight of her bags and missing the American soldier who had helped her the last time.

"Al-Hamra?" Zoe asked the driver.

He looked up and glanced around, then smiled and said, "Ten dollar."

She felt in her pocket and handed him the money, dragging her bag to the nearest seat. There was no air conditioning, and the heat in the bus made it hard to breathe, but it looked like a regular city bus, which, Zoe thought, would at least make them less likely to come under attack on the airport road. Another passenger climbed onto the bus, glanced warily at Zoe, paid and took his seat. Two more passengers came. None of them spoke; they all sat alone. The driver started the bus, which rattled consumptively, and they set off. As they passed out of the checkpoint, Zoe braced herself for the airport road. The driver was

289

accelerating steadily, the bus shaking with the effort and making a terrible noise. She looked out of the windows, scanning the verges for any sign of danger. She had hoped that once they were moving, the draught from the windows would cool her, but the air blew in stale and hot. The other passengers stared nervously out. Eventually they reached the Baghdad traffic: they had safely negotiated the most dangerous stretch of road in the city, and Zoe turned her mind to what lay ahead.

The news had kept coming as she travelled from London, and Zoe had caught it in snatches from television screens in airport lounges and radios in taxis. Although an American helicopter had been shot down, a fragile ceasefire was holding in Fallujah, and it looked as if the Americans might have lost their nerve and backed off from their assault on the town. Elsewhere, they were still in a stand-off with the Mahdi Army across the south, insisting they would arrest Sadr, but not going after him. An American hostage, captured on the road outside Fallujah, had given an impromptu interview to an Australian television crew when they stumbled upon his kidnappers—twenty-four-hour news coverage had come of age when hostages under threat of death were allowed to say a few words for the camera. Hostages were being taken all over Iraq, so quickly that the news media couldn't keep up. When a British hostage was freed, it was the first anyone had heard of him: no one even knew he had been kidnapped. The deadline for the other hostages, the Japanese and the American, had passed without news. No one knew if they were alive or dead.

The bus had reached the checkpoint outside the Palestine Hotel, where the other passengers gathered their luggage and got off, but the driver signalled to Zoe to stay where she was. One of the Iraqis manning the checkpoint peered in at her. Once the others were gone, the driver pulled away, back into the streets, and she was alone with him. Zoe realised she had made a mistake: people were being kidnapped off the streets every day, and her only defence was a bus driver she had no idea if she could trust—in fact, he could easily kidnap her himself. She had paid him $10; the hostage-takers would pay him a lot more than that for her. For that matter, he could drive her down a back alley, steal the rest of her money and kill her—it was easy enough to explain away a disappearance in Iraq. She looked out of the windows to reassure herself. She had driven between the Palestine and al-Hamra hotels many times, and she hoped she would recognise the route. But she didn't know the streets they were on.

They turned into a quiet, residential street, then off that onto an even quieter road, the sound of the traffic in the distance now. Zoe wondered whether she should try to jump from the bus. They were moving fast enough that she would probably be injured, and she had no idea what she would do alone in these unfamiliar streets. She moved towards the door and glanced at the driver. He was looking back at her in the rear-view mirror. She stared out at the black road moving by. Then, to her relief, she saw the familiar shape of the al-Hamra ahead.

She wondered if the driver had guessed her fears. If he had, he gave no sign of it. The hotel guards recognised Zoe. One of them came to help with her bags, and she was up the steps and through the door, past the gift shop still selling the souvenir cigarette lighters of American bombers, and there, waiting, was Jack.

"Hello, Zoe Temple. Good of you to drop in."

He didn't kiss her or embrace her in front of the Iraqis lingering around the reception desk, but he touched her arm gently and took her bag from the security guard. Ali and Mahmoud were waiting too, and she had to sit and exchange news with them, though she was impatient to be alone with Jack. Eventually she pleaded that she needed some rest after her journey and arranged to meet them later. She made love with Jack in the familiar room, with the sounds of Baghdad in the background. It wasn't until they were lying tangled in each other's limbs that she realised she hadn't called the paper to let the foreign desk know she had arrived safely. Jack was running his fingernails softly down the inside of her thigh. A loud explosion from outside made the glass rattle in the window frames, and she looked up anxiously.

"It's nothing," Jack said. "They're going off all the time."

"Seemed close."

"Mmm. Not close enough to worry about."

They ordered lunch in the room, and over an unappetising plate of chicken Jack told her about the situation.

"It looks as if the ceasefire's holding in Fallujah. But you still can't get anywhere near the place. I managed to speak to some refugees who got out this morning. They're in an old air raid shelter outside Baghdad. The stories are horrific—people walking for miles to safety, but I doubt they'll keep your desk any happier than mine. They want action stories, not refugees, but it's virtually impossible to get any. I've had Adnan trying to call people up there, but it's hard to get through. And anyway, looks like the action may be shifting south. The Americans have been moving troops to take on Sadr's guys, and there's talk of a move on Najaf."

"Can we get there?"

"Don't know, but if it's anything like Fallujah, no chance."

"What about the hostages?"

"Nobody knows. We don't even know how many they've got. There're more reports every day. A group of Czechs picked up, a Canadian missing. The wire guys are trying to compile lists like they used to keep of the hostages in Beirut, but the situation's moving so fast they can't keep up. The good thing is they haven't killed anyone yet—it's only been threats. And when they have picked up journalists, they've let them out once they proved they were press. But…" He trailed off.

"But?"

"But…well, I'm not sure it's going to stay that way."

Zoe drove to the air raid shelter and interviewed some refugees for the paper. As Jack had predicted, it didn't satisfy Nigel, who wanted drama from the frontline. Ali and Mahmoud were subdued—Ali in particular seemed nervous of the roads, and when she asked him about the situation, he sounded depressed.

In the evening by the poolside, however, the reporters were excitable, riding the edge of the crisis, full of stories of their attempts to reach the action—and none had tried harder, and with more dramatic consequences, naturally, than Janet Sweeney. Zoe found Kate and Mervyn full of energy, planning how to reach Najaf. Zoe forgot Jack's pessimism and Ali's gloom. The story was moving fast, and they were right on it.

"What shall we do?"

Even though it was the news Mahmoud had been expecting—and dreading—for so long, he felt as if it had knocked the breath out of him. He sat in silence for a while, looking across at Saara, unable to speak, to think even, or to understand what she had just said. At first, when things began to unravel across Iraq, he had let himself believe it might be good for her, that the extremists would be too busy fighting the Americans in Fallujah to trouble themselves with an unimportant Christian family. Saara had seemed re-energised by the crisis. It was as if she felt that, by virtue of the threat that had been hanging over the small house spreading across the entire country, she was once again involved in life and no longer cut off from the outside world. Whenever he visited, as long as the power held, the television was tuned to the news, and she would often hush him so she could listen to the latest developments. But now she was ignoring the latest footage from Fallujah and staring at Mahmoud.

The warning, this time, had come not in the form of an anonymous letter pushed under the door, but from friends her father trusted: it was not safe for the family in this neighbourhood any more. The friends didn't want it to be that way, they said, but it was, and the best they could do now for the family was warn them to get out in time. And so Saara's father had done what he had sworn he never would: he turned to the Americans. As Christians, they could get asylum in America. Within weeks, perhaps days, Saara would be gone, to America, where Mahmoud could not follow—he would not get a visa. He had hoped the family would move to an Arab country where he could at least visit, but the opportunity to live in the US, safe from the whims of Arab governments who might send them back to Iraq without warning, or turn against the Christians themselves, was too good for Saara's father to pass up. Mahmoud wanted the Americans to refuse to take them, or for the paperwork to be delayed, so she would stay longer in Baghdad, yet at the same time he felt guilty for wanting to keep her in danger. He sat in silence, looking at her across the room, her words echoing in his ears: "What shall we do?" He had no answer.

--※◎◎※--

The attack on Najaf did not come, the ceasefire in Fallujah held, and Zoe began to fear she had returned to Iraq at precisely the wrong moment, as the crisis calmed and the story began to fade. First it dropped off the front page, and then, with no new developments, news reports gave way to lengthy analysis pieces, and finally, in an infallible sign that the story had gone cold, to speculations and predictions. The bodies of the four contractors whose deaths had sparked the Fallujah conflagration were found, and American troops continued to mass around Najaf, while their commanders made sporadic warnings to the Mahdi Army's leader, Moqtada al-Sadr, but there was an uneasy calm. The hostage story alone continued to run—the one story the reporters at the al-Hamra wished would quietly resolve itself, because it cut too close to home. Another video was released, this time showing four kidnapped Italians. None of the journalists cared to make predictions about what would become of the hostages; they all knew it could all too easily be them in the video, with kidnappers holding guns to their heads and swords to their necks.

Then, amid news that the Japanese hostages had been released, came a crushing blow: one of the Italian hostages had been killed, and his murderers had released a video of his death to an Arabic television network that refused to broadcast it, saying it was too gruesome. Although everyone denied having a copy, detailed accounts quickly made their way around the al-Hamra. The Italian had died a hero's death: his captors had forced him to dig his own grave, but when they tried to make him wear a hood and kneel, he had refused, struggling free and declaring, "I will show you how an Italian dies." They shot him in the neck.

Two days later came yet another video. This time the insurgents had taken an American soldier hostage. If they could capture a heavily armed soldier, Zoe wondered what chance the unarmed journalists would stand against them. The mood at the al-Hamra grew sombre. The reporters sat around the pool quietly, all of them, Zoe was sure, asking themselves the same question: if it came to it, would they have the courage to die like the Italian, or would they act out the part scripted for them by the masked killers, kneeling meekly to die?

Zoe had stopped using her room for anything but work, and she spent her nights in Jack's room. A strange place to start living with a man, she thought, in a dingy hotel room in occupied Baghdad. A few days after the Italian's death he told her, "I think it may be time to start thinking about getting out of Iraq."

Zoe looked at him in surprise. They were sitting together on the balcony of his room, sharing a bottle of wine as the last light of the day faded. Jack had been in a solemn mood all afternoon, but the suggestion he might leave Iraq seemed to come from nowhere, and Zoe felt deflated. She might have been unnerved by the killing, but she still believed in the work she was doing in Iraq and had begun to let herself think of a future with Jack—and now he was talking of leaving.

"Seriously?" she asked. He nodded.

"They've crossed a line. Now that they've killed a hostage, it's that much easier to kill the next one. And not just for this group of insurgents, for everybody. There are going to be more killings; other groups are going to copy it, to prove they're serious. I wouldn't want to be one of those hostages right now."

"But to leave? I mean, this is important work. Sure it's risky, but that's part of the job, isn't it?"

"Well, I'm not talking about getting on a plane," he said. "I just mean it's good to have a plan for how to get out of here if things get too nasty. You don't want to end up desperate to get out of Baghdad with a paper that wants you to stay and have to choose between your job and your life. Now's the time to start thinking about ways out."

He didn't mention the idea again in the days that followed, and Zoe thought it had probably been the whim of a passing moment, brought on by the horror of the Italian's death. Behind Jack's carefully constructed facade, Zoe was convinced, lay a sensitive man—though Kate had laughed when Zoe told her.

"Sensitive? Jack?" she had said incredulously. "You must be in *love.* Maybe he's sensitive where you're concerned, but not about anybody or anything else."

⋅⊱⊶◉⊷⊰⋅

Adel's hand hovered over the computer keyboard. He was in an unfamiliar Internet cafe once again, where he would not be recognised. He had not logged into the hotmail account he used to send the email to the foreigner for months, and now he hesitated, fearing what he would find: perhaps a message from her, a missed opportunity from months ago. Or, worse, some sign that she had discovered him, or that the Americans were onto him. But when he pressed the key there was nothing, no new messages, all that was in the inbox was the solitary message from her which had so enraged him, saying his father's death wasn't interesting enough for her newspaper.

Since the humiliation of the day of the attack on the American convoy, Adel had been tortured with shame. He had been a few metres from his father's killers, with a gun; they had been pinned down by fire; and yet he had turned and run, like a frightened child. He would not run again. If he could not get inside Fallujah to fight, he would do something else. His thoughts had returned to the journalist. There were so many foreign hostages being held in Iraq now that Adel had lost count. If so many others were capturing foreigners, then so could he. He was angry he had given up on the idea so easily: it turned out it was something any resistance fighter in Iraq could do. The problem was to think of a way of getting her attention, and drawing her to him. He sat and wrote:

> Dear Zoe, I am Zaynab, do you remember? Are you still in Iraq? I hope you are OK. The situation in Iraq is very bad now, as you know. I am wondering if you are OK? Please do not go close to Fallujah, the situation there is very serious.
>
> If you need any help please tell me. I have some interesting news maybe for your paper. Did you publish the story about me yet?

Night was falling across the camp. Cigarettes glowed red here and there against the expectant twilight, and as Benes gazed across the tents huddled together, the wind whipped the dust up, stinging his eyes. Benes had never noticed the wind in Baghdad, but out here, in the desert, there was no mistaking it. It picked the dust up and danced it across the horizon. Benes looked back at the men busy around the tents; they had been swept up by the same wind and were being danced across Iraq from battle to battle, as so many armies had been down the centuries.

The battalion had abandoned Kut just when they were beginning to make their temporary camp there comfortable. With Kut secure, the order had come to move to Najaf, where the Mahdi Army was still holding out in larger numbers, but while the commanders drew up their plans, the troops were being held in the desert outside the city. A year in Iraq, and they were camping in the desert like an invading army. Benes wandered through the camp, looking at the men keeping themselves busy as best they could, some huddled around an MP3 player hooked up to speakers, others listening to a long-wave radio, trying to make out the news through the shrieks and hisses of the ether, a tenuous thread back to civilisation. Snatches of conversation drifted towards him from open tent flaps.

"…I got some in Sadr City, mother thought he was hidden, firing at us, lit him up…"

"…when I get back I'm gonna fuck for a week without stopping…"

"…dumb Hajji motherfuckers…"

Outside their tent, Moon and Zivkovich were talking. They were about to get to their feet when they saw Benes coming, but he motioned them to stay where they were and sat down beside them.

"What's up?" he asked.

"Not much, sir," Zivkovich replied.

"The usual," Moon said. "Just sitting waiting."

"We should be into Najaf and in better accommodation in a couple of days," Benes said.

"I don't know," Moon said. "I kind of like it out here." Benes couldn't make out Moon's expression through the gathering gloom; he could just see the dim outline of his face, and the glow of his cigarette. "You can see the stars at night. And it's quiet. In the cities, you know you're in Iraq. But here, we could be anywhere."

In the distance, the wind picked up across the desert.

⟶⟩▪◉ ◉▪⟨⟵

It was late morning and Zoe stretched luxuriously in bed. The sunlight spilling through the thin curtains fell warm on her face, despite the air conditioning. Jack had left early for an interview, but Zoe lingered in bed. The paper was planning to run a lengthy feature she had already written, so there was little for her to do unless there was a breaking news story, and she had allowed herself the rare luxury of a lie-in. Then the memory of the email she had received the previous evening from Zaynab returned, unwelcome. This time, Zoe had not replied immediately, but had put it off. She felt guiltier than ever. She couldn't see how she could get Zaynab's story in the paper with everything else that was happening in Iraq at the moment: no newspaper would run the story of an Iraqi family that had been killed the best part of a year ago while Western hostages were being murdered. But Zaynab said she had news, and Zoe knew she would have to reply. She glanced at her watch on the bedside table and, yawning, got out of bed, pulled the sheet around her instead of bothering to dress and crossed into the small kitchen area. She put a saucepan of water on to boil for coffee, the wet pan cracking and hissing on the electric ring, and switched on the television to check if there was any news. A political report from Washington was showing, so she turned to breakfast. Jack had left fresh rolls on the counter, and there was fruit in the fridge. The thought of Zaynab's email returned again and, unsure what to do about it, Zoe felt a flash of anger. The table was covered in the usual litter of Jack's notes—no matter how often she cleared them, the sprawl returned—and in her irritation she set about clearing a space, glancing at the papers as she swept them away:

old press releases from the CPA that announced rubbish collections had recommenced, grainy photocopies of Arabic typescripts that were allegedly old intelligence ministry records—Jack told her they had been selling them by the kilo after the fall of the old regime—and his own scribbled notes from interviews.

As she moved them into neat piles her eyes fell on a folder that was labelled "Selim Abdullah" in Jack's handwriting. The name was familiar. She tried to recall where she had heard it before, and then it came back: the boy Jack wrote about who had lost his leg in the village near Mahmudiya. Curious, she flipped it open, expecting to see his notes from the original interview, but instead there was what looked like a print-out of an email. She glanced down it, her mind half on the television, which was airing a report from London.

"Dear Mr Wolfe," it read, "thank you for your phone call earlier today. As I indicated on the phone, I may be in a position to help financially with some or all of the cost of providing a prosthetic leg for the boy Selim Abdullah. I would be most grateful if you could let me know the details of the Baghdad clinic you mentioned, as well as how it would be possible for me to contact the family. In the meantime, this is my email address, and here are my other contacts."

All thought of the television report forgotten, Zoe looked through the rest of the folder. There was a printed document in Arabic with Jack's handwriting scrawled across it: she made out the name of the prosthetic clinic in Baghdad she had heard about, together with two doctors' names and telephone numbers and a series of what looked like prices in US dollars. Underneath that she found what seemed to be Jack's notes from the original interview and, tucked behind the rest, a badly scratched DVD or computer disc. She looked back at the date on the email: it had been sent before her visit to Mahmudiya, back when Jack was insisting to her he didn't even remember the boy's name.

Zoe hesitated. The television was showing the news from Baghdad now, but she barely registered it. She looked down at the folder in her hands. A part of her was pleased to discover Jack had been helping the boy after all, but she couldn't help wondering why he had gone to such lengths to hide it from her.

He hadn't just denied it: he had gone out of his way to give her the impression he couldn't care less. She looked at the disc. She knew he hadn't wanted her to see the contents of the folder and that she was intruding on his privacy, but her curiosity overcame her, and glancing guiltily behind her to make sure she was not being watched—though she couldn't possibly be—she switched on Jack's laptop and slipped the disc inside it. After a moment, a video began to play on the screen. To Zoe's surprise, it was old footage of the war, pictures of the American tanks advancing into Baghdad that she remembered watching on television the previous year. Wondering why he had bothered to keep it, Zoe was about to eject the disc when the picture jumped, flickered and changed to a young man in uniform, being held down by masked men who were looking up at the camera and saying something. Zoe felt a chill spread through her. The recording quality was poor and there was no sound, but she knew it was another hostage video. She watched, unable to take her eyes off it as one of the masked men took out a knife and put it to the throat of the young soldier, who gasped as the point went in and the dark blood started to come. Zoe wanted to look away, but she couldn't. The soldier was bracing himself, trying to cope with the pain, as the masked man pushed the knife in deep and pulled it forward, and the blood began to pour out, and then they were hacking the head off altogether and holding it up for the camera. They were cheering and chanting something, and Zoe felt she had somehow violated the young man by watching his death, which should have been private and had nothing to do with her.

But the real question, she knew, was what a new hostage video, which none of the other reporters had even heard about, was doing lying in a folder in Jack's room. If he had a scoop, why hadn't he published it? She watched the video again, wondering if the soldier was the American who had been kidnapped. The quality was very poor, and it looked as if it had been copied several times, and the soldier looked nothing like the pictures she had seen of the captured American.

Other things came back to her, which she had pushed to the back of her mind: Jack had known about the insurgents in

Mahmudiya, he had known that the mortars were about to fall in Karbala. And now he had a video of a hostage being beheaded sitting in his room, a video no one else knew about. Thinking he might have been so eager to get a scoop he had hidden it even from her, she went across to the Internet cafe to make sure he hadn't somehow written about it behind her back the previous day, but when she checked the *Daily Post* website there was no mention of the video. She even checked back through previous days, to be sure she hadn't somehow missed it, but there was nothing. She decided to confront him, and ask for an explanation, though she wasn't sure she really wanted to hear it, and she settled down uncomfortably in the room to wait for his return.

Chapter Twenty-Five

Picture Postcards from Abu Ghraib

25–29 April 2004

THE ANSWER, WHEN it came to Mahmoud, was so simple he couldn't believe he hadn't thought of it before. If Saara could not stay in Iraq, then he would have to leave with her. The problem was how to do it: there was little chance the Americans would give him asylum, and he didn't see how else he could accompany her. Then she told him one day that the family needed a driver and asked if he knew anyone they could trust. They needed to get to Jordan to catch a flight to the US, but with the mounting expense of the journey, they couldn't afford a flight out of Baghdad. The road, which ran past Fallujah, was more dangerous than ever, they had sold their car to raise funds, and her father didn't want to go with an unknown taxi driver.

Mahmoud immediately said he would drive the family himself; it would give them a few more hours together. Delighted, she said she would get her brother to recommend Mahmoud to her father as driver, so it didn't look as if the idea was hers. That night, awake in bed, the answer came to him: he would marry her in secret. If they were married, perhaps the Americans would let him in—and if they wouldn't, he would persuade her to stay in an Arab country, where she was safe, as his wife. The Christians, he knew, did not recognise such marriages the way the Muslims did; their marriages had to be blessed by their priests, but even if her family refused to recognise the marriage, the Muslim Arab governments would let them stay together. He knew he could get a visa for Jordan as a professional driver. All he had to do was persuade her.

Once he had it worked out, he couldn't sleep for thinking what her answer might be, and he lay awake, impatient for the dawn. He thought, guiltily, of his own family. He might not see them for a long time, but when he compared that to the thought of being parted from Saara, he knew what he had to do. He would have to take his savings with him, and that felt like stealing from his family, even though he had already given more than half of what he earned to his parents. He felt he had no right to leave them without his income as a driver; he would send them money from abroad as soon as he could. If he made it to the US, he would be able to send plenty. He couldn't tell his parents anything of what he was planning—he could tell no one, not even Ali. He would disappear from their lives, leaving only messages to explain.

Even when the tentative dawn began to pick out shadows around the room, he knew it was too early to go to her house. He thought of calling her, but he didn't want to tell her over the phone. He sat in silence at the breakfast table, watching his mother, thinking how she would react the morning he didn't come down, when she went to his room and discovered he was gone, and for a moment he considered giving up the plan, but he thought again of life without Saara. When he left, he headed not towards the al-Hamra, but to Saara's house. On the way, he called Ali and lied that there was a problem with the car and asked him to apologise to Zoe and tell her he would be at work as soon as it was fixed. He knew there would be no signal in the window—she would not expect him in the morning, and they used the signal less now they both had mobile phones—but he didn't want to call in case she told him not to come. He checked the road for her father's car and decided to chance going to the door. If her father was in, he would say he had come to offer his services as driver.

It was Saara's mother who answered. For a moment, she looked at him in surprise, and then she greeted him warmly and, without questions, showed him in. Saara was watching the news on television. Surprised to see him at such an early hour, she looked up in concern and asked if anything was wrong. He shook his head, and her mother left them alone. For a moment he delayed, asked her how she was, and she stared at him in confusion and asked why he had come in the morning. He turned the television up loud, as if they were listening—it was showing, by luck, a report from Fallujah—and, speaking softly so her mother would not hear, he told her his plan. He had expected her to argue and resist when he spoke of marrying in secret, and he had come prepared with arguments to convince her, but she just smiled and said, "Is this your idea of a proposal?" When he tried to stammer a reply, she stopped him and said, "How do we do it? Do we need witnesses?"

"No, we just say the words."

"Just the two of us?"

"Yes."

"Then why will anyone believe us?" she asked, and before he could answer, she went on, "Never mind, if it works. If it keeps us together. My parents will never accept it, but we can marry properly later. When do we do it?"

"We can do it now."

She hesitated. "Not here," she said, "not in this house."

"Why not?"

"It's not right, not in my parents' house."

"Where then? You are always here."

"We'll find a chance. On the way perhaps, or before. Don't worry," she said smiling, reaching out to brush his cheek with her fingers. "It's a wonderful idea. I thought I was losing you."

⊷⊶⊷

Benes ducked into the shadow of the sandbags when he heard the first mortar being fired in the distance, the blast only slightly muffled by the buildings all around. He stood for a couple of minutes, then heard the rush of air as the mortar came in and felt the shockwave as it landed, not far away, followed by a loud explosion that set his ears ringing. Up above, the snipers started firing. He waited a few moments, listening carefully for any more mortars, and then decided it was safe to come out of cover. When he was in the open, he heard the blast of another mortar being fired and, cursing, began sprinting for the building, counting off the seconds, a part of his mind academically wondering if he'd make it or be blown to pieces. And then he was through the sandbags and safe inside the building. He heard the second mortar landing somewhere in the distance. He almost wished they were back in the desert, sleeping in tents, where at least there were no mortar attacks. Here death was ever present, rushing out of the sky.

They had moved into Najaf, to a base in the old CPA building, although strictly speaking the building was not inside the Najaf city limits, which allowed the army to say it had not entered the holy city. The building lay in a thin strip of land between Najaf and Kufa, a small town that almost joined the city and which was where Moqtada al-Sadr, the leader of the Shia insurgency, was holed up. In theory, the American presence was supposed to intimidate Sadr into backing down; in practice, it meant the soldiers were trapped between concentrations of Mahdi Army fighters in Najaf and Kufa, a sitting target for mortar attacks, which came in night and day. Benes often woke in the night to the sound of a mortar landing, followed by the guns in the nest above his room starting up in reply. Usually, they just shot harmlessly into the night. Fearful of Shia sentiment in the holy city of Najaf, the army had designated the mosques, shrines and other religious sites exclusion zones, which the soldiers could only fire into if they were under direct attack from inside them, but in Najaf and Kufa, almost every other building was a mosque or shrine of some sort, and it was easy for the Mahdi Army to fire on the Americans from the open, then duck into the sanctuary of a shrine.

To Benes, it felt as if the Americans were trapped in some old movie, holding out in a lone fort against the marauding enemy. Some of the men had even started calling the compound the Alamo, and in his darker moments Benes found himself imagining a desperate last stand, a few soldiers defending the smoking ruins of these buildings as the hordes advanced from all sides, until the helicopters came to take the survivors from the burning roof. Of course, it couldn't end like that, he told himself, not with the firepower the US had.

A short distance from the compound where Benes was stationed, across the low rooftops and dusty streets of Kufa, the call to prayer was going up from a rather more ornate complex of buildings at the heart of which lay the Kufa mosque, where Nouri was preparing for prayers with his fellow fighters from the Mahdi Army. As they knelt to pray, the sound of gunfire echoed from outside, but neither Nouri nor any of the others flinched. Nouri wouldn't be surprised if the Americans defiled the mosque by firing into it, but he would not allow them to interrupt his prayers.

Nouri had been glad when the announcement went out that the militia was looking for volunteers to come to Najaf and Kufa—there was little left to do in Sadr City besides defying the American patrols by carrying arms in public. The fight had moved south, and he wanted to be part of it. Life in the compound was harsh. They slept forty to a room, crowded close together on the bare floor, and queued for meals, sitting to eat in whatever dusty corner of the floor they could find free—but that was easy for Nouri, who had been in Abu Ghraib. He had not told the others about his time in prison. Some of them knew he had been there, but he never spoke of the things that been done to him inside.

The sound of the guns and mortars was constant, day and night, and Nouri often lay awake at night, unable to sleep, and thought of his family. Before he left, he had argued with his father, who didn't want him to leave Sadr City. His place was with the family, not far away in Najaf, his father had said, and when Nouri refused to back down, they had parted on bad terms. Now he thought how he had been taken away from the family once already, when the Americans sent him to Abu Ghraib, and had returned only to leave again. He wondered if his mother lay awake at night worrying about him and if it was the same for her as it had been when she worried about him in prison.

⇥⇤

"What's this?" Zoe held up the disc to Jack.

"Don't look at that," he said.

"I already have. What is it, Jack?"

He had been longer returning than she had expected. There had been reports of another bombing, and Zoe had wanted to go and check them, but Mahmoud had arrived late. There had been some sort of problem with the car, but Zoe had taken out her frustration on Mahmoud, surprising herself with her sudden anger and apologising to him after.

"It's a video the insurgents are passing around—"

"What are you doing with it? Are you trying to get some sort of exclusive? Or…" She trailed off, reluctant to finish the sentence.

"Exclusive?" He seemed surprised. "No, I got hold of a copy in a cafe where I used to go, in Adhamiya."

"They cut a man's head off, Jack."

"Yes, I know—"

"Who is he? Is he American? Why hasn't anyone else heard about it?"

"No, look, hold on, Zoe. It's an old recording, of a Russian soldier from Chechnya. I got it months ago, before they even started taking hostages here. There were stories going round of a video of an American being beheaded, so I checked it out. It turned out the stories were wrong: it's an old video from Chechnya that the foreign insurgents brought in. Presumably in the hope it might serve as inspiration."

Zoe stared at him in silence, going over his explanation in her mind.

"So why didn't you write about it?"

"I did, but the paper didn't run the piece. They weren't interested. They said Chechnya was old news, and they only wanted new developments from Iraq. At that point there were no hostages here. It didn't look like anyone was interested in copying those tactics. You can see the piece I wrote if you like." He opened his laptop and turned it to face her. "I can show you the emails I sent the paper as well if you want."

Zoe read the story on the screen, which described the video.

"So how come no one else has heard of this?" she said.

"I don't know, it's just something I heard about. I was hanging out in this cafe in Adhamiya. Last year, before things got so fraught. It's a sort of rebel cafe, a place a lot of pro-insurgency types hang out. And I heard about this video."

"Adhamiya? What were you doing there?"

"Back then you could move around a lot more easily. And I'm not American or British, Zoe. A lot of Iraqis like the Irish; they see us as fellow victims of the Brits. So I could hang out in places where you wouldn't be welcome, speak to people you couldn't."

"What about that time in Karbala? How did you know about the attack?"

"What?"

"How come you knew it was about to start and to go down that side street?"

"What are you accusing me of?" He looked more hurt than angry. "We all thought there was going to be an attack. We were talking about it for days beforehand. I got nervous in the crowd."

She ran it over in her mind. It was just like the road through Mahmudiya. She had made assumptions and let her imagination run away with her, building suspicions out of nothing. She looked up at him, fearful she might have damaged things between them.

"It's OK," he said, and put his arms round her. "This place gets to us all sometimes. And this fucking thing's enough to freak anyone out," he added, holding up the disc. "Where did you find it?"

Zoe remembered the file marked "Selim Abdullah" and the e-mail from the mysterious benefactor.

"In your file on that…Jack, why didn't you tell me you were helping that boy, Selim Abdullah?"

"Oh, you found that as well?"

"You told me you didn't care what happened to him, you couldn't even remember his name, and all the time you were finding some rich guy to pay for his leg."

"It wasn't quite like that. The rich guy contacted me. He'd read my piece and wanted to help. I just put him in touch with the family and the clinic."

"But why didn't you tell me?"

"I didn't know if it would work out. To be honest, I didn't know the kid had got his leg until you went off to Mahmudiya and found out…and nearly got yourself killed in the process."

"It was your article that did it."

"No, it was the rich guy."

It was some time later when Zoe realised she had completely forgotten about Zaynab's email. She sat deliberating over a reply. She knew she must not raise the woman's hopes falsely again. In the end, she decided Zaynab had given her a way out by asking if she was still in Iraq. She wrote:

> Dear Zaynab, it's good to hear from you, and that you're safe. I'm afraid I'm not in Iraq at the moment, I'm in London. You said you had some news. Can you tell me what it is?
>
> I hope I'll be back in Iraq soon. Keep safe. Best wishes to you and your daughter.

Zoe felt guilty at lying, but she thought it was the best option: she didn't want to make any more promises she couldn't keep, or humiliate Zaynab by telling her the newspaper wouldn't use her story. This way, if Zaynab's news turned out to be something she could use, Zoe could write back and say she had just flown in.

⤞∰⤝

When Mahmoud returned to Saara's house, the signal was in the upstairs window, and he went confidently to the door. But when Saara's sister showed him inside, it was not Saara sitting waiting for him in her familiar place on the sofa, it was her father, Abu Yusuf. He must have found out. Was he going to tell Mahmoud he couldn't marry his daughter, warn him off, threaten him?

The old Christian smiled up at him and asked him to sit down. Mahmoud mumbled his way through the usual pleasantries, wondering when it would come and if Saara's mother had overheard them, or if Saara herself had given them away in a moment of guilt. Abu Yusuf had let his hair and moustache turn grey without dyeing them, and Mahmoud found it hard to believe this was the man he had feared meeting for so long. There was nothing he could do to Mahmoud, his family could not touch

Mahmoud's—he could do nothing except forbid Mahmoud to see Saara, and that was everything. Mahmoud watched warily as he stood up and crossed to the bookcase and felt for something behind the books. For a moment Mahmoud wondered if he was going to pull out a gun, but the old man turned instead with a bottle of wine in his hands and held it out in offer. Mahmoud declined politely and touched his hand to his heart.

"So," Abu Yusuf said, returning to the sofa, "my son says you have offered to drive us to Amman?"

"Yes."

"It is good of you. It would be a great burden from my mind if you are our driver."

Mahmoud wanted to shout with joy, but he kept control.

"It is the least I can do."

"Of course we will pay you," Abu Yusuf said, and Mahmoud tried to look embarrassed at the mention of money, when in truth he would happily have paid to drive them. "My son says you are a good friend, and we need friends now," Abu Yusuf said with a look of sincerity, and Mahmoud felt a stab of guilt that he was planning to take this trusting old man's daughter away. "And I think you are a friend of…others in my family," Abu Yusuf added with a knowing smile that made Mahmoud start. "Don't worry," Abu Yusuf said, reaching out and touching his elbow gently. "I am happy you are our…friend."

Mahmoud felt uncomfortable. He wasn't sure what the old man was saying, whether he was trying to let him know that he would welcome him as a son-in-law, or only that he accepted him as an admirer of his daughter who would help the family for her sake and then be gone from their lives. Saara did not appear, and after agreeing the details of the drive to Jordan, Abu Yusuf showed him to the door.

In the days that followed, Mahmoud made his preparations. Getting a visa for Jordan was easy. Money changed hands—not only at the official rate. More money was needed to get the car's paperwork in order, but Mahmoud was ready before Saara and her family, who were still waiting to hear from the American Embassy. He would have to carry his cash with him on the journey, hidden around his body. There was a risk he would be robbed at gunpoint and lose it all, but there was no other choice. He waited for Abu Yusuf to tell him the day of departure. At meals, he read accusations in the faces of his mother and father across the table, though they knew nothing. He heard reproach in his father's questions, felt it in his mother's glances; even the house seemed to be calling out to him. The creak of the door asked, "Where are you going, Mahmoud?" The click of the lock on the drawer where he kept his passport said, "What do you need these papers for?" The silence of the walls at night said, "And will you never come back?"

Adel was dismayed by Zoe's reply. His hostage had slipped through his fingers, she had left the country. He debated making up some "news" to send her, in the hope it might lure her back, but he had no idea what sort of thing would do that. His plan had been to say he could only tell her the news in person, and arrange to meet, so that he would never have to concoct a story. Now all he could do was wait for her return, and he wrote to say he would tell her his news when she was back in town, and to be sure to let him know when she was coming.

An air of despondency filled the al-Hamra. It wasn't just the sense that the story had gone quiet for the moment—it was still impossible to get into Fallujah, even though the fighting was over there, and the Americans were waiting in the south, building up their forces without moving against Sadr. There was a nervousness in the air. The reporters knew they would have to take bigger risks to get stories that would make the papers or the television news. And all the while, the killing of the Italian hostage and the unknown fate of the others hung over them. Perhaps that was why it came as a relief when, one evening by the pool, an overweight South African security contractor made the mistake of placing his considerable bulk rather too swiftly onto one of the hotel's flimsy white plastic chairs and it exploded in a shower of broken shards, leaving him rolling on the floor. Zoe had to duck inside the lobby to hide her laughter—several of the other journalists were not so polite.

Then, one morning, Zoe woke to find the mood in the hotel transformed. Reporters pushed past her on the stairs. The hotel staff seemed distracted. Puzzled, Zoe went to her room—Jack was still asleep and she didn't want to wake him—and switched on the television. She got the tail end of a report: something had happened at Abu Ghraib, and it must have been big because it was dominating the news, but she missed the details. Too impatient to wait for the bulletin to come round again, she hurried to the Internet cafe to find more, but all the computers were busy with reporters scanning the news. Kate was at one of them, and Zoe asked her what had happened.

"Haven't you heard? The Americans have been torturing prisoners at Abu Ghraib. Look at this shit." And she started scrolling through a series of photographs on the computer screen. In one, a man was standing on a box with a black hood over his head and what appeared to be electrodes attached to his body. In another, naked men were being made to stand in a row wearing hoods over their heads while a smirking American woman soldier pointed at their genitals and gave a thumbs-up to the camera. In a third, naked men were piled on top of each other in a pyramid while American soldiers in uniform looked on.

"Where'd this come from?" Zoe asked.

"CBS ran an exclusive in the States last night. It's kicked off a fucking shit storm; this is going to be massive. What were the Americans fucking thinking? I mean, in Abu Ghraib, where Saddam used to torture Iraqis?"

"What are the Americans saying?"

"That it's bad apples, an isolated group of soldiers acting without orders, that they've been arrested and are going to be tried. But I doubt that's going to convince the Iraqis. These pictures are all over the TV. There's going to be murder. This is the last thing the Americans want after they fucked up Fallujah."

Benes crouched under the concrete shelter, half-deaf with the noise of the machine gun as Jackson fired into the night. The air shuddered around him as another mortar came in. It was a particularly heavy bombardment, and Benes thought it probably had something to do with the news from Abu Ghraib and the pictures that had been on television all day and all over the Internet. Several of the mortars had landed close enough to send soldiers scurrying out of the building below, thinking it might have been hit; at one point Benes had even seen the colonel running for one of the concrete shelters surrounded by a group of senior officers. Jackson was shouting something as the tracer fire arced up out of his gun, but Benes couldn't make out his voice through all the noise. Two helicopters passed low overhead, heading out in search of the mortar men. Below them, the artillery fired.

Benes wished he could send the soldiers of Abu Ghraib out into the night to make their own peace with the mortar men of Najaf. The soldiers who had taken those pictures had endangered him and his men as surely as if they had fired with their own hands the mortars that were coming in now—they had endangered them and dishonoured them. He had not endured a year in Iraq, in the heat and the dirt, trying to keep his men alive, had not watched Gutierrez die, so an American soldier could stand on a helpless, naked prisoner's neck or take photographs of a woman pointing at a prisoner's genitals and grinning.

⋅⋅⋅◉⋅⋅⋅

Nouri kept low in the dark, passing mortar shells from the box at his feet to the fighter in front, who was loading them into the tube and launching them. They worked quietly and efficiently, speaking little. The other fighter didn't warn Nouri when he was about to fire; Nouri had to watch his hands through the dark to know when to shield his ears for the blast and keep his mouth open so his eardrums didn't burst. There was a low wailing, like someone whistling softly, or a ghost, as another artillery shell came in from the Americans, then a muffled thud and a patch of lighter grey against the night where the shell kicked dust up into the air. They were getting closer. Nouri hefted another mortar shell in his fingers.

He had heard about the pictures from Abu Ghraib, but he had tried to keep away from televisions or newspapers where he might see them. At one point he had caught a glimpse of a picture of a naked man in the newspaper over someone's shoulder, but to his relief, it had not been of him. When some of the other fighters who knew he had been in Abu Ghraib asked him, he told them he knew nothing, that he had heard rumours of torture like this in some other part of the prison where he had never been.

⇥⬤⇤

When the phone rang, Mahmoud was at the dinner table with his parents. He and Saara were used to hiding their calls from anyone who might overhear by speaking in codes only they understood, but when Mahmoud heard Abu Yusuf's voice he was nervous the old man might give him away.

"We got the papers today," Abu Yusuf said. "Can you go tomorrow night?" Mahmoud glanced at his parents; they were engrossed in the television news.

"Yes, that would be fine," he said cautiously. "I'll make sure the car is ready."

"Good. See you tomorrow then." Abu Yusuf rang off.

"Who was that?" his father asked.

"Ali," Mahmoud lied. "The journalist wants to go to Basra tomorrow. I'll be away for a day or two." His mother looked across at him.

"Are you sure it's safe?" she said.

"It's fine."

"Be careful," his father said. "The south is dangerous now, with Sadr's people out."

"We're always careful, and Ali knows people there," he said. "Don't worry, we'll be fine. First sign of trouble we'll turn back." His father nodded, but his mother looked concerned, and Mahmoud felt guilt twist its knife in his stomach.

Chapter Twenty-Six

Saara

30 April–1 May 2004

WHEN MAHMOUD LEFT the house on the last morning, his mother stood in the doorway, her eyes fixed on him, her hand outstretched, as if she somehow knew. Watching her retreating form in the rear-view mirror of the car, he felt like a traitor. She had made him eat a good breakfast before his journey, and he had promised to bring home dates from Basra. But no one can be loyal to everybody—sooner or later you have to choose who you betray.

He had left a letter for his parents, in a drawer where they wouldn't look until he had been missing for a few days, together with as much money as he could spare. The rest he had hidden on him, in his socks, and in a pouch tucked inside his trousers. To avoid raising their suspicions, he had just a small bag of clothes with him—there wouldn't be room for more with all Saara's family's possessions anyway. The day moved slowly towards their appointed meeting time in the evening. He drove the journalist around the city, aware all the while it was the last time he would go through these familiar old routines. Often he glanced at Ali in the seat beside him and wished he could confide in his friend, but he knew he couldn't—another betrayal—and wondered what Ali would think had become of him when he disappeared. He had never even told him of Saara's existence, and the thought came to him that Ali too could have a girlfriend he had never mentioned somewhere in the city, and he wished they had spoken of it.

In the evening, when they were finished with the journalist, he dropped Ali home as usual, and when they pulled up outside the house, his friend invited him in for tea.

"I can't," Mahmoud said, "I have to be...somewhere."

"Your family won't miss you for half an hour. Come on," Ali urged him.

"It's not my family," Mahmoud said awkwardly.

"Oh, a girl," Ali smiled, "in that case I mustn't delay you. We mustn't make her impatient."

Mahmoud tried to smile back. "Let's have tea tomorrow?" he said.

"Of course."

Darkness was falling as he drove across the city, and the lights were coming on. Some of the shopkeepers were already shutting, for fear of looters or other disturbances. The old men were coming out of houses with plastic chairs to catch what little evening breeze there was. As Mahmoud passed the river, the moon was gleaming off the water, below the watchful American guns on the opposite bank. He was leaving, and he had no idea when he would return to the city that had been his only home. He saw an American convoy ahead and slowed instinctively, letting a more impatient driver pass, so there would be another car between him and the convoy. The soldier on the rear Humvee looked jittery, swinging his gun from side to side and glaring aggressively at the drivers. He looked over in Mahmoud's direction, and Mahmoud looked down quickly, avoiding eye contact. The traffic was moving smoothly. Mahmoud thought of the difficulties that lay ahead: he and Saara were still not married, and Abu Yusuf could easily pay him off and send him away when they reached Amman, or earlier still, at the border, where he could hire a Jordanian taxi for the rest of the journey. He would have to try to find a moment alone with Saara on the way, but it would be difficult.

There was a flash from ahead, and Mahmoud felt his blood stop. He knew what it was before the sound of the explosion reached him, and he was already braking hard and pulling over to the side of the road. Someone had attacked the Americans. There was the sound of gunfire. The American on the gun was swinging it wildly—he had no idea where the attack had come from and he was firing all over the street. Mahmoud knew the bullets could hit him at any moment. He wanted to put the car into gear and drive away, but he knew the best thing was to stay still. That way, the Americans didn't think you were a threat to them: move and they shot you.

There was a sound of squealing tyres and a straining engine, and looking out of the side window, he saw some fool trying to drive away. The car swerved and was heading straight for him. For a moment Mahmoud could see the driver's face clearly through the windscreen, the wide-eyed look of terror and astonishment on his face as he hit the Mercedes side on, then Mahmoud watched as the glass in his window shattered into a thousand pieces and the door bulged towards him, then there was overwhelming pain and darkness.

⊷⊶

When Mahmoud woke up, all he was aware of was the unbearable pain in his arm. He could feel that it was hanging at an impossible angle and, panicking, tried to reach for it with his other hand, but he was being held by someone. There was shouting all around and he was moving—being carried. The pain was too much, and he forced his whole body round somehow and grabbed at the arm, pulling it back into place. Somehow that was better, though the pain still seemed impossible, and he realised he was going to be sick and tried to tell the men holding him. It was only then he realised he had been screaming aloud. He couldn't make them understand and turned his head to one side and vomited.

"Nearly there," one of the men was shouting at him. "Hold on!"

They were trying to push their way through a crowded doorway, and his arm was badly jostled several times, sending shocks of pain through his whole body. He tried to cradle it close against his stomach; he could feel the vomit drying on his lips. There was electric light, and more people were pushing around him.

"No! No!" he called out. "I can't wait, I have to be somewhere!"

He felt them lift him higher and then lower him onto a bed,

and at least the moving had stopped and he could hold his arm still, safely against his stomach.

"My car!" he called as the men started to leave.

"It's no good," one of them said to him. "The Americans have cordoned the area off; there's no way to get to it. You're lucky we got you out."

Then they were gone and people in white were moving around him. One of them took hold of his arm—he tried to stop them—and moved it, and the pain was terrible and he felt the world slipping away again.

⊷•⟊•⊶

When he woke up again, he saw he had somehow kept his arm cradled to his body. The pain was still there, but he didn't seem to mind so much; he felt strangely disconnected from the world.

"We've given you something for the pain," someone said above him, and he looked round to see a young man's face. "It looks like it's broken, I'm afraid. Is there someone who can come for you?"

"Broken? No, it can't be. I have to…there's something I need to do tonight."

"Not tonight," said the young man. "We'll X-ray it for you. But I'm sure it's broken."

Mahmoud felt the weight of the news crushing down upon him and laid his head down on the bed.

"You're better off than the other driver," the young doctor said. "The Americans shot him. He's dead."

When he had gone, Mahmoud felt in his pocket for his mobile phone. He had to let go of his arm to do it, which was agony even through the fuzz of whatever they had given him, and he quickly cradled it again, gasping at the pain. He dialled Saara's number and, wincing, managed to get the phone to his ear.

"Mahmoud? Where are you?" Her voice came urgent down the line. "We were worried you weren't coming."

"There's been…been an accident."

"What?"

"Americans, I'm OK, I'm…I'm at the hospital."

"What? What happened?"

He realised he hadn't thought through what to say, but he knew he had to delay them, stop them leaving until he could get out of hospital and get the car back.

"It's OK, nothing serious. The doctors say I'll be fine," he lied, trying to keep the pain out of his voice, "but the car's a bit damaged. Can you wait one more night? I don't think I'm going to be able to make it tonight."

"Hold on."

He could hear muffled talking down the phone. Someone came over and tried to tell him to hang up, but he motioned them away. A new voice came down the line, her father, Abu Yusuf. Mahmoud explained there had been an accident, the Americans' fault, that it was minor, and he would still be able to drive them, but he had to get the car fixed, so he couldn't leave that night. Abu Yusuf reluctantly agreed—he had little choice; it would be hard for the family to find a replacement driver at such short notice—but asked Mahmoud to come round in the morning.

"They are coming for you?" the young doctor asked when he had hung up.

"What? Yes," he said distractedly. "I have to leave." He tried to get up, but the arm stabbed at him again.

"Wait, let us X-ray it first, and then we'll put it in plaster," the doctor said.

"My car, I have to go."

"You're not going to drive it like that. Wait till your friends arrive."

Mahmoud looked down at his arm and knew the doctor was right; there was no way he could drive in this condition.

"When will I be able to drive?" he said.

"Not for about six weeks, I imagine," the doctor said. He must have seen the reaction on Mahmoud's face, because he added more gently, "Let's wait and see the X-rays?"

Crushed again, Mahmoud lay back on the bed. Then a thought came to him, and he sat up and dialled another number on the mobile. His cousin Barzan was a driver; he was always asking Mahmoud to put work his way. Better still, he owed Mahmoud a favour: Mahmoud had sold him his old car when he bought the Mercedes, a battered Oldsmobile, but it would do the job if the Mercedes couldn't. He explained the situation quickly and asked Barzan to go straight to the crash scene and make sure the Mercedes was all right, then come for him at the hospital. A plan was forming in his mind: if he couldn't drive, he would get Barzan to drive the family and offer to come himself as a guarantee they could trust him. He wasn't sure they would agree to him coming along as a passenger, but it was his best hope. When the call was finished, he felt nervously for his money, worried someone might have taken it while he was passed out, but it was still there, and he was grateful he hadn't hidden it around the car, as he had thought of doing. He felt better now that he had a plan.

The X-ray confirmed what the doctor had said, that the arm was broken. Mahmoud tried to protest when they wanted to put his arm in plaster, but the doctor told him his humerus was completely shattered, and if his arm wasn't in plaster it would never heal and would be so painful he would have difficulty walking. It was the last detail that decided him; he needed to be able to make the next day's journey. They gave him a sling too, which at least meant he didn't have to hold the arm any more.

Barzan arrived with the news that the Mercedes was safe—the local shopkeepers had watched over it—and looked like it wasn't badly damaged. As soon as he had dropped Mahmoud home, he would go back for it. It was then Mahmoud realised he would have to go back to his parents' house with his arm in plaster, but there was no avoiding it, and he made up a version of events for them on the way. He wondered whether he should tell Barzan of his real plans, but decided it was better to wait and made Barzan promise to call for him the next morning, regardless of what his parents said, holding out the prospect of a lucrative driving job to the Jordanian border.

At the house, his parents made a dramatic scene, his mother crying and his father demanding to know who was responsible. Mahmoud pleaded the pain and managed to get away from them to his bedroom, where he saw they had not discovered his farewell letter. Exhausted with pain, he lay down and drifted in and out of morphine dreams in which he was with Saara, punctuated by stabs of pain from his arm that woke him more times than he could remember, until he woke to light spilling in through the window, the daze of the drugs gone and his arm horribly painful again, feeling heavy and massive and full of tiny splinters and one overwhelming raw ache all at once. He glanced at the clock. Barzan would arrive in half an hour, and he had to get past his parents. He decided to pre-empt them by getting washed and dressed unaided, so he sat up, but the wrench of pain from his arm left him rasping for breath. Getting out of bed was excruciating; he had to use his good arm to cradle the broken one, and that made it almost impossible to balance. Somehow, though, he managed it.

His parents at first refused to countenance his leaving the house, but eventually he won them over, lying that he needed to introduce Barzan to the journalist or he would risk losing his job and promising to come straight back. It cost Mahmoud some effort to get into the car—the Mercedes was in no state for a long journey, so Barzan had brought the Oldsmobile—and once they were under way every jolt and bump in the road sent new agonies coursing through his arm. On the way, he told Barzan a degree of the truth. He had decided he couldn't trust him with the whole story, but would have to risk some of it, so he said that he liked Saara and wanted her safe, but mentioned nothing of his marriage plans. Barzan gave him a knowing smile to say that he, a man of the world, understood.

Mahmoud knew he still had to persuade Abu Yusuf to take him along as a useless passenger with a broken arm, and that would be the hardest part of all. As they got closer to the familiar neighbourhood, he saw black smoke hanging in the air ahead and wondered if there had been a fire. Every turn they took, the black smoke lay ahead of them, and Mahmoud began to fear. As they turned the corner he knew so well, he saw the house in blackened ruins before him, smoke still rising, the upper floors partly collapsed, the window where she used to hang a ribbon for him a hole onto open air like the empty eye of a skull, the room behind it gone.

"Saara!"

Somehow, despite the pain from his arm, he was out of the car and running to the house. He could feel the heat coming off it before he even reached the door; when he touched it, the wood of the door burned his good hand, and he backed away. He forced himself to go forward again, despite the heat he could feel crawling across his face and tugging at the roots of his hair, but before he could plunge in he felt himself being held back by Barzan.

"Easy, easy, Mahmoud. You can't go in there."

"But Saara," was all he could sob, "Saara."

"They're gone," a voice said quietly beside them. Mahmoud looked up, and through the tears he recognised Saara's neighbour Ridwan, a man he had met once or twice.

"What?" he asked.

"They're gone," Ridwan repeated, his face pale, his eyes haunted. "It happened last night."

"What happened?" Mahmoud said, although he was already beginning to guess.

"It was the extremists," Ridwan said. "They came in the middle of the night. Abu Yusuf and his family were supposed to leave last night, everyone knew that, but for some reason they didn't; at the last minute they stayed. It was around three o'clock in the morning, and the noise woke me up. I could hear loud voices coming from their house, and then screaming. Someone was shouting, 'Help, help.' I didn't want to go; I knew they'd been getting death threats, but Abu Yusuf was my friend. Twenty years I knew him, and now he's gone. I saw his children grow up."

He tailed off into silence. Mahmoud stared at him, wanting and not wanting him to go on. Ridwan seemed to come back from wherever his mind had wandered and continued, "I took my Kalashnikov, and I went into the street. I couldn't see anyone around, and the noise had stopped. I went to the door. I had my gun with me, but there was nothing I could do, nothing. They were waiting, and I was no match for them. As soon as they opened the door they had their guns on me. They took my gun and made me go inside, with the others. Abu Yusuf and his son were there, kneeling on the floor in the middle of the room, while they stood around them with guns. There were three of them, all wearing masks so we couldn't see their faces. At first they told me to kneel with the others, but Abu Yusuf told them I was Muslim, and they questioned me about it, and then told me to get down on the floor some distance away from the others. When I asked them why, they said nothing. Then I saw the women on the other side of the room, Abu Yusuf's wife and his daughters, Saara and the little girl, standing in the corner. Abu Yusuf's wife and the little girl were crying, but Saara, she was different, she had this hard look on her face, as if she were angry, but keeping it inside. She just kept watching them, with this…look in her eyes. She had her arms around her mother and sister, and she was comforting them. She was speaking softly, but I'll never forget the look in her eyes.

"And then I realised what was happening, and why Abu Yusuf and his son were kneeling on the floor like that. They were going to kill them there, in front of the women. They were going to kill Abu Yusuf and make his wife and daughters watch, and I was going to have to watch as well. When I realised I tried to get up, told them not to do it, told them Abu Yusuf was a good man, how everyone in the neighbourhood respected him and his family, but one of them hit me hard in the stomach so I fell down again, and they told me to be quiet or they'd kill me too. Then I saw they weren't going to shoot Abu Yusuf; no, it was worse than that. One of them took out this long knife—it was shining; they were going to cut their throats there, in the middle of their own home, while the women watched. And as I looked over, Abu Yusuf's wife—she was praying, she kept repeating some prayer of theirs—she turned the little girl away and hid her face in her skirt so she didn't have to see. But Saara, she didn't say a word, she just kept on looking, and that's when he made his mistake, the one who was guarding the women. He turned away from them to watch Abu Yusuf's throat being cut, and that's when Saara did it. She had a knife hidden under her dress. I don't know how—she must have taken it from the kitchen when the gunmen came in, and the moment his back was turned she took it and plunged it in his neck. I couldn't believe her strength, the way she pushed the knife in against his muscle. And that look in her eyes…I never want to see that look again. But it was all Abu Yusuf and his son needed. The other gunmen ran to help their colleague, who was on the floor with the blood pouring out of his neck, and in the confusion Abu Yusuf leapt up and knocked the knife from the hand of the one who was going to kill him and threw his arms round the man's waist so he couldn't go for his gun. Yusuf did the same with the one next to him. I rushed over to help, expecting to die—one of them could have got to his gun at any moment and started shooting us all—but Yusuf shouted at me to get the gun from the one Saara had stabbed. He was lying on the floor, the breath hissing out of the wound in his neck and making bubbles in his blood. He was twitching, but there was no strength in him and I took the gun easily and levelled it at the others. Just then there was the sound of a shot, and Abu Yusuf stopped moving. The one he was fighting had got to his gun and shot him. Abu Yusuf fell back, and I pointed the gun and fired at the gunman before he could shoot again. Yusuf had the other one under control, but I wasn't taking any chances so I told Yusuf to stand clear and I shot the one he'd been holding. When we went to see how badly Abu Yusuf was hurt, he was dead; my friend was dead. But he had saved his family—he was a hero, Abu Yusuf. His wife was in shock; she kept muttering what sounded like gibberish and staring around the room. The little girl was shaking, but Saara was standing over the one she had stabbed, with his blood all down her clothes. He was still alive, and his fingers were clutching at her, but she stood over him and looked down at him with this cold look in her eyes. I only heard her say one thing in all that time, and it was to the man who lay dying at her feet. 'You will not rob me of my wedding night,' she said, but I don't think he could hear her by then. It was a long time before we got her to move away and come and look at her father's body. I don't think she knew he was dead until then; she had been lost, but when she saw Abu Yusuf lying there, that was when that terrible cold finally went out of her eyes and she wept daughter's tears for her father, cradling him in her arms and hugging him tight to her chest.

"When we got the gunmen's masks off, they were just children. I doubt one of them was twenty. If they'd been older or more experienced, we would never have survived. They'd taken the family by surprise, coming in the night, and got to them before they could get their gun. But they made stupid mistakes, not tying the men's hands and not even searching the women for weapons. We were lucky, but I knew it couldn't stay that way, and so did Yusuf. He wanted to bury his father, but I knew the news would travel fast and the family was in danger, and they had to leave immediately. I told Yusuf to go and that I would bury Abu Yusuf. I called a friend of mine to drive them and they took what they could and left."

Mahmoud stood in silence.

"She's alive?" he asked, his own voice sounding strange. "She's alive?"

"They were all alive except my friend, Abu Yusuf. They left for the border. I took Abu Yusuf's body to the morgue this morning. When I got back, the extremists had already been for their revenge." He gestured at the burning remains of the house. "But with the family gone, this was all they could do. I'm moving my family. We have a tribe to protect us, but all the same I am going to my brother in Samarra."

"She's alive," Mahmoud repeated. In the last few minutes, he felt he had died more than once, listening to Ridwan's story, only to hear that she was still alive, his love, the enemy, his Saara.

"We should go," Barzan said. "They could be watching this place." He led Mahmoud back to the car.

"We have to follow them," Mahmoud said.

"Are you crazy? They're gone," Barzan said. "They left hours ago; they'll be at the border by now."

"I have to see her."

"Let her go, Mahmoud, she's gone. At least she's alive, that's what matters. Let her go."

As they drove away Mahmoud realised it was true: she was alive, his Saara, but he would never see her again.

Chapter Twenty-Seven

Hollywood Part Two

11–22 May 2004

THE RUMOURS STARTED in the afternoon, rumours of a hostage no one had heard of, stories of a body found hanging from a bridge in Baghdad. Zoe heard it from Kate, Jack heard it from his translator, Ali heard it from the drivers, and nobody was sure if it was true. Janet said there were always rumours like these that generally turned out to be untrue, and Zoe wanted to believe she was right. Several hostages had been released unharmed, and there was the American who had escaped his kidnappers, but small developments had been adding to her sense of unease. A week and a half before, Mahmoud hadn't turned up for work. It turned out he had broken his arm in a car accident, and he sent his cousin Barzan in his place in another car, but Zoe felt a little less secure with an unfamiliar face. Then there had been the afternoon she had found Jack exploring the kitchen entrance at the back of the hotel: when she asked him what he was doing, he said he was looking for an escape route in case the insurgents attacked the hotel. And now this story of a body found hanging from a bridge. As the afternoon wore on, there was a new detail: it was a body without a head. Still the journalists tried not to believe it. The hours passed and more details came: a name, grieving parents in the US, official confirmation.

"There's a video," Kate said, breathless at the door.

"What?"

"There's a video of this guy being killed."

Zoe thought of the disc of the Russian soldier being killed.

"Where did it come from?" Jack asked.

"Nobody seems to be clear on that," Kate said, "but we've got a copy if you want to see it."

"No," Zoe said. "No, I don't want to see it."

But she did, they all did, sitting on the bed in Kate's make-shift editing room, watching on the monitor as the poor-quality image flicked and jumped. The American was made to sit on the floor, his hands and feet bound, powerless. Men dressed in black stood over him, their faces masked with headscarves and balaclavas, guns at their sides. The American was made to give his name—Nick Berg—the names of his parents, of his brother and sister and his home town. Then there was a long statement in Arabic and the masked men closed in around him. He screamed as he saw the knife, and it was done.

It was a clever, cruel little piece of propaganda, with Berg dressed in a bright-orange jumpsuit like those worn by prisoners in Guantanamo Bay. An answer to the pictures from Abu Ghraib too, vicious image for vicious image, except it went one better: a video instead of still pictures, complete with soundtrack. An American made to kneel helpless, waiting for the knife, made to drag the names of his father and mother into it. But Zoe saw something else in those images, not the carefully honed propaganda of the killers, not the death of an American at the hands of Arabs, but a young man, bewildered, afraid, and, when the awful truth dawned, dying in panic and terror. According to the reports that were emerging, he had come to Iraq as an idealist, hoping to take part in the reconstruction of the country—his speciality was communication towers. A little naive, perhaps, to be roaming around such a dangerous place looking for work, but Zoe thought of someone else who had come to Iraq a little naive and idealistic. They had all thought Iraq was lawless, a war without rules, but now she realised there had been rules, a sort of tacit understanding of where the limits lay, but that it had died in Fallujah and Abu Ghraib and in the video of a young man dying before her. It was impossible to say who was reacting to whom any more; they were just responding to each other in a dance of escalating cruelty, and the dance was getting faster.

In the days that followed, Zoe began to worry about Jack. He seemed restless and preoccupied, frustrated at being forced to stay in the hotel, unable to get close to the action. One day he ventured south to Najaf and came back to say that the Americans were fighting the Mahdi Army inside the great cemetery of Wadi al-Salaam. He described extraordinary scenes, like something out of a movie, fighters dressed in black firing on the Americans, then retreating amid the tombstones. But the journey had been dangerous; more than once he got stuck in traffic and had to wrap his face in his headscarf and curl up pretending he was ill, and he said it wasn't worth trying to get south again. The crisis came a few days later, when they were alone in his room.

"I think it may be time to get out," he said quietly. She didn't want to reply, but kept her eyes fixed on her glass and on the drops of condensation forming on it. "We can't even do our jobs any more," he said. "We can't talk to people on the streets, we can barely leave the hotel, travelling outside Baghdad is taking your life in your hands. And it's only going to get worse. You're going to be out of here in a couple of weeks and, well, it's not up to me but…but I don't think you should come back."

"What about you?"

"That's what I wanted to tell you. I've applied for chief reporter on the paper. Mike Davies is going to Washington so I've put in for the job."

"I see." Zoe was disappointed and a little hurt that he had applied for the job without discussing it with her. "And if you don't get it?"

"Then I'll think of something else."

"Right. Are you…are you sure this is what you want, Jack? I mean, it's just you've been covering Iraq from the start. Don't you want to see it through?"

"I've done my bit. Someone else can have a go. I've done more than a year here. And you can't cover the story properly any more."

"But do you really want to be chief reporter? Somehow I can't…I mean, it isn't you." He'd make a lot more money, but he'd be reporting on celebrity scandals and politicians cheating on their wives.

"Why not? It's a good job."

"Yes, it is, of course, it's just…it's just I always imagined you staying here. I mean, you belong here, Jack. Out here, you can make a real difference; you're not just churning out the American line—you're telling the real story."

"We can't do that any more," he said quietly. "Nick Berg's not going to be the last. Now that video is out there, there are going to be more killings like that. The streets are crawling with armed men. Anyone can drag you out of your car at gunpoint. How long until you're at a checkpoint and they look in the back, find you're a Westerner, and that's it, you're dragged off and end up in a video like that? I don't want to die like that."

"No," Zoe said, shuddering.

"I don't see how we can do our jobs under pressure like that. We'll just end up stuck in the hotel, rewriting the official line."

"We'll find a way, Jack, we always do. I mean, you're the one who says there's always a way."

"I'm not sure there is any more. Face it, Zoe, time's up. We just can't cover this story properly."

"Well, if it's what you want."

But she left the thought that troubled her the most unspoken: he might want to leave, but she didn't. She didn't want to cut and run just as her career was blossoming, and more than that, she felt a responsibility to keep telling a story that mattered now more than ever. For the next few days they avoided the question. Jack didn't mention it again, and Zoe hoped she had dissuaded him. Their lives in Baghdad had changed. In the wake of Berg's killing, the reporters' world had become more circumscribed. Leaving the hotel carried new risk, and where before Jack and Zoe had often lunched out at restaurants around the city, they stopped altogether, leaving the hotel now only for work, travelling direct to an interview or the site of an incident to report, and returning as quickly as possible. The other reporters were doing the same; no one wanted to risk word of their presence getting to potential kidnappers. Leaving Baghdad was even less inviting an option, since all the roads out of town ran through dangerous areas. Some of the journalists had taken to lying down in the backs of their cars—the danger with that was that if someone spotted you, they knew you were hiding. Zoe started going more often to the American press briefings inside the Green Zone, even though it meant queuing for hours in the sun at the dangerous entrances to clear security. Inside the drab neon-lit conference hall, the spokesmen droned on about how the security situation was improving, while they were guarded by men hunched behind concrete blast walls with guns pointing out.

Film and images were dominating the news in more ways than one. More victims of the Abu Ghraib abuse came forward to say they were the men in the pictures: grown men trying to hold onto their dignity while they identified themselves naked in pictures where an American woman soldier pointed at their genitals and smirked. The Americans bombed a wedding party out in the remote desert by mistake, killing more than forty people. The generals denied it had been a wedding, claiming they had attacked a safe house used by foreign fighters crossing in from Syria. There was no way the reporters could travel there safely and find out for themselves, but they were finding new ways of uncovering the truth, as Zoe had predicted. A couple of videos emerged: the first the usual shaky home wedding video, shot with a little portable camera, of children playing and musicians entertaining the guests; the second, filmed with the same camera, showed the bodies of the same musicians and children, dead. The military continued to deny it had been a wedding.

The video of Nick Berg left unanswered questions. It emerged that he had been arrested in Iraq and held for more than a week by the Americans, and then let go before he was kidnapped and beheaded. There was no clear explanation of why he was held or why he was released. There were strange reports that, years before, he had accidentally run into one of the 9/11 hijackers on a bus in the US and lent him his laptop. No one ever got to the bottom of all that.

Zoe would have been content with the new limits of covering Iraq, but for Jack. She could see he was growing increasingly frustrated; used to following his own leads and stories, away from the crowd of the journalists, he wasn't happy spending long hours in the hotel, reporting and analysing the day's developments. He wanted those stories from out on the edge, stories of how ordinary people's lives were affected. He even went back on his previous resolve to avoid leaving the city and tried to drive south to Najaf again, only to come back more badly shaken than the previous time. She wished he would understand the source of his frustration and give up the idea of a dull London job that would make him more bored and unhappy. But one evening, two days before she was due to leave Baghdad, he told her, in the same quiet tones as before, that he had news.

"I got the chief reporter job," he said.

"Right," she said. "I mean, congratulations. It's what you wanted."

"I'll be staying on till they get a new correspondent set up here, then I'm moving back to London, in a couple of weeks or so...Don't look like that, Zoe, it's for the best. We've had a good run here."

"But." She hesitated. "But what about me?"

"You'll be out of here in a few days, and I'll be with you a couple of weeks after that. I mean, that's why I held out for this job. They offered me Washington, but I turned it down because I wanted to be with you." Washington correspondent was a better job than chief reporter. It was one of the best jobs on the paper. But that just made what Zoe had to say even harder.

"But, Jack, the thing is, I don't want to leave Iraq."

"What?"

"This is *the* story. The biggest story of our time, and I want to be here. It's not just a question of my career, it's that, well, this is journalism I believe in. I don't want to go back to writing little nothing stories in London."

"You won't, after everything you've done here."

"But I want to stay, Jack. I want to keep coming here and see it through."

"Right," he said, looking disappointed. "I mean, well, it's up to you of course. I'd never try to...But think about it, Zoe. Please think about it. Because it's only going to get more dangerous, and I think it's going to happen very fast."

"Right."

She wanted to ask him to stay on in Iraq, to stay with her, but knew she wouldn't. It wasn't as if they were splitting up; they would be together in London, but it wouldn't be the same. Feelings she hadn't acknowledged began to surface, feelings of disappointment, as if he hadn't quite lived up to the man she had thought he was. They didn't speak of it further, and she tried to make the most of their last days in Baghdad together, but the sense of disillusionment lingered. When the day of her departure came, he insisted on driving with her to the airport, even though it meant a needless return trip along the dangerous airport road, and he told her he'd see her in London.

<hr />

Mahmoud sat and stared at the wall. His arm ached. There were new pains every day, sometimes like tiny splinters of bone pricking all through the inside of his arm, sometimes a great dull ache, sometimes a raw feeling. He couldn't move his fingers. The doctors said it was temporary, that the nerves would grow back, but it felt like a foretaste of death. It wasn't that it hurt to try to move his fingers, or that he didn't have the strength. When he tried to move them, nothing happened. Nothing at all. No matter how hard he concentrated—and he did, until the veins stood out on his forehead and the sweat poured—he couldn't get the message from his brain to his fingers. At times, in bed at night, he woke to a sensation like his fingers had somehow all got twisted in a knot with each other, and he threw off the covers in a panic to find they were all in place. He thought about his arm a lot, to block out the other pain that was worse, and that he knew was not temporary, but it was no use. As he stared at the blank white wall, he could see images moving against it: her face, her hair, her body, the way she used to hold it so the shape showed even through her loose clothes, her mocking smile, the way she turned away abruptly when she was annoyed, the way she had looked the first time he kissed her...

He knew he shouldn't think of these things, that they only brought pain, that she was gone now. His mother and father spoke to him. He murmured replies, but he didn't hear, not the part of him that mattered anyway. That part was watching her on the wall, fading images that were all that was left of his life now.

Chapter Twenty-Eight

A Hero's Death

12 May–4 June 2004

BENES CROUCHED BEHIND the wall of the tomb, listening hard over the sound of his own heart beating. Cautiously, he raised his head and peered over the top of the stonework. The cemetery stretched on as far as he could see, tomb upon tomb, some simple, some the size of small houses, all of them ghostly and insubstantial in the green of his night vision, but there was no sign of movement. The lead Humvee lay ahead where it had been hit. Hernandez and Steele crouched alongside it, behind the wall of the next tomb, but to reach them Benes would have to cross exposed ground, at the mercy of the enemy's guns. He was on the edge of the city of the dead, long after midnight, and somewhere among the graves, the enemy was watching him. He tried to put it from his mind and edged slowly forwards.

Something flew into his face, a blur of movement and a leathery brushing at his cheeks, and he dropped to the ground. Just a bat, he saw, as it fled into the night. The attack had come, as they always did, at the spot where their patrol route led them alongside the cemetery, the lead Humvee hit as they turned the corner. Benes supposed he should be grateful it was only sniper fire and not an IED or a rocket-propelled grenade: none of the men had been injured. The lead Humvee was disabled, that was all, but it meant they were stranded until backup could arrive. Benes glanced at the grove of palm trees opposite: the enemy snipers liked to sit in the palm trees, but tonight they were empty. The danger would be from the cemetery. He looked back at Gibbs, a few feet behind, and signalled him to give covering fire. Gibbs opened his mouth to protest, but Benes was up and moving before he could speak, crouching low in a mad run across the exposed ground, expecting every moment the first bullets to come in. He was almost across when they did, cracking loud in the air around him until he threw himself, grateful, next to Hernandez behind the shelter of the tomb.

"You OK, sir?"

"Yeah. Want to light that fucker up for me?"

"Which one, sir? You got half the cemetery firing at you."

"Fuck, I don't care. Any of them."

It could only be a matter of time till they brought out the RPGs, or worse. The firing stopped; they were moving again. The Mahdi Army could move around invisible as ghosts inside the cemetery, hidden in the dense network of tombs. Benes scanned the sky, looking for any sign of the helicopters. Benes and the platoon were being used as bait. Wary of attacking the holy sites around Najaf, including the cemetery, the higher-ups had resorted to sending unarmoured patrols of Humvees to lure the enemy out of hiding and then take them out on open ground, but the problem was the Mahdi Army always attacked in places like this, on the edge of the cemetery, where they could disappear among the endless tombs, and Benes and his men weren't allowed to follow.

Benes heard the sound of helicopters approaching and looked up gratefully. With their cover from above, the platoon was safe again. At the sound of the helicopters, the Mahdi Army would already be melting away.

--◦●◦--

Nouri made his way through the narrow alleys of the cemetery in the dark, running to keep ahead of the helicopter he could hear moving somewhere above. There was no moon, but Nouri knew the tombs so well by now he could find his way blindfolded. He had to keep moving fast so he could get under cover before the helicopter found him. He felt the ground give beneath his left foot and his shin hit hard against stone, but he kept silent. The ground was treacherous: it often gave way around the tombs, and Nouri had heard stories from the others of seeing bones, though he didn't believe them. He pushed himself round the last corner and, looking up to make sure the helicopter wasn't too close, swung under the small opening into the tomb, where he had to duck under the roof. The others, Sa'id and Ammar, were already there. He could just make them out in the dark, sitting towards the back of the tomb.

Nouri put his rifle with the others, shuffled in and sat down. There wasn't room to do any more. The helicopter was growing louder overhead, and Nouri feared the pilot had seen him entering. They sat in the dark, listening. Eventually the sound faded into the distance and the helicopter left. They sat on for a time, until Ammar switched his electric torch on, filling the tomb with a light that cast eerie shadows across the stone roof. There was no body inside the small stone space: it was buried beneath; this was just a symbolic tomb. All the same, the others said they were unnerved at night, thinking of the body below. Nouri tried not to think of it. He and the others had been living here for some time; much of the space was taken up with ammunition and RPGs, piled up along the rear wall, and with their blankets and food and water supplies; guns and a smaller store of ammunition were kept at the entrance, ready to be used in a hurry.

Other men were posted as look-outs that night and would pass the message if there was another patrol, but Nouri doubted there would be one. At least one of them had to stay awake, and he volunteered, knowing the others would not relish a night alone with the ghosts. He watched them bed down, and some time after, he put out the light. In the middle of the night, when he thought they were both asleep, he heard Sa'id's voice, speaking softly so as not to wake Ammar.

"Nouri?"

"Yes?"

"What's it like in Sadr City?"

Sa'id was younger than Nouri; he came from Najaf and had probably never been to Baghdad. Nouri told him about it.

"Will you go back there when this is over?"

"Insha'Allah."

She had begun to haunt his sleep again, what little sleep Benes could get between the mortars and the gunfire that were the constant song of the Alamo: the girl with no eyes. It seemed she was there whenever he slept, a wet smear of red flesh where her eyes should have been, watching him. He hadn't thought of that night in Baghdad for months. When he had lain awake, unable to sleep, it had been with other sentinels of the night, Gutierrez's lifeless body, riding alongside him in the Humvee, or Dr Afaf, her imagined dead body bloody and naked, punished for speaking to him, cut in unbearable places. But when he slept during those nights in Najaf, it was the checkpoint in Baghdad that came back to him, the mother keening from the back of the car, the father blinking in incomprehension as he died, the light glittering off the tiny crystals of glass embedded in the flesh of the girl with no eyes. The dream came so much she began to haunt his waking hours as well, until he felt she was walking every step with him in Iraq.

He was worried about the men's morale. They had been stretched to the limit, and he feared they were about to start breaking under this relentless deployment that had gone on, month after month, as they got sucked ever deeper in. Even the military couldn't keep them here forever, fighting in circles in a war that had been officially declared over before they had even arrived. But Benes knew the men were starting to wonder if they'd survive long enough to get home. At times, in the madness of those days in the Alamo, he even wondered if they were all already dead and in some hell where they were being punished for their sins, sent in the same circles with no way out. He didn't understand how the war was taking place in reverse, the fighting getting worse, the enemy getting stronger, and all the while the Americans were being pulled further into Iraq, fighting around alien shrines that meant nothing to them. They were getting stranded in the quicksands of Iraq.

And then they were ordered into the cemetery.

Benes knew he had made a mistake. No solid mausoleum wall to shelter behind this time, just an old and crumbling gravestone that wouldn't last more than a few minutes against sustained fire, and his path of retreat was cut off. It was broad daylight, but still he couldn't see them amid the tombs, yet he knew from the gunfire that had raked in a minute before that they were all around, cutting off every path of advance. They were waiting over there, somewhere beyond the tombs, for him to make a move. He glanced back to the others, sheltering behind their own tombs and bits of stonework, where they had ducked for cover when the shooting began, but there was no way they could reach him. He felt a movement, a disturbance in the air directly over his head. A puff of dust kicked up from the top of the tombstone and he heard a crack. That one had been so close he had felt it moving; the slight contact with the tombstone might have been be all that had saved him, deflecting the path of the bullet a fraction of an inch away from his head. He hunkered in closer to the old stone. Any words that had ever marked it were long worn away, not that he would have been able to read them anyway. There was no shade and the heat was intense. He saw a flicker of movement from behind the tombs, and there was the crack of another bullet, not so close this time. He fired back.

Someone in the chain of command had decided he'd had enough of letting soldiers get picked off by an enemy who could retreat into the safety of religious sites that had been designated exclusion zones by a general back in Baghdad. He had decided to provoke a confrontation, so he'd lined up his tanks outside the cemetery in daylight and waited for them to be attacked. When the Mahdi Army took the bait, he threw everything at them: tanks, helicopters and several platoons on foot to hunt them down. Benes had led from the front, running through the narrow alleys into the maze of the cemetery, only to find he'd led his men into an ambush. They were deep inside, lost in the biggest cemetery in the world.

—•→●→●←●←—

Nouri watched the American soldier behind the nearest tomb. One more move, and he would have him. The bullet must have missed by the smallest of fractions. Nouri glanced across at Sa'id, behind the tomb a few feet away. They had been waiting for this moment, planning for it, but Nouri was still angry the Americans had entered the cemetery. He saw movement from behind the tomb and fired, but he missed again. His arms ached from the weight of the rifle, and his legs had gone numb from crouching too long in the same position. Looking up at the sky, he saw two of the helicopters on the edge of the cemetery turn towards them, the sun glinting off their bodies. Nouri gripped his gun and fired at the Americans: there wasn't much time, the helicopters would soon be upon them, and he would have to fall back.

"Nouri," Sa'id hissed at him, gesturing up at the sky. Nouri nodded and kept firing. The helicopters were a thunder approaching overhead now. Nouri tried to ignore them.

"Nouri," Sa'id hissed again, and he looked up. The helicopters were almost on top of them. Nouri reluctantly shouldered his gun and followed Sa'id through the alleys of graves, running at a crouch.

⇥⊛ ⊛⇤

"I got some! I got some!"

"Lit the fucker up! Smoked him!"

Outside the cemetery, the soldiers were regrouping around the Humvees, congratulating themselves on enemy kills, but Benes stood apart, the sense of how close he had been to leading the men to their deaths sharper now that they were out of danger. The helicopters hammered overhead, turning in arcs over the cemetery. Benes saw something flick briefly across the corner of his eye, then land on the ground with a soft thud beside him and roll under the Humvee.

"Grenade!" he shouted. The soldiers scattered. Benes was still running when he felt the blast lift him from his feet and drop him hard to the ground, the heat washing around him before he heard the sound of the explosion. He turned and saw the Humvee in flames. The firing started up. Instead of retreating deep inside their graveyard, the Mahdi Army were coming back to attack the Americans' main position. Benes picked himself off the ground and began shooting back in the direction of the enemy fire. The Humvee was still burning, and the heat it gave off made it hard to keep his eyes open. He waited for the order to fall back, but instead Captain Parks's voice came over the radio telling them to defend the burning Humvee.

"Defend it?" Benes asked.

"Roger that, defend the Humvee. Do not let the enemy approach."

And so they held their positions, defending a wreck that was long past any chance of repair. When Captain Parks ran, at a crouch, to join Benes, he explained that they didn't want to let the Mahdi Army film themselves celebrating next to the destroyed Humvee.

The fighting at the cemetery went on for days, and they had to snatch what little sleep they could in the armoured cars. At times Benes woke disoriented in the strange subterranean lights of the armoured cars, as if he had been buried in some sort of mass coffin, and he had to get out for air, despite his exhaustion. After a few days, fatigue became the overriding sensation, every minute an effort to stay awake and focused.

—◦—

Moon was trying to say something, but Benes couldn't hear him above the sound of the tanks and the helicopters. They were on the edge of the cemetery, and the wind was blowing the thick black smoke streaming from somewhere nearby across their faces, so it was hard to see. They were watching for any sign of the Mahdi Army, but Benes didn't think they would come, not after the hammering they had taken in the last few days. Moon was still trying to get his attention and Benes signalled irritably that he couldn't hear.

He turned and looked back over the expanse of tombs, searching for any sign of movement. After Fallujah, everyone had been terrified of urban combat, but for the soldiers in Najaf it had been necropolitan combat—even the dust beneath their boots was probably made of the bones of long-dead men that had spilled out of these tombs. He felt something move through the air and turned and saw Moon with a look of shock on his face, even as he heard the crack of the bullet. There was a patch of red blossoming at Moon's throat, just above the protection of his flak jacket, and Benes was running and caught Moon just before he fell. The red was flooding out now, soaking Moon's clothes under his flak jacket, as the sound of the return fire went up around them. Benes clamped his hand over the wound to stop it and looked around desperately for help. Forgetting the fighting, he picked Moon up in his arms. He could hear someone screaming at him to get down, but there wasn't time. He started running, as fast as he could with Moon's weight, back towards the armoured vehicle where the medics were. He could feel bullets slapping the air around his head. Doc Martinez ran out to meet him, clamping something hard over the wound in Moon's neck—the blood was streaming out between Benes's fingers. Benes looked at Martinez, but he could see it in his eyes. No need to speak: there was nothing they could do for Moon.

"I'm cold," Moon murmured. Benes, still holding him, pulled him closer. They were all around now, Hawkes pressing in on one side, Gibbs on another.

"It's all right," Benes said. "You're going to be fine."

"Is it bad?"

"No," Benes lied. "It's nothing."

"I'm dying," Moon said.

"Don't talk crazy," Benes said. "Doc's going to fix you up. You're going to be all right."

"Mom!" Moon said.

"Hey, remember that day with the lions?" Benes said. Moon couldn't smile any more. "You fucked with those guys good."

Moon moaned. Benes held him tight and felt the life go out of him. It happened slowly, and the boy's last words turned to a series of unrecognisable moans. After they took the body from him, Benes sat a long time in the dust, covered in his friend's blood. He wished he had heard what Moon was trying to say to him earlier. Would it have made any difference? Probably not; he didn't see how it could have, but he would have liked to have known what it was.

Sa'id and Ammar both died in the fighting. Ammar died first, hit by fire from a helicopter as they were running through the cemetery. Nouri heard him cry out and, looking back, saw him fall. An instant later and he would have ducked safely under cover of one of the tombs. Nouri and Sa'id waited there till they were sure the helicopter had gone; then they went back for Ammar, but he was dead, lying in a large, dark patch his blood had made on the ground. There were more helicopters, so they moved the body quickly. Sa'id died later the same day. He and Nouri were both pinned down by American fire in a narrow defile, the Americans so close Nouri could see their faces across the tomb tops. There was no question of surrender, Nouri knew, as his and Sa'id's eyes met, not after they had seen Ammar die. Nouri knew it was only a matter of time and prepared himself to face death.

Sa'id was hit first: his gun abruptly fell silent, and looking round, Nouri saw the blood spreading from his head. Sa'id looked at Nouri as if he was trying to say something, but Nouri didn't know what it was. Somehow Nouri crawled to him between the tombs and the American bullets, but when he got there Sa'id was dead. The Americans were calling something, but it was in English, and Nouri fired at them from the spot where Sa'id had been hit, expecting death. After some time, he ran out of ammunition, and having nothing left to fight with, he lay down and played dead. The American guns fell silent. He waited for the Americans to come and check his body, but nobody did. When, eventually, he decided to risk looking up, they had gone, the fight had moved into another corner of the graveyard, and unable to move Sa'id's body on his own, he ran back through the alleys to the tomb where he and the others had lived. Night was falling and Nouri lay down, exhausted. The tomb was empty of their voices, the voices that had irritated Nouri and kept him awake at night. He glanced at the corners where they slept, at their bedding, still lying there ready for them. Outside, the sound of the battle went on. He had barely known them, but he felt as if his oldest friends had died and left him alone in the world.

Eventually he gathered up the remaining ammunition and went to find others, to collect Sa'id's body and rejoin the fight.

In the end, they had to demolish an entire section of the cemetery wall. That robbed the Mahdi Army of the cover the grave-yard had given them: they could still disappear among its endless tombs and alleys, but they couldn't get close enough to attack the American patrols passing outside without being seen. There was a great deal of Shia anger at the damage to the cemetery, and even more that the main shrine had been hit in the fighting. The Americans and the Mahdi Army, of course, each accused the other, but to the American commanders, the broken wall and bullet-holes in the golden dome of the shrine meant that the exclusion zones had been breached and there had been no massive civil strife—on the contrary, the operation had been a success. So they turned their attention to Kufa, where the leader of the Mahdi Army was holed up inside the large mosque complex, a mortar's throw from the Alamo.

There was little time for Benes or the men to grieve for Moon. No sooner had they returned to the Alamo than they were preparing for a final push on Kufa. Benes did, however, see some reasons for optimism. With the exclusion zones less of an issue, there would be no more need for unarmoured patrols to serve as bait. And if they could succeed in getting Moqtada al-Sadr out of Kufa, there was a chance it could end the fighting across the south, and they could be on their way home at last. People began to speak of it as the Final Offensive.

In the calm between storms, Benes finally managed to sleep—he slept so deeply that he woke in confusion, forgetting where he was. The shape of the room, the walls, the smell, the sound of gunfire were all unfamiliar and frightening, and when he remembered that he was in Najaf he began to panic, asking himself how he had got there when he was supposed to be at home with Maria and Juan.

In the hours before the operation began came the news that the Mahdi Army was withdrawing from Karbala, which meant

Kufa was the last remaining battleground. As night fell, the whole Alamo was on edge: this was the start of the battle that could end the war, for them at least, that could take them home. Benes watched as the men sat and listened to favourite songs or stood in small groups, shifting nervously from foot to foot.

The plan was to send a few tanks on an exploratory drive through Mahdi Army territory and see how far they could get. Benes knew it wouldn't be long before they came under heavy fire, and then he would be sent out with the platoon to engage the enemy in the dark, in unfamiliar territory. Once the tanks were under way, he sat in the operations room and listened to the voices of their crews coming in over the radio.

"They're in every fucking alley."

"We've already taken six hits, they're everywhere."

"Take that fucking position out!"

⊷⊶⊷

Nouri watched from the rooftop as the tank burned below. The young fighter next to him was shouting in excitement, but Nouri knew the American tanks; he had seen them in Sadr City. Even in flames, the tank was still advancing; there was nothing they could do to stop it, and even if they did, there were more coming behind.

The flames lit up the night sky. The fighters on the rooftops all around were black against the red of the fire. Down below, he could see more fighters running up to the tanks and throwing grenades, while the great guns of the tanks swung round. Several of the fighters were cut down by machine-gun fire.

And all the while Nouri could see Sa'id and Ammar, the way they had fallen in the cemetery, the last look Sa'id had given him, as if he had something to say. He wished the Americans would send foot soldiers.

⊷⊶⊷

Benes didn't even have to leave the Alamo. The colonel didn't send them out to fight; he let the tanks handle it. The enemy threw everything they had at them, but the tanks kept going, smashing their way through the gates and into the mosque complex itself, before turning round and heading back to the Alamo. When they got there, only one of the tanks was still usable. The other two were damaged beyond repair, but they had made their point. The Mahdi Army had taken heavy casualties trying to fight against battle tanks. When Benes ordered the men to stand down and went to bed, he feared the operation's success would just mean a bigger operation the next day, one that would include the platoon.

But the morning brought news that the tanks' sortie had been even more of a success than he'd thought: the Mahdi Army had offered a ceasefire. Benes knew that could mean the end of the fighting; the others knew it too—he could see it in their expressions as the news spread through the Alamo. Hawkes was less optimistic.

"Ceasefires have been known to be broken," he muttered, and he insisted on keeping the men battle-ready, even as the nightly mortars fell silent.

-⇥⊜⊜⇤-

On Friday, the commander decided to test the Mahdi Army's sincerity by sending a patrol across the bridge into Kufa. There had been no trouble since the ceasefire, and no one was particularly concerned, but the colonel still sent out a full company-sized unit, Benes's platoon among them. They were in unarmoured Humvees, but they had some firepower with them, including tanks up front, and the Mahdi Army had learned to fear tanks after the night raid on Kufa, so Benes felt relaxed as they turned onto the bridge. The traffic was heavy, the civilian population out on the streets in force. The ceasefire was holding. It was a brilliant morning, the Euphrates River indigo and gold where the sun flashed off the water, the heat of the day not built up yet, the breeze cool through the Humvee's open windows. Gibbs was in an expansive mood at the wheel, grinning out at women as they passed.

"Hell yeah, come to daddy, baby," he called out. "Last chance to get some all-American action."

In the back, on the gun, Jackson laughed. As they eased their way up the street towards the mosque, the loudspeakers attached to the minarets crackled into life, not the familiar call to prayer, but a speech of some sort in Arabic, and Benes was wondering why someone was making a speech when the firing started coming in at them from all sides. The civilian crowd scattered. There was an explosion as a grenade went off and sounds of panic, Jackson swinging the gun, voices over the radio, confusion, gunfire.

Another rocket-propelled grenade came in, exploding just a few feet away, and Benes saw they were the only Humvee with a clear path to the alley it had come from. He told Gibbs to head there and called over the radio for the Humvee behind to follow. As they turned into the alley, Jackson firing all the way, Benes saw black-clad fighters running. Two of them managed to make it through the door of a house, but the third was too slow and couldn't make the ground to the house. He turned to face them, a teenager with a scruffy half-beard and a look of terror in his eyes. Benes was about give the order to take him alive when he raised the RPG launcher in his hand and pointed it at them. Jackson opened up on him, and he fell.

Gibbs was reversing back out of the street when something slapped the air past Benes's eyes. There was an explosion, and Benes turned to see that the Humvee that had followed them into the alley had been hit. Worse, it was blocking the way out. Gunfire was coming in from above and, looking up, Benes could see Mahdi Army fighters on the rooftops: the alley had become a trap.

⊷▪◍ ◖▪⊶

Nouri watched from the rooftop as the Americans drove into the dead-end alley. He wasn't concerned for the fighters down there; on foot they could easily escape over the rooftops. But he saw an opportunity and fired at the Humvee that tried to follow. As the smoke cleared, he saw it wasn't a direct hit, but he had managed to disable it, and it lay skewed across the road, blocking the only way out of the alley. He called the others to follow and ran lightly across the roof. He could see the Americans trapped below. Abbas wanted to use the RPG launcher, but Nouri refused. In the cramped alley it would hit a house and kill civilians. So he knelt and fired his Kalashnikov. Bullets hit the roof inches from where he was sitting. The American kneeling on the ground behind the Humvee had seen him. Nouri concentrated on him.

⇥⊙◈⊣⟵

Benes knelt behind the engine block for cover, firing up at the enemy and shouting into the radio for help. Mahdi Army fighters were streaming onto the rooftops around the alley, surrounding them. Benes knew they were in trouble and shouted into the radio. He could see Hawkes running through the entrance to the alley, followed by Hernandez and Steele, but they were cut off by a wide expanse of open ground where the Mahdi Army snipers could pick them off. He needed helicopters. Then he saw her.

A little girl, she couldn't have been older than four, had run out into the middle of the street. She must have come from one of the houses. She looked down the street and her eyes met Benes's, a frightened child, confused, not sure what to do. Her mother was leaning out of a doorway, shouting to her to come back, but the girl was terrified and couldn't move. She was right in the middle of the shooting. Benes looked at the mother, wanted to tell her it was safe to come out, that he wouldn't shoot, but he feared someone else might. Whether they couldn't see or didn't care, the Mahdi Army fighters were still firing. *One of you go and get her,* he wanted to say to them, *she's yours, one of your people.* But no one came. It could only be a matter of time till she was hit.

And then, in the middle of that narrow alley, amid the sound and anger of the guns, Benes knew what he had to do. With an enormous feeling of weariness, wishing it didn't have to be him, that there was someone else to do it, he put down his gun and got up out of the cover of the Humvee, ignoring Gibbs, who was shouting at him to get down, ignoring Hawkes calling from the other end of the alley, walked into the middle of the street, and, feeling faintly embarrassed at what he was doing, picked the girl up in his arms. She was frightened, and he tried to murmur something reassuring to her. Over her tiny shoulder, he could see the mother screaming frantically. She probably thought the American was stealing her child. But he kept walking slowly towards her.

⋯⊙⋯

Nouri watched as the American picked up the child. He must have thought he could use her as some sort of human shield, that he would somehow walk out of there alive. Nouri aimed carefully. He wasn't sure he could hit the American without hitting the child. He couldn't see the child's mother, but he could hear her cries. He thought of Sa'id and Ammar, and of those nights in Abu Ghraib, and he pulled the trigger.

⋯⊙⋯

When the bullet hit Benes, it didn't hurt as much as he had expected; it just felt like being hit very hard, so that it was difficult to keep going. He was grateful the child hadn't been hit—that would have made it pointless. As he went on, it seemed to take a lot of effort even to move a single leg. The distance to the child's mother was getting bigger and bigger, and he wasn't sure he'd make it, and that was the one thing he wanted now, the only thing he wanted, to make it these last few paces. All the colours seemed to have gone from the world, and it was hard to focus or be sure exactly what it was he saw, but he felt there was someone watching over him, a girl with her eyes torn away. The mother was still so far away. He knew the last steps would take all he had left, but he forced himself on and, falling to his knees, held out the girl to her mother, who looked at him in confused gratitude, then took her child as, all around him, the world died.

⋯⊙⋯

Nouri did not see Benes hand the child to her mother because his view was blocked by the roofs. But he saw that his shot had hit the American and missed the girl, so he was grateful that he had killed an American officer and saved an Iraqi child's life.

⟶•◉•◀

When the commanders in Baghdad heard of the circumstances of Lieutenant Benes's death they thought it best hushed up, for fear it might get into the press and give the wrong image or, worse, start a chain of copycat incidents of soldiers putting down their guns to rescue stray children or carry out other random acts of kindness to the civilian population. Instead it was put out that he had died a hero's death, defending two of the men of his platoon from an enemy ambush. But his own men heard what had happened from Gibbs and Jackson and from Hawkes and the others who had seen it from the end of the street, and the story spread by word of mouth. Not everyone who heard it believed it, but Benes's platoon, who had known him, did. At his memorial Sergeant Hawkes said, "Even if the circumstances of his death were not quite as some would like us to believe, it was no less a hero's death, no less worthy of a true American officer."

The fighting continued in Najaf for a few days until the Mahdi Army finally gave in. After that, Benes's platoon was able to go home at last.

PART FOUR

Summer 2004

Chapter Twenty-Nine

War Is Good Business

6 June–7 July 2004

THINGS WERE DIFFERENT between Jack and Zoe from the moment he returned to London. They tried to pick up where they had left off in Baghdad, but his decision to leave Iraq hung over them. He moved in with her while he looked for a flat to rent, but their life together was full of awkward silences and unspoken thoughts, and there was a distance between them. They began to quarrel over small things, but the real reason, though neither admitted it, was always Iraq. Although Zoe didn't like to acknowledge it, even to herself, she was angry with him: things had been good, and he had changed them. She felt irritated, too, that he had assumed she would go along with his plan for them both to leave Iraq and be in London together, without ever really consulting her, or considering that she might want to keep going to Iraq. He had applied for his new job before he even spoke to her about it. Now, although he wasn't trying to stop her, she was sure he resented her determination to return to Baghdad, and there were several times she thought he wanted to say something but forced himself to keep silent.

It didn't help that she was having her own misgivings. According to the reports coming from Baghdad, the situation was getting worse by the day; there were more kidnappings and more hostages held under threat of death. But she felt she couldn't change her mind when everyone at the *Informer* was expecting her to go—she'd got used to being referred to by the Editor as "the fearless Zoe"—and she didn't want to back down after she had made an issue of it with Jack. The moment she came closest to changing her mind was when one of the hostages, a South Korean translator, was beheaded. She reluctantly agreed to watch the video of his beheading in order to write a piece about it for the paper. The Korean pleaded again and again before the knife came down, and Zoe returned home that evening feeling sick and frightened.

Unfortunately, that was the evening Jack chose to break his silence: he had seen the video as well, and before she could begin to tell him of her doubts, he started furiously trying to talk her out of going back to Iraq, insisting it was too dangerous. She felt as if he had been waiting for the opportunity, which only renewed her determination to go back and prove him wrong. In the days that followed, he repeatedly tried to talk her out of it. He tried one too many times, and they fought. The next day they patched the quarrel up, but after the third or fourth fight, in a flash of anger she told him that perhaps they would be better apart, and he moved out. Bitterly disappointed, Zoe focused her energies on her trip back to Iraq. He called her the night before she left, but the conversation was awkward and stilted. The last thing he said was, "Be careful."

Something had changed in Baghdad. Zoe was aware of it the moment she arrived: not a physical change, but something you sensed in the people. It was in their eyes, the mistrustful glances they gave you, the way no one held your gaze but kept looking around them all the time. She saw it in Ali and Barzan when they met her at the airport—no one used the bus any more. They were tense and wanted to get moving as quickly as possible, Ali ushering her into the back seat of the car, no time for the effusive greetings of old. It was in the way Barzan drove into the city, refusing to slow for any reason, driving up the hard shoulder when there was traffic, cutting through red lights and across intersections. When Zoe asked him to slow down, Ali cut her off, saying it was safer if Barzan drove that way. When she asked about Mahmoud, Ali's answer was vague; he said only that Mahmoud was still recovering from his injury, and Zoe got the impression he didn't want to talk about it.

The Americans had theoretically handed over power to a new Iraqi government, but on the way into town Zoe saw what looked like new American checkpoints, complete with tanks and razor wire. They had signs in English and Arabic that said they would use "lethal force" against anyone who so much as approached them, and the traffic kept a nervous distance while the American soldiers glowered at the cars that passed. Even on that first ride back into the city, as Ali constantly checked the mirror and gave short, urgent instructions to Barzan, Zoe began to fear she had made a mistake coming back.

The change was there at the al-Hamra too, though she didn't notice it at first, the hotel deserted as it always was in the afternoons. As night fell, there was no sign of the returning journalists, no familiar laughter out by the pool, nobody working urgently to meet a deadline in the Internet cafe. Instead, the hotel seemed full of security contractors, walking the corridors and sitting around the pool with guns by their sides, glaring at her suspiciously. Zoe was beginning to despair of seeing a friendly face when she heard someone call her name and looked over to see Kate and Mervyn with a small group of reporters huddled around a table far from the pool, in the shadows off to one side.

"Where is everyone?" Zoe asked.

"This is it," Kate shrugged. "Our fast-dwindling band." Looking around the table, Zoe recognised Janet Sweeney and Alain the Journonator. She was even glad to see Peter Shore, so few of the old crowd were there.

"What happened?" Zoe asked.

"Pulled out for safety reasons," Kate said. "Some of them wanted to stay but their editors insisted, claimed it was insurance and all that. Others were only too happy to go."

"What about all these contractors?"

"Soon as the reporters moved out, they moved in. There's more of them than us now; they pretty much dominate the place."

Everybody wanted to know about her journey in, anything she'd seen on the airport road. It seemed most of the reporters were nervous about travelling around the city. Over a bottle of wine someone had managed to get hold of, Kate filled her in on the situation. There had been so many kidnappings and bombings that you took your life in your hands just driving across town to the Palestine Hotel to buy a ticket on the flight out. No one went to the press briefings in the Green Zone if they could avoid it because the checkpoint at the gate had been hit by suicide bombers so many times. The kidnappers were growing ever more confident: they had even started setting up their own impromptu checkpoints around the city, searching cars for foreigners. Sometimes they had police uniforms, and some of the journalists even suspected they might really be police making a little money on the side selling foreign hostages to the highest bidder. There was a market in hostages, and they were often kidnapped by one group only to be sold to another—and it was said the highest bidders were the extremist groups who wanted victims for their beheading videos. A lot of the journalists had taken to travelling with two cars, a second following at a discreet distance, so that if the first came on a kidnappers' checkpoint, the reporter could get out and run back to the second—but it only worked if there was a queue for the checkpoint in front of you. Some of the reporters barely left the hotel at all, Kate said, and relied instead on their translators, sending them to report in places where it simply wasn't safe for a foreigner to venture and writing up their stories from the notes they brought back. There was even a rumour of a reporter for one of the wire agencies who had suffered some sort of nervous breakdown in his room up on the eighth floor and was barricaded in with a Kalashnikov, facing the door, ready to shoot Them when They came for him, a grenade by his side to take Them with him if it came to it. No one had ever been up to investigate if this was true, for fear of getting shot.

In the days that followed, Zoe learned that the hotel was no sanctuary. One morning she was boiling coffee and watching the news on the television when she felt the room shake and there was a blast that rattled the windows so hard in their frames she felt sure they would break. She looked out from the balcony, but all she could see was a pall of black smoke rising from the end of the car park, near the entrance from the main road. She went to see what had happened, but it was too dangerous to venture even a step outside the guarded hotel complex on foot, so she went in the car with Ali and Barzan. On the street outside there was a crater blown in the road with the twisted metal wreckage of a car inside. It looked like a suicide bomb that had gone off too early. No one knew the intended target, but the car could easily have been heading for the al-Hamra. The only casualty apart from the bomber, Zoe learned, was a boy who used to sell chilled cans of Coke and Pepsi to passing motorists. She had often stopped there with Ali and Mahmoud to pick up a drink on their way back to the hotel, and the boy had always joked and laughed with the men in Arabic. He couldn't have been much older than thirteen.

A lot of the journalists were convinced the al-Hamra enjoyed some sort of special protection. Certainly, it was the only hotel that hadn't been hit: all the others had been targeted with rockets or car bombs. There were rumours of some connection between the owners and the insurgents, but Zoe didn't believe them: she felt it was only a matter of time before the hotel was hit and found herself going over escape routes, as she had once found Jack doing. For some reason that nobody understood, most of the car bombings took place in the mornings, between eight and nine, and at first Zoe tried to make sure she was always awake by then and ready to run. But she got tired of sitting with her nerves on edge, waiting for the attack, and learned to sleep on deliberately through the danger hour, so that by the time she woke at nine the worst was past.

Through all this, though she didn't like to admit it to herself, it was Jack's absence that Zoe felt most. It wasn't that she was pining for him, but she missed having someone to share the danger and the risks. Things they would have laughed at together were grim; things that would have been grim anyway would have been easier to face with him. She resisted the temptation to phone him.

The security situation was creating difficulties for her work as well. With little news to report, Nigel was demanding big features from Iraq, but it was almost impossible to go anywhere and research one. Whole sections of the city were too dangerous, and leaving Baghdad was out of the question. Even where they could venture, Ali told her they couldn't afford to linger for more than ten minutes, in case someone sent word of their presence to the kidnappers. The *Informer* balked at the cost of renting a second car to follow, which limited her movements even more. Zoe cast around for ideas for features she could write, but Iraq had already been covered exhaustively. In the midst of this, Nigel called to say the Editor wanted a piece on Western businessmen fleeing Iraq because of the kidnappings and the reconstruction effort collapsing. After several days of unsuccessful enquiries, Ali tracked down an American businessman who was prepared to talk.

"Do you think it's safe?" Zoe asked.

"I think it is," Ali said. "He was recommended to me. It's a big Western company. And it is close to here."

The "office" was in a deserted residential building. They had some difficulty finding it at first, just one in a long line of villas, not particularly grand or expensive-looking, with no indication that it was used as an office. As they were searching, an armed man stepped across to the car.

"He is a guard here, it is OK," Ali explained. "He says it is this house."

Zoe followed Ali to the front door, where he pressed a buzzer. Zoe noticed a security camera she had not seen from the street, directed straight down at them. A voice came over an intercom and Ali spoke briefly with it. There was a click and the door opened. They stepped into a small vestibule, with a second door beyond, this one reinforced with bars of iron. When the first door had clicked shut behind then, the second opened, and they walked into a large hallway, more opulent than the nondescript exterior of the house had suggested. The floor was white marble, and there was a grand arc of stairs, paintings and gilt-framed mirrors, and small objets d'art on the coffee tables. Muscular security guards were sitting around on elegant armchairs, rifles across their laps, as if they were on a break. A smaller man in an expensive-looking suit spoke with Ali, then turned to Zoe and asked her for a visiting card. For the first time in Iraq, she felt underdressed. He ushered them through a door to a large office and introduced the man she had come to see, Dan Mitchell, a sleek American in open-neck shirt. Across from him sat another man in a crumpled checked shirt and jeans who was not introduced.

"So, how can we help you?" Mr Mitchell said, gesturing her to a chair.

"Thanks for agreeing to see me," Zoe said. "This is my translator, Ali. You don't mind if he sits in with us?"

"No problem."

"Basically, I'm researching a story on how foreign businessmen are getting out of Iraq—"

"But they're not," the second man, the one in jeans, interrupted.

"I'm sorry?" Zoe looked from him to Dan Mitchell, confused.

"They're not leaving," the man in jeans said. "We're here, as you see."

"Yes, of course, but, I mean, you're an exception, aren't you? I thought, after the kidnappings and killings—"

"Yes, yes, I can see why you would *think* that," the man interrupted her impatiently. "That's what they want you to think. They want the people who are behind these kidnappings to think it. But they're not leaving; they're all still here. They're just keeping a low profile." His accent sounded American, but there was something formal and stilted about his English that was more like an Iraqi's. "There is still huge competition for every reconstruction contract that's handed out. I know, because I'm bidding for them."

"You, er," Zoe looked from him to Mr Mitchell, who had remained silent, again.

"We work together," the second man said, in explanation.

"I'm sorry, I didn't get your name."

"My name isn't important." He smiled.

"I need a name for my interview."

"You have my colleague's name. You can use that."

Zoe looked at Dan Mitchell dubiously, but he nodded. "You can say your interview was with me. Everything he says, I say. We speak as one," he said with an expansive gesture and a smile.

"Are you partners?"

"You could call me an adviser," the nameless man said. "I advise my friend Mr Mitchell."

"You work for him?"

"I *advise* him. But I don't appear in your piece. OK? Or this interview is over."

"No, no, that's fine, I'm just trying to understand."

"I know Iraq. I have connections here. I advise Mr Mitchell's company on the local situation."

"You're Iraqi?"

"I know Iraq. But let's get back to your article. You want to know why people are staying?" He paused. "Money, that's why. There is still an enormous amount of money to be made here."

Zoe glanced back at Dan Mitchell: he seemed happy for the nameless man to dominate the interview.

"But isn't it dangerous to be here?" she asked.

"You've seen the security we have."

"All the same, it's dangerous."

"Yes." The mysterious man nodded. "It's *very* dangerous. But you're still here."

"Well, it's my job."

"And this is our job."

"You can do business anywhere."

"Yes, and you can report the news anywhere. But the news is here so you're here," he said, smiling. "It's the same for us: the big money's here, in Iraq. That didn't change just because it got dangerous. But you could say the people who are interested changed. You're a specialist at what you do, right? You cover wars, emergencies, dangerous places? It's the same with us. There are businessmen who operate in safe places. But we specialise in these situations. You know why? Money. We're taking a risk, I won't deny it. We're taking a big risk. But we're doing it because the rewards are so great. Look, if you want to do business somewhere safe like America or the UK, maybe you'll make ten per cent, if you're lucky. Here, it's not safe, we're not just risking our money, we're risking our lives—but there are guys making 200 per cent, 300 per cent, in just a year. And it doesn't end after that year. Some of these reconstruction contracts are guaranteed for years."

"But there doesn't seem to be any reconstruction going on."

"That's because the Americans aren't handing out the contracts fast enough. There have been a lot of private deals, and there are a lot of people here who want to work but aren't getting the business. You probably heard about people pulling out? But that's because the American government has made deals with favoured companies. They made them in private, before the bidding process even began, so there's nothing left for the others to bid for. That's why they've pulled out. But I tell you, there are people getting very rich in Iraq. Look, there's one thing you have to accept, whether you like it or not. I don't expect you to like it. I'm not even saying I like it. But I accept it because it's true. War is good business; it's as simple as that."

Zoe looked over to Dan Mitchell, who nodded and said, "That should just about cover it, I think? You got enough? Only we've got a meeting we have to be at."

Zoe thought she had uncovered a real story, of furtive contracts and businessmen still in Iraq despite the risks, but Nigel, or someone at the *Informer*, didn't agree, and the paper ran it as a small piece at the bottom of a page, where it was swiftly forgotten. The next evening Zoe had an email from Nigel that ran:

> Zoe, your safety is our first concern and you must not take any undue risks or go anywhere unsafe. But within those limits it is imperative you find strong features to file asap. The Editor is demanding strong hits from Iraq.

Frustrated, she went to the poolside to look for Kate, but she wasn't around. Zoe looked across the courtyard for someone she knew among all the security contractors. The only face she recognised was Peter Shore, sitting at a table by himself. She hesitated for a moment, then crossed over to him.

"Evening, Peter. OK if I sit here?"

"Zo! 'Course it is," he said, pushing out a chair for her. "How're you doing these days?"

"Not too bad, considering. And you?"

"Oh, I'm fine," he said, reaching to the bag at his feet and pulling out a bottle of Johnnie Walker. "Whisky?"

"Thanks."

"A little more civilised than the beer they sell here," he said, pouring her a generous measure and offering a can of Coke as a mixer. She poured the Coke up to the top.

"It's good to see you still around, Zo," he said. "Our numbers have been thinning somewhat of late."

"Yeah, well, got to keep on going, haven't you?" she said.

"I see Jack left town," he said.

"Yes," she said, trying to sound neutral. Peter shrugged and smiled.

"Good to see you're still here," he said. "I remember when I first met you. It was a year ago, right here; you were so new to it all. And now look at you, a hardened war hack, still up for it when more experienced reporters have lost their nerve and run." He raised his glass. "Here's to you, Zoe."

She smiled, raised her glass and drank. He leaned over and refilled it.

"Not so much for me," she said, but he went on pouring.

"Helps get you through the days, I find," he said. "So how're you getting on with stories?"

"I don't know, it's not easy at the moment." She hesitated to tell him of her difficulties.

"Tell me about it. I've got my lot on the phone morning and night, wanting features on this, in-depths on that, and we can hardly leave the bloody hotel. You try doing it with a camera, Zo."

"No, I know."

"I've told them we just can't do these stories, but they don't listen. They just say find us something you can do."

"It's the same with my guys," she said, glad to have someone to share her frustration with. "I've just had a message saying, 'Don't take any risks, but get us features.' How'm I supposed to do that?"

"I know, it's crazy."

"I'm beginning to wonder if it's worth being here. If we can do our jobs at all."

"It's not that bad, Zo. I mean, we all bitch, but we can still get the job done. These are the situations when you make your name, when you hang in there. Thing is, there's always a way round it, always some story you have tucked away somewhere you've forgotten about, that you can do. You search and search, and all of a sudden you realise it was there all along. What sort of thing are your guys after?"

"Just a feature of some sort."

"How about a snapshot of everyday life in Baghdad? Always a good fall-back."

"Yeah. Problem is the interviews."

"There must be some contact you've got from an earlier piece you can go back and interview. Someone you know will be safe."

"My fixer, Ali, seems to reckon we can't trust anyone, and he knows Iraq better than any of us."

"Ah, you always get this with fixers when things start to get tough, even the best of them. He doesn't want to be the one who tells you it's OK to go somewhere, and then you find it's not. It's fair enough. I'm afraid in these situations you have to take charge and make the decisions, not the fixer." He looked across at her. "But look at you. You've changed so much."

She noticed he had filled her glass again while they were speaking. The whisky had taken the edge off her nerves and she felt exhilarated to be in Baghdad again. The guns echoed in the distance.

"I still remember that first night," he said. "I won't pretend I don't wish things had turned out differently."

She laughed. "Oh come off it, Peter. You couldn't care less."

"That's not true. You know it's not."

Her head was swimming now, and when the few others scattered around the tables had all gone, and the waiters wanted to clear up and close for the night, and Peter suggested one more drink in his room, she found herself agreeing. Found herself letting him kiss her and undress her and lead her to his bed again. After all, it was just one of those al-Hamra nights.

Chapter Thirty

The Trap Closes

8 July 2004

MAHMOUD SAT AND looked at the photograph of Saara. It was the only one he had of her—all he had left of her now, besides his memories, so careful had he always been to destroy every letter, every note that his parents or others might find that could lead back to her. The photograph he always carried in his wallet, it was a simple passport picture, left over from a set she had made when she worked at the ministry. He looked at her staring earnestly into the camera from under the headscarf, so much life in those eyes, hungry to see the world and be a part of it, not locked up forever in her parents' house. She must be somewhere in America now. He wondered how it felt to live in the country whose invasion had driven her from her own—had driven her from him. For weeks, he had checked his email and his phone several times a day, waiting for some message from her, had rushed to answer the door despite the pain from his arm, thinking it might be someone with news of her. She was on his mind so much that he watched the television news half expecting word of her, a report on Iraqi refugees in America, or some political opposition to the war, with a fleeting glimpse of her somewhere in the background. But there was nothing. At first he stopped going to the door, then he checked his messages only once a day. She had started a new life and had to leave him behind. It wasn't what either of them had chosen, it wasn't what they had wanted, but it had happened and it couldn't be helped.

His arm was all but healed. He could move it again, and the doctors were insisting he do several difficult and painful exercises every day. He had agreed with his parents that he would not go back to driving when it was fully recovered. The Mercedes had been repaired, and he had found another cousin to drive it. Mahmoud was making a good living, passing on work to his cousins, and he was already planning to buy another car, which he could hire out with another driver. Life was safer as a businessman than as a driver, and his parents, convinced he had been working when the Mercedes was hit and would never have been hurt if it weren't for the crazy foreign journalist, had been insistent. Life should have been good—he was making money and had a future—but all he thought of was Saara.

Then, a few days before, his mother had told him the news. It was time he got married, she said, and she had found him a suitable wife. His heart had lurched; he hadn't known what to do or say. He had known he would have to marry some day, but the thought of marrying anyone other than Saara was unbearable. His mother had told him the girl's name and shown him a picture, but he was blind to her; he could see no one but Saara, hear no name but Saara. In his confusion, he didn't know what to say; had tried to stammer that he wasn't ready to marry. Surprised, his mother had asked if he preferred some other girl, and he had thought for a wild moment of telling her, but realised he couldn't, and said no. Then she brooked no argument, and at a loss, Mahmoud had agreed. In a few days he was to meet the girl. He did not know what he would do. He looked at the picture of Saara again and lost himself in memories.

⤛⟡⟡⤜

Nouri staggered under the heavy load he was carrying. Setting it down on the road, he wiped the sweat out of his eyes and turned to look back at the others. His chest stung from the effort, but after only a few breaths he shouldered the heavy bag of cement again and staggered forward. It wasn't the sight of the foreman watching that made him go on; Nouri knew he would have let him rest a little longer. Nouri was a veteran of Najaf, and people treated the militia with respect. Abbas had told him the work on the building site was beneath him, that he shouldn't have taken it. Nouri replied he needed the money to take care of his father,

363

whose health was getting worse, but the truth was that Nouri was content to be busy.

On his return from Najaf, he had been greeted by his old friends in Sadr City as a hero. People spoke as if coming back from a place like that alive were some sort of achievement. They wanted to hear stories of the fighting, wanted him to tell them how it had been in the cemetery, what it was like fighting tanks. Nouri tried to tell them at first, but he felt he could not make them understand, so he gave up and pretended he didn't want to talk about it. Away from their gaze, he lay awake at night haunted by memories. He often heard Sa'id and Ammar talking in the dark, their voices echoing the way they had in the old tomb as they talked to ward away the fear.

He sought out the company of fighters who had been in Najaf and spent his time hanging around the militia's buildings. There was still work to be done, but it was not enough to occupy a man who had been living at the limits, and he found himself spending long hours doing nothing. He sensed his parents looking at him with a reproach they would not voice, because he was not working to provide for the family. He knew the militia would not let them starve, that he could provide for them better as a veteran of Najaf than by manual labour, but he went out looking for work all the same, to fill the hours, and took the job on the construction site. Between his work for the militia and heaving bags of cement, there was little time left to think. His mother had started talking about finding him a wife. He longed for the simplicity of the fighting again, for a life where there was nothing to think of but carrying a gun and staying alive. He yearned for it and feared it, his body cried out to be back in Najaf, but the ghosts of Sa'id and Ammar came in the night.

It was murderous heat in which to be carrying such a heavy load, and Nouri could feel the bag slipping on the sweat that was pouring from his neck and shoulders. He reached the bottom of the ladder and, without pausing for breath, started up it with the bag across his shoulders, feeling his calves screaming with the effort. Anywhere else in Baghdad there would have been a crane to lift it, but this was Sadr City, and it was only a slum house they were extending, so the cement had to be carried up.

Yet Nouri loved the feeling of strength in his body. For someone who had lain on the floor of a prison cell at the mercy of pain inflicted by others, the pain he chose was a kind of freedom.

From time to time, he noticed people stopping to point him out. He knew what they were saying. He was the fighter who had saved a child's life in Kufa, when one of the Americans tried to use her as a human shield; he was the sniper whose perfect shot had killed the American and not harmed a hair on the child's head. Nouri would not meet their gaze. He would let his eyes drop to the ground, and heave another bag of cement on his shoulders. They must have thought he was modest; none of them could know it was a lucky shot, fired in anger. None of them could know that when he thought of Najaf and Kufa, he did not see the American with the girl; he saw Sa'id and the look on his face, as if he wanted to tell Nouri something as the blood spread from his head.

⤝⊶⊷⤞

Zoe woke to the lingering sense that she had something to regret. With her head throbbing and her mouth paper dry, for a moment she hoped it was just hangover remorse, until the world blinked back into view and she saw Peter Shore lying beside her. He was still asleep, so she got up and dressed quickly and quietly and crept out of the room without waking him. There was no one in the corridor, and she took the stairs to avoid running into anyone she knew in the lift. The whisky was exacting its price; she felt queasy and was sweating profusely, and there was nothing she wanted more than to go back to her own room, sleep the hangover off and not think about what had happened. But looking at her watch, she saw she had overslept and Ali would already be waiting for her, and more pressingly, she still had no feature idea to offer Nigel, who would be arriving at the *Informer* office in London in a matter of hours. She managed to slip across the courtyard back to the second building without meeting Ali and went up to her room and showered, letting the water run over her face, trying to think of some feature proposal she could give Nigel. But her mind was reeling from the whisky fug, and she could think of nothing but stories she'd already written, of the children's hospital, of the road through Mahmudiya, of that first day in Sadr City. She didn't want to think about Peter. She would have to try to avoid him for a few days.

Downstairs, she found Ali waiting in the Internet cafe. She checked her email and saw a message from Jack. She considered for a moment, her hand hovering over the mouse, then left it unopened and signed out. She looked through the news wires, trying to think of an idea for a feature as she scanned the headlines. There were reports of another kidnapping—a truck driver this time—and a number of killings in a mixed area of Baghdad, where both Sunnis and Shia lived. An American general had said the security situation was improving. There was nothing she could safely research, no story it wouldn't be suicide to investigate. She asked Ali if he had any ideas; he said he'd asked around, but there was nothing that wasn't too dangerous. Zoe glanced at her watch: less than an hour till Nigel would reach the office and she had nothing. Her head pounded and she wanted to sleep. Reluctantly, she thought back to the previous evening's conversation with Peter: he had suggested some contact from an earlier story, someone she knew it would be safe to revisit. She thought back over the stories she had written. There was the children's hospital, but Dr Afaf had disappeared, and Zoe had never been able to find out what became of her: just another of the thousands of Iraqis who had vanished amid the chaos and violence, leaving their loved ones to search in vain. Afaf's disappearance would make a good story, of course, but if she was in hiding it might endanger her: Zoe couldn't write it unless she knew Afaf was safe—or dead. She could try to find out if there was any news of the doctor, and Zoe knew the chances were she would learn nothing: she had searched exhaustively before. Besides, it would be time-consuming, and she needed a story to offer Nigel today. She wondered whether Lieutenant Benes had heard anything of Afaf, and realised he would make a good story himself if she could persuade him to talk, an American officer disillusioned with the occupation—but then, she thought, the chances were he was long gone from Iraq and safely home with his family in the US. She emailed him, asking about Afaf, and whether he was still in Iraq, but there was no immediate reply and she knew she'd have to think of something else in the meantime. She thought back to her first confused days in Iraq: there must be someone.

Then, as she sat and stared at her emails, hoping Benes would reply, it came to her: Zaynab. It was perfect: she could finally fulfil her promise to Zaynab and get her story in the paper. All she needed was an up-to-date angle, and there had to be one: the story of a widow's life in occupied Iraq, a year on, and what had become of those of her children who had survived. Zaynab would readily give her a new interview. She searched back through her emails for Zaynab's, and told Ali, who was scrolling through the Arabic news sites looking for a story. But he was reluctant.

"I don't think it's safe," he said. "We don't know this woman. We don't know who her friends are."

Zoe thought again of Peter's words the night before, that in situations like this Ali would see danger everywhere rather than risk leading her into trouble: it was up to her to take a lead.

"I don't know. I met her and sat in her house alone," she said. "It was fine."

"It was different then, things were calmer. You don't know how her situation may have changed in the last year. Even I am careful where I go now."

"But we know this woman, we know her background. And you've said many times if we don't stay anywhere too long, then it's safe. By the time word spreads of our presence, we'll be gone."

"I said it's better, I didn't say it was safe."

"Well, we have to do something, Ali. And I can email ahead, and make sure it's safe for us."

"How did you get her email?"

"She wrote to me months ago, asking if the story had been in the paper."

Ali frowned. "But she doesn't speak English."

"She got a friend to write."

"When did she write?"

"What does it matter?"

"I want to be sure no one is trying to trap us somewhere."

"It was months ago, Ali, in April."

"And she hasn't written since?"

"No."

He sat silent, considering for a long time.

"If you really want to go, this is not the best way to do it," he said. "If you send an email, then someone can find out you're going to be there. They can have people waiting for you. If you really want to speak with her we should go directly and see if she is there."

"OK."

"But I still think it's better if we don't," he said.

Her head hurt, and she was tired of the argument. She couldn't see how the widow could be a threat to them. "I think it's OK."

"All right," Ali said reluctantly. "But we must not stay more than ten minutes."

"OK, ten minutes," Zoe agreed, thinking she could stretch it a little if it seemed safe when they got there. "When can we leave?"

"You want to go today?"

"Why not?"

"At least let me ask some questions, find out if it's safe."

"You said yourself that will only advertise our presence ahead of time. Better to go straight there."

He looked unhappy, but he agreed. Zoe wrote a quick email to Nigel saying she had a potential feature and was looking into it, and that she'd call as soon as she knew if it would work. There was still the problem of pictures of Zaynab, and Zoe took her small camera with her: if it came to it, she would have to take her own, though she was no photographer.

Ali remembered the place. He could have lied and told her he couldn't remember the way, but he directed Barzan straight there. Zoe recognised the house and saw herself, a younger, more naive reporter, looking at it the first time and hesitating before she stepped inside. The street was deserted: no one who could avoid it was out on the streets of Baghdad any more.

"Remember, ten minutes," Ali said. "And if there is any problem, we will leave."

"OK," Zoe said.

She had her headscarf wrapped tight around her head—no one would be able to see she wasn't Iraqi unless they came up close—and her notebook and camera were hidden under her long, loose coat. Barzan stayed in the car and parked close to the house in case they needed to leave in a hurry. Ali rang the door-bell, Zoe close behind, wondering if she was making a mistake. When the door opened, it was the young girl who answered, the daughter. Her face was still scarred. She seemed nervous, and as Ali spoke with her she looked anxiously at Zoe. She showed them into a room Zoe recognised from the year before, seats around the walls, the embroidery of Mecca, and gestured them to the chairs and left. The house was very quiet.

Zoe glanced nervously at Ali, but he said nothing. She remembered that the year before Zaynab had not allowed Ali into the house without a man present. Perhaps the son was here this time, or maybe Zaynab trusted them after their previous meeting. She felt time passing and wished Zaynab would hurry. The door opened and she stepped in, looking much as she had the year before. She didn't seem all that happy to see them, though: she looked frightened, and Zoe wondered if she'd done the right thing coming. She had thought only of the risk to Ali and herself, but now she realised she might be putting Zaynab in danger. Ali spoke to her a little in Arabic, then turned to Zoe for the first question.

"Thank you for your emails, Zaynab," Zoe said. "I'm sorry I was so long coming back."

When Ali translated that, Zaynab looked confused, but Zoe felt their ten minutes passing, and quickly asked her next ques-tion. "How has your life been, the last year? Is it safe for you, living here without your husband?"

Ali translated and Zaynab began to speak, picking threads from her dress. As she spoke, Zoe had the unnerving feeling someone was watching and listening from behind the door, which was just ajar, but told herself not to worry: it was probably the daughter who had shown them in. Zaynab spoke at length, and Zoe was horribly conscious of the pressure of time; she was using up their precious minutes answering a single question. When Ali translated, there was something that seemed slightly wrong about her answer, but Zoe couldn't make out what it was. At any rate, there was little she could use in it: Zaynab had spoken of the deaths of her husband and children. She held out the same photograph of her children she had shown Zoe a year before. It seemed a little more dog-eared; she probably carried it everywhere with her.

"How do you think life in Iraq has changed since the Americans came?" she asked. Again, a long, rambling answer, nothing new. Zoe had to resist the temptation to glance at her watch. She was beginning to think she would have to tell Nigel the idea had come to nothing.

"But what about the situation in Baghdad now? Is it better or worse than a year ago? Safer or more dangerous?"

The answer this time at least provided some material she could use: complaints of kidnappings in the street, local Iraqis being held for ransom, of a neighbour's husband who had disappeared without trace one day after he left for work. But as Ali translated, Zoe realised what was troubling her about the answers: they didn't sound like Zaynab. Or rather, they didn't sound like the emails she had sent. Zoe felt a chill stealing down her back, but told herself to ignore it. People were often different when they wrote.

"Zoe, it is ten minutes," Ali said. "We must leave."

"OK, I just need a picture."

"There isn't time."

"I'll be quick. Please ask." Zaynab posed next to a photograph of her dead husband. Zoe took the picture quickly. It wasn't good but it would have to do, unless she could talk a photographer into visiting the house. She packed up her camera and notebook and, with Ali in front of her, slipped out of the door and walked quickly across the street to the waiting car. Barzan watched anxiously as they got in. As soon as the doors were closed, he pulled away without speaking. As they moved off, a car cut across the road in front of them, blocking their path. Barzan changed gear and tried to reverse, but another car blocked their way in that direction. Men were getting out of the first car, carrying guns, their faces hidden in headscarves. Zoe looked at Ali, wondered if she should get out and run, but the gunmen were upon them. One of them opened the door and reached in for her. Ali grabbed at her other arm, but it was hopeless as the gunman dragged her from his grasp. She tried to resist, but he was too strong for her. She could see his eyes through the narrow opening made by the headscarf and hear his breathing. Ali shouted, and she turned to see him getting out of the car, trying to help. One of the gunmen shot him. It happened very fast; the masked man held out his gun and fired and Ali went down, blood spreading across his shirt and trousers. Zoe watched him fall, her mind in a daze. Then Barzan was out of the car and they shot him too. She saw the red bloom where the bullet hit him in the head. Two of them had hold of her now; they were dragging her to the car. *Do something*, she thought, *you have to do something.* But her mind was frozen. They were forcing her onto the back seat at gunpoint, and as they drove away she looked back at Ali and Barzan lying there in their own blood in the road and realised she was a hostage.

Chapter Thirty-One

Waiting for the Knife

8 July 2004

ZOE SAT IN darkness, alone. From somewhere, she could hear the faint sound of a television and the noise of an old electric fan. The darkness was complete. They had bound her hands with plastic wire that cut into her wrists, but she could reach out with her fingers and feel behind her. They had left her legs free, and she had felt her way around the room until she came to the door, but of course it was locked. The only furniture in the room seemed to be the old bed she sat on, which she had discovered when she hit her shins painfully against it during her search. It was impossible to tell how long she had been in there: an hour, two hours, more. They were going to cut off her head. The thought came back to her, the one she had been trying to avoid, and in a surge of panic she stood up, though there was nothing she could do, nowhere she could run. She sat down and tried to think; she had to make a plan, had to find some way to escape or get word out of where she was.

They had taken her mobile phone, of course, and the satellite phone she still carried around Baghdad. If there were a window, she could try to bang on it to attract attention or get some sort of message out, but she had been round the room three times and she couldn't find one. Were they going to torture her? Don't think about that. She had to let them know she was a journalist. The kidnappers had let journalists go before. She had tried to tell them, shouted the Arabic word Ali had taught her, but they had not responded. Would they rape her? Think about something else. Anything else. They were going to kill her. She realised she was shaking.

Ali. The image came back to her across the dark: Ali leaping from the car to save her as he had saved her so many times, and she had believed he would do it again, and then the sound of the gun, Ali stopping in his steps with a look of surprise on his face and turning to look at Zoe before he fell. Barzan, whom she hardly knew, following him out of the car to help her, even though he must have known it was hopeless, that he was following Ali to his own death for a woman he barely knew. She had killed them as surely as if she had pulled the trigger herself. She had insisted on returning to Zaynab's house for an interview that hadn't even been any use. Ali had warned her. He had known there was something wrong with those emails. She thought how difficult it would have been for him to refuse to come with her, when the paper was paying him far more than he could have hoped to make in any other job. His family probably needed the money—he couldn't risk losing it. And then she realised he had not come for the money; he had come because he was her friend. And she had killed him.

She thought back over what had happened, trying to remember any detail that could help her, any means of escape, any way she could get word out, any clue as to where she was. They had blindfolded her and tied her hands when they got her in the car, and then pushed her to the floor behind the front seats. They drove for some time, during which none of them spoke to her. She kept telling them she was a journalist, that she wasn't with the Americans, until one of them hit her to silence her. They only spoke a few words to each other in Arabic. When they reached their destination, they pushed her roughly from the car and in through a doorway. From the sounds of their feet and voices, she got the impression they were in a small building, perhaps a house. They led her up a staircase—she stumbled on the steps at first—and into the room where she now sat. There was a brief moment of blinding light as they tore the blindfold off, then they had closed the door behind them and she had been left in darkness. In the pitch black, and without windows, the room felt like a sort of cellar, but they had led her upstairs. There was nothing, she realised, that could help her. They were going to kill her.

She thought back to the emails, trying to remember any clue, anything that could help, but there was nothing. How had she been such a fool, to believe those emails had come from the help-less old widow, to think Zaynab would have been busy sending her messages when she had enough to do taking care of her daughter? But then how had the kidnappers known, when she hadn't emailed to say she was coming? Perhaps it had nothing to do with the emails, and was just a horrible coincidence.

She had heard them speaking among themselves, and though she didn't understand Arabic, they sounded nervous and fright-ened. She wondered if she could break through to one of them, make them understand that she was a journalist and had nothing to do with the occupation. She needed to make them search for her articles on the Internet; if she showed them what she had written about the children's hospital, about American attacks on civilians, they would understand. They were going to cut off her head and film it. They weren't just going to kill her—they were going to film it for the world to see, for her mother to see.

Zoe thought of her mother, alone in the house with all its memories, and of how she would react when she heard that her daughter was missing. She wondered if she was officially missing yet. Probably not: unless someone had found the car and Ali's and Barzan's bodies in the street, the chances were it would be a few hours yet before someone at the al-Hamra noticed her absence and raised the alarm. Would her mother hear about it on the news, turn on the television to hear her name in sudden horror, or would someone from the *Informer* think to call and tell her? She pictured the scene at the *Informer*: the awkward meeting in the Editor's office, everyone, with eyes on the floor, agreeing there were more important things than the day's news, the paper's sole priority now to get its reporter out safely, but a big story on the front page couldn't hurt, could it, and do we have a picture of her looking vulnerable? Oh, and Nigel, you'd better call her mother. Does anyone have the number? She even smiled at the thought of Nigel's consternation. She thought back to that first phone call, when she had told her mother she was going to Iraq, and she remembered the unease in her mother's voice. She heard men's voices somewhere in the building; it sounded as if they were arguing. They were going to kill her. They had killed Ali and Barzan and now they were going to kill her.

Adel couldn't believe it when he saw the foreign journalist in his house. His foreigner, the one he had dreamed of capturing, had tried so hard to entice back here, and now, when he least expected it, she had walked through his door. His sister had come to tell him a man and a strange woman had come to see his mother, and he had watched from behind the door as they spoke in the front room. He recognised her immediately: the headscarf and coat didn't make her look Iraqi, not with the way she walked, the way her eyes wandered as his mother spoke. It took him only a moment to decide. He had thought of this so many times, he knew exactly what to do. While they were still talking, he telephoned Selim, whispering down the line, telling him there was a foreigner in his house and to come quickly with a gun. He fetched his own Kalashnikov and hid it in a hold-all, listening all the while to be sure the foreigner was still there. He didn't want her to leave before he was ready. He couldn't risk taking her in his mother's house; it had to be in the street outside as she left; he had planned that long ago. He called Ibrahim—as much as insurance against Selim as because he wanted another pair of hands. He heard the translator urging the foreigner to hurry, speaking in English so his mother would not understand, and glanced in through the barely open door again. He willed Selim to hurry—there was no way Ibrahim could make it in time. He looked out from behind a curtain and saw the journalist's car, the driver waiting behind the wheel. The fool was not watching the road—he was too busy smoking a cigarette and looking idly around. Adel slipped out the back of the house to meet Selim before the foreigner's driver could see him. He walked swiftly down the street, the rifle heavy in the hold-all, knocking against his leg as he walked, resisting the temptation to turn back and make sure the foreigner didn't leave, for fear he might attract the driver's attention.

Before he could round the corner, he heard the sound from a horn and looked up to see Selim in the front passenger seat of a car he didn't recognise. The man at the wheel had his face hidden in a headscarf. Adel crossed the street to the car, forcing himself to stay calm. For a moment, he thought Selim had brought one of Abu Khalid's foreigners, but when he got in he recognised the driver as Daoud, a friend of Selim's from the cafe. Both he and Selim, he saw, had Kalashnikovs by their knees.

"Can't you be quiet?" he said, his nerves pushing him to anger. "Her driver's just outside my house."

"Calm down," Selim said. He looked anything but calm.

"Let's go then," Daoud said and reached for his Kalashnikov, but Adel touched his arm.

"Wait," he said. "They're still inside. Drive as if we're leaving, then wait round the corner, out of sight. We'll stop her as she leaves."

"Let's just go in and take her," Daoud said.

"No," Selim said, "Adel's right, we'll be recognised." Daoud drove round the corner, and Adel and Selim wrapped their faces in headscarves. "I thought it was better to bring Daoud's car," Selim said when they were in position. "Too many people round here know mine."

Adel nodded; he didn't want to be distracted. He watched the street, waiting for the foreigner. She had to come this way; it was the way to the main road. In the other direction the street only led to more houses. But there was no sign of her, and he wondered if the foreigner had out-thought him and gone round the long way. He took off his headscarf and got out of the car.

"Get back in," Selim said, "you'll be seen."

Trying to look casual, Adel strolled back to where he could see his front door. The foreigner's car was still there. The door opened, and he saw the foreigner coming out, followed by her translator. He walked quickly back to the car.

"They're coming," he said. Daoud panicked and over-revved the engine, driving back round the corner with a squeal of tyres as Adel hastily reknotted his headscarf. They blocked the path of the foreigner's car. It started reversing away, and Adel thought it would escape when Ibrahim's car arrived from behind, cutting off its path of retreat. Adel got out and walked towards the foreigner. He could see her there, on the back seat, looking out at him with frightened eyes. She was cornered, trapped in a car, just as his father had been. Adel opened the door and pulled her roughly from the back seat. She was like a startled animal, too shocked to act. The translator started up after her. There was a gunshot, and Adel saw that Selim had shot him. The translator stared at them stupidly as the blood spread on his shirt, and then he fell in the street. The driver came at them, then, and Selim shot him too. Adel hustled the woman into the back of Daoud's car and they drove off, Ibrahim following. Looking back, Adel saw Ibrahim hadn't thought to cover his face and hoped he hadn't been recognised. He hadn't planned to kill the Iraqis, but he wasn't sorry Selim had done it. They had no business working for the foreigner, and this way they wouldn't be around to identify him or the others. There was no way to connect him to the kidnapping; it would look as if she was snatched off the street by a random group.

They took her to Daoud's house. Selim said it was safest, because Daoud was the least close to Adel, if anyone started making connections with the fact she was taken outside his house. Daoud's father was dead, and his mother could be relied on not to speak. They locked the foreigner in a small room upstairs with no windows and only one way in or out. Adel sent a message with Daoud's young brother to his mother—it was too risky to phone—saying he had seen the foreign woman being kidnapped outside their house and telling her to say he'd been out of town, so the Americans could not accuse him and the family would not be dragged into it. The fourteen-year-old boy returned, flushed with pride at carrying a message for the resistance fighters, to say Adel's mother was frightened and had said he should stay away as long as he felt necessary.

Selim wanted to hand the journalist over to Abu Khalid and his foreigners. At first Adel had been so completely taken up with capturing the foreigner that he hadn't thought what to do once he had her, but now that he had a hostage he didn't want to give her up so quickly. She was his prisoner, his revenge for his father's death, and he didn't want to hand her over to a group that had no use for him, that hadn't even let him fight.

"Why should we hand her over to foreigners?" he said. "This is an Iraqi war. Are they going to teach us how to fight?"

"We are all one nation," Selim said. "Don't you think there are Iraqis with Abu Khalid? You think no Iraqi has been fighting in Fallujah?"

As Adel had expected, Ibrahim took his side, and to his relief Daoud backed him as well. He hadn't been sure where Daoud's loyalties lay: Adel had heard him and Selim talking about Abu Khalid and the foreigners, but he'd also seen Daoud working with Abu Mustafa when he was delivering ammunition. Still, Adel knew that Selim wouldn't let the matter drop, that he could easily tell Abu Khalid they had the woman, and that if he did the foreigners might come looking for her. He had to make his own plans. He sent Daoud's younger brother out on another errand, to the market, to buy a video camera.

"We'll make our own video," he told Selim. "Hollywood. Remember?"

--→●○●←--

Zoe heard the sound of footsteps approaching and wondered if she should try to get past as the door opened and make a run for it. She heard the sound of a key turning in the lock, but as the door opened the bright light that flooded the room blinded her. The shape of a man blocked the doorway, and there was no way past him. As her eyes adjusted to the light, she saw he wasn't wearing his headscarf any more. He wasn't as frightening without the scarf: he looked young and nervous. But if he wasn't bothering to hide his face, he wasn't worried she could identify him, which was probably a bad sign.

"Please," she said, "please, I'm a journalist. I'm not part of the occupation. I'm a journalist. Press."

He stood and stared at her silently.

"My name is Zoe Temple. You can look me up on Google, you can see what I've written."

He said nothing. Zoe was sure she recognised him from somewhere, this young man with intense eyes standing over her, but she couldn't remember where she'd seen him. She wondered if he had been in one of the hostage videos she had watched.

"Come," he said and took her by the arm.

"Please," she said. "Please don't hurt me."

But he was surprisingly gentle, guiding her out of the room and down the staircase. Was this the way they led you to die, gently, so you wouldn't panic?

"Please, I wrote a story about the children's hospital, al-Iskan. My story made the Americans clean it up. All I wanted was to help the Iraqi people. I wrote against the occupation. I was trying to help."

He said nothing. She remembered what the other journalists had told her about the experts' advice for if you ever got kidnapped: don't get aggressive or try to fight and don't try to befriend your kidnappers, just be grey, be neutral. And whatever you do, don't look them in the eyes, but in her panic she couldn't help it. He looked back at her, and she wondered what he was thinking. At the foot of the stairs he pushed her into a room where the other three were waiting, guns in their arms. They were wearing their headscarves, and when Zoe saw the camera on the other side of the room, she knew. She felt the strength go out of her legs.

"No," she heard herself say. "Please, no."

The young man pushed her into the room. She didn't want to die, didn't want to walk forward, take the last steps. He made her kneel in the middle of the room, in front of the camera, with the others standing behind her. He slowly wrapped his face in a headscarf. She waited for the knife to come from behind; she didn't want to look back in case she saw it. She forced herself to think of something else, to look into the camera and think of her mother, and not to let it show on the video that she was afraid. The one who had brought her down pushed a sheet of paper at her.

"Read this," he said and took his place behind her. She looked down at the paper: they had written out a message for her to read.

"My name," she read out, and she heard the shaking in her voice. They had left a blank space for her name. "My name is Zoe Temple, I am a British journalist." She found herself correcting the English, they had written *I am Britain journalist*. She tried to keep her voice steady. "I am being treated well." *I am treat good.* "But unless you agree to these demands I will be killed." She faltered, then forced herself to go on, "You must release all prisoners from Abu Ghraib. If you do not do this in four days, I will be killed." It was not yet then—she had four days. "You must take these demands serious…seriously. Please take them seriously." She balked at the last sentence but read it out. "I do not want to die."

They made her hold a newspaper in front of the camera to prove the date, and the one who had brought her down read out a long statement in Arabic over her head while they stood behind her. She knelt before them, her body shaking with relief that it hadn't come yet, that there was still a chance. When they had finished, the same man took her upstairs again. She found she could barely walk.

※

Adel sat in the Internet cafe. They had burned the video onto a computer disc, and he had brought it to email it to the Arabic news channels. It wasn't safe to send it from Daoud's house. First he checked the old hotmail account, to see if the journalist had sent a message to say she was coming; he was angry with himself for not checking it more often. There was no message from her, which was good: it would make it harder for the Americans to trace anything back to him. He signed out of the account and created a new one. It would be safer to do this from another Internet cafe, but there wasn't time. Adel didn't want to leave his hostage alone with the others for too long. He wanted the address kidnapper@hotmail.com, but it had been taken, and he had to settle for kidnapper with a long number after it. He knew there was no chance the Americans would give into their demands and release the prisoners from Abu Ghraib. He didn't even know why he'd made that demand; he just knew you had to make a demand, had to give them a chance. He knew, too, that he still faced a struggle with the others over what they would do with the woman. Selim had gone to take care of some family business, and as soon as he was out of the house, Daoud had revealed his true reasons for not wanting to hand her over to Abu Khalid.

"We can get good money for her," he said. "The foreign groups pay for Western hostages. Why give her to Abu Khalid for free when we can sell her for thousands of dollars?"

"No," Adel said. "This is not about money. This is about revenge for what the foreigners have done, this is about Iraqi honour."

"Be reasonable," Daoud said. "If we sell her to them, they'll still kill her. Only this way we make money as well."

Adel knew he had to be careful: he needed to keep Daoud on his side, not least because it was Daoud's house they were using to hold her. But he realised he could use this to his advantage: if he pretended to go along, Daoud wouldn't let Selim hand her over to Abu Khalid, which would mean Adel wouldn't have to watch over them all the time: he could set them to guard each other. So he told Daoud to put the word out, cautiously, and find out how much they might get for her, but warned him not to breathe a word to Selim, who would see it as treachery. It was Ibrahim who suggested they could find another use for her.

"Why not?" he said. "She's a good-looking woman. Shame not to use her before we kill her."

Adel found it hard to control his anger.

"This is about honour," he said, "not a chance for you to fuck some foreign woman. You don't touch her."

Adel quickly uploaded the video and emailed it. He had to get back: he didn't like to leave the others alone with her. As he hurried back to the house, he seemed to hear his father's voice calling out to him, but he couldn't make out what it said.

⟶⟟⊙⟟⟵

Zoe sat in the darkened room and waited. The sense of reprieve when they had not killed her had passed. She had four days left to live. She had been over everything she had seen of the house where she was being held a hundred times in her mind, searching for a way out. The room she was in was always kept locked, and even if she managed to get past one of them when they brought her meal and made it down the stairs, the others would be waiting there for her. There was no way the Americans would meet their demands. Her only chance now was that somehow she would be found, that the Americans would track her down and come for her. The video of her must have been released by now, and that at least meant they would be looking for her—but she knew it was a slim hope she would be found. The kidnappers had all of Baghdad to hide in, and she didn't even know where she was.

They would all have seen the video by now: her mother, her friends. She hoped they would not be able to see her fear; she had tried to hide it. Even though they would know she must be afraid, she didn't want them to see it.

She heard the sound of footsteps on the stairs and braced herself. It must be night, because when the door opened there was no flood of light, just the dim glow of a low-powered light bulb. The same man as before came up, carrying a tray of kebabs and bread for her. She tried not to flinch.

"Did you look up my articles on the Internet?" she asked. "Please look me up. My name's Zoe Temple. From the *Informer* newspaper. I've been writing pieces against the Americans and the British, against the occupation. I've been trying to help."

"Eat," he said, pushing the plate of food towards her. Again, she had an overwhelming sense she recognised him from somewhere.

"At least give me a light," she said. "Please."

On one of her searches she had found a light switch, but either there was no bulb or it was burned out. He did not reply, and the door closed behind him. She felt in the dark for the plate of food. At first, she didn't want to touch it, but the smell made her realise she was hungry, in spite of everything.

There was a sound, and the door opened again. It was the same man, carrying a bulb. Without speaking, he screwed it into a light fitting, working by the dim light from the hall. She glanced at the door, wondering if she could make a run for it, but her eyes met those of one of the others, standing outside waiting. She looked back at the first. His face was half in shadow, but when he finished with the bulb and flicked the switch, it caught the sudden light and she remembered where she had seen him before, in the dog-eared photograph Zaynab had pulled out of the folds of her clothes and shown her both times she visited. He was her son. She quickly looked away, before he could see that she had recognised him. But as he left, she realised it made no difference and he was going to kill her anyway, so she called out, "You're Zaynab's son, aren't you?"

He stopped and looked back at her.

"It was wrong," she said, "what happened to your father and your brother and sister. It was a crime. I wanted to write that. I wanted to help your mother."

He said nothing, then pulled the door closed behind him and locked it. She wondered if he had been the one who sent her the emails. Now at least she had a light, but it only showed her she was right, that there was no way out of the room except the door: no window, no vent, and there was nothing she could use as a weapon to fight her way out. The room was completely bare except for the old bed. She lay down on it. Eventually she must have slept, because she dreamed she was home again in her parents' house, and her father was alive, and she was sitting talking with him as she had when she was a little girl while he smoked his cigarettes, flicking them off in his old brass ashtray, the smell of whisky about him. He held her and told her it was all right, that she was safe, and she believed him because she had always believed him. He was her father, and he could keep her safe. And then she was awake and wondering where she was, with a terrible pain in her wrists, and it came back to her: she was in Baghdad, she was a hostage, and in four days she was going to die.

Chapter Thirty-Two

The Search

9–11 July 2004

THE DOORS TO the lobby of the al-Hamra Hotel opened, letting in a brief blast of hot air. The small knot of security contractors looked up from their conversation at the man who had just entered, weighed down with bags, but they quickly turned away and resumed their talk, uninterested. The newcomer crossed to the reception desk and spoke with the clerk. It would have been clear from the clerk's apologetic expression and outstretched hands, had any of them cared to notice, that he was telling the new arrival the hotel was full, and that there were no rooms available. The man persisted, and the clerk went through a door to the back office. After a short time he re-emerged and handed over a key, though he took it from a drawer, not from the rack behind the desk. He offered to help the new guest with his bags, but the man shook his head and, gathering them up, made his way across the lobby, still ignored by the security contractors. As he stepped through the door that led to the courtyard by the pool, another guest emerged from the lift just in time see him. She stopped in her footsteps and stared after him with undisguised curiosity. Janet Sweeney hurried after him, eager to be first to tell the other journalists the news that Jack Wolfe had returned to Baghdad.

"Jack!" she called out, "didn't expect to see you back in town. But then," she added in a tone of concern, "with this terrible business of Zoe—"

"Have you heard anything?" he cut her off. "Is there any news?"

"Nothing, there's been nothing since the video."

"Any idea who might be holding her?" There was no sign he was distressed or upset.

"No, we all talked about that last night. None of us has a clue. It really is the most terrible situation, you must be feeling—"

"Any idea who might have known where she was going that morning? Did she mention anything to anyone?"

"There was nothing, Jack," Janet said. "We went over it again and again. I'm sorry. Has…has the *Post* sent you out specially? I mean, it must be horrible for you…" A particularly keen observer would have seen her hand make a tiny movement towards her notebook.

"Did she say anything that might give us a clue? Anyone she'd been in contact with, any story she'd been working on?"

"No, I can't think of anything. What about you, Jack? How are you coping?"

"I'm just focusing on trying to find her."

"Yes, of course, well, I know the Americans are doing everything they can—"

"Has anyone noticed cars being followed? Could someone have followed her there from the hotel?"

"No, the Americans have been through all that and there was nothing like that. Do you want to talk about this? I mean, you must be going through a lot, you should—"

"I'm sorry, Janet, I can't right now, I've got to get to an appointment. But if you hear anything, anything at all, please let me know."

"Yes, of course, I—"

She tried to call after him, but he hurried on his way.

⋅⇒⊨◉⊨⇐⋅

Within half an hour, the hotel was alive with curiosity at Jack Wolfe's return so soon after Zoe's disappearance. The journalists had tried to track him down without success, eventually coming to the conclusion he had gone out somewhere. Jack, however, was to be found at a table in a far corner of the restaurant, which was barely used in the summer months and where none of them thought to look for him. There were three people at the table besides him: his old translator Adnan, smoking and playing nervously with a half-drunk glass of tea; Kate, a haunted expression on her face; and opposite her a figure who might have been a ghost—he was certainly pale enough—Ali, his side heavily bandaged.

"When the bullets hit me, honestly I'm telling you I thought I was dead," he was saying. "I thought there was no way I could survive. But when I saw the car drive away with Zoe in it, and I was still conscious, I realised there was a chance and somehow I dragged myself from there. I don't know how I did it. I was in so much pain; I felt so weak. I went first to Barzan, to see if I could do anything for him, but he was dead. The bullet had gone straight to his head. He was a good man, he didn't deserve to die."

The others murmured in agreement.

"When I saw he was dead I felt helpless again," Ali went on. "Zoe was gone, and there was no way of knowing where they had taken her. But I had to do something. I dragged myself to the nearest house. Thank God, I was lucky with the people there. If it had been some other house, they would have been afraid and stayed inside, but they came out and helped me, called a doctor and took me to hospital."

"I've passed on to the Americans everything Ali was able to tell us," Kate said. "Where it happened, the description of the car. It should help narrow the search."

"I wish I'd been able to see one of them or get the car's licence number," Ali said. "But their faces were covered."

"Thank God you're alive, Ali," Jack said. He still had one of his bags with him, a small hold-all he kept at his feet. "So we have no idea who they are?"

"No."

"It was very quick for them to get a group of gunmen together. You say you were there just ten minutes?"

"Twelve at the most."

"What about the people you went to visit?"

"It was an old woman and her daughter; the girl had been badly injured."

"The Americans spoke with them," Kate said. "There's a man who usually lives there, a son, but he was out of town and he hasn't returned. The neighbours confirmed he hasn't been around. The Americans don't think the family were involved."

"Well, I suppose we can rule them out. What about the cars?"

"I spoke to the neighbours, the ones who would talk," Adnan said. "None of them knew the car they took her in. One had seen the other car once before, but he didn't know who it belonged to."

"The Americans haven't got anything on the cars either."

"What else are the Americans saying?"

"Not much," Kate said. "They keep me posted, but they haven't found anything. They've got plenty of guys on it, I know that much. They've been looking at the…the video," she added, looking down at her hands, "going through it for any clues. The problem is there's such a wide area to search."

"We've got three days," Jack said. "We can't rely on the Americans to find her. We need to make our own enquiries, go over everything we can. We might find something they missed; we might have sources they don't. Plus we have options they don't. They can't pay for a hostage's freedom, but we can."

"You mean pay a ransom?" Kate said.

"Lots of the kidnappings are for money: they take foreigners hostage and then sell them up the line to the extremists."

"Sure, but you saw the video, these guys want to kill her—"

"The video may be just to let everyone know they have the hostage," Adnan said. "You don't get the big money unless you let people know her life's in danger. No one has heard of this group before. I have asked everywhere, but no one has heard of it, even among the resistance. It's completely new. Their accents on the video are Iraqi. Most of the previous killings have been by foreigners from the other Arab countries."

"So there's a chance they may be looking for a buyer," Jack said.

"Even if they are, where are we going to get that sort of money?" Kate asked.

"Let me worry about that," Jack said. "I've got a contact who might help. Look, I'm not saying this will work, but it's worth trying. Get the word out to everyone you know that we're prepared to pay to get her back," he said to Ali and Adnan. "But we still have to work with the possibility that they really mean to kill her. So we need to find out anything we can. And we need to keep the pressure on the Americans. Kate, can you do that?"

"Yes," Kate said. "I've been speaking with the *Informer* in London, and I'm liaising with the Americans for them until their guy gets here."

"He's not here yet?"

"No, he's due in tomorrow."

"Who're they sending?"

"David Wilson. Look, there's one thing, Jack. I mean, not that it's a problem for me, but just so I know, in case it comes up, exactly what capacity are you here in? Did the *Post* send you, or…" She trailed off.

"They don't even know I'm here. I left London as soon as I got your call. So it might be best if you don't mention me, but I'll leave it up to you."

"OK." She looked uncertain, but she nodded.

"Well, we don't have much time," Jack said. "We can't afford to lose a minute, so let's get started right away. I think we should go back to where it happened. Ali, are you OK to come back there?"

"Of course."

"Jesus, Ali, you're bleeding," Kate said. Blood had begun to seep from under his bandage and was dripping onto the floor.

"It's nothing, I'll get it seen to." His face was terribly pale.

"Are you sure you're up to this? You look like you should be in bed."

"I cannot rest until we find her."

"Good," Jack said. "Let's get started."

‐‐‐◈‐‐‐

At first no one took much notice of two Iraqi men in Zaynab's street, one of them carrying a small hold-all over his shoulder, going from house to house as if they were looking for a particular address. But the neighbours watching from behind their curtains grew nervous when they saw the men linger at more than one house. Several called out to their wives and children to keep quiet and not to answer the door. Their fears did not abate when they saw a third man join the other two. He had a limp, his side was heavily bandaged, and he bore a striking resemblance to one of the men who had been shot down in the street the day the foreigner was kidnapped. When he came into view, one man shouted to his wife to switch off the lights and the air conditioner so no one would think they were home. After the kidnapping, the American soldiers had passed from house to house asking questions, and everyone in the street was on edge. Almost no one opened their doors to the strangers.

There was no answer when they called at Zaynab's house, even though they waited and rang the doorbell more times than was polite. The only place they were answered was at the house where the wounded man had been taken on the day of the shooting, but even there, the watching neighbours saw with satisfaction, they were hurried away.

After that they were seen calling at the car mechanic's work-shop a few blocks away, but those who witnessed it said the mechanic who spoke to them was unhelpful and accused them of being American spies, and they had to leave in a hurry.

⟶⊜⟵

The cafe in Adhamiya was alive with the evening crowd. Cigarette smoke floated in the light, and the air was thick with conversation and the click of backgammon pieces being slapped against boards. The sky was darkening outside, so that the shadows on the players' faces were picked out by the yellow electric lights. The hour when no outsider dared be found in Adhamiya was fast approaching, so when the door opened and two strangers walked in, the sound of backgammon fell quiet, and every eye was on them. It did not help that one of the strangers had a look about him that wasn't quite right—he had a small hold-all bag over his arm, for one thing. One or two of the regulars remembered seeing these men in the cafe many months before and muttered to those around them. The strangers walked across the room, a little uncertain under the gaze of so many eyes, and were about to sit at a table when the cafe owner intercepted them, leading them back towards the private part of his house, behind the curtain. Seeing them welcomed as guests by the owner, who smiled and shook them by the hand, most of the regulars relaxed and returned to their backgammon and their tea. Few noticed that the owner did not take the strangers all the way into his home, but just ducked behind the curtain, out of sight, where he spoke with them in hurried, hushed tones, standing up. One man, who chanced to be sitting at the table nearest the curtain, did notice this strange behaviour and, leaving his companions to their game, leaned across to eavesdrop on the conversation.

"What are you doing here?" the cafe owner was asking, his tone not as friendly as it had been in front of the customers. "I told you it was not safe for him to come here. It's not safe for him, and it's not safe for us either."

"I'm sorry, but we had to come," one of the strangers replied. "He has a real emergency, and he has to request your help. His wife has been kidnapped."

"His wife? When?"

"That woman, on the news, the British one. She is his wife."

"His wife is British? I thought he was Irish."

"He is, but his wife is British. She is not with the British, she is with him, but she was born there."

"Then it is even more dangerous for him to be here. You have to get him out. They will take him as well. They don't make any difference any more between Irish and British—all the foreigners are the same to them."

"But he has to find his wife."

"I don't know where she is."

"He is ready to pay a ransom if she is released unharmed."

"I tell you I don't know who has her. Some of the resistance, they come here, it's true. But they don't tell me who has done what, and certainly not who has a hostage. Anyway, it's probably the foreigners who've got her, the Saudis."

"Their voices were Iraqi."

"Well even then, I still don't know who they are."

"But if you hear anything. Anything at all."

"Because he is a friend, yes, if I hear I will let you know. But *you*…not him. Don't bring him again."

"And you will let people know we will pay?"

"How can I do that? They'll think I'm with you."

"Just spread the word around."

"I'll try. But get him out of here."

The eavesdropper saw the curtain stir as they were about to come through it and quickly looked away. The owner led the visitors back out through the cafe, smiling and shaking hands with them again at the door, sending them out into the uncertain night.

→—◦◉◦—←

The reporters at the al-Hamra, unable to find any news about the kidnapping of Zoe Temple, devoted much of the day to trying to find out which room Jack Wolfe was staying in. Eventually, by means of a bribe to a hotel employee, they discovered that because the hotel was full, he had been given a staff room on the ground floor. It was an unprepossessing room, difficult to find, and hardly worth finding when you reached it: the window had been bricked up for security reasons, so that the only light was from a bare bulb overhead. All the furniture seemed to be broken, and the carpet was threadbare and tattered. The moment Jack got back from Adhamiya, he was besieged by journalists. Exhausted as he was, he spoke with all of them. No sooner had one group left than another would appear at the door. Most came offering their condolences at first, but sooner or later reached for their notebooks. Jack gave them noncommittal remarks they couldn't make a story out of and asked them if they knew anything that might help in the search for Zoe—but none of them did. Peter Shore came by and said that Zoe had been frustrated by the difficulty of reporting in Baghdad. One awkward visitor was Rob Tucker, who had taken over from Jack as the *Post*'s correspondent in Baghdad and was distinctly frigid at first. But once Jack had assured Rob that he hadn't been sent out to take over the story, or to "bigfoot" him as the journalists put it, that in fact the paper didn't even know he was there, Rob softened. Jack asked him not to tell their editors in London he was there. Rob said he'd try, keeping his eyes fixed on a patch of threadbare carpet, but he left with the air of a man about to telephone his office for instructions.

Eventually they had all been answered and dispatched from the room, and Jack called Kate, Ali and Adnan to join him.

"The Americans have been through her emails," Kate said, "and they've found some suspicious messages."

"Go on," Jack said, leaning forward.

"They were sent some time ago, the last one was back in April, but they look like they come from the woman she went to see, Zaynab. Only when the Americans asked her about them she was confused and didn't seem to remember sending them."

"Zoe told me about these messages," Ali said. "I was suspicious because they were in English, but Zoe said Mrs Zaynab got a friend to send them."

"That's them," Jack said. "That's the kidnappers."

"Looks like it," Kate said. "They were all sent from the same hotmail address, and it was only ever logged into in internet cafes. Various different cafes around the city. But it was logged into from the same place the ransom demand was sent from, just a few minutes before."

"Well, that's great. They can find them."

"It's not so easy, Jack. There're no security cameras in these Internet cafes, and no record of the people who've been using them. No one remembers the guy. Anyone can set up an email account. There's no way of tracing them."

"There has to be something."

"They're trying."

"Is there any way we can get this email address?" Jack asked.

"No way. The Americans aren't giving it out."

"I wish I'd thought to look through her email before they froze it," Jack said. "Keep trying. See if you can get it from them."

"I'll try."

"Other than that, I suppose we just keep going."

"There's one other thing," Adnan said, a little hesitantly. "Ali and I were speaking and...well, after what happened in Adhamiya, well, we think it might be best if you don't come with us tomorrow."

Jack looked up at him.

"It's too risky," Ali added. "Adnan and I can do the work more safely without you. Maybe they will even tell us more if you are not there. But if someone recognises you, there could be serious problems."

"All right," Jack said. "You two keep asking around tomorrow. I've got some other contacts I can speak to. Anyone you can talk to, Kate? NGOs, embassies?"

"I think I've tried everyone, but I'll ask around again."

"Whatever we do, we have to stay focused and keep going. We've only got two days left to find her."

The others nodded silently.

⋅▸═◉═◂⋅

"There's a group in Mahmudiya who are prepared to pay ten thousand."

Adel sat and played his fingers around his tea glass, considering his response. He and Daoud were alone in the room. Selim and Ibrahim were away trying to keep up some of the routines of daily life to avoid raising suspicions. They had all decided it was bad enough that Adel had to pretend to be "out of town" at the time of the kidnapping: indeed, he had made a point of "returning" home that afternoon and being noticed by his neighbours. Now they were taking it in turns to guard the house and watch over their hostage, while the others made sure they were seen around their usual haunts.

"That's...worth considering," he said.

"Come on, that's serious money." Daoud was excited, Adel could see it in his eyes. "They'll kill her, you can be sure of that. This way she dies, and we get two and a half thousand each." Adel had no intention of letting Daoud trade away his hostage, but he couldn't afford to tell him as long as they were using Daoud's house to hold her.

"Let's wait a bit. Maybe they'll offer more."

"Why wait? Ibrahim says people have been asking questions. They went to Abu Noor's asking about the car. What if they trace us here, what if the Americans come?"

"They're not going to trace us here. They found nothing."

Adel had been watching from behind the curtains when the visitors called at his house that afternoon. When he saw the translator who had been shot dead standing alive on his doorstep, for a terrible moment Adel had wondered if he was some sort of vengeful ghost, before he noticed the bandages and realised the translator had survived. That detail hadn't been in the press reports he had read. He had warned his mother not to open the door. That was just as well, he thought: if she had recognised the translator she might have lost her mind and let slip that Adel was there that day.

But the moment of danger was past; they had discovered nothing. The hostage had made a lot of noise the first night, so much that he worried he would have to gag her for fear the neighbours might hear, but the threat of a gag had been enough and she had been quiet since. The problem now was keeping hold of her in the face of Daoud's desire to sell her and Selim's determination to hand her over to Abu Khalid.

"We'll wait a little longer," he told Daoud. "We can get more for her. And remember, say nothing to Selim about this."

⋆⟶⟩⟨⟨⟵⋆

The room where Jack Wolfe was staying looked no different in daylight, save for one or two tiny chinks where the light broke through the makeshift brickwork that blocked the window. But this was not enough to relieve the pall of gloom that hung over the room beneath its solitary light bulb. There was a knocking at the door, and after a short time Jack emerged from the bathroom, pulling a shirt on.

"Who is it?" he called out.

"A friend," a voice came from the other side. "Richard Nichols, from the British Embassy. Can I have a word?"

"Sure. Just a minute."

Jack opened the door to a tall blond man who stooped incongruously, as if he felt uncomfortable with his height.

"Jack Wolfe? Of the *Daily Post*?" he asked, holding out his hand.

"Sorry about the room," Jack said, shaking his hand. "It's all they had at short notice."

"Not at all, we all have to rough it in Baghdad. Delighted

to meet you at last, Mr Wolfe. I've been an assiduous reader of yours for the past year or so." He handed Jack a business card.

"Thank you."

"Really enjoyed your stuff. I think it's safe to say you got a handle on the way things were going here ahead of some of your colleagues. Yes, you were pretty much required reading over at our mission in the Green Zone. I was sorry when I heard you'd left your posting. Was surprised to hear you're back in town though…" He left the sentence hanging.

"It's only a brief visit."

"Oh yes? Here for a particular story?"

"Yes."

"Mm hmm." Nichols shifted uncomfortably in his seat. "Doesn't your paper have another correspondent here now?"

"Rob? Yes."

"Yes, nice guy, we've had a couple of drinks. So the *Post* have sent you out just for the one story?"

"I'm a little confused as to why you're so interested."

"Oh, well, you see sometimes our American friends get a little concerned about why people are in town. So sometimes, if Brits are involved, we think it best to have a word."

"I'm not a Brit, Mr Nichols."

"No, no indeed. But, uh, your employer is."

"Well, I'm just here for a few days looking into the kidnapped journalist, Zoe Temple, seeing what I can find out from my contacts."

"And your employers are happy about that, are they, Mr Wolfe?"

Jack did not reply.

"You see, this is a slightly delicate matter, but we've heard you've been putting it about that you're prepared to pay a ransom for Ms Temple. And you see, the thing is, Mr Wolfe, we, that is to say HMG, would consider it rather ill-advised of you to do that."

"Why's that?"

"Well, as I'm sure you know, it's always been our position, HMG's position, not to make deals with terrorists. The feeling is that if a ransom were to be paid, and that information were to get out, which by the nature of things it probably would, then that would only encourage further hostage-taking for ransom. Do you see? And I wouldn't normally be authorised to tell you this, but in the circumstances, well, I happen to know that the Americans have got some pretty good intelligence on where Ms Temple is being held and will be in a position to go in and get her pretty soon. So can we agree that you'll leave off this whole ransom business and leave this one to the professionals?"

"Where's she being held?"

"I'm sorry?"

"You said you knew where she is."

"Well, obviously I can't share information like that, you understand—"

"When are the Americans going in?"

"I don't know operational details—"

"If they know where she is, why haven't they gone in already?"

"Look, it really would be best if you left this to us."

"Best for who?"

"Look, Mr Wolfe," his voice hardened, "we happen to know you're here without the authorisation of your newspaper. You're not working as a journalist, you're in Iraq under false pretences, and by rights you could be deported. Now, if you'd like to be able to stay on while the operation to find Ms Temple goes on, we could turn a blind eye if you just sit tight and don't do anything that's going to jeopardise the search to find her—"

"I thought you said you knew where she was?"

"Mr Wolfe, I'm sorry to have to put it like this, but if you can't cooperate we'll have no choice—"

"You'll have me thrown out of Iraq? That would look great on the front pages. And I'd be sure to quote you in person."

"What makes you think you'd still have a job at the *Post*, Mr Wolfe?"

"Any paper in London would happily print the story. The *Informer*, for instance. It's their reporter we're talking about, after all."

"I am asking you on behalf of Her Majesty's government—"

"As I said, I'm not British."

"You work for a British paper."

"Who would be very happy to know the details of this conversation. If the Americans know where Zoe is, what I'm doing won't make any difference. They'll go in and get her. If they don't, and I find out where she is, then I'll be the first person to share it with them. But if I can't find that out and money will get her out safe then, yes, I'll go down that route. I'll do whatever I have to do. All I want is to get her out safely."

"Mr Wolfe, if you insist on choosing your own path, I can't force you. But I think I should warn you that Baghdad is a very dangerous city these days."

"Can I quote you on that? I don't think we've got any more to discuss, Mr Nichols."

⊶⊙⊷

Despite his agreement the previous evening to leave the search to Ali and Adnan, Jack was seen coming and going from the al-Hamra several times during the day. As he came back in towards evening, he was met by Kate, who looked concerned.

"Jack, David's arrived from the *Informer*. He'd like a word if you've got a moment."

David Wilson was sitting at a table in the cafe with Jack's colleague Rob Tucker sitting across from him.

"Jack, good to see you," David said. "Awful business, this. Kate's been filling me in."

"What's the latest?" Jack asked. "Any news from the Americans?"

"Nothing, I'm afraid. Look, Jack, well, the thing is…" David hesitated. He had his hands folded on the table and he was looking down at them. "We're all very grateful for you rushing over like this. I know my guys, right up to Henry Haight, really appreciate what you've been trying to do. But we really think it would be best if you left this to me now. I'm liaising with the Americans and the Brits on this, I've been speaking to London all day, and the feeling is it's best to leave this to the professionals."

"Right, I see."

"It's just we risk clouding the issue," David said. "My guys have spoken with Zoe's mother in the UK and she's on board. We're all agreed, we need to back the Americans on this."

"I understand."

"The editor wants you to call him, Jack," Rob said from across the table. "I'm not supposed to know this, but from what I understand the Brits have been on to him at that end. The word is, if you get on a plane back to London now, he's willing to forget about the whole thing."

"OK. I'll give him a call." Jack got up. "You'll let me know if you hear anything."

"Of course," David said, getting up and putting a reassuring hand to Jack's arm. "We all know what you're going through."

⤙⤚⧳⤙⤚

"Sell her? *Sell her?*" Selim was furious. "And you *agreed* to this?" he asked Adel.

Daoud's impatience had got the better of him and looked in danger of upsetting all Adel's calculations: anxious for an answer to his Mahmudiya offer, he had made the mistake of mentioning it in front of Selim and, worse, implying that Adel was in favour of it. Now Selim, angry at what he saw as a betrayal, was rounding on Adel.

"You told me we would do this ourselves," Selim said, "and the moment my back is turned you start scheming to sell her off to the highest bidder! If we're going to pass her on, it should be to Abu Khalid!"

Adel was exhausted; he had barely slept.

"We're not passing her on to anyone," he said. "Not for money, and not to Abu Khalid."

"But—" Daoud started.

"No, I didn't say we'd sell her. We didn't do this for money. And we didn't do it to be Abu Khalid's messenger boys either," Adel said, turning on Selim and cutting him off before he could speak. "I didn't do this just to hand her over to someone else."

"Are you crazy?" Daoud said. "This is $10,000!"

"It's not about money!"

"Well, if that's your decision you can't do it here," Daoud said. "It's not safe for my mother. People are already asking questions. What if someone recognises the house from the video?"

"Fine, then let's hand her over to Abu Khalid and be done with it!" Selim said.

"No," Adel said. "We're not handing her over. I've got another place to do it. It's all prepared."

"Then take her there," Daoud said.

"Not yet, it's not time. But we won't do it here, I promise you."

Daoud subsided into muttering. But Adel knew Selim was the dangerous one.

"We're doing this," he said. "We're killing her."

⋯⊷⊶⋯

As evening turned to night and uneasy dark fell over the al-Hamra Hotel, Kate made the same journey she had made the previous evening, only this time she took care that no one saw where she was going and waited for the small lobby of the second building to be clear of guests before she slipped down the corridor to Jack's room. Ali and Adnan were already there.

"Anything?" Jack asked. His calm resolve of the past two days was faltering; for the first time there was anxiety in his voice.

"No, sorry," Kate said. "The Americans have got nothing. They've been searching the city, but they've got no idea. The political people I was speaking to before aren't letting on, and David's dealing with them now. But I managed to speak to a guy I know in the military, and he was a lot more frank. They've got nothing; they're just searching the area around where she was picked up."

"And the emails?"

"Nothing new. And no, they're not telling me the address."

"Adnan and Ali got nothing either," Jack said. "I spoke to a few people I know, but they knew nothing. The trail's completely cold. And we've had no takers on our offer of money."

"Right." Everyone in the room was downcast: Adnan was studying his shoes, and Ali looked exhausted. "When are you leaving?" Kate asked Jack.

"I'm not."

"But—"

"I spoke to my editor this afternoon, told him I was on my way back to London as soon as I could get a flight. That should keep them off our backs for a little."

"Jack, you'll lose your job."

"Probably. I'm going to have to keep a low profile, but nothing's stopping the rest of you heading out again tomorrow. Any ideas?"

The others shook their heads

"In that case, we'll just have to go back to the beginning," Jack said. "Go back to the street where it happened. This wasn't a chance pick-up—we know that from the emails. It was planned to happen there. See if anyone will talk, see if there's anything. And do the rounds of the cafes again."

"OK," Adnan said.

"We have to keep going. We've got one day left. Just keep going."

⋯⋯⋯

The next morning there was an insistent knocking at the door of Jack's room. He opened it cautiously, as if he feared a return visit from Mr Nichols of the British Embassy, but it was Ali, out of breath and excited.

"We've found…someone," he said. "Says…says he knows… where she is."

"Who? Where?"

"Adnan's with him…I can take you…he wants…wants money."

"Let's go."

They left the hotel via a back entrance near the kitchen, where Ali had a car and driver waiting.

"Make sure we're not followed," Jack said. "The last thing we want is the Americans blundering in with guns blazing before we find anything out. And switch off your mobile; they can trace the signal. So who is this guy?"

"I don't know. He contacted Adnan last night. He wants to meet in a cafe. To be honest, it could be dangerous."

"We have to take the risk."

"He insisted on speaking with you. I'm worried they may be planning to kidnap you as well."

"I'll have to take the chance; she only has one day."

"Yes."

"Are you sure you're OK to come, Ali? I mean, after what happened."

"I have to come. We have to find her."

They drove far out into the suburbs, where the streets gave way to scruffy buildings, with few people around, and large open areas of wasteland. They pulled up outside a cafe that looked, from the outside at least, much like the one in Adhamiya. Adnan was waiting, and he came over to the car.

"What do you think?" Jack asked him.

"I'm not sure. But he says he has something and he wants to speak to you. I…don't know if it's safe, but he says he'll only speak to you."

Inside, the cafe was more basic than the one in Adhamiya, just a few plastic tables and chairs, the floor dirty and unswept. An old man sat to one side with a small portable electric fan directed at him, a boy was wiping down tables, and, at the back, a young man sat waiting. There was no air conditioning, and the old man wasn't sharing his fan. The air was hot and stifling.

"Please sit," the young man said in English, gesturing Jack to a chair. Adnan introduced Jack, the young man gave no name.

"It's OK, it's safe," he said, with a crooked smile, offering Jack a cigarette. "You look for the British woman, the hostage?" Jack nodded. "You can pay?" Again Jack nodded. "We have her," the young man said.

Jack looked at Adnan in surprise.

"I not tell your friend, I tell you," the young man said. "We have her. Ten thousand American dollars. If you pay, we let you take her. If not…" He let the sentence hang.

"OK. Let her go and we'll pay," Jack said.

"No," the man said, shaking his head and smiling ruefully. "First you pay. Then you take her."

Jack inhaled the cigarette slowly.

"We'll do it at the same time. An exchange," he said.

"No. Money first."

"How do we know you'll let her go?"

"You have to trust. It's your only chance."

Jack looked at Adnan, then at Ali.

"I don't have the money on me," he said. "I didn't bring it."

"You can go for it. I will tell your friend here a place to meet."

"How can I be sure you have her?" The young man said nothing. "You were there when she was taken off the street?" The man nodded. "What was she wearing?"

"What?"

"To prove you have her. What was she wearing when you took her?"

"You expect—"

"I have to know."

"OK. Jeans. She was wearing jeans. And a white shirt."

"OK. I'll get the money. You'll call my friend with a place to meet?"

"Yes." Jack stood up and shook hands with the kidnapper, then walked back out to the car, followed by Ali and Adnan. It wasn't until they had driven several blocks that Ali spoke.

"He's lying," he said.

"I know," Jack said. "He described what she was wearing in the video."

"When they took her, she had her headscarf and the long coat," Ali said.

"So this guy is just lying? To get the money?" Adnan asked from the front seat.

"Can we risk it?" Ali asked. "He might have made a mistake."

"When he calls, tell him we don't believe him. Ask him to prove it. If he's serious and he sees us slipping away, he'll come up with something."

But when Adnan asked for further proof, the young man hung up on him. That evening, they met for the last time in Jack's room. Their faces were lost in shadow under the electric bulb. Kate told them that her military source said the Americans still had nothing, and David Wilson had told her privately that he was not optimistic. Adnan and Ali had spent the rest of the day going back over everywhere they had visited, but they learned nothing new. Their time was up. If the kidnappers kept to their schedule, they would kill her the next day.

"They don't always do what they say," Adnan said. "A lot of the deadlines have passed, and the hostages have not been killed. If they want money they'll hold out."

"We have to keep going," Jack said. "Even if the time's up. We go on to the end. I will not abandon her. We just keep going until we find her. Or..."

He didn't complete the sentence. For a long time they sat together in silence.

Chapter Thirty-Three

Hollywood Part Three

12–13 July 2004

THOUSANDS OF MILES from Iraq, rain was falling over the graves, persistently enough that all but a few of the visitors to the cemetery had taken shelter under the green canopy of the trees. The wind was blowing gently, and the leaves were whispering secrets to each other overhead. The visitors watched as a few umbrellas moved in the distance, and one man who had no covering walked on, searching among the tombstones, oblivious to the rain that had soaked through his clothes and was streaming from his hair down his face. They watched with sympathy: the flowers clutched in his hand were drooping from the force of the downpour. He must be newly bereaved to endure the elements like that, yet from the way he looked at the inscriptions, it was clear he didn't know where to find the grave he was searching for, as if he had been absent from the funeral—estranged from the family perhaps, or a secret lover. Eventually he stopped at a plot that looked new, the grass only just beginning to show over the dark earth, fresh flowers piled on top, the tombstone clean and sharp-edged, death unsoftened by time. He stood a long time alone before it, even as the rain grew heavier and the sound of thunder rolled in the distance. It was growing dark and most of those watching gave up their own visits, some sprinting quickly to leave flowers, others heading for their cars, promising to return when the weather was kinder, so few were there to see when a woman came to join the man at the new grave and offered him the shelter of her umbrella. He took it and held it for both of them, taking care to shield her.

"Thank you for coming," she said.

"It was the least...I mean, I wanted...I had to come," he said.

"Rick would have appreciated it."

"Yes." Sergeant Hawkes's voice faltered. "He was a good man. He was the best…best officer I served with. Best man I knew."

"Thank you." Maria Benes looked at him sadly. "He often told me about you, how good a sergeant you were. He really appreciated you, you know. He spoke about all the guys. It's only you who've come, the guys from his platoon. Of course a few officers turned out for the funeral, and the honour guard. But no one from the higher-ups, no one from the government. It's like we don't exist."

"I wish I'd been at the funeral."

"He'd have liked the platoon to be there. You were stuck in Iraq, we understood. But so many of you have come since you got back. It means a lot to me, to know the guys felt that way about him."

"I hope he knew. He was a good officer. And the way…I mean…he was a hero. The way he…when I saw him pick that kid up, I, well, I don't know anyone else who would have done that."

"Yes. But if he hadn't…" She trailed off into silence. "I miss him, I really miss him. It hurts, you know."

"Yes."

"Well, I can't…I have to go, my sister's with Juan. Usually I'd bring him but, with this weather."

"Yeah, I know. Let me walk you."

They disappeared into the sound of the rain. On the tombstone, the newly cut letters read "Lieutenant Rick Benes, beloved husband and father". In the distance, the wind moved among the trees.

⸻

When they came for her, Zoe knew it was the hour. All four of them came, masked in their headscarves and ready. It was no meal this time, no opportunity to use the bathroom. Though she had no way of telling the time in her windowless cell, she had counted the meals they brought and watched the daylight come and go beyond the door with their visits, and she knew her four days were up. She had accepted it in the long watches of the night, when no one came and there was no rescue attempt. She had always known she would die—she would rather it had not been now, but still it would have come. She was not looking forward to the pain, and she hoped it would be quick. She wished she could spare her mother and her friends the video they were going to make of her, but she would not let them see that she was afraid. These men could choose the hour of her death and the manner of it, but they could not decide the way in which she faced it. It was a little, a very little, but in the end it was all that was left to her. When they take everything else, all that remains is the way we die.

"Well?" she asked. Her throat was dry.

None of them spoke. Zaynab's son—she could tell him apart, even in his headscarf—held out a blindfold. She had thought of making a run for it, but there was no chance with all four of them blocking the door. He tied it around her head, so that it dug into her eyes, and she felt a gag being tied around her mouth. One of them took her arm and guided her towards the stairs. She had been determined to remain calm, but robbed of sight and unable to make a sound, she felt panic rising and her legs gave way beneath her. Two of them took her then, one on each arm, and carried her down the stairs as she fought to regain control of her body, to make her legs respond. They reached the foot of the stairs: a few more steps into the room, then the camera, and the knife. It was hard to breathe. But they were still moving; they had taken her past the room where they made the video. She felt a change in the air, heard the sound of cars, and realised they had taken her outside. They lifted her up and put her down roughly in a lying position. She flinched for the knife.

"Keep your head down!" one of them said. She heard the sound of metal closing over her and the sound of an engine starting. They had put her in the boot of a car—they must be taking her somewhere else to do it. She wondered how she could think calmly about her own execution. Every minute was another minute of life, yet there was nothing to do with it but fear the moment that was coming. She tried not to think of it, to think back to her childhood, her father's arms, the smell of his cigarettes and whisky, her mother, walking in the fields near the house, the sun slanting through the trees. She felt the car stop, and the engine cut out, dragging her cruelly back. She heard footsteps approaching and knew it was now, the moment we spend our lives trying to defer, to postpone, not to think about.

Now.

She heard the boot being opened over her and felt hands reaching across her body. She was lifted out; someone tore the blindfold from her eyes and there was a blinding white light. She could feel the ground beneath her feet, but someone was holding her up. A voice said, "It's all right, you're safe now."

She looked around and saw Jack, but that was impossible. Beside him was Ali, who couldn't be there because he was dead. She wondered if she was dead too.

—————

Adel sat in the car, clutching the hold-all full of money, while Daoud drove. His mind was a turmoil of emotions. He had just let his vengeance go, yet through his confusion he was somehow certain of one thing: that his father would approve of what he had just done. The money that sat in his lap was an excuse. Almost from the first night, when he had gone up to her room to bring her down and she had spoken to him, Adel had begun to have doubts. When he looked her in the eyes, he didn't see a foreign invader or his father's murderer. He saw a frightened woman. He had tried to ignore it, to concentrate on the task ahead, but when she recognised him and spoke of his father's death, he felt as if his father were reaching out to him through this woman. When he went back to his house, to keep up the appearance of living a normal life, he heard his mother speak of her horror and shame that "that poor young woman, who only wanted to help" had been taken from the streets after visiting her. Once, in the makeshift prison cell, bringing the girl her food, he had seen her trying to pretend she wasn't afraid, and for some reason he had thought of his own sister, Rana, who had died. Rana had only been a girl and this was a grown woman, but if Rana had lived she could have been this woman before him, and he knew she would have tried to hide her fear the same way. It was one thing, he knew now, to think of her as an abstract idea, someone at the end of an email, it was something else when she was before his eyes, trying to hide her fear. He could hate the journalist who wrote an email saying his father's death wasn't important enough to go in a newspaper; he couldn't hate this helpless woman.

He had thought, then, of handing her over to Abu Khalid or selling her to Daoud's contacts in Mahmudiya, but he had known it would be the same as killing her himself, only it would be a coward's choice, and he was not a coward. What he had begun, he would finish, either he would kill her himself, or he would let her go—but he had no idea how to let her go. It wasn't until the evening when, sitting in the cafe in Adhamiya, he had seen the two men who had been outside his mother's house, that he found a way out. Eavesdropping through the curtain as they spoke with Arif, the cafe owner, he overheard them say they were prepared to pay for her release. If they paid enough, he could easily get Daoud and Ibrahim to agree, which would only leave Selim to worry about.

But he prevaricated, uncertain whether he should go through with it after all, whether, the moment she was gone, he would regret that he had passed up the opportunity forever. On the final evening, he knew he had to come to a decision: it had been hard enough holding out against Selim and Daoud's demands, and there was no way he could keep it up past the deadline he himself had set. He went out for some fresh air, leaving the others with her, and before he realised what he was doing, he found himself walking towards the cafe. Inside, he asked Arif for the number of the man who had come asking for her. He fended off Arif's questions and took the number. All the way back to his house, he debated whether to call. He sat for some time in his room, staring at his mobile before he dialled. Time was passing; the chance was slipping. He dialled, and when someone answered he almost hung up…almost. He asked for $50,000, expecting to bargain—he knew he had to get more than the $10,000 Daoud had been offered from Mahmudiya—but the man on the other end of the phone agreed immediately. That made him suspicious that it might be an American trap, and he almost backed out, but something about the way the man spoke convinced Adel he was genuine. Adel returned to Daoud's house, and when Selim had gone home to sleep, he told Daoud about the deal. Daoud was visibly relieved; he had lost his nerve and was ready to take any way out at that stage. Even the $50,000 didn't interest him as much as the thought of getting her off their hands. When Ibrahim arrived for his shift as guard in the early morning, he was as easily persuaded: it turned out he had been having the same doubts as Adel, and he didn't want to go through with it either.

Selim would be the problem. Adel knew that since they had kidnapped her, Selim had taken to carrying a handgun at all times. He made his plan with the others. When Selim arrived, Adel said they were going to move her to the place he had prepared to film her execution, and he suggested they take two cars in case of any trouble. He and Daoud would take the first, with Zoe in the boot, and Selim and Ibrahim the other. Selim agreed, and they left in convoy. All he had to do was give the second car the slip in traffic, which was harder than Adel had thought it would be, but he managed it and drove to meet the foreigners in an empty street on the city edge as agreed. He was nervous the foreigners would have betrayed him and the Americans would be waiting, but there was just a car, two Iraqis and a foreigner. He handed over the woman, took the bag of money and left.

He knew he would have to disappear for a while, in case the woman identified him. He had made up his mind to tell Abu Mustafa that he needed to get out of Baghdad and ask him to put him in touch with the resistance in some other city, preferably in Fallujah or elsewhere on the frontlines. Giving up his revenge did not mean giving up the fight against the Americans. There would be arguments with Selim, but nothing they would kill each other over; they had known each other too long for that. Besides, the money would soften the blow, especially when Adel told Selim that he was donating his share to the resistance.

Yet as Daoud drove, Adel felt curiously defeated. He knew he had done the right thing, and that his father would approve, yet it brought no satisfaction or sense of justification, only a sense of relief that felt almost shameful.

It was some time before Zoe got the whole story of her release. At first she was too bewildered to understand much of the explanations. She had given up all hope and prepared to die and, finding herself unexpectedly alive, found she felt almost nothing at all, as if her exhausted mind could produce no further emotions, and she could do no more than sit and breathe and watch uncomprehending the world around her. Jack and Ali hurried her into the back of a car, and they drove away from the spot where Zaynab's son and the others had released her. The others seemed nervous and kept looking around. When they reached the al-Hamra hotel, they found American officials and people from the British Embassy waiting, none of whom seemed at all happy to see her alive. There were television cameras and photographers as well—Kate, she later learned, had made sure of that, so that the Americans and British couldn't simply spirit her out of the country.

Robbed of that possibility, they had contented themselves with separating her from her liberators, Jack and Ali, and taking her alone to the Green Zone, where they questioned her at length and generally gave her the impression that she had caused them a great deal of inconvenience. They gave her a comfortable room at the British Embassy, but they refused to let her leave, saying they were concerned for her safety. They had her things collected and brought over from the hotel. Zoe told them all she could about the identity of her kidnappers and where she had been held. The officials were most insistent that the circumstances of her release, and in particular the fact that a ransom had been paid, must never be allowed to get out. They wanted to know where the money for the ransom had come from, but Zoe was able to tell them quite truthfully that she had no idea—in all the confusion, she hadn't even known Jack had paid a ransom. David Wilson from the *Informer* came to tell her everyone at the paper was delighted at her safe release, and she was allowed to speak to her mother by telephone. It wasn't until she heard her mother's voice that the near trance she had been in broke, and Zoe began to feel again how close she had been to death.

Amid all this, Zoe didn't know how she felt about Jack Wolfe's unexpected return to her life: it had been too sudden, and in circumstances that were too extraordinary. The authorities refused to let her speak to him: Mr Wolfe, they said, was in very serious trouble and being deported from Iraq and, they were reliably informed, in all probability fired by his newspaper as well. But despite their disapproval, Zoe could make out from what they said that it had been he who had saved her life by paying some sort of ransom to her kidnappers. She may not have known how she felt about him, but she wasn't about to let the man who had saved her life be thrown unceremoniously out of Iraq, and in no mood to be bullied, she refused to cooperate any further unless she was allowed to speak to him. They told her she was worn out by her ordeal and needed some rest. In the night, she dreamed she was in the darkened upstairs room again, waiting for the knife, and heard their tread on the stair, coming for her, the turn of the key in the door—and she woke up clutching at the air in panic.

The American officials returned to tell her that they had raided Zaynab's house but found her son gone—Zaynab had not known where. When she asked about Jack, they said Mr Wolfe's circumstances were being reviewed, but in the meantime she had a visitor, and they showed in Kate, who threw her arms around Zoe. Kate filled her in on all the details she didn't know, how Ali had survived, how Jack had flown to Iraq as soon as he heard she'd been kidnapped, how he'd remained indefatigable when everyone else had given up hope, and how he'd come up with $50,000 in ransom money—Kate had no idea where he'd got it—to buy her freedom. When Kate asked about her ordeal, Zoe was aware of how curiously flat and devoid of emotion her answers sounded, almost as if she were bored or embarrassed by the whole thing.

"It's all right," Kate said, "it's just a delayed reaction. You're probably still in shock. In a couple of days it'll all come out."

The embassy officials told her a flight back to the UK had been arranged for her. The media had been clamouring to speak with her, they said, but it was considered best to get her back home safely first. Doubtless the press would want to speak to her on her return, and she herself would probably want to write about her experiences, but they impressed on her again how important it was that the fact a ransom had been paid for her must not get out. If it did, it would only expose other journalists to the risk of future kidnappings. Zoe felt that was an opportune moment to raise the question of Jack again, and they told her he would be deported from Iraq, but that she would be able to see him.

Zoe was happy to leave Iraq: she knew she would not be able to return to the country any time soon, but after all that had happened she wanted only to get home. She still wasn't sure how she felt about seeing Jack again, though. It was one thing to try to defend him from deportation—that at least she felt she owed him—but amid the emotion of her narrow escape, she wasn't ready to decide how she felt about him after all that had happened, and she was particularly uncomfortable with the thought that she was in his debt after he had paid so large a ransom for her.

One thing, though, she insisted on before she left: to be allowed to see Ali and thank him for all he had done. And so he came to the embassy to see her off with Kate, and Zoe hugged him, careful not to press too heavily on his wounds, and told him how sorry she was about Barzan, and said she would stay in touch. After that she was bundled into a waiting car and driven out of the Green Zone, without a chance to set foot in the al-Hamra again or see any of her other friends. When they pulled up to the airport, she thought the officials had lied to her about seeing Jack, but she was shown into a small office where he was waiting for her.

"Zoe!" He got up and came towards her, but Zoe, feeling awkward, stood still.

"So you came back," she said.

"Yes."

"Thanks. For saving my life, I mean."

"It was the least I could do."

"But it doesn't mean—"

"Of course not."

"Don't think because you paid all that money—"

"Wouldn't dream of it."

And she found herself in his arms, and despite all the confusion, it made sense. It appeared that American and British officialdom had decided that, since they couldn't keep her and Jack apart once they were out of Iraq, they may as well send them home on the same flight. Sitting on the plane beside him, she asked, "Where did all that money come from?"

"I'd been saving to put a deposit down to buy a flat."

"Is it true the *Post* are firing you?"

"It seems so."

"So you've lost your job and you've spent your life savings?"

"Yes. But I've sold the story of how we found you to a rival paper for a very tidy sum. And my agent reckons there's a book deal in it."

As they took off, she looked out of the window at the fast-retreating city where she would probably never return. In the streets below, they were still queuing at checkpoints, driving nervously past American convoys, wondering who they could trust, trying to survive as Arab turned against Kurd, Muslim against Christian, Sunni against Shia, neighbour against neighbour, brother against brother. Down there, they were getting ready for the storm.

⇒■❦■⇐

Nouri was working on the construction site when a shadow fell across the ground before him. Turning, he saw Abbas, his old comrade from the militia.

"This is no work for a veteran," Abbas said, as he always said.

"We take what we can."

"But there is more important work to be done. Our brothers in Najaf are preparing for a new battle. The Americans will not win so easily this time. But we need experienced fighters. We leave the day after tomorrow, Insha'Allah. Put things in order here and be at the compound by seven."

Nouri stood staring after him for a long time after he left. It was what he had wanted and what he had feared. He stood as the sun slipped behind the ragged palm trees and the evening breeze blew the dust in little eddies around his feet.

Mahmoud stared at the computer screen, scarcely able to believe it. After so long, after he had stopped checking his email for it, after he had given up even hoping it would be there, it was: a message from her, from his Saara. At first he was too nervous to look, afraid it would tell him that she was married or that she somehow blamed him for what had happened, but he made himself read the words on the screen:

My dearest, I hope that you are well and that your arm is better. I would have written before, but we have had a very difficult time of it after all that happened. We had terrible problems reaching here, but I am safely in America with my mother and brother and sister now, living in a place called Chicago. Did you hear about my father? I suppose you must have come to the house the next day to find us gone. They came to kill us that night, my poor father died to save us from them. After that we had a lot of problems, my brother had trouble with the police in Jordan and it took weeks to get him free, we had a lot of problems with money, my mother was in shock after my father's death and couldn't do anything. But finally we reached America and we're safe here now.

How are you, my Mahmoud? Write to me and let me know you are OK. I suppose by now you have found some other girl and are married. I forgive you if you are, but please don't tell me. Let me still believe that I am your love and your wife. And hope that perhaps, one day, you can come to America, or I can return to Iraq, and we can be together. Please tell me that you are safe and well.

All of my love
Your wife
Saara

He knew then that he would have to break off the engagement he had agreed to with a girl his mother had chosen—would have to break it off even though there was no way he could get a visa to travel to America and no way Saara could return. Even though his parents would not allow him to forestall marriage indefinitely, and if he broke it off this time, would only start pressing him to agree to another bride. All the same, he knew he would do it. Her message represented hope, the tiniest thread of hope through the darkness.

He got up and looked out of the window. A couple of American helicopters were flying in the distance, low over the rooftops in the dying light of the sun. The sound of gunfire echoed over the city. Mahmoud had sensed for some time that what the country had lived through in the past year would be nothing to the storm that was coming. In the years that lay ahead, hope would have to be enough.

Justin Huggler was born in the Channel Island of Jersey. A former foreign correspondent for the *Independent* newspaper, he covered the occupation of Iraq from 2003 to 2004. He has also covered the 2001 war in Afghanistan, the second Palestinian intifada, the 2004 Indian Ocean tsunami, the overthrow of Slobodan Milosevic, and the Nepalese revolution. He lives in London.